Also By H.R. Kemp

Deadly Secrets

Lethal Legacy

H.R. Kemp

Copyright © H.R. Kemp 2022

All rights reserved. No part of this publication may be reproduced or transmitted in any form or by any means, electronic or mechanical, including photocopy, recording, or any information storage or retrieval system, without permission in writing from the author.

PAPERBACK ISBN 978-0-6487663-6-0
EBOOK ISBN 978-0-6487663-7-7

This book is a work of fiction. Names, characters, businesses, organisations, places and events are either the product of the author's imagination or used fictitiously. Any resemblance to actual persons, living or dead, events or locales is entirely coincidental.

H.Schuster Publishing
PO Box 413
Glenelg, SA 5045,
Australia

For Jesse, Zara, and Clayton

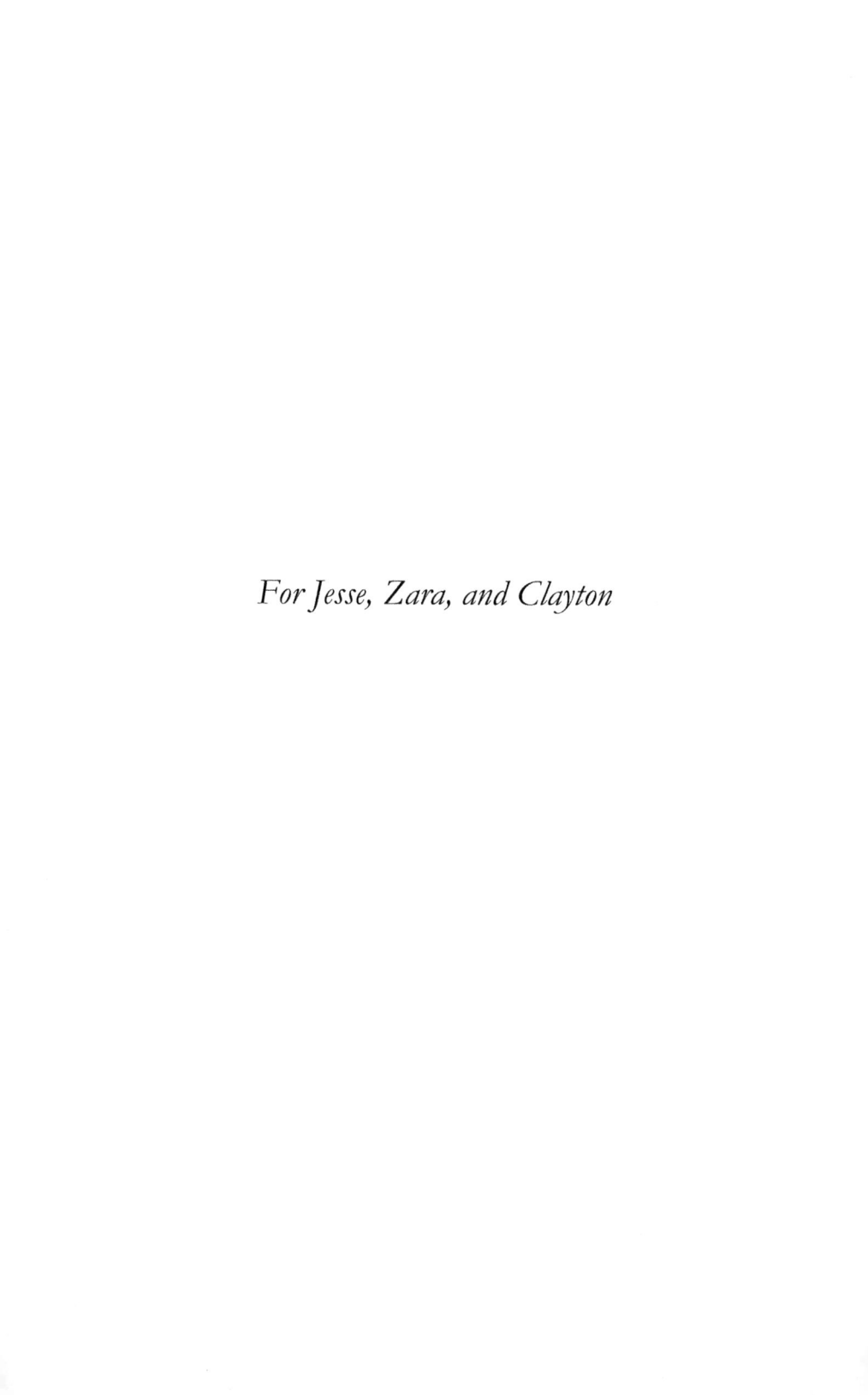

"The price of liberty is eternal vigilance"

- The RSL (Returned Servicemens' League) motto.

"Blind belief in authority is the greatest enemy of truth."

- Albert Einstein German-born physicist and founder of the theory of relativity
1879 - 1955 Letter to Jost Winteler (1901)

Chapter 1

Adelaide, February 2006.

The crowd slithered snake-like through the usually deserted Victoria Park. It crackled with the same excitement Laura felt. On the horizon the dusk skyline shimmered like a grey scrim curtain with pink highlights and she drank in the vivid colours. Attending the Music festival free opening concert was a rare treat but then she glanced at Tom and frowned. Laura fought to stave off the contagion of his sour mood.

Finding their friend Peter and his second wife, Abbie, would be difficult in this throng and Tom suggested they stop at the rear of the outdoor venue. His reluctance again provoked her annoyance. After thirty-seven years of marriage, it should be easier. The laughter and friendly banter of other couples and family groups made her heart ache.

She rang Peter. His cheerful voice restored her joyful anticipation, and she followed his shouted directions deep into the crowd until she saw him waving from the main aisle. Abbie stood beside him, unsmiling and rigid, and Laura hesitated. Eva, Peter's first wife, was Laura's best friend, and it created tension with Abbie.

Peter kissed Laura's cheek and gently squeezed her shoulder. His hair had greyed since she'd last seen him but his tight smile was the same. Tom maintained his angry silence. He left Peter's projected hand unclasped, grunted a greeting to Abbie then set up his chair at the outer edge of the space.

'Are you OK?' Abbie asked Tom. 'You look pale.'

'Just a headache and a sore arm from lugging all this stuff,' Tom grumbled.

Laura struggled into the low beach chair. She rummaged in her handbag, extracted painkillers, and offered them to Tom. He barely nodded an acknowledgment, then turned and stared ahead. He obviously wasn't ready for peace yet.

It hadn't always been like this. His retirement, eighteen months ago, hadn't gone to plan, at least not for her. Instead of day trips, lunches with friends, or spontaneous fun, Tom burrowed away in his study, researching and investigating a mystery he didn't share with her. She'd expected them to draw closer once the children were grown and had left home, but instead, he'd become surlier and more withdrawn. He hadn't been ready to retire, even if his office said he was. Now, his hurts, disappointments, and needs, dominated their lives and she admitted to her resentment. She was losing patience.

She moved her chair closer to Abbie and Peter to hear better, and the gap between her and Tom became a chasm.

'Where's Katie tonight?' Laura asked, hiding her hurt behind small talk.

Abbie's first child, Katie, was Peter's third.

'She's with Peter's boys tonight. They're here for his birthday,' Abbie explained.

Peter's sons, from his first marriage to Eva, were close to Abbie's age, with families of their own. Living in Brisbane meant they seldom encroached on Peter's new life and Laura rarely saw them.

'They've taken her and the grandkids to visit Eva.' Abbie smirked and then laughed. 'McDonald's or KFC tonight, probably.'

'Now, now, that's enough,' Peter mumbled.

Laura looked away. Abbie's animosity perplexed her, after all, Peter chose Abbie over Eva and his family. Laura accepted a glass of wine. Peter stepped behind her and offered Tom a glass too, but Tom declined ungraciously and sunk further into his beach chair.

Peter clapped him on the shoulder. 'Let it go. We're here to enjoy a social evening.'

'You'd like that,' Tom replied.

As Peter moved back to his seat, his hand brushed along Laura's shoulder and its warmth was reassuring. She glanced at Tom's huddled figure. He was at war with everyone. Tom's anger at his old workplace, and Peter, intensified with the Cole Commission hearings that had started last month. The investigation into the Australian Wheat Board corruption was stirring up their old conflict and its findings would prove one of them right. Tom took the moral high ground and railed against their company adopting the Wheat Board style contracts with their illegal transport component paid straight to Sadaam Hussein's agents. Tom argued that ignoring the UN rules was both unethical and immoral, but Peter supported the approach and sided with management.

Laura and Abbie's conversation fell back on Laura and Tom's four adult children. As they talked, Abbie poured a glass of wine and offered it to Tom. This time, he accepted.

In front of Laura, the multiple stages rose in wedding cake layers with several smaller stages nestled beside them. Tall gum trees formed a majestic backdrop. The lights dimmed, and a hush settled over the crowd. She yearned to reach out and touch Tom's arm, or better still, cuddle into the crook of his armpit and call a truce, but the look on his face warded her off and she turned her attention to the artistic director's opening address.

The floodlights dimmed and the throb of drums cascaded into the night air. It drew her in. A fire wheel swirled arcs of flame as performers strutted into the light, fire flared from their heads and backs, and a tribal rhythm underscored the dancing. Flames licked and danced in time to the music. She stared, transfixed. Strong unwelcome emotions rose unbidden and threatened to overwhelm her. She fought the urge to get up and run; to be carefree and careless. Instead, she watched as the dancers threaded gracefully around the stages, some on stilts and all aflame; their control and precision almost suffocating. Their white fire suits eerily juxtaposed with the dark backdrop and the towering trees. The crowd's gasps filled any brief silences.

Through the evening, the acts spun intricate patterns and tunes, each different from the one before yet eerily the same, creating a harmonised yet diverse performance. Smoke laced the air. Laura's attention was commandeered by long trumpet-like instruments wailing into the air, rising above the drums, and she lost herself in the noise and spectacle. Her heart raced as flashing flares of flame and light illuminated everything, even the dark corners of her mind.

A flare briefly cast light across the audience, and she glanced at Tom. She thought she saw him smile and finally, Laura smiled too. He was enjoying himself at last. She let the furious beat and dancers pull her attention back to the show.

Then, as the evening drew to a close, it burst into a crescendo of the biggest fireworks display she'd ever seen. Colours and light sprayed patterns across the inky sky. A familiar lump choked in her throat and she fought back tears. Fireworks made her emotional; she didn't know why. Blossoming streaks of colour erupted onto the dark backdrop, turning it grey with tufts of smoke. The colour and whizz of the golden rockets overloaded her senses. The crowd oohed and aahed, erupting into applause as the hour-long show came to an end. Laura closed her eyes, trying to imprint the unbelievable beauty of the fireworks on her mind and capture forever the spectacle in her memory.

As the applause subsided, Laura reluctantly opened her eyes. The area spotlights' glare blinded her momentarily, and she resisted the pull of those around her as they gathered their belongings and prepared their exodus. She looked up at Peter, confused by his open-mouthed stare and followed his gaze. Tom, his strange pallor revealed by the full lights and that grimace she'd mistaken for a smile, fixed on his face, sat still. His arm hung limply at his side, touching the ground in an unnatural pose. His head tipped back. If his eyes had been closed, she'd have thought him asleep.

She reached out and touched him, murmuring, 'Tom. Tom, it's—'

He didn't stir. She recoiled, struggled out of her chair, then shook him. He was asleep, wasn't he?

At her touch, he slid sideways and slumped to the ground. It couldn't be happening.

Peter was on the phone. The people immediately beside them stood and stared while the crowds beyond them pushed and jostled as they tried to leave.

Chapter 2

People helped with first aid. The ambulance slowly navigated through the streaming crowd. But all was in vain. Peter held Laura close and Abbie took charge, clearing the space around Tom, organising and arranging.

Laura sank into Peter and Abbie's care. Tom had had a heart attack. It didn't seem possible, but he was dead. She choked as she spoke to her children. At first, the words wouldn't come. He's dead; he died; so final. Three times she'd uttered those words and each time she summoned all her reserves, to calm the shock and horror for herself and her children. Only Robby didn't know yet. Tears streamed down her face. Peter and Abbie waited with her at the hospital until the second and quietest of Laura's four children arrived. Mel bundled Laura into the car to take her home.

They drove through the city. Twinkling lights punctured the darkness, while groups of young people transited between nightclubs; their laughter and raucous carousing ringing through the air, oblivious to her pain. For them, nothing had changed. But Laura's life, and that of her children, would never be the same again. They drove in silence. There were no words left to say.

Her sense of loss, knowing she couldn't press replay or atone for being cold and indifferent, added to her grief. All her efforts couldn't change anything now. He was gone, and with him went the life she knew.

Tears filled Laura's eyes. 'I was so angry with him …and now—'

'Dad knew you loved him,' Mel whispered.

'He'd changed his mind again. He didn't want to go to the opening, and I got cross … he always had some excuse. I didn't believe he was unwell. And now…'

At home, Mel parked while Laura went on ahead and unlocked the front door. A faint thump sounded inside. The hairs on her arms stood rigid.

Mel stepped up behind her. 'Is everything alright?' she asked.

Laura put her finger to her lips. She cautiously clasped the bedroom door handle and nudged it open. Nothing. She scoured the living room, but everything was in its place. It didn't feel right, but it looked untouched. She hesitantly motioned for Mel to come in.

As she turned to lock the front door, a clunk sounded from down the hall. The hairs on her neck bristled. There was someone in Tom's study.

'Hello,' she called out.

Silence.

She called again, but no one answered.

They crept down the hall. Laura reached forward tentatively and gently pushed the door ajar. A faint beer odour perturbed her. She had no time to adjust to the darkness before the door was wrenched from her hands. Laura flew forward. A blow to her shoulder sent her crashing to the floor. Something jabbed her side and her hands flew up in protection. Material brushed her fingers but eluded her grasp. Mel cried out, followed by a thud and footsteps receding down the hall. The front door slammed.

Laura moaned as she struggled upright.

'Are you alright?' she called out to Mel.

'I think so.' Mel rubbed her head. 'What about *you*?'

'I think I'm OK.'

Laura wrapped her arms around Mel before reluctantly dragging herself away to limp to the front door and lock it.

Blood trickled down Mel's forehead.

'It's nothing,' Mel insisted as Laura steered her into the bathroom to examine it more closely.

When the doorbell rang, Mel clutched a walking stick from her father's collection, and together they approached the door. The sight of Laura's best friend, Eva, on the doorstep made them both relax.

Eva examined their injuries, then phoned the police while Laura checked her jewellery box and keepsake drawer. Nothing was missing. Only Tom's office had been disturbed.

When the police arrived, Eva took charge. Laura couldn't provide a description, and Mel only recalled a balaclava-clad thief in black clothing. There were no signs of a forced entry and the police suggested Laura had forgotten to lock the front door. At first, it seemed plausible, until she remembered unlocking it when she arrived home.

The police dusted the door handles, window locks, and surfaces in Tom's office for fingerprints and searched for clues. The laptop and Tom's old work satchel appeared to be the only things missing.

'One of my officers found a key under the hall table. Is it yours?' the short, squat, police officer asked.

'It must be the spare from outside,' Laura suggested. Hers was still in the back of the door.

'It could be how they gained entry,' the police officer said. 'They might dump the laptop and satchel somewhere nearby if they're not valuable. Make sure you lock up after we leave and don't leave a spare key outside.'

Laura shivered. Was he suggesting they might come back?

He handed her the paperwork with a reference number. 'They don't appear to have taken anything valuable. It could be identity fraud,' he suggested.

The top two filing cabinet drawers were open and there were spaces in the previously crammed second drawer, indicating files were missing. The locked desk drawer had been jimmied open and was now empty. Tom stored his most recent precious concerns in there.

November 2004

He'd been in his study all morning, again. Laura brought him a cup of tea to encourage him to take a break. Maybe they could go out for lunch. Tom hunched over his desk, scribbling furiously and adding to the angry red scrawls defacing the document in front of him.

'How about taking a break?' She softened her voice to not startle him but he startled anyway.

'I'm busy, I can't...' he muttered.

'For goodness sake.' Would he ever let work go?

'It's important. I can't work it out.' He glanced at her, then at the cup, as though seeing both for the first time. 'It's all in jeopardy. How has this happened?'

'Is this about work again? Surely the senior people will sort it out. That's what they're paid for. You don't work there anymore. Why don't you give it to Peter and let him deal with it?'

Tom shuffled the papers and used his pen to circle some figures on the first and second pages. He rested his head in his hands. 'It has to be sorted but—'

'Will we ever have a retirement together?' Laura raised her voice, trying to break through.

He glared. 'I raised my concerns about the Wheat Board scandal with management and you see how that turned out. I was punished for asking questions and standing up for principles. I won't let that happen again.'

Laura stormed out and went out for a light lunch by herself.

***

Even after Tom retired, he worked tirelessly in his home office, keeping the details secret. He'd hinted it was dangerous more than once, but he and Peter tended towards the melodramatic. They'd often joked, "If I tell you, I'd have to kill you."

The police left and Laura sat on the sofa with Eva while Mel paced the lounge.

'My jewellery and other valuables haven't been touched.'

'They didn't get the chance,' Eva suggested.

'Dad's satchel was pretty old. Was there anything in it?'

'I don't know.' An icy shiver ran up Laura's spine. 'We interrupted him.'

The office was an odd room for a thief to start and the list of items stolen – a decrepit old satchel, an ancient laptop, and Tom's papers – raised questions.

'Do you think there could be a connection?' she asked no one in particular. 'Could the break in be related to what he was working on?'

'What?' Eva asked.

'Tom's files being stolen on the same night he died.'

'No.' Mel frowned at her mother.

'It's not like…no, I don't think so,' Eva said.

Were his papers important enough for someone to break into the house to steal them? She pressed her fingers against her eyes. What was he doing and what were the papers about? If the thieves wanted them this badly, good luck to them. They were no use to her.

'You can't stay here tonight, Mum. I'll fix up the spare bed at my place,' Mel said.

Laura packed an overnight bag and closed the study door before she left. Outside, she checked under the third rock in the flower garden. The spare key was still there. What key had the police found inside?

Chapter 3

John Masters strode across the shaded courtyard, stepping over the debris from Sunday's violent winds across Sydney. A large branch had speared a café divider, its end resting precariously across an outdoor table. With the café closed on weekends, no one was hurt. The office workers, or as he preferred to call them, bludgers, were back, sitting among the dishevelment as though nothing had changed. He smiled. As usual, they pretended to work while sipping their coffee and boasting about their cleverness. He heard them; anyone walking past could hear them, and he suspected it was their intention, this was their verbal CV.

John nodded to familiar faces. He enjoyed being recognised and people cultivating his friendship, although he rarely bothered to remember their names. His hard work paid off, and he was proud of owning a successful transport company by the age of forty-five. Now his sights were set on the next step.

He flashed his pass at the security desk, and the elevator doors pinged open as he approached. He stepped inside. The mirrored walls were freshly polished, and he scanned his reflection, fluffing up his brown hair and dabbing at the moisture on his brow. The scars on his chin had faded nicely, and the one on his lip added an interesting and menacing touch. Otherwise, the surgery had healed well. It successfully transformed his features; his father might not even recognise him now. The multiple surgeries made him look new, but inside, he was still the same.

The expensive suit sat well on his medium frame and he ran his hand over his almost flat abdomen with satisfaction. The elevator shuddered and jerked to the fifth floor. When the doors opened, his eyes squinted to adjust to the dimness. Meeting rooms, alcoves, and partitions bordered the corridor. All the natural light was cut off and the windows at the end were overshadowed by a new building next door. The top floor office had recently become vacant and John coveted the commanding view across Sydney harbour and the abundant natural light. It was more appropriate for his status.

Fleur, his receptionist, looked up, and her delicate lips curved into a coy smile.

'Good morning, Mr Masters,' she said.

She'd only started working for him last month, but he'd noticed that look before. His eyes swept over her face and body, the old-fashioned floral dress denying any hint of what was beneath. She wasn't his type, too plain and perhaps too young, but she had a warm smile. He nodded acknowledgment and walked on past.

'I've printed the important emails for you. They're on your desk,' she purred. 'Would you like a coffee?'

'Thanks.' John appraised her slightly rounded body. 'I think you can call me John when we're alone.'

He felt her eyes follow him as he walked into the even darker office. He was a summer creature, the sun and its warmth imbued him with a sense of wellbeing. Greyness settled over him as he slumped in his chair.

Turning to the pile of papers on the edge of his desk, he selected the first file. Fleur already had his daily routine set up the way he liked it. His aversion to technology had been a constant battle with his last personal assistant, but Fleur didn't fuss. She printed everything he needed and put it in neat stacks for his attention. It was a perfect system. He knew technology would probably win in the end, but he was buying time.

John worked through one file; two South American shipments were delayed for the second time in the last six months. His contacts were embroiled in another feud with their competitors, and these ego-driven disputes were hampering business. John clenched his fist. He'd paid handsomely for officials to turn a blind eye, yet there was always another official, another payoff. Smuggling drugs should have been easy money. It was for his little sister, Dimi.

Dimi's Iraqi supply wasn't affected by the petty issues he dealt with in South America. He'd get his revenge. He'd make his move to take over soon. It was fitting. The family business should have been his all along.

His mind wandered. John's business, especially transporting large-scale construction equipment, was thriving, thanks to unofficial military contracts in Iraq. That and the sensitive weapons business channelled his way by the arms manufacturer, Wayne Skollov. It was good, but not enough. John wanted more, and an introduction to the latest crop of politicians would open more doors.

You could never have too many friends and allies within the government. The current government didn't have factions, but they had tribes, and at the moment, they were warring tribes. The PM's sudden heart attack, during one of his early morning walks, sent the party machine into chaos. They couldn't decide anything without him taking charge. The jostling for position had been ugly to watch, but somehow, an outsider took over as PM. Luckily, his allies were also John's contacts.

The mobile's shrill ringtone interrupted his musings and John fumbled his private phone out of his pocket.

'Giovani, ah John?' Carlo's deep voice faltered.

John scowled. Carlo's carelessness was unforgivable.

'Watch your tongue. I'm John Masters now, remember that,' John scolded. Carlo had worked for the family long enough and should know better.

'Sorry,' Carlo said insincerely. 'It's confirmed.'

John stretched his legs and leaned back. 'So, tell me.'

'He's been silenced.'

'How?'

'You don't need to know the details, but it's settled.'

'Good.' One less impediment to deal with. Dimi was too indecisive and let that complication get out of hand. 'And the documents?'

'I think we have them. We're making sure.'

John shook his head. He'd make sure issues like this were dealt with quickly once he took over. 'What about the girl?'

'She's been frightened off.'

'Bloody Hell! That's it? She could ruin everything.'

'The boss is on it.'

John clenched his jaw. Carlo had promised this before. He was too protective of Dimi, and always had been. His agreement to be John's inside man still surprised him. John expected Carlo to resist more, to require more inducements to switch his allegiance away from Dimi. As long as Carlo didn't bullshit him. Maybe he felt loyalty to John, the son and traditional heir, but then again, maybe Carlo was double-dealing.

'The *boss* has cost us time and is jeopardising that business. Don't be taken in by the rhetoric. You need to act.'

'It doesn't affect you, not yet,' Carlo said quietly.

'If you screw this up, we're all screwed. That means you too. At this rate, there may be no business left for me to take over and you could be out in the cold.'

Carlo sighed, obviously unable to think of a witty retort. Of course, his talents lay elsewhere.

'Keep me informed and remember, keep your trap shut.' A year of aggravations and slip-ups made John edgy. He'd enough to think about without Dimi's stuff-ups. 'Now for my plans. Business plans,' he added.

'What about them?' Carlo sounded no more ready to move forward than the last time.

'I'm not waiting much longer. As soon as Dimi's mess is sorted, I'm moving forward,' John insisted.

'It's too risky. I don't like it,' Carlo protested. 'If it ain't broke, don't fix it.'

'I can't…no I *won't* wait. I have to strike while the iron is hot.' John smiled. He could match proverbs with Carlo anytime.

John was not a patient man, and he'd already waited far too long. He clenched and unclenched his fist.

'You don't need to overstretch and risk everything. I—' Carlo grumbled.

'It's not your decision.'

'Yeah.'

'You do your job and I'll handle the rest.' John hung up. He welcomed Carlo's advice and ideas, but there was a limit.

He stood, walked to the window, and quietly studied the office block next door. It was time for action before his little sister stuffed it up completely. He smiled, imagining Dimi's face. She'd finally learn that she wasn't rid of her big brother. Then he'd have his revenge.

Chapter 4

The weeks flew by in a blur. The arrangements, cards, and condolences blended into an amorphous movie, one in which Laura felt like a bad actress being prompted and cajoled into place as the action swept around her. Regret, anger, and sorrow swirled into a mix of emotions that were constantly misinterpreted by family and friends. She'd been in limbo waiting for the autopsy, but the results left her breathless. An overdose of an illicit drug had triggered a heart attack. Guilt again clutched at her chest. If he'd been depressed, she should have seen it; known; helped; shouldn't she?

She walked into his office. Three weeks since he'd died and, at times, she still expected to see him sitting at his desk. Conflicting emotions tossed her like a rudderless ship. At times she ached for Tom, but enjoying the tranquillity and relief at not having to cope with his moods brought debilitating guilt.

His office reflected a sense of crisis with piles of papers stacked high. His collection of notebooks, newspaper clippings, and official documents appeared haphazard, but Tom was anything but haphazard. There'd been a system, one she wasn't privy to. Why had Tom locked himself away in here for hours, even days, at a time? What was he working on? And what files had the thief taken?

The space was now clearer than she could remember; the thief managed what she couldn't. Three notebooks lay at the base of the filing cabinet. Flipping the pages, a cartoon strip of jumbled jottings flickered past her eyes. Tom's form of shorthand was incomprehensible. Turning to leave, she spotted the corner of a brown envelope poking from behind the cabinet. She dropped the notebooks onto the desk, grabbed the letter opener and tugged it free.

'Commercial-in-confidence' was stamped across the documents. Familiar red-ink scrawls tracked along the invoice margin, and question marks with short commentaries scored the pages.

She and the family were painfully aware of Tom's unhappiness at work. After the takeover, the culture he so disliked was replaced by one he found even more difficult. His benefits and status were reduced, and he was bullied into accepting a less than satisfactory package. They transitioned into the Australian Pharmaceutical and Agriproducts Trading Organisation, or APATO for short. He hated it at first, but with time, he settled into a complaining acceptance.

These papers were six years old, from the time when APATO ran joint missions to Iraq with the Wheat Board, and Tom first voiced concerns about their use of illegal transport arrangements which contravened the UN Oil-for-Food program rules. He lobbied senior managers, but finally, let it drop. Once the Iraqi invasion began, there were no more joint missions and Tom settled into a more affable routine, although Tom's regrets smouldered.

Three years ago, he again fumed over an issue at work and it was worse than before, but by then, she'd lost patience. The Volcker report last year and the eventual establishment of the Cole Commission into the Wheat Board's practices stirred everything up as well. Even though APATO was exempt from the investigation, Tom's warnings were vindicated, and he seemed to blame himself for not persisting, not stopping what he'd known was wrong. He became cynical and disenchanted.

Perhaps his anger or regrets had plunged him into a black hole, deep enough to turn to drugs. Laura couldn't accept that answer. It made her culpable.

A rising tide of anger burst from deep within her. His brooding, preoccupation, and withdrawal took him away from her and his family, and for what? These files consumed him while he was alive, but she wasn't going to let his issues commandeer her anymore. She swept her arm over the desk and scattered the notebooks across the floor. The desk was clear, but her anger remained. Her simmering resentment felt foolish and useless. It was all too late.

May 2004

Laura carried her shopping bags into the house, surprised that Tom was already home.

'Did they throw you out?' she joked.

He smiled a weak unconvincing smile that only crinkled the corners of his mouth.

'Well, funny you should say that.' A fake levity tinged his voice. 'I've been offered a redundancy package. They're cleaning out the 'deadwood' as they call it.'

'Maybe it's for the best.'

His eyes clouded and again he tried to smile, although it didn't work.

'Is the package any good?' Was he unhappy about the money or losing a job he hated?

'I'm getting some financial advice, but on the surface, it looks generous.'

'That would be a first, for them to be generous, I mean.' Laura remembered the haggling over pay and conditions even while Tom was travelling to dangerous places and risking his life for the job.

'To work there you have to be a believer, but I stopped believing some time ago.' He screwed up his face as though he was eating a lemon. 'It's time I accepted it and adjusted.'

'What do you mean?' Laura asked.

Tom shrugged. 'Never mind'

Laura unpacked the groceries and smiled. This was a new beginning.

***

At first, Tom seemed resigned to retirement, but slowly he began working on a project. It started with internet searches and phone calls and progressed to meetings. Before long, a cloud attached itself to him again. Work had been difficult, but retirement was worse. She couldn't convince him to stop, and the life she'd planned slipped through her fingers. He was troubled by more than his no longer being needed, but he wasn't telling. Laura believed they'd get over this phase, like the others. What a fool she'd been. Now there would be no next phase.

She'd never seen the pill bottle the police found in their bathroom and she didn't know where that key was from. The police were investigating, but what, if anything, would they find? And could she live with the answer? She hugged herself, pushing the guilt from her thoughts while sadness numbed her brain. She turned her attention outward to the desk.

The third drawer was jammed, and she gave up. As she moved away, she tripped on the notebooks at the base of the desk. This year's dark blue diary sat on top. It was mostly empty. There were no birthdays or anniversaries marked like in hers. The coded entries in the months before his death baffled her. 10th January 'meeting with CL' and 'phone PF re BL consignment.' Peter's initials were PF, Peter Fairbrother. Oblique numbers, similar to those on the documents, accompanied initials and times. The pages oozed secrecy and furtiveness. On the day he died, he'd been ensconced in the study, as usual, when she left for the supermarket. But an appointment with CL was written against 9.30 a.m. and the word *liar* and *he knows?* was scrawled in blue ink below the initials. The other doodles on the page were illegible.

She threw the diary on the desk and it skittered across the surface, coming to rest next to the envelope. She lowered her head into her hands. Was this about work or drugs? She would never know.

Finally, Laura stuffed the papers back into the envelope. The Tom she'd fallen in love with hadn't been paranoid or hysterical. He'd been systematic, a problem solver. What had happened to him? And to them? And now, what would happen to her?

Laura slowly wandered into the kitchen, opened the fridge door, then closed it again. She didn't want to cook for one. She opened the pantry door, scanned the contents, and took out a loaf of bread. The toasted sandwich didn't take long, and she hunkered down in her chair in front of the TV and flicked the remote control. Nothing happened. She shook it, pressed a few buttons, then threw it down when the phone rang. Abbie's voice was soothing, but Laura was tired and grumpy. She used the excuse her dinner was getting cold to cut the conversation short. But, with the phone back in its stand, she stared at her cold toasted sandwich and at the uncooperative TV and tears edged to the corners of her eyes, finally trickling down her cheek. The trickle turned into a flood as the emotions pushed through the widening gap in her resolve and she couldn't stem the flow. Her shoulders shook, her face screwed in pain, and the tears took with them some of the tension that became such a burden, but the sadness remained.

When the doorbell rang, it startled her. She grabbed a tissue and swiped at her eyes. Her reflection in the hall mirror was scary, the red eyes and blotchy skin told on her. She saw Peter through the peephole, smoothed down her hair, and pulled herself upright. His face took on a strange combination of grimace and smile when she opened the door, as though he couldn't decide which he should use.

'Abbie told me you needed help.' He leaned forward and pecked her cheek.

'Oh?' Then she remembered, 'Oh yes, the TV.'

'Let's have a look at it.'

He sat in Tom's chair and studied the remote control. He pushed some buttons, walked to the TV, and pressed the on button. It flashed into life. He fidgeted with the remote control and laughed.

'Have you got some AAA batteries?'

Laura found two in the laundry cupboard and, as soon as Peter replaced them, the TV obeyed his directions.

He stood up and patted her shoulder. 'It'll be alright now.'

His hand remained gently resting on her shoulder, and she sat down.

'You look beat.' He turned off the TV and grabbed two wine glasses from the cupboard. He lifted a bottle from the wine rack into the air. 'Shall we?'

Laura hesitated, then nodded.

Peter poured two generous glasses of rich red wine and handed her one.

Laura breathed in the aroma, swirling her wine distractedly. They clinked glasses and Peter muttered, 'To old friends.' Were they toasting each other, or Tom?

The wine swept over her palate and she realised with surprise that this was the first glass of red she'd consciously enjoyed since Tom's death. She settled back in the chair and Peter sat on the sofa. His eyes studied her intently, and she became self-conscious.

'You look wrung out. Are you OK?' The tenderness in Peter's voice almost opened up that crack again. She fought the imminent tears and, not daring to speak, nodded.

'It's been rough, I know.' He leaned towards her. 'Do you need help with anything else?'

Under control now, Laura met his eyes. 'No, but thanks. I haven't…it doesn't feel…real. One minute he was here, the next—I sometimes expect him to walk through that door, but then I remember.' She shrugged.

That was the part of the story she was willing to share. She couldn't share the darker feelings and her need for answers.

Peter sat back again and crossed his legs. 'Tom wasn't easy.' He chuckled, then saw her look. 'Sorry, that was tactless.'

Laura hid behind her wine glass and took another sip. 'What do you mean?'

'It was obvious he was taking his frustrations out on those around him. He brushed off my attempts to talk to him. He was in a shit about being made redundant and you took the brunt of it.'

Laura tensed, but her rigid control was loosened by the red wine, or perhaps Peter's acknowledgment. It was loosening her tongue, too.

'We never talked anymore.'

'It's not unusual. Even Abbie and I can have weeks when we hardly talk. She's busy, I'm busy, it happens.'

'But I was mean. I feel guilty,' she blurted out. Why was she telling him?

'Don't Laura.' He edged forward on the sofa and reached over to touch her arm. 'You can't feel guilty. He was impossible that day. We both know he could be a real prick when he wanted to.'

Laura pulled away, feeling disloyal, and Peter muttered an apology, 'I didn't mean to bad-mouth him, but it's true.'

With a smooth movement, he refilled her glass. Laura hadn't realised it was empty.

'It's been hard on you. I saw what was happening and felt for you.'

'But… I could have…' Laura didn't know how to finish it. The fun-loving, passionate, caring Tom she'd loved had morphed into a different, angrier version. She understood change was inevitable. She'd changed too, but it had created a wedge between them. Even though their marriage became strained, they'd still loved each other. Hadn't they? She believed it, but believing didn't necessarily make it true.

'What are you thinking?' Peter's prompt lapped over her remembrances.

'I was thinking about how different we were at university. You remember, don't you?' They'd been a fun-loving foursome, Tom and

Laura and Peter and Eva, long before Abbie.

'We were idealistic; naïve.'

Peter's emphasis brought images flooding into Laura's mind; Tom standing on the soapbox arguing antinuclear messages despite his fear of public speaking. Emotion forced him to create the kind of fuss he hated, pushing him into the limelight. It seemed like only yesterday. The quiet and principled Tom she'd fallen in love with had made her heart sing.

Peter interrupted Laura's thoughts. 'Do you remember when he fell off the podium?'

'Yes, I remember.' She chuckled at the image summoned by the memory. 'He swore he wasn't drunk, but we knew better.'

'We certainly did. I topped up his glass when he wasn't looking, to give him some Dutch courage.'

'You didn't?' Laura exclaimed.

Peter winked at her. 'He was too controlled, and we needed one of his rallying speeches.' A sparkle in Peter's eyes danced as he shook his head gently. It reminded her of his younger self, all energy and bravado, the one Laura had found attractive. 'I guess I went a bit far,' he added.

'We even missed the march when we took him to hospital.' Laura sighed. 'We used to believe in things, anti the Vietnam War, and nuclear weapons. What's happened?'

'You still have causes.'

'I've been distracted, raising a family and making a living. I sign the occasional petition, but I'm wrapped up in my own life and busyness. Tom was serious enough for both of us, although—'

'He became bitter. Work knocks the edges off you if you don't conform, especially these days. Tom never learned to protect himself and forge on. That's why I beat him for promotion and eventually, why he was asked to leave.'

'Asked to leave?'

'It wasn't a general cleanout. You knew that, didn't you? Patrick felt he was a liability and … he should leave.'

'Patrick?'

'You know, Patrick Furness, the minister in charge. Didn't Tom tell you?'

'I knew something was troubling him, but he kept it to himself.' Tom said it was a cost-cutting exercise, not that he'd been singled out.

Silence sent her thoughts into areas she preferred to avoid. Why was he targeted? What had he done? Did she really want to know?

'Have you cleaned out his study yet? Did he have any classified documents?' Peter interrupted.

Laura nodded. 'You know some were stolen the day he…'

'That was frightening for you. Did they take much?'

Laura shook her head.

'Promise me, if you find any documents, files, or other materials, you'll let me know. He wasn't himself anymore. In fact, why don't I save you the bother and clean out his study, just in case?'

She shook her head. 'It's OK.' Then she remembered the bundle of documents sitting on the desk. 'I found some behind the filing cabinet today. Do you want them?'

Peter nodded.

Laura left to collect them. She handed him the envelope, and he flicked through.

'Thanks.' He put them down beside his chair. 'These are old. There isn't anything else, is there?'

'If I find anything, I'll let you know, but I need more time.' She preferred to sort through Tom's office. She didn't know what she'd find.

'It's important you don't handle confidential material or throw it out. It's an offence. Let me deal with it. It's no trouble. I'm happy to help.' He sipped his wine and continued. 'Tom was paranoid. You don't need to trouble yourself with that stuff. He was in…*had* trouble with change and needed to let go of his…bugbears.'

She thought back to the papers in his office, his bugbears, as Peter called them. 'Like you did?' she said. 'You became a good corporate citizen, didn't you?' Tom complained about Peter's preparedness to do what the company wanted without question.

'Of course, Tom would say that.'

'He didn't say much. Only that you and he disagreed a lot recently. He thought you took the company line too much.'

'There are rules and there's a hierarchy. I know when to keep my mouth shut.' Peter sipped again, studying Laura.

'And your eyes, maybe?'

Peter's hand twitched sharply, and he almost spilled his wine.

'That's not fair. Tom had his own agenda.' Peter smiled, but his voice remained tight. 'Anyway, is being a good corporate citizen such a bad thing? I faced reality, the world changed, and I changed with it.'

'Is that why you met with Tom in January?'

Peter frowned. 'January? We hadn't seen each other since before Christmas. Anyway, why would we meet? I didn't talk to him about work anymore and these days we weren't mixing socially without you and Abbie.'

Why would Peter lie? Maybe the PF in the diary wasn't him. Her head ached, and she watched Peter watching her. 'Did you know he was taking drugs?' she asked.

Peter looked down at the wine swirling in his glass and sighed. 'I never saw him take anything, but his behaviour became strange.'

'There were illicit drugs in his system as well as heart medication.'

'I heard. Perhaps he was self-medicating. That combination can produce a sense of euphoria and wellbeing. It can make people feel invincible.'

'That doesn't describe his mood.'

'It can affect people in different ways, I guess. Maybe, in Tom's case, they induced paranoia. That's possible too.'

'You seem to know a lot about these drugs.'

'You forget, working with pharmacists, we pick up information all the time.'

'Surely, not about illicit drugs?'

'Well, no, but we talk about what's out there. That synthetic drug, E-bomb, or Euphoria, as it's sometimes known, is new and causing problems on the streets, so of course, we talk about it.'

'I still can't believe Tom would take drugs.' What else hadn't she noticed?

They sat in silence, each looking at their glass of wine and lost in their thoughts. Tears pricked at Laura's eyes, but she bit them back. Peter leaned forward, breaking the spell.

'He became sour. We talked from time to time, but not much anymore. Work became a barrier.' He stared up at her. 'He did love you.'

She scanned the photos around the room. 'Just not enough,' she whispered.

The love between her and Tom had struggled for expression or even acknowledgment in the last few years. It had to be taken on trust, but the lack of confirmation had left Laura adrift. She'd withdrawn and their ties to one another weakened. It added to her guilt.

'He didn't *appreciate* you, though.' Peter slid forward in his seat, this time resting his hand on her knee.

'We were both guilty of not appreciating each other,' Laura admitted.

Peter didn't move his hand. His animal magnetism got him into trouble. She, like many other women, had found him attractive. She'd been charmed by him in the early days and, as if seeing him for the first time, Laura understood why. Despite getting older, he exuded energy and life, even when perfectly still. His eyes twinkled and the spiky grey hair added boyish charm, not age.

Leaning further forward so his breath puffed lightly against her face, he whispered, 'You're a beautiful, smart, and strong woman.

I've always admired you. You know I've always been attracted to you. Tom beat me to it.'

He stood, and taking her hand, pulled her out of the chair. Their clothes brushed against each other. Her skin tingled with the nearness of him; his subtle pine-scented aftershave reminded her of university days when they were young and carefree. His lips found hers. She responded involuntarily, remembering that time all those years ago. A craving for affection and touch stirred in her. He wrapped his arms around Laura, pulling her close as his kisses became hungrier and stronger with her response. Her mind disengaged and a low moan escaped her lips.

Then, for no reason she could identify, she pushed him away. Gasping for breath, she stared at the familiar face of their family friend and shook her head violently.

'No.' There was only the beginning of resolve in her quiet voice.

'Laura.' His hands reached for her, to drag her back, but she shook him off.

'No.' This time, her voice resonated with more force and determination.

'Laura. You want this too; I can feel it.' He pleaded with his eyes, 'I've wanted this for a long time. We could—' He read her answer as she stepped back. 'Why not?'

'We're different people now. There's Eva, Abbie, Katie.' She couldn't let this happen.

'They need never know. It can be our secret. What about us?'

'No, I can't.' Laura turned, almost knocking the empty wineglass off the coffee table. 'It's late, you'd better go.'

Peter's eyes turned fierce. 'You can't do this, Laura.' He stepped towards her, then stopped. 'There won't be another chance.'

A laugh tickled at Laura's throat. She was becoming used to missing second chances, but she was certain she wouldn't regret this.

Peter moved towards the door, trying to turn on the charm again, but she knew him better than he perhaps knew himself. He'd be over the rejection by the time he'd started his car. Strangely, the look on his face was more anger than disappointment.

Chapter 5

John edged his sedan into the remaining space. Skye's Audi was parked at a careless angle, forcing him closer to the wall than usual. Inside, he called out to Skye, but there was no reply. He strode through the atrium, loosening his tie. With a flick of the wrist, he threw it through the open doorway and watched it slither off the bed onto the floor. In the kitchen, he again called out, but there was still no answer.

With no Skye to distract him, he grabbed a glass, threw in some ice, and fixed himself a generous Campari with vermouth and a dash of soda. He opened the fridge, lifted the lid off the prepared dinner left by the housekeeper, and sniffed. It smelled good, but tonight, he preferred pizza.

He slid gently into the soft leather sofa and gazed out onto Bondi Beach. The glistening, choppy water traced white froth patterns across the waves. He drank deeply and relaxed back against the cushions.

His phone pinged with a message; the latest shipment was underway, but a search at the departing Guatemala City airport resulted in an extra *fee*. Again! He frowned. Another bribe. These altered arrangements, dishonoured contracts, and constant hiccups took a toll. He was tired of working with these gangs.

Dimi's easy market appealed more than ever. Dimi, short for the diminutive one, was his nickname for his little sister, a term of either endearment or insult. John smirked. His intent was rarely endearment. He itched to call her, but he couldn't blow his cover. Not yet.

He hurled the phone onto the sofa. He'd never been good at delayed gratification, but it was necessary to safeguard his plans.

John gulped down his drink, then made another. He swirled it vigorously, and the melting ice sent the red liquid dangerously close to the edge. That's exactly how he felt.

The front door clicked and high heels tapped across the front entrance.

'Hello,' Skye's husky voice called through the house.

'In here,' John directed, disappointed that she was home already.

'Hi, honey.' Skye staggered slightly in her impossibly high heels. Her long, shapely legs accentuated the shortness of her skirt. She bent down and kissed him sensuously on the lips before toppling onto the sofa. She giggled.

'I thought the photoshoot was at lunchtime.'

Skye waved her hand casually in the air. 'I hung around with the crew afterwards.' She turned and focused her eyes on him, then pouted. 'What? Can't I have a drink and be sociable sometimes?'

He hated the childish voice she used when he challenged her.

'Drinks?' He clenched and unclenched his fist, pumping his annoyance down. 'I'm warning you. If you're taking that shit Anton's into, we're done.'

'I'm not!' Skye turned away. 'I went for a drink,' she protested.

He didn't believe her. It was classic Skye, lying and trying to cover up.

'Listen, Babe. I'm not telling you again. Stay away from that stuff. You don't know where it's from or what's in it.' He should know. This was his business line after all.

Skye avoided his eyes and shrugged. 'It was a few drinks,' she insisted and laid her head on his shoulder.

'Anton can help your career. Don't screw it up. Keep it professional,' he warned. Fucking Anton. 'He's good for your exposure, but I won't stand for you getting involved in that shit.' John wasn't going to work through these issues again, not with anyone.

Her head lay heavily on his shoulder and she didn't move.

'Did you hear me?' he shouted at her hair.

Skye flinched and nodded gently, without lifting her head. It had been a mistake to call in the favour from Anton. John jerked his shoulder up hard, and Skye suddenly sat up.

'You're paranoid. I said it was a few drinks. That's all it was.'

'Don't call me paranoid. I know what I'm talking about. I can see the signs.' He clenched his fist.

'Have it your way.' She glared at him and stood up. 'But you're wrong.'

He glared back. He didn't like the argumentative Skye.

'I'm going to have a shower and freshen up. What's for dinner?' She looked away from John, towards the kitchen.

'There's something in the fridge but I'm ordering pizza,' he said.

Skye pulled a face. 'And a salad?'

He shrugged. 'I'll order.' She ate like a bird anyway.

Her heels clipped down the hallway, then muffled as she stepped onto the carpeted bedroom floor.

She was gorgeous, and her success was guaranteed, if only she'd focus on the endgame. Those legs and her tight arse got him hard, and those breasts. They'd cost him a fortune, but they were worth it. Although, he wouldn't let her become a liability.

He'd seen it before. Careers ready to fly only to be shot down; uppers, downers, appetite suppressants, happy pills before getting onto the hard stuff. First, you'd see it in their eyes, and their skin, both becoming dull and lifeless. Cosmetic surgeons could only do so much. The vain attempts to hold back the ravages, not of time, but loose living, were expensive. He couldn't go through that again.

A face from the past leaped into his mind. Harper. Young, fresh, and full of life. That's the way he liked to remember her, the way she was before the drugs drained her energy and turned her into a hopeless liar. His heart ached at the thought of her. He'd loved her more than anyone before, or since. He'd wanted to save her, but he'd failed. Her addictions stole the woman he loved, and his life was changed forever. He hung his head and stared into his empty glass. The accident killed the one thing that mattered to him. He stroked the faint scar along his chin. In hospital, alone and grieving, he'd vowed to never allow himself to be hurt like that again.

John refreshed his drink. That crash had almost killed him, too. During his recovery, he'd become morose, despondent, lost, and hadn't known how to get out of the black hole. It took determination and, of course, his best friend, Kleb's help and support, both personally and professionally. John had surprised himself, too. He grasped the opportunity and become a new man with a whole new identity. He hadn't been known for his perseverance or strength, rather for the opposite traits. But this time, he'd beaten the odds, and no one was going to ruin it now, not even Skye.

His mind pulled down the curtain on Harper and he stowed the memory back out of reach. It would weaken him. She was in the past and nothing could change that. Instead, he focused on his challenges. He smiled. He'd start with Dimi, then he'd sort out Skye. One challenge at a time.

Chapter 6

Arranging the funeral, organising the will, notifying friends and businesses, and completing paperwork and forms, had successfully tied up Laura's thoughts for weeks. She'd swatted away the occasional bout of grief and focused on her busyness, consoling the children, and dealing with others. She was good at putting herself last, and others simply followed her example.

Laura plumped and fluffed the cushions for the third time and straightened the painting once more. Robby and Shayida were late. Robby wasn't constrained by time, but she'd hoped his new girlfriend might have a more positive influence. Of her four children, the twenty-one-year-old twins, Robby and Becky, were the youngest in more ways than age.

Laura checked her image in the mirror and threaded her fingers through her uncooperative hair. She wasn't sleeping well, and it showed. The doorbell made her jump.

Shayida's high heels lifted her to Laura's eye level, and the waft of expensive perfume floated ahead of her through the doorway. Her long blonde hair feathered past her shoulders and waved and flicked with every movement of her head. She shook Laura's hand firmly. None of Robby's former girlfriends had been so formal, but then, none had been brought to the house to meet her either. Was he getting serious?

Robby trailed Shayida into the lounge. She scanned the room, chose the armchair, and sat down elegantly. Robby stood for a moment, looking awkward and uncomfortable, sauntered to the three-seater sofa and sprawled across it. Something about Shayida's manner didn't feel right.

'Can I get you anything?' Laura asked.

'A glass of water would be fine,' Shayida replied.

'I'd love a coffee,' Robby said.

'Maybe you should get them, Robby, and let your mum sit down,' Shayida cut in before Laura could respond.

Robby dragged himself off the sofa with exaggerated heaviness and Laura stifled a smile.

'Shayida's a lovely name.'

'Thank you. It's a family name.'

'Robby's kept you a secret. Have you known each other long?'

'We've been going out for a couple of months. Although, we met at my brother's workshop, about a year ago, when Robby brought his car in. We got talking and —'

'It's all very secret, but she was going out with someone else then. Now she's going out with me.' Robby said from the doorway. He grinned, seeming pleased with himself.

He placed a glass of water in front of Shayida and sat down with a mug of coffee and a packet of chocolate biscuits.

Shayida cleared her throat. 'What about your mum?'

Robby scowled but didn't argue. Laura was impressed.

'What do you want?' he asked in his least generous voice.

'I'll have a coffee thanks, Robby.' Laura turned back to Shayida. 'Your brother's a mechanic?'

Robby had been tight-lipped until now, so most of what Laura knew about Shayida had come from Becky.

'He helped me get a new car. Well, new to me anyway. It's great. Red, sleek, and reliable too. Nick owns the garage, and he has tattoo parlours and night —' Robby began.

Shayida's steely look cut him short. 'Nick has several businesses.'

A chill crept up Laura's spine. The mention of tattoo parlours conjured up thoughts of bikie gangs. Becky's description of Nick made it worse.

'He has businesses in Sydney, Melbourne, and even a couple in Brisbane.' Robby ignored Shayida's stern look, then left to make the coffee.

'I hear you're studying accountancy. You enjoy working with figures?' At least Shayida was pursuing a career.

'Working with money,' Robby answered as he set a mug on the table in front of Laura.

Laura sipped the weak, milky coffee and grimaced.

Robby dunked a chocolate biscuit in his coffee. 'Damn,' he exclaimed as the end broke off and fell into his cup. Grabbing a spoon from the sugar bowl, he swirled his coffee until finally raising a shapeless blob of biscuit. He swallowed it. It took all his concentration. The corners of Shayida's mouth turned down in disgust, but when she caught Laura's eye she shook her head with that 'boys will be boys' look.

'Are the rest of your family in Adelaide?' Laura hoped her fishing exercise would distract Shayida from Robby's.

'My parents live on the east coast. Dad's only connection to Adelaide now is us. He's in property development, so he's pretty busy and can only visit now and again.' Shayida scanned the large lounge room and added, 'This is a lovely place. Robby says you're selling up. Have you found somewhere to buy?'

'I'm still looking.'

'I'm sorry about Tom. It must have been a shock. Robby told me what happened. I'm sorry I didn't get to meet him.'

Laura nodded. 'I've lived here for almost thirty-five years. I'm not sure how I'm going to clear it up by myself.'

Despite not having a timetable to work to, she felt a strange urgency.

'It would be a big job after all those years,' Shayida said quietly.

'Dad's office is the biggest chore,' Robby said.

'I've cleared out a lot, but the biggest chore is the stuff you kids have left behind.'

'You'll have to help your mum,' Shayida suggested.

They sat quietly, then Robby turned to Shayida. 'Shall I show you my room?'

Shayida nodded, and they strolled down the hall. Laura smiled. Robby hadn't lived here for two years, but it was still *his* room.

After Laura tidied the kitchen, she walked down the hall to put away some books. Voices came from Tom's study. Why would Robby go in there? She gently opened the door, and the voices stopped. Robby sat in Tom's chair, flicking through one of the diaries while Shayida stood facing the filing cabinet. The top drawer was slightly ajar.

'The door was open,' Robby explained.

Laura remembered deliberately closing the door to confine the unpleasant memories.

'This is a lovely office. There's a lot of storage space. I guess it wouldn't have spilled over into the living areas like my study materials. It must've been hard work clearing it out.' Shayida smiled at Laura, but her eyes didn't reflect her smile.

'How are your studies going, Shayida?' Laura shook off her unease.

'I have exams coming up. I'll have to hit the books again soon.'

'What about you, Robby? Will you return to your studies?' Laura poked at a sore point.

'No way. It's not my scene. I can do better than that.'

'What do you mean?'

'I'm no good at studying,' Robby said irritably. 'We have to go.'

Shayida nodded, and they both moved towards the door.

Laura stepped back. 'I'll need you to sort through your boxes in the garage soon; I'm going to need the space.'

Robby looked at his watch. 'It'll have to wait; we're already running late.'

'Don't leave it too long. I need to prepare for open inspections.'

'I could drop by some time,' Robby explained, 'but I need a new key. I lost mine.'

He'd assured Laura he had it on the morning of the funeral.

'When did you first miss it?' Laura asked.

'I don't know.' Robby followed Shayida into the hall. 'I haven't used it in ages.' Robby shrugged.

As they walked through the lounge room, Shayida pointed to the coffee table. 'We've got time to clear up.'

'What?'

Daggers passed between them but Shayida shrugged, picked up the glass and biscuit packet and took them through to the kitchen. Robby followed.

'Don't worry about that,' Laura said.

Shayida shrugged. 'It's no problem.'

When they'd finished clearing up, Shayida left to use the bathroom.

'Shayida's family…are they…' Now she was alone with Robby, Laura couldn't find the right words.

Robby didn't help.

'Be careful, won't you?' Laura continued.

'Stop trying to run my life. I can look after myself.'

Robby's attempts at managing his own life, so far, had fallen short of the mark. She'd be ready to catch him when, not if, he fell, although she'd prefer to prevent a fall. Unfortunately, it wasn't her choice.

Shayida reappeared. She leaned in to kiss Laura on the cheek. 'It was lovely to meet you.'

Laura watched them leave. Robby's red Toyota sedan was a step up from his previous beat-up Suzuki. Hopefully, Nick's help didn't come with conditions.

Shayida and Robby were an improbable match. She radiated confidence and self-assurance, and he was immature. Laura had devoted a lifetime of love and energy to her family, nurturing and caring for them, yet, for the twins, especially Robby, she was simply their mother. She was subject to expectations and rules, but what Laura felt or wanted was immaterial and they swatted away her expectations of them. She'd been easier on the twins, softer and less demanding. Maybe this had lowered their ambitions, too. The eldest two, Mark and Mel, were different. They saw her as a person in her own right and understood, even when they didn't agree.

Once back inside, Laura started up the laptop. The search engine did its magic, listing references for Nick and his father. A newspaper article reported the father maintained a close relationship with both state and federal politicians. His company was rumoured to donate to both major parties and some minor ones. What was he getting in return? His business was embroiled in a controversy involving substandard imported cladding used on high-rise flats. Despite the higher fire danger putting lives at risk, he denied any responsibility. Laura sighed. It wasn't fair his business profited by using the substandard materials, but purchasers were charged thousands of dollars to fix the mistake and wouldn't be compensated.

Nick's turbulent history featured numerous court appearances without convictions. He was either being victimised or employed good lawyers. He reputedly held a powerful position in a bikie gang, too. Shayida was mentioned once. She'd provided an alibi for a rival gang member, known as 'Bulldog', in a 2004 shooting at a car repair garage. He was released without charge. The report inferred Nick would not be pleased with Shayida's "interference".

Did Robby know about Shayida's family? He seemed impressed by them, but did he know what the family was involved in? Was Shayida different, or was she biding her time?

Laura rang Eva.

'I've met Shayida, Robby's girlfriend. She seems nice enough, and she's studying accountancy.'

'A serious girlfriend who's studying might help him find his way.' Eva laughed.

'I wish. I worry about him.'

'It's natural. Our parents worried about us too and look at how we turned out. You never know what'll get Robby back on track.'

'We seemed more mature, or am I deceiving myself? Both Becky and Robby seem trapped in being young and dependent. I sometimes think I should call them Rebecca and Robert and see if it encourages them to grow up.'

'If only it were that simple.' Eva chuckled. 'It sounds like you have some reservations about Shayida.'

'That's why I'm phoning. I need your help.' As an ex-journalist, Eva had resources.

'Oh, not for my scintillating conversation then?' Eva laughed. 'Fire away, what do you need?'

'Robby's girlfriend is Shayida Saviento. Does that name mean anything to you?'

There was silence at the other end.

'The Saviento family? The head of the family is a property developer who's a bit … dodgy. He has important connections, if you know what I mean. There are rumours of mafia links, especially the Italian Mastriani family, but nothing has ever been proven.'

'Her brother, Nick, has connections to bikies.'

'That's the same family. He's allegedly president of the Python bikie gang and runs tattoo parlours, brothels, you name it. Is she one of those Savientos?'

'I think so.'

'They're dangerous. They've been involved in recent inter-gang trouble; people have been killed. I hear there's more trouble brewing.'

'I've never heard of them. I don't know how embroiled Shayida is in the family businesses, but I don't like Robby being involved with them.'

'I'd tread carefully and warn Robby. You don't want to get mixed up with that family.'

'If only he'd listen to me.'

'I could talk to him and spell out the seriousness of it.'

'He might listen to you.'

Eva promised to call once she'd talked to him. If he didn't listen to Eva, what could she do?

As soon as she put the phone down, it rang again.

'Hi again.' Eva must have forgotten something.

The only sound was soft breathing.

'Hello?'

Nothing.

She was about to hang up when the caller cleared their throat.

'I need to warn you. They think they've got everything, but if you find more, don't tell anyone. They're watching,' a woman's voice whispered.

'Who is this? What are you talking about?' Laura asked.

'Laura, be careful.'

She flinched at the use of her name.

'Keep Tom's files safe. Any tapes, DVDs, papers, no one must know if you find them. It's dangerous. They will kill to keep this information secret. Don't take any chances.'

Laura's mind reeled. 'I don't understand. What DVDs? Who are *they*?'

'I'll be in touch again once I'm sure of what to do with the information.'

There was a click, followed by a continuous buzz. They'd hung up.

Laura stared at the phone. This wasn't a prank? She could feel it. What had Tom become involved in that people would kill for the information?

Chapter 7

John breathed deeply, letting the cool, moist air fill his lungs. In front of him, Sydney harbour shimmered. Sunlight glistened on the water and his eyes followed a yacht skimming the wash near the heads, its sails billowing in the breeze. It was almost flying.

John turned at the sound of footsteps on the gravel path. The first thing anyone noticed about Kleb Sharpe were his piercing eyes and protruding nose. Just like his mother, although that was their only similarity. Combined with his athletic frame, Kleb reminded John of a panther. The easy-going manner on display today was his preferred public image, his lawyerly persona, but John had seen him at his brutal best and was glad to be his ally. They had history, but their friendship was a closely guarded secret. Kleb helped him recover from the accident, the multiple surgeries, and medical procedures, and was instrumental in getting John back on his feet business-wise. Of course, Kleb had his own motives and would also benefit from John's success. It wasn't only about friendship.

'This is a nice spot.' Kleb sat beside him on the bench seat. 'So, what's happening?'

'The usual South American issues. They're fleecing me at every turn,' John complained.

'What do you want to do about it?'

'I'm not sure what I can do.' John didn't like to declare defeat, but he was out of ideas. 'Their split into competing factions is affecting my supplies and the price.'

'I'll bet Skollov doesn't suffer these issues. He introduced you to them but didn't warn you or help in any way.' Kleb's dislike of Wayne Skollov surfaced.

'It's not his fault. He doesn't run their businesses for them,' John protested. Skollov's introduction to the South Americans had established the drug importation arm of his business. It had worked well at first.

'You're sure about that? His business interests span many territories and it's more than arms trading and security services. I don't trust Skollov, he's too cunning.'

John laughed. 'Are you saying we're not cunning?'

Kleb grinned. 'No, but his arrogance will bring him undone. Make sure he doesn't pull you down with him. It's a pity the politicians think the sun shines out of his proverbial. Skollov's gained access to inside information on defence and security. He must have something on them. If I can get you closer to the political inner circle, maybe we can prise him loose.'

John smiled. Kleb's introductions and a word in the right ear opened doors that John could never open by himself.

In front of them, the boats skipped across the water, and in the distance, the ferry trailed towards Manly. The breeze whipped up a discarded piece of paper near the bin and settled it at John's feet.

'How's the *Dimi* issue going?' Kleb smirked at the nickname.

'It's close. Taking over that business could solve my South American troubles. I don't like relying on the cartels. Maybe they'll play nice once I have the Mastriani name behind me. It would give me more clout. At least Dimi's eliminated the hitch.'

'Good. The takeover will set us up.' Kleb chuckled. 'I can't wait to see her face.'

John's takeover of the family business was personal for Kleb, too.

'Babbo should never have given Dimi control of the Australian arm of the business.' The sting of injustice pricked John again. He was the eldest, and the son. He should have been the natural heir, but no one could make his father see reason. The nickname Babbo suited his father perfectly. It was both an endearment and an insult, after all, his father was rarely a loving father but often a fool. 'Babbo was wrong. I'm more courageous, more forward-looking, and I'd have made the business thrive. He called Dimi a safe pair of hands, but we don't need safe right now. The business needs my entrepreneurial flare.'

John gritted his teeth. Dimi always had the dream run, while John was burdened with his father's unrealistic expectations. Babbo never forgave or forgot John's mistakes. Now John would show them both, and Dimi would finally pay.

Kleb shrugged. 'Babbo's ruthless, just like all his ilk. He wanted to pull you into line but probably would've caved in, if you'd … survived.' He grinned.

'Babbo never backed down.' John admired his father's tenacity, except when it became stubbornness.

John's memories flashed; the car accident, the white pristine hospital rooms, the pain, the operations, and recovery. It felt like only yesterday, especially the pain. Kleb kept John's recovery and rehabilitation secret. All in the name of revenge.

'You're right. Babbo won't listen to reason. He let my father …' Kleb's eyes flickered with an intense fire before fading to their controlled normal.

Kleb and John grew up together. Kleb's father was like an uncle to John. He'd also been Babbo's right-hand man before the rumours. But their strong and long-held friendship hadn't proved strong enough. Despite Kleb's father swearing on the bible that he hadn't met the prosecutor and insisting he'd been set up, Babbo didn't believe him. When Babbo denounced him, years of friendship and loyalty were destroyed by one rumour.

Kleb's father's murder was a warning to others that no one was above the rules of allegiance. Although Babbo denied involvement, John knew the truth. He'd overheard Babbo ordering his henchmen to 'Get it sorted. No one squeals.' Babbo refuted it, but John knew he was responsible.

Kleb was banished from the business. However, it didn't stop John and Kleb's friendship. In Babbo's eyes, it was further proof of John's weakness. John's loyalty to a traitor was unforgivable.

For Kleb, the fire of revenge simmered deep inside, waiting to be released. He'd loved and admired his father and would never forgive or forget his murder. He held Dimi responsible for the rumour. John wasn't going to set him right.

'I've got news.' Kleb was again calm and businesslike. 'There's a special, secret defence project. I hear it's big. I've arranged for you to attend Wayne Skollov's next soiree. The decision-makers will be there.'

John smiled. Until now, his business dealings with Skollov hadn't brought John into Skollov's influential circle. This was an important development.

Kleb continued, 'Paddington will be there, too. Be careful around him. He's powerful and influential, and his media empire has killed a few careers. His loyalties are simple; his top three priorities are No.1 Paddington, No.2 Paddington, and No.3 Paddington.' Kleb counted them off on his fingers. 'If you remember that, you can't go wrong. Get my meaning? I'm sure the lovely Skye will beguile them. Convince the decision-makers you're the man for the job, and don't get on the wrong side of Paddington, and we could secure a role. Keep your ears and eyes open.'

A nervous tremor travelled up John's spine. Paddington was not a man to trifle with. His media empire wielded powerful control over the political parties. He could make or break them with a few well-chosen articles. His opinions accepted no challenges. John needed to step carefully indeed.

'Anything I should say or not say?' John asked.

'You can handle it. I'll let you know if I learn anything.' Kleb stood. 'I need to make tracks. I'm flying to Singapore early tomorrow.'

'Some financial fine-tuning?' John asked.

Kleb's other business, besides corporate law, dealt with the ins and outs of tax minimisation offered in Singapore and locations like Panama. It made him more valuable to the business community, and John hoped to take full advantage of it, eventually.

'Nothing too complicated,' Kleb explained as he crunched back along the path.

Chapter 8

The detritus of a long life lived in one place filled Laura's cupboards. This careless accumulation of things had to be reckoned with, sooner or later, and it was a good time to start. She'd lived in this home for over thirty years, yet it felt like only yesterday when she'd first glimpsed the dim interior. Back then, its dull-brown cigarette-smoke tinged paintwork didn't blunt her enthusiasm, nor did the original-condition kitchen. With no money for renovations, they'd bought it anyway and patiently turned it into a family home. Now, decluttering and repainting, the way the agents recommended, was transforming her warm home into a sparsely decorated, depersonalised, and neutral living space.

After the phone call, Laura searched Tom's office but found no DVDs. The space in the filing cabinet drawers convinced her the thief had taken the much sought-after files. Frustration niggled at her and she slammed the door shut on the office, turning her attention to the dining room sideboard instead. She stacked an assortment of glasses and platters, including her favourite blue and white plate, into a box for the children to pick through. Then Laura focused on the ornaments. Memories transformed these cheap mementos into treasures. Two beer steins decorated the middle shelf. Their first overseas trip flooded her mind with images as she lifted the heavy glass stein with the Hofbrauhaus insignia on the front. They'd been young and carefree, enjoying a European adventure, an Australian rite of passage back then. She remembered sitting in the Munich Hofbrauhaus, filled with noisy tourists, the way they liked it.

Munich Hofbrauhaus, June 1969

'I'd like one of those,' Tom said, jabbing at the menu.

The waiter bent down low and peered at where Tom pointed. He straightened, smiled strangely, and shook his head. 'No,' he said firmly.

Tom asked again in a noticeably firmer tone.

'No,' repeated the waiter, then grinned and leaned in close. 'If you want a small glass of beer you should go to a restaurant. Here, our best beer is the stein.'

'But…it's on the menu,' Tom argued, outrage straining his voice.

The waiter laughed, 'Ah, yes, but it is not a nice beer.' He leaned in close again and with a softer voice said, 'It is for old men with kidney troubles. You would not like it. A stein is better.'

His laugh and conspiratorial tone made Tom visibly relax, and he ordered a stein.

'And for you, madam?' The waiter moved to her side of the table.

Laura wasn't a beer drinker, but she didn't mention it. 'I'll have a Radler,' she said, not sure she'd manage a stein but content that the shandy had less alcohol. The waiter didn't argue with her choice.

Two steins arrived, and they both laughed. Drinking this quantity of beer at 11.30 a.m. seemed bizarre. Unlike the Japanese tourists trying to skol their beers, they lingered over theirs and people-watched.

The waiter returned with a small glass, only a quarter full of amber liquid, and offered it to Tom, who sipped it and immediately screwed up his nose.

'See, for old men with kidney troubles,' the waiter said.

They spent a happy hour watching lederhosen-clad locals, drinking steins of beer with a schnapps chaser and gnawing at pork hocks in between. It appeared to be a regular event and the locals laughed and joked with the tourists. The comradery made better for the alcohol surging through their systems. Then the oomp-pa-pa band filled the mural clad hall with music and everyone sang and laughed.

Laura loved the funny Tom that emerged that afternoon. He was relaxed and fun to be with. When they returned to the hotel room for a short break, the beer took its toll. Instead of continuing to the museum as they'd planned, they slept a few hours and were still a little tipsy when they headed out for dinner.

***

Laura chuckled. That trip was peppered with adventures, laughter, and romance. She must find space for the steins in her new home.

Tom had once loved to travel, but work trips changed that. At first, he'd regale them with anecdotes, lamenting that she couldn't accompany him. Later, he grew tense in the weeks before and after a trip. He never confided in her, but it was clear the negotiations and meetings in Iraq greatly distressed him.

Memories again slowed Laura, but she had to resist. Clearing out wasn't simply spring cleaning the house, it was also spring cleaning her life, ready to make a new start. It was good for her. They'd bought the second ceramic stein later that same trip. She flipped open the lid and saw a wad of paper wedged inside. She extracted a sealed envelope.

It contained a folded slip of paper and a small, copper coloured key. A rubber loop threaded through a hole in the key's red circular head and a faint inscription read L132. What was this for? The code printed neatly inside the note 'B1002MSC' was gibberish too. Tom hadn't mentioned a safe deposit box or locker. She'd never seen this key before.

'Damn you, Tom,' she muttered.

Laura sighed. This puzzle would have to wait; she'd couldn't let herself be constantly distracted. She jammed the key and paper back into the envelope, stowed it in her pocket and returned to clearing out the sideboard. She worked for another hour before the doorbell interrupted her concentration.

Eva grinned as she hoisted a bottle of champagne. 'The

publisher said yes.' Eva twirled as she stepped into the house. 'Although there'll be edits and changes.'

'Congratulations.' Laura hugged her and added, 'Sorry about the mess.'

'Is it OK to interrupt? I brought this to celebrate. I know it's not quite midday but I couldn't resist.' She looked around the dining room. 'Shall I come back later?'

'No, silly, this can wait. We have to celebrate your success.'

'Potential success,' Eva corrected as Laura grabbed a platter from the dining table. 'At least I'm over the first hurdle.'

Laura arranged some smoked cheese and crackers on a plate while Eva grabbed two glasses. They carried them out to the patio.

'Congratulations, Ms Eva Tonique,' Laura said as they clinked glasses.

'The revisions will be a ton of work.' Eva threw up her hands in mock horror. 'It's causing me angst already. I have to replace two stories and rework three others.'

'Why do you have to replace real stories?'

'It's political. The government failed to convict one of my subjects as a people smuggler. It's *controversial.*' Eva sighed. 'His story is one of the reasons I wrote the book.'

'If the conviction was unsuccessful…'

'I'll do whatever it takes to be published. The other stories need to be told too.'

Laura sipped her sparkling wine, enjoying the bubbles tickling her nose. She popped a cracker with cheese into her mouth and Eva did the same. She watched a pigeon land on the roof next door, strut along the tiles, and eventually slip under the neighbour's solar panels. She was sure they were building a nest and causing damage.

'It's ironic. The war opened Iraq up to terrorism, destroyed their infrastructure, and yet we won't help them. We ignore the damage it did,' Eva mused.

'You'll show that refugees are human and victims.' The first time

Laura read Eva's draft, she'd cried. 'We're a country of immigrants. Each wave has struggled for acceptance.'

It wasn't theoretical for Laura. Tom's parents emigrated from Germany after the war. While Tom's father gained a grudging acceptance through his work, his mother struggled with isolation and loneliness. Tom was bullied and tormented as a young schoolboy. With a name like Schultz, he couldn't hide, and Laura suspected it fired his advocacy for justice. Laura's family avoided direct discrimination by anglicising their name to Gynne and refusing to speak anything but English at home.

'I can't see an end to the fear campaigns.' Eva leaned forward and refilled both their glasses. She popped another cracker and a sliver of cheese into her mouth. 'I'll keep fighting, but I have to be smarter.' Eva waved her hand towards the dining room. 'How's the clean up going?'

'I'm exhausted.'

'Once you've finished, you'll feel good … lighter somehow. I didn't miss my stuff once I cleaned out.'

'Tom's office is a nightmare.'

They sipped their wines. The clock ticked loudly, and the leaves rustled in the wind. There was a change coming.

'Tom never told me anything, but I didn't ask either.' A sense of helplessness weighed Laura down.

'Maybe he was shielding you?'

'Maybe.' Maybe she'd avoided looking too deeply.

'I've heard criminal gangs and terrorists are vying for control in Iraq, especially in the outer provinces. They're well-funded. My interviewees hint that Australian companies, maybe even our government, are involved in dubious deals.'

Laura shuddered. 'Ethics is almost a dirty word these days. Tom deeply regretted not standing firm on the Wheat Board kickbacks issue. He was bullied into silence but…' Had Tom given up entirely?

'Peter winning the promotion didn't help, but something more happened, didn't it?' Eva asked.

'One minute they were friends, then they weren't. I maintained a link but…' The sparkling wine was going to her head and Laura nibbled a slice of cheese. 'I'm sorry that Tom let work matter so much to him when he mattered so little to his work. I've culled his papers and I'll sort through what's left after I've moved.' Maybe by then, she'd be ready to face the truth.

'Why are you keeping them?'

'Perhaps I'm deluding myself, but they might … give me some answers. I know, it sounds silly but—'

'His papers and notes are unlikely to help you, you know.'

'I know in my head, but not in my heart. I want to believe he was distracted by something so important, that it's understandable that—'

'Oh, Laura. Don't torture yourself.'

'I need time … I need … I don't know what I need.' Laura remembered her discovery in the beer stein. 'Besides, since his death there have been odd things, a weird phone call telling me to hide any of Tom's papers and …'

She dug the envelope out of her pocket and handed it to Eva.

'Who was the phone call from?'

'I don't know. It was probably a prank, but I'm not sure. I found this inside one of the steins today,' Laura explained.

Eva pointed at the code. 'What does it mean?'

'I've no idea.'

'A Post Office box or a luggage locker?' Eva suggested.

'I hadn't thought about luggage lockers. Do they still have them?'

'The interstate train or bus station might.' Eva frowned. 'What are you going to do?'

'It feels important.'

'Laura, be careful. He might have had good reasons for hiding this.'

Laura shivered. Maybe Eva was right.

'Peter dismisses Tom's concern as paranoia. He says the drugs made him see conspiracies, but what if Tom stumbled onto something important?' This was a more palatable explanation. She needed to break the past's hold on her, but without answers, she couldn't move forward. 'I don't know what to think.'

'Promise you won't do anything dangerous.' Laura shivered at Eva's stern expression.

'I promise.' Laura would try. That's all she was promising.

They sat quietly, enjoying each other's company without needing to break their silence. The pigeon reappeared. She knew it was technically vermin, but its soft repetitive cooing soothed Laura's nerves.

'I thought retirement would be different,' Laura mused. 'I was looking forward to more freedom. I don't know what happened.'

'Tom happened. He retired and cramped your style.'

'I let him commandeer my attention. I felt … responsible … like I needed to jostle him out of his moods.'

'No chance.' The finality in Eva's voice echoed Laura's thoughts. Laura's dream retirement hadn't happened. Now, it never would.

'I should find something to occupy my time,' Laura said quietly.

'Getting a job at sixty is impossible, especially for women. Experience isn't valued.'

'Even for a woman of fifty-nine!' Laura laughed, then added seriously, 'the office environment seems too toxic and stressful for me now.'

'You could try volunteering. They always need people to work with refugees or migrant families.'

'I know.' Laura was ambivalent. Everything felt too hard, and she was already too emotionally volatile.

'I met Peter and Tom's Iraqi regular driver the other day. Tom helped him with his visa application. Working for the allies made him and his family a target for insurgents.'

'I remember Tom fuming at a convoluted visa process he was

working on.'

'It's sad. Fayyaad's father died in prison and people-smugglers helped Fayyaad and his family escape.'

'He's safe now?'

'For now, the changes to government policy ...' Eva drained her glass. 'He was upset to hear about Tom and insists he needs to talk to us urgently. He wouldn't explain but says it's important. He might answer some of your questions. It can't hurt.'

'Am I crazy to dig into Tom's issues?'

'Tom's death left you with loose ends. I can understand why you need to know. It's called *closure*.'

'I'll think about it,' Laura said.

'Don't tell anyone, Laura.'

'Who would I tell?' Instead of deterring her, the mysterious request intrigued. She'd had so many strange issues to ponder lately. Maybe he'd provide answers. But were they answers she wanted to hear?

The phone rang.

'Hi, Abbie,' Laura said. Eva waved her hands in an elaborate charade and she added, 'Can you hold on a moment?'

'I just noticed the time. If you go on a locker search, let me know what you find.' Eva grabbed her things.

'I have time on Saturday. Maybe then.'

'Tom's mystery continues.' Eva hugged Laura and left.

'Can you come for dinner on Friday night?' Abbie asked. 'Willow and Ivan are in town and I thought you'd enjoy seeing them.'

Ivan worked with Tom and Peter before taking up a position in Canada, and Laura remembered them as a friendly and fun-loving couple. She accepted the invitation.

'You don't need help with your clean up? Tom's hoarding would make it a big job. The rest of your house is enough of a challenge,' Abbie continued.

Laura tightened her grip on the phone. Her house was not a

challenge. 'It's been…cathartic, a way to draw a line under things.'

'Good. No use twisting yourself up with Tom's issues. It's time to put it behind you.'

Laura bit her lip. Abbie's manner grated today.

They finished with small talk before saying goodbye.

She'd lost her momentum for cleaning and instead, she made herself a cup of tea. Laura watched the pigeons line up on her neighbour's roof. Their repetitious cooing was calming, but also lulled her into complacency. They were vermin, and opportunists, and could cause damage. Just like some people.

The phone rang again.

'I got the scientific intelligence officer job.' Mel's voice sang with uncharacteristic joy.

'What does it involve?' Laura injected enthusiasm into her voice despite a niggling dread. Mel's field was potentially dangerous.

'I'll be assessing documentary evidence and testimonies. It's a promotion and draws on my qualifications.'

'That's great. Does that mean a pay rise?'

Mel laughed. 'I haven't got all the details, but it does.'

'Is it dangerous?' Laura choked back her barrage of questions.

'I'll be based here. There's occasional travel. Some training in Canberra and Sydney and I might be going to New York at the end of the month.'

Laura breathed a sigh of relief. Tom's travels to Iraq gave her sleepless nights. The thought of her daughter travelling to countries in conflict, those dangerous places that needed so much of Australia's military attention, made her shiver.

'I'll know more when I've talked to the professor tomorrow. He recommended me.'

'Congratulations, I'm so happy for you. How about dinner together? We could open some champagne and celebrate properly.'

'I have a seminar tomorrow, but maybe Wednesday.'

Laura smiled. Mel's career and romance woes were a source of worry, but maybe now Mel's career was on the right track.

'I've also been researching the drugs in Dad's system. They're not known to cause paranoia. E-bomb is a synthetic drug that's recently flooded the market. No one knows where it's come from. It's potent and affects individuals differently, with some becoming excessively pliable and others imagining wild adventures, even hallucinating,' Mel explained.

'I never saw Tom hallucinating.'

Mel sighed. 'I don't understand the demand for illicit drugs. They're dangerous, and this only requires a tiny amount to overdose.'

'Me neither,' Laura concurred.

'Honestly, terrorists don't need weapons. They can flood a country with recreational drugs, kill people with overdoses and get rich in the process. The Taliban fund their activities with opium and the South American drug cartels grow rich from heroin. Why does no one ask where the drugs come from or where the money goes?'

Mel's animated tirade reminded Laura of Tom in his younger years.

'I'm sorry, Mum, it gets me riled.' Mel sighed again. 'Anyway, the other drug, digoxin, is used to treat heart irregularities. I didn't know that Dad had heart problems?'

'He didn't.' Had he kept this information from her too?

'Digoxin can trigger a heart attack in someone with a healthy heart. Why was he taking it?'

'They said the heart attack was probably caused by the combination of drugs. I should have noticed, should have—'

'There were no signs of long-term use or damage,' Mel said. 'Mum, none of us saw this coming.'

Laura and Mel arranged a time for Wednesday night and hung up. Laura struggled to believe Tom would take drugs, but the proof was in the report.

Memories filtered through her resolve. Tom's conscientiousness and ethical streak were infuriating at times, but she'd admired him for it too. The corporate world had challenged his principles. She'd seen no signs or sudden changes in behaviour to suggest Tom's drug-taking, only a gradual decline of mood, and she'd put that down to work stress. Was that the clue she should've seen? She'd let him down.

Laura's fingers brushed the back of Tom's favourite armchair. She could still smell the goo he used on his hair since going to the new hairdresser. The dips and worn patches made it unsaleable. Could she let this go? Tears welled in her eyes. The past was not finished with her. Sometimes she felt strong and capable and sometimes she didn't. Her fingers touched the headrest. She could see him, engrossed, either listening to his music or watching the news or a documentary.

She rubbed her neck, making small circles under her hairline. If only she'd helped him. Remembering the phone call, she shivered. There was more to this. Had he become depressed by the battle? Maybe the key held answers or talking to Fayyaad would help.

Suddenly, she straightened up and, in the kitchen, she poured her cold tea down the sink, grabbed a wine glass, selected a bottle from the wine rack and poured herself a generous glass of Shiraz. She put on an Elvis CD, sat down in her favourite chair, and let the music remind her of happier times. Still, her mind wouldn't rest, puzzling over the phone call, the mysterious key and the drugs found in Tom's body. It pointed to more sinister answers than she was prepared to admit to.

Chapter 9

As Skye sashayed into the room ahead of John, the other men barely hid their lust. Wayne Skollov, the arms dealer, and his ex-model fiancé stood by the entrance. They were a strange contrast; her beauty and elegance next to his squat, beer-bellied shape. His penchant for brightly coloured jackets was on display tonight and he'd matched it with a bright blue, red, and black tie. Combined with dark-rimmed glasses, he looked old fashioned and almost comical. It was a façade. He was shrewd, and John admired the way he'd wheedled out of tight situations. Arms-dealing provided many challenges.

Skye gently nudged John in the ribs and whispered, 'Is that Lucinda Murphy?'

He nodded. Here was a collection of the most powerful men in Australia and she picked out the ex-model. 'Lucinda Skollov doesn't quite have the same ring to it, does it?'

'Why would she change her name? She's well known in her own right.' Skye chuckled. 'Fancy becoming Lucinda Skollov. It sounds like seafood.'

John's head jerked up. Luckily, no one had overheard. 'She could do worse. It would open doors.'

'She doesn't need him for that.' Skye was a dedicated follower of fashion and believed models had a universal celebrity.

They approached the host and hostess.

'Glad you could make it,' Skollov said.

John's hand disappeared inside soft flesh, although the handshake was firm.

They introduced their partners, and John grabbed Skye's arm as she began to curtsey. Both Skollov and Lucinda smiled before turning to greet Barton Paddington, the media mogul, and his plump and very loud wife. Paddington looked haggard and older in real life, and his tired jowls sagged, pulling his mouth down into a grimace. His deeply creased forehead folded down over his eyebrows, but his eyes were fierce. His name and roundness evoked the famous bear, but the resemblance ended there. They hadn't met before, but John was well aware of his reputation. His arrogance and toughness were legendary, as was the power he wielded. His control of the biggest share of the Australian media, both print and TV, could direct public attention for or against anything. Politicians in Australia, the US, and the UK, and possibly Russia, listened when he spoke. John straightened and lifted his head. He needed to be careful. Paddington was a powerful ally, but a brutal enemy.

John nodded a greeting.

'Haven't seen you at these gatherings before,' Paddington said.

'I hope to change that.' John only just kept the tremor out of his voice.

'We could use some new blood.'

John wasn't sure what he meant, but Paddington and his wife moved on before John could respond.

Bernard Casterlow, the Minister for Defence and Security, stood in the corner. Grey-white tufts of hair surrounded his shiny pate and formed a luminescent halo. He stretched up in conversation with Patrick Furness.

The new PM's staunch ally, Bernard Casterlow, avoided being dumped as Minister of Defence and Security. Favours or pay up time, no doubt. John's promising relationship with Casterlow assured him of access to more Iraqi contracts. As a bonus, it also brought him closer to Dimi's business.

Surprisingly, Furness was still Minister for Trade and Imports after the reshuffle. He looked stylish in a tailored suit, a change from his usual crumpled appearance, and his tall frame physically dwarfed Casterlow. Although, in John's estimation, Furness was the lesser man. Unfortunately, the overlapping responsibilities in Iraq meant John was required to work with both.

Over dinner, Casterlow talked mostly to Skollov, while Paddington entertained and impressed the ladies with tales of the movie stars attached to his media stable. Furness looked uncomfortable. His tendency to lick his lips was on display as he concentrated on eating and drinking.

After dinner, they crossed the cavernous atrium. The women filed into the sitting room while the men moved to the library.

'Remember what we said,' John whispered into Skye's ear.

'I *know*,' she hissed and pulled her arm away.

'She'll be safe with the ladies, John, although I can see why you might not want to leave her,' Paddington said with a lecherous leer.

'If you say so.' John almost bit his tongue. His first opportunity to impress with a witty riposte and he'd failed.

There was something old fashioned about the men retiring to the library, and John liked it. Luckily, there weren't any female MPs to upset the routine. The *boys'* network maintained power where it sat most comfortably, and John agreed that it didn't need to change.

Skollov removed his brash jacket and offered drinks, mixing them himself. When John asked for a martini, Skollov frowned over his thick black glasses.

'You'll need to develop more refined tastes if you're going to mix with this lot. My scotch is top-shelf,' he said.

'I never developed a taste for scotch,' John admitted. 'Vermouth or Campari are my drinks of choice.' Surely he didn't have to conform down to the right drink.

'I like a man who knows his own mind. Not like the politicians who sway with the breeze so much it's hard to know what they think.' Paddington jabbed his finger out in front of him to emphasise his point.

'I thought you and your newspapers told them what to think.' John smiled at his witty response, but their sober faces worried him. Had he overstepped the mark? They unanimously burst into a guffaw, and he relaxed.

'Well, he's got you there.' Furness raised his glass at Paddington. 'Last week you scuttled that good deal with a few headlines, despite it being to our advantage. We missed the boat on it now. Instead, we've had to commit to the more expensive US contract which offers less.'

'Someone has to tell you when you get it wrong,' Paddington said. 'Rule number one: reward our friends.'

Paddington's smile contrasted with the hard edge in his voice. He barely concealed his distaste for Furness and John took note.

Skollov sat in the big armchair next to John. 'How's your business these days?'

'If it weren't for the latest Iraqi insurgent attacks interrupting my transports and causing delays, it would be fine.'

'At least we're trading again,' Skollov said. 'It's been a dog's breakfast so far.'

'You've had plenty of advantage, and the attacks have helped you extend your private militia, too.' Paddington smirked and his jowls tensed.

Skollov glared at Paddington. A clash of egos. John hadn't heard about Skollov's private mercenaries. Had Kleb?

'I was sure the Iraqi infrastructure would be rebuilt quickly although, discontent is good for my business. All that money and still the rebuilding has stalled.' Skollov laughed. 'Now the Coalition Provisional Authority's bribery scandal is being investigated it will delay progress,'

'You're not caught up in it, are you?' Casterlow's eyes burned into Skollov.

'Those contracts went only to US companies. I was willing, but they weren't interested.' Skollov chuckled.

The latest scandal involved bribes paid to the authority to award Development Fund contracts to preferred US companies. Questions were being asked about where the money was being spent, especially when most of the contracts had been paid but not completed. Many of the infrastructure rebuilding programs hadn't even started, which meant the conditions wouldn't improve anytime soon.

'With the essentials; electricity, water supply, and fuel still unreliable, the surprise attacks posed a huge threat,' John emphasised. He hadn't even benefited from the cash being handed out.

'The attack at *Tall Afar* was too close for comfort,' Casterlow said, lost in his thoughts.

John leaned forward. *Tall Afar* wasn't near any sites he knew about. Was this related to Casterlow's secret defence projects?

As though reading John's thoughts, Skollov asked, 'How many Australian operations are there in Iraq now?'

Skollov should know the answer. Didn't his security force protect Australian sites?

'We have what we need, for the moment.' Casterlow's face turned impassive again.

John frowned. Skollov didn't appear to know what the secret project was either.

'To the victor go the spoils. Our government stuffed up by letting the US set up the Provisional Authority and take all the rebuilding contracts. We should have fought harder to extract benefits. Rule number two: Always have a plan B,' Paddington growled.

'We developed plans A, B, and C but in the end, we needed a plan D,' Casterlow insisted. 'Luckily we have God on our side.'

Furness smirked behind his glass.

'My media rallied public support for the Iraqi war by amplifying the weapons of mass destruction scare, but you're wasting the opportunities,' Paddington sneered and stabbed his finger at Casterlow.

'No matter that you didn't find any,' Skollov mocked.

Furness waved his hand expansively. 'Well, our political philosophy is "Lie now, pray later," isn't it Casterlow?'

Casterlow scowled. 'I'll grant we were outmanoeuvred, but we haven't lost all our advantages.' He smirked, then added, 'At least, Skollov, you've eked out a trade advantage.'

'You could bloody-well do more to help.'

'You've had enough help.' Casterlow swigged his drink.

John scanned the faces. The power plays in the room played out in looks and frowns. There were competitive pressures and egos at stake, but the underlying tensions ran deeper and he needed to understand them if he was going to infiltrate this power circle. Casterlow wasn't giving anything away. Was that why Paddington appeared hostile, or was it his natural disposition?

'The insurgent attack on Abu Ghraib late last year was daring. Are they gathering momentum?' John asked, underscoring he knew about the latest developments and was prepared.

'I could provide stronger protection,' Skollov offered.

'It's the only Iraqi detention centre in the combat zone, so it's inevitable but the casualties inconveniently focus public attention on human rights,' Paddington said. 'Luckily, there's only a handful of lefties protesting.' He hesitated. 'Another rule for you; the public accepts indefinite detention and even torture of *terrorists*.' Paddington drank the last of his scotch. 'If you tell people it's about security and the terrorist threat, no one can challenge you, not even the opposition, but *you* have to do more of the hard work, not leave it all to the media.'

'Your media campaigns are as much about spreading your

opinions and influence as they are about supporting the government,' Furness quipped.

'As long as our interests coincide, you're safe. Although, the latest polls aren't looking good for you.' Paddington bated the politicians. 'A media campaign on the terrorist threat or the *flood* of asylum seekers, or both could help you. The Iraqi war has delivered two for one with those issues.'

'People must be tired of scare campaigns by now. They're a dime a dozen,' Furness said.

'Fear fatigue? I don't think so. You underestimate the power of fear at your peril,' Paddington insisted.

'Scare campaigns work. Remember children overboard and Tampa, they won an election,' Skollov said.

The media campaign supporting the government's hard-line position won over public opinion. The refugees rescued by the Norwegian captain of the Tampa were denied entry to Australia and despite the world's condemnation, it was a vote-winner. The PR surrounding that incident had taught John valuable lessons. Having the right friends, people with influence, was critical to success, and it didn't hurt if they had flexible ethics.

'Certainly, belief is stronger than logic. Once people have faith in something or fear something, they act on it regardless of the proof.' John ventured. It was a safe comment and earned a nod from Paddington and a frown from Furness. A good result.

John's father, Babbo, used fear to his advantage for generations, even against John and now, John would use any means available to gain success.

Their conversation lingered on reminiscing past successes. The strategies that brought public acceptance of unpalatable policies. Paddington's chest puffed up with pride, recounting his influence on each issue.

'Although, in the Tampa and children overboard situation, the government got caught red-handed,' Furness added and licked his lips. He seemed determined to bring the mood down.

'That was four years ago. No one remembers that the October 2002 Senate Committee found the government misled the public. No one cares. There's been no backlash.' Paddington jabbed his pointer finger towards Furness. 'There's your lesson. Facts don't matter, you just need good PR. Even the latest Wheat Board findings will be forgotten quickly.'

'Those lefties won't let the public forget the Wheat Board debacle too quickly,' Furness insisted.

John hadn't been paying much attention to the Wheat Board scandal, only that Dimi's new drug supply was somehow connected to the Wheat Board's partner organisation.

'We can handle protestors and do-gooders. We have the law on our side, especially with our latest legislative amendments. The Wheat Board issues don't matter. My concerns are focused on the future and our developing situation with pacific neighbours. I'm adamant. Once they accept our aid, we own them, but now they're threatening to pull out of the mining expansion agreement,' Casterlow explained.

John thought the deals with Indonesia were signed off, although the latest mining mishap, cyanide poisoning of a main river system, had triggered a serious pull-back.

'It should be easy to fix,' Skollov said. 'Do you want my help?'

'I don't need your heavy-handed approach. We've had a beneficial relationship with the current leadership, but they're losing public support by backing our policies. The opposition Muslim parties are talking tough and they're more popular with voters, but it would be a disaster for us if they won.' Casterlow glanced at John and nodded. John didn't understand what it meant, but it was a positive sign. Was this issue part of the secret project?

'Tell me what you need. I'll help if I can.' Paddington smirked.

'We need more than a media campaign.' Casterlow stared at his empty glass and mumbled, 'I have a possible answer.'

The conversation splintered into a series of separate discussions. The men finished their drinks then returned to the sitting room. Skye sat beside Lucinda Murphy looking forlorn and neglected while the other wives talked animatedly. John frowned. Skye was more often the centre of male attention and didn't cope with being on the sidelines. He needed her to cultivate connections and invite gossip from the wives, otherwise, she was no asset.

As John stepped forward a hand touched his elbow.

'I want to run something past you. Can we arrange a meeting?' Casterlow said.

'I have to travel to Brisbane tomorrow.'

'No rush. The PM thinks you have,' Casterlow paused, 'potential.'

'Really?' John frowned at his own inadequate response. The prime minister thought he had potential and that was all he could say?

'My secretary will arrange something. There's no urgency,' Casterlow moved away.

Skye stumbled as she stood and John grabbed her arm. At least he'd accomplished his mission tonight, Casterlow was inviting him to a bigger role. Now if only he could get Skye to overcome her insecurities and become the asset she needed to be.

Chapter 10

Change was within Laura's grasp. The Glenelg apartment had everything she needed, three bedrooms and good storage, but it was the view across the water that clinched it. That, and the cafés and restaurants within walking distance. The idea of living there drew her forward into a different life, walks on the beach, eating out, having coffee in the cafés, and exercising, with a gym and pool right there in the complex. Moving was exciting, but also daunting. If she made an offer, she'd have to put the house up for sale immediately. Was she ready?

She parked outside Peter and Abbie's house and glanced in the rear-vision mirror. She grimaced. What had possessed her? She prodded at the lopsided haircut. It suited her but felt unnatural, especially since a mid-length bob was an integral part of her identity until now.

Abbie and Peter's rambling brick mansion was big for the three of them and even big enough to accommodate Peter's sons, although Abbie didn't welcome them into their life, especially once Katie was born.

At the door, Peter greeted Laura, leaning forward to kiss her cheek. She pulled back. She'd deliberately avoided him since that encounter.

'Nice look.' He stepped back to let her in and she handed him the bottle of wine she'd brought. 'You know I didn't mean anything by my … I got the message. I was out of line and I'm sorry. We're still friends, aren't we?' he whispered.

'There'll be no repeat. I don't want you … to get the wrong idea,' Laura said sharply.

'I promise it won't happen again,' Peter vowed. Laura was reassured until he added, 'I've missed you.'

In the kitchen, Abbie looked up from slicing cucumbers. 'What have you done to your hair?'

Laura blushed.

'It's different.' Abbie studied Laura's face, then turned back to her cutting board.

Did that mean Abbie liked it or not? From the look, Laura thought not.

'I like it,' Peter said as he left the kitchen.

As usual, Abbie declined her offer to help. Laura handed Abbie the chocolates she'd brought as a thank you gift, then propped on a kitchen stool at the bench. The tantalising cooking aromas made Laura's stomach grumble. When Peter returned, he handed Abbie and Laura a glass of wine each.

'Can you believe Willow and Ivan have been in Canada for almost two years now?' he said.

'They're bringing a friend … colleague. He's here on business. We haven't met him before.' Abbie hesitated. 'He's divorced.'

The others arrived, and they all moved into the lounge, where Peter organised pre-dinner drinks.

'This is Jacques.' Ivan introduced the tall, grey-haired man beside him.

Jacques was about Laura's age. He stood tall, although a slight protrusion showed around his middle, like someone who lived well. They shook hands. He leaned forward to kiss her ceremoniously on each cheek, but Laura turned her head the wrong way and they almost clashed noses. His eyes crinkled in amusement. Laura's face warmed.

When Ivan and Willow offered their condolences, Peter placed a consoling hand on her shoulder. She shrugged it off and moved away.

'Have you enjoyed Canada?' she asked Ivan and Willow.

'I was thrown into overhauling their contract systems as soon as we arrived,' Ivan explained.

'Ivan was too busy with work, so I settled us,' Willow added. 'It's hard to adjust to the different climate.'

Jacques pulled a face. 'Winter this year was especially harsh.'

'Thank goodness the heating systems cope, but I'll never get used to those icy winds. It's just too cold,' Willow said.

'They didn't let you settle in if you're already overhauling their contracts,' Peter commented.

'They … *we* need to win more contracts. It's become more complicated with the war and the corruption scandal and I needed to learn fast to take advantage of the new conditions.'

'What contracts?' asked Peter.

'Premium agricultural products mostly. Australia's been beating us, especially with wheat sales, you'd know that. The investigation into kickbacks could change the landscape dramatically, though. Are you involved in the inquiry?'

Peter grinned. 'We're not being investigated.'

'How come you're so lucky.' Ivan raised his eyebrows. 'Canada will be more competitive now. Has APATO broadened its operations now they're not partnered with the Wheat Board?'

Peter smirked. 'You'll get no information from me.'

Abbie brought in platters of finger food and arranged them on the table. Abbie and Peter took the seats at each end of the table while Willow and Ivan sat on one side and Laura and Jacques on the other.

'You're living in Ottawa, is that right, Willow?' Abbie asked.

'It's so convenient. The government departments are there,'

Ivan said.

'How do you know Ivan and Willow, Jacques?' Laura asked

'We met through work. Jacques helped us settle in,' Ivan explained.

'What do you do?' Abbie asked Jacques.

'I freelance for different organisations.'

'Oh, like who?' Abbie responded.

'It's too boring to spoil a lovely dinner party with.' Jacques' eyes sparkled. He had a warm smile.

'I'm sure it wouldn't be boring.' Abbie smiled and unleashed a charm Laura hadn't often seen.

'It must be hard to move between projects,' Laura said. 'It's not very secure.'

'I enjoy the variety and I go where the work is. I'm not often without work.'

'Are you based in Ottawa too?' Peter asked.

'Lately, I've mostly worked out of New York and Geneva. I'm seconded to the UN on a short-term posting, working on their charity initiatives.'

'That sounds noble,' Abbie commented and sipped her wine.

'My daughter will be in New York soon for her new job. She's never been before,' Laura said.

'What does she do?' Jacques asked.

'It's a new role examining microbiological intelligence. She's very excited about it.'

'That sounds important. She's done well,' Willow said.

Jacques offered Laura his card. 'If she needs help in New York.'

Laura noted his title, 'Senior Adviser, Centre for Humanitarian Dialogue and Re-settlement' before pocketing the card.

'You didn't tell me Mel had a new job,' Peter almost whined.

'I thought I had,' Laura lied.

Peter glared and if she didn't know better, she'd think he was acting territorial.

Ivan turned to Peter. 'You're still travelling to Iraq for work? I may have to go. I've never been before. Any tips?'

The mention of Iraq brought back unpleasant memories for Laura, even though she'd never been there. She remembered another dinner with Tom, Abbie, Peter, Willow, and Ivan; in the early days, before the war, but after their first missions without the Wheat Board.

November 2002

'Iraq is so poor.' Tom shook his head solemnly. 'The middle class are selling their furniture and anything of value to survive.'

'Because of the sanctions?' Ivan asked.

Tom nodded. 'Burned out army trucks, tanks, and car wrecks, rust by the side of the road. More than once, I've wondered if we would run off the road and join them. It's better now we have our regular driver, Fayyaad,' he said. 'Our trucks have ended up there. Hopefully, that'll change when the new transport company takes over.'

Peter cleared his throat.

Tom continued, 'It's tough doing business there. No one wears seatbelts and the chain-smoking drivers are maniacs.' He waved his hand to disperse the imaginary smoke.

'It sounds too awful,' said Willow.

'You can be miles from anywhere, no visible signs of civilisation, not even a skerrick of water, just the desert, the road, and the vehicle wrecks, and from out of nowhere, a Bedouin in long white robes appears, herding camels. Or you'll see one of those massive, notorious prisons in the distance.' Tom shook his head.

Peter again cleared his throat.

Despite having heard the stories before, they still made Laura uncomfortable.

'It doesn't sound safe,' Ivan observed.

Tom continued. 'There are bandits everywhere and when we travel to remote areas...'

'Our driver showed us the ancient gun hidden under his robes. It didn't make me feel secure!' Peter said, and winked at Laura. 'No wonder I've

developed heart issues.'

'I wasn't sure you had a heart,' Tom laughed at his own joke.

Peter sighed and shook his head.

'Where do you stay?' Willow worked for the Hamilton hotel chain.

'We stayed in the 5-star hotel in Baghdad.' Peter winked at Tom. *'There are only two hotels for westerners; the other is 4-star.'*

'At least you enjoy some comfort,' Willow replied.

'I'm pulling your leg. It's a rat-hole. The carpet is putrid, the walls dirty and crumbling, the doors don't lock and heavens know what the beds have in them. I'm only now getting over a rash on my back.' Peter screwed up his nose and Willow mimicked his expression.

'Ew,' she said loudly.

'They have oil wells, yet the electricity cuts out regularly and there's not enough fuel to run generators.' Tom shook his head *'Yet they have a top-class health system and produce top-quality pharmaceuticals.'*

'So, is your business conducted in Baghdad?' Ivan asked.

'Mostly, although lately—' Tom began.

'Everything is done in Baghdad,' Peter interrupted.

'How do you cope with the different cultural expectations, especially the not-so-subtle bribery?' Ivan asked.

'We have our rules for negotiations but…' Tom answered.

'We hold our own,' Peter explained.

After a short silence, Tom continued, *'Our meetings are conducted over feasts, always at night. Given the poverty, the dinners are embarrassingly lavish. I wish I could invite Fayyaad in to share it.'* Tom grimaced. *'They treat us as important.'*

'We are.' Peter raised his glass in a toast.

'Well, not really. For example, they asked us to—'

'I don't think we should bore people with the details,' Peter interrupted.

Tom glared at him and continued, *'They think we can influence government decisions, like break our ties to the USA.'* An unreadable look passed between Tom and Peter.

***

Laura's reminiscing reminded her of the tensions between the two men back then. She'd waved them away as tiffs, but now she wasn't so sure. She looked up at the sound of her name. Peter was frowning at her. She'd missed the ongoing conversation.

'Have you cleared out Tom's office?' He sounded impatient and annoyed.

Laura shrugged. 'I threw out a lot, but I've been distracted.'

'You have to be ruthless. No point in hanging onto stuff you don't need. I stay on top of it so we don't end up with that problem,' Abbie suggested.

'Yes, I know.' Laura thought of her emotional attachment to all the *stuff she didn't need*; if only she could be more ruthless. 'Did I tell you about my mysterious phone call a few weeks ago? The caller said Tom's files were dangerous, and *they* – whoever *they* are – would kill for them.'

Willow gasped. 'Oh my God, Laura.'

'That's absurd,' Peter said adamantly.

'Why would Tom's files be dangerous?' Laura asked Peter.

'It must be a prank? Someone is playing with you,' Abbie suggested.

'It didn't feel like a prank. She knew my name.'

'*She?*' Peter echoed.

'Anyone could find out your name. It's a nasty joke,' Abbie insisted.

It was plausible, but Laura didn't believe it. 'I don't think it's funny.'

'Did you report it?' Jacques asked.

'It's too late now.'

'Laura, don't let this worry you. It's a prank. Give me anything you find and I'll make sure it's dealt with appropriately. No one would kill for whatever Tom hoarded in his office.' Peter's laugh sounded hollow and strained.

Laura remembered the key. 'Do you have keyed lockers at work?'

Peter frowned. 'No. Why do you ask? Did you find anything?'

'Not really. I—' Laura didn't want to tell him about it but couldn't find an excuse for her question.

'You what?' Abbie enquired.

'It's nothing.'

'Was he always a hoarder?' Jacques asked.

'No, but the last few years … he didn't cope well.'

'What did you find?' Peter persisted.

'Nothing.' Laura swatted away the question, hoping to make an end of it. 'I promise I'll give you anything important.'

'If he'd used safety deposit boxes, it could have been worse,' Abbie suggested. 'You'd have to do a lot of running around.'

'He might have been keeping things … secure,' Peter said.

'Did he tell you he had one?' Did Peter already know about the key? 'If he used a safety deposit box, why did he keep so much stuff at home?'

'I was asking, in case…' Peter studied her.

'Is your house ready to sell now?' Willow asked.

'I might need a temporary storage lock up. The kids have so much stored in my garage, there's no room and I'm sure they won't sort their boxes out in time.'

'Peter can help. He has contacts in that line,' Abbie offered.

'Thank you,' Laura said gently, atoning for being difficult.

After dinner, they moved back into the lounge. Peter topped up the wine glasses while Laura sat down on the sofa next to Willow.

'You're all old friends?' Jacques asked.

'We go way back, don't we, Laura? We've known each other since university.' Peter raised his glass to Laura.

'We were a foursome,' Laura explained. 'Peter, Tom, me and Peter's ex-wife, Eva.'

81

'I haven't maintained any of my university friendships,' Jacques mused.

'Some people just fit,' Peter said.

Laura laughed at the absurd picture he created.

Abbie shot Peter a cold stare. 'How long will you be in Australia, Jacques?'

'About a year. Most of my time will be spent in Adelaide.'

'Most big companies are on the eastern sea-board rather than Adelaide,' Laura noted.

'Some of my key people are here, so Adelaide is more convenient.'

'Can I help with anything?' Peter offered.

'No, but thank you.' Jacques leaned towards Laura. 'Negotiations here are slow.'

Willow tapped Ivan on the arm. 'Time to go. You have an early meeting tomorrow.'

They thanked Abbie for dinner and Jacques turned to Laura. 'Maybe we could meet for lunch or a coffee sometime when I get back.'

The invitation caught her off guard, but the look on Peter's face decided it for her.

'Why not?' she said.

Jacques gave her another card, and she gave him her phone number. He was attractive, and she liked the twinkle in his eyes. Accepting his invitation was pure mischief and Peter's look was her reward, but also, she'd enjoy getting to know Jacques better. Guilt wrapped itself around her thoughts, but she forced it away. They were only having lunch.

Laura helped Abbie clear up.

'Jacques seems mysterious; the serious type.' Abbie smiled weakly.

'I'm not into the serious type,' Laura mused, not sure what Abbie meant.

'You were.'

Had Laura preferred a serious Tom, or was that just the way it turned out? She'd loved his funny and playful side, but it was lost under work pressures and adult responsibilities.

Saying goodbye to Peter at the door, Laura said, 'You seemed put out by Jacques?'

Peter flinched. 'I hate self-important officials. Ivan's in the industry, but I don't know about Jacques. Perhaps you can let me know if you find out anything.'

She smiled. She wouldn't tell Peter anything she learned.

Chapter 11

John Masters swore under his breath. His day couldn't get much worse. He experienced unexpected bouts of light-headedness and a throbbing pain behind his right eye ever since the accident. It was there this morning. The news that one of his trucks had crashed en route to Adelaide, and the Queensland state government was lodging an inquiry into truck maintenance, made it worse. Now, a change to his meeting with Casterlow meant he was meeting that dolt Patrick Furness instead. Casterlow hadn't explained why or given any excuse.

He left his office early and detoured into the quiet oasis of Centennial Park. John passed the kiosk filled with retirees and young mothers enjoying coffee and cake. The chilly air bit the back of his throat and he sat on a shaded seat, letting the calming view over the water towards Sydney Harbour Bridge ease the headache. Light flickered from the waves as ferries skimmed through the heads.

Across the lawn, a young woman propped on a bench shaded by a spreading fig tree. She was pretty, in a carefully groomed way, with wispy dark hair framing her face and a close-fitting blouse revealing gentle curves beneath. She fidgeted, almost dropping the folder she carried. Placing it carefully on the seat beside her, she scanned the park and John instinctively pulled back into the shadows. As he was about to stand, a man stopped in front of her. His ill-fitting suit draped loosely over a tall but solid frame. He shook her hand, then sat down beside her, although his rigid pose suggested he was ready to flee. It was Furness and John could imagine him vigorously licking his lips between sentences. John sat back to observe.

They sat uneasily, heads bent in conversation when, suddenly, her posture stiffened and John sensed a strained or shrill tone infecting their conversation. She presented Furness with the folder and he scanned the park surroundings before accepting it. John again pressed back against the wooden seat. Furness opened the folder and casually flicked through it as the young woman talked. He slumped enough for John to notice. The young woman stood, offered Furness her hand, and he placed the folder on the seat to grasp her hand with both of his. He spoke, still holding her hand, and now she was the one who was poised to flee. Finally, Furness let go, grabbed the file and they walked away in opposite directions.

A shadow moving along the trail caught John's eye. A familiar figure followed Furness. Another shadow trailed the young woman and John's mind whirred with questions. Who was she? And why were so many people interested in this meeting?

After they'd gone, John walked down to the water's edge. He stopped at the café near the exit gates and ordered a sandwich. He ate without tasting it. When sufficient time had passed, he grabbed his phone, scrolled to the number he wanted, and pressed call.

'I saw you today. Your surveillance skills need upgrading,' John said. It would unsettle Carlo to know he'd been observed following Furness.

'Today?'

'You were, shall we say, strolling in Centennial Park. Nice day for it.'

'It couldn't have been me.' Carlo's bluff didn't work.

'What's going on?'

'Nothing,' Carlo protested, then sighed. 'I was keeping an eye on our gal, Corrinne.'

John sat up. 'That was her? I thought you said she'd been frightened off.' If he'd known this was the girl threatening Dimi's business, he'd have paid more attention. 'Why's she meeting Furness?'

'We think she's enlisting his help.'

'Will he?'

'Of course not, he's in it up to his neck, but I don't think she knows that. Maybe she thinks he can be persuaded.'

'She's more of an issue than you expected. You haven't scared her off at all,' John growled. This was worse than incompetence.

'It's in hand,' Carlo suggested and added, without emotion or sentimentality, 'We'll fix it properly.'

'What about the files?' John asked.

'We're working on it.'

John gritted his teeth. If Dimi kept mismanaging this, it could blow that business wide open and then what would he have?

'For fuck's sake. Get it sorted,' he ordered and hung up.

Why was such a pretty young woman risking so much to expose the E-bomb supply? Was she idealistic, or was she using the information for her own gain? She couldn't win. He admired her gumption, but no one could help her now.

A wave of tiredness washed over him. He ordered a coffee and closed his eyes. These inconvenient bouts of weariness and flashes of memory assailed him too often these days. After five years, he'd expected it to change, improve somehow. His mind played with the images of the past. If only he and Harper had started their life together, there in the Greek Islands, away from Babbo, the family business, the hassles, and the intrigue, they might have had a chance. Life would have been simple and happy. John shook his head and laughed. It was a fantasy. The simple life would never have truly satisfied him, no matter how much he tried to convince himself. Perhaps Harper knew it too. Her hesitation, her slide into depression, and her use of drugs all pointed to a loss of hope. He'd have done anything to stop it from happening. He'd even promised to give it all up for her. He clenched his fists. He couldn't blame himself for her decline. It was not his fault. It was time to move on, focus on the future, and reclaim what was rightfully his.

He checked his watch, paid his bill, and strode to the busy main road. The pedestrian lights flashed red, but a few daring people played with death and darted through the traffic. Cars sped past. One sounded its horn, and John shook his head. Some of the running pedestrians came close to a mishap. They were taking foolish risks. He preferred calculated risks, where the gain was great and the chance of failure slim.

At Furness' office, the male secretary showed John to a waiting area. John smirked. Politicians usually employed pretty secretaries; presenting a diversion from time to time. Maybe Furness didn't trust himself. Then again, maybe he preferred a male. John would check it out.

Since expanding his APATO contracts, he'd dealt with Furness' office more often, but luckily, he didn't have to work closely with Furness himself.

Furness shuffled in, carrying the file. His crumpled suit looked worse up close and matched his face, which looked wrinkled, beaten, and cowed down. His habit of constantly licking his lips was in action, and it made John queasy. Either he was preoccupied or uncomfortable; John suspected it was to do with the woman and that file. The receptionist pointed at John and Furness glanced at him. He looked surprised, recovered, then beckoned John to follow him. Inside his office, Furness stowed the file in the bottom drawer of his desk.

They started with small talk, pretending they liked each other enough to care about how they spent their days. Furness talked of yachting and being South Australian, following Australian rules football. He was pompous and haughty, and John bristled at his allusions to his rich family, private school education, and political connections, to establish his credentials. He seemed overly impressed by them himself although Furness' strong belief in his own superiority wasn't often shared by others, especially not John.

'How's the commission inquiry mess going?' John asked, enjoying seeing Furness squirm.

'It's a storm in a teacup. It's inconvenient, there is no *mess*, as you call it. The Wheat Board issue is sorted.'

'Given Canada, the UN, in fact, the world, are watching the proceedings closely, it's a lot more than inconvenient, I would have thought,' John said confidently.

'We've done nothing wrong. They're barking up the wrong tree. It's a scurrilous attempt by other countries to gain trade leverage and steal our advantage.'

'That's not how it looks.' John hadn't read all the reports, but the government appeared open to charges of corruption. The terms of the inquiry, set by the prime minister, confined the damage. Key ministers couldn't be cross-examined and get themselves into trouble. Furness was protected and wouldn't have to incriminate himself.

Furness licked his lips. 'What's your interest in this?'

'I'm a good corporate citizen and have a civic interest.' John stifled the smirk teasing at his lips. He enjoyed baiting this pompous ass. And he was curious. Did that file provide information about the scandal, or was she exposing Dimi's E-bomb imports?

Furness' face darkened and his eyes flashed a warning.

'Enough idle chit chat. Time is money. I need to discuss a new construction project with you. It's a closed tender to transport additional equipment, but—' He smiled a half-smile. 'To cover our bases, the usual arrangement will apply. Submit your application, no need to rewrite it, but this way, we get the best of both worlds. There can be no suggestion of undue advantage.'

Furness seemed pleased with himself, he'd charted through his spiel being vague yet clear.

'Who's we?'

'Casterlow and I agreed. Although, I'm still to be convinced of your…credentials.'

John shrugged. Furness didn't count while the important decision-makers, Casterlow and the PM, were on his side.

'I've successfully handled numerous jobs for you.'

'Not me, the government. I don't want you to bite off more than you can chew. You're very young to be heading up a company. Tell me how that happened.'

'Nothing to tell. I'm a self-made man. I worked hard and reaped the reward.'

'Surely you had help along the way.' Furness smirked. 'There's no such thing as a free lunch. Who do you owe?'

John leaned back and stretched out his legs. 'I'm my own man. What about you? Who do *you* owe?'

A cold mask flashed across Furness' face before the insincere smile returned. 'Very funny,' he muttered.

He shuffled papers, withdrew a small file, and handed it to John. 'These are the details you'll need for a successful tender application. But keep them under wraps. We need to remain circumspect about it.'

'We're meeting in your office. That's hardly *circumspect*, is it?' What a pompous moron.

'That can easily be explained away. You have current contracts and are handling other business for us.'

'Maybe next time we could meet in the park. Be more discreet,' John teased.

Furness flinched. His eyes narrowed. 'What!' He licked his lips. 'Let's concentrate on this project and conclude our meeting. I have other appointments.'

They discussed the details of the new contract, its similarities and key differences. Instead of delivering the large machinery and specialised equipment direct to site, for this project he'd deliver into a central warehouse. John wondered why it had been changed, but Furness couldn't, or maybe wouldn't, explain. Technicalities out of the way, John sat back and watched Furness rearrange his desk and tidy the files.

'I didn't think there would be additional work.'

'I didn't either, but you may as well make hay while the sun shines,' Furness admitted. 'It's become…necessary. Bernard's operations are expanding.'

'Is there anything I should know?' John asked in case the candour was continuing. He desperately wanted more information on Casterlow's projects.

'Not at all.' Furness shut down.

Furness and Casterlow worked together on joint projects, but there was noticeable tension between them. John assumed they were personality-based or related to ideology and was glad that Casterlow's connections should prevail in any power contest. At least he hoped that was true. Politics was a strange game, and he didn't understand how the party men thought. They manoeuvred, even if it wasn't in the interests of the party, the country, or the people. Self-interest was defined so broadly it was hard to work out what the next move would be. John preferred to ruthlessly steer towards what benefited him and leave others to look out for themselves. At least Kleb was better at the politics and would watch John's back, but it made him uncomfortable to be this far removed from the decision-making mechanisms.

Chapter 12

Both counters in the joint post office/news agency were busy; one with lotto hopefuls, the other with elderly patrons clutching payment notices and wads of cash. The postal staff maintained a steady pace, with a quick chat and a smile, they whittled down the line. When it was her turn, Laura stepped up to the counter.

'Hello. I thought you'd moved,' the mousey-haired assistant with the large wire-framed glasses said.

His eyes darted to the growing line of customers, then watched her rummage in the zippered section of her handbag.

'I'm hoping you can help me.' Laura dropped the key onto the counter. 'Could this be for one of your boxes?'

He reached forward. 'May I?'

She nodded. His face folded into itself in a thoughtful grimace, then he shook his head.

'It's the wrong shape.'

He turned the key over for one last look and handed it back to Laura.

'Do you have any ideas?' she asked.

He again glanced at the line building behind her.

'I found it among Tom's things.'

'Sorry,' he said before turning his attention to the next person in the line.

Laura sighed and stowed the key back in her bag.

She drove out of the carpark and turned onto Anzac Highway. Slowing to 25kph past the roadworks, she glanced in her rear-vision mirror. The driver behind her waved his arms and slammed his hands against his steering wheel in obvious frustration. Once past the roadworks, he swerved out, roared up beside her, and gestured rudely before speeding off. Her knuckles turned white, but she focused on the road in front.

She pulled up beside him at the next traffic lights and was tempted to gesture back, but resisted. Glancing in her rear-vision mirror, she saw the number plate on the car coming up behind her and chuckled. N.U.T. seemed an appropriate judgement.

The main office at the railway station was closed, but a bank of lockers spread along one wall of the waiting area. Most with their doors wide open.

The attendant hovered on the platform.

'Excuse me. I wonder if you can help me.'

'If I can,' he said warily.

'I found this key in my late husband's desk and wondered if it fits one of your lockers.'

He frowned. 'Is there any reason you think it's from here?'

'I'm clutching at straws. There was a note too.' She showed him.

'Our lockers are only for temporary use; we empty them regularly. Long-term storage isn't allowed. Security, you know.'

Laura's hopes sank. 'Do you have any suggestions?'

'There aren't many places with lockers.' He studied the key again 'What makes you think it's worth finding?' He laughed softly.

It was a good question.

'You could ask a locksmith. They might know,' he suggested.

She was unsure about what to do next. She already had enough on her to-do list without pursuing this mystery. Why was she bothering? She could throw the key and note away and forget she'd ever seen them. But then she'd never know what was in that locker or if it was important.

At home, she unlocked the front door and froze when she heard footsteps coming up behind her.

'Hi.' Peter walked up the driveway. 'Abbie told me to bring these around.' He lifted a plastic carry bag. 'Preserves.'

'Thanks.' She swallowed down her fright and reached to take them, but Peter pulled the bag out of her reach.

'Would you like to come in?' she asked reluctantly.

'Yeah, sure.' He followed her in and set the bag on her kitchen bench. 'A coffee would be nice.'

'Only if you behave,' she cautioned.

Peter raised his hands in surrender. 'I promise.'

They took their coffees outside and settled into a comfortable banter more reminiscent of years ago.

'I'm not sure why you've been so tetchy about letting me help clear out Tom's stuff. I thought you'd be glad to let someone else deal with the mess.'

Laura shrugged. His persistence irked her.

'What happened, Peter? Help me understand.' Perhaps he could explain and she could put this mystery to rest.

'I'm not sure I know any more than you. Tom and I were a bloody good team. We broke new ground. Admittedly, our first Iraqi forays were pathetic.' Peter chuckled at his memories. 'We were outplayed by the big US pharmaceutical companies, even Canada was beating us. Without the necessary contacts or political connections, nothing worked, even though we were bloody aggressive. Tom's brainwave to run joint missions with the Wheat Board clinched it. It was a win-win. The bosses were pleased, but that was before everything changed. Tom blew it and it all came crashing down.'

'What was he worried about?'

'It's touchy. The commission hearings.' He sighed. 'Tom insisted the transport component was irregular and that the *oil-for-food* program guidelines meant it was illegal. He wouldn't let it rest.'

'Did he eventually get a satisfactory answer?'

'I thought it was, but of course, Tom didn't. He threatened to involve the UN. That was the beginning of the end. The Wheat Board cancelled our joint missions and our bosses were livid. That's when management gave Tom his first warning. It didn't stop him. He niggled at contracts and delved into the details. He was holding things up, so we cut him out of the loop. Once he wasn't as involved, he eased up and finally, he accepted it. A couple of years ago, he changed again. He became cynical and morose. He withdrew, kept secrets; and management was fed-up. He'd become a liability; he was unpredictable and erratic.'

'Did you suspect he was taking drugs?'

'The autopsy result shocked me too. We'd been on opposite sides of the argument for too long. He accused me of being a management stooge and said he couldn't trust me.'

'The Volcker report suggests he was right about the Wheat Board contracts. Maybe he had legitimate concerns again.'

'Let it go, Laura. Yes, the trucking fee paid straight to Saddam Hussein's regime shouldn't have happened, but we wouldn't have won the contracts if we'd refused.'

'The sanctions were set up to avoid that.'

Peter nodded.

'And you didn't think it was a problem?' Laura's voice raised a notch.

'Look, it was a commercial reality. I got nervous too when the government started spruiking for war with Iraq. They claimed they had weapons of mass destruction and, of course, we knew the Wheat Board alone was channelling hundreds of millions of dollars to Hussein via the transport component of our contracts. We weren't as big, but who knew what he was doing with the money.'

'Nervous? Nervous? We were planning to send troops into Iraq while Australian companies were handing Saddam Hussein millions that could be spent on weapons to kill our soldiers. You don't think that was worth worrying about?'

Peter hung his head and examined his hands.

'That's how business is done with these countries. It's a fact of life and there's no point in going on about it,' he said firmly. There was no sign of contrition.

'It was OK to ignore UN Sanctions and the *oil-for-food* program. Corruption is alright so long as you get the business?'

'That's a bit strong. I don't imagine we were the only ones. But corruption? It's a commercial reality in those countries; you have to grease palms to win the contracts.'

'The word is *bribe*.'

'OK. OK. I don't want to argue about it. I was trying to explain.'

'I still don't understand. Tom raised issues that everyone dismissed despite him having sound reasons for his concerns. Yet the Wheat Board issue was almost four years ago. Something else was bothering him; something that surfaced about a year after the Iraqi war. He was concerned and even though he was right about the Wheat Board, he was sacked.'

'He got sacked because he was disrupting business. I don't know what he was doing or keeping secrets about. Ministers directed the company to sort it out, and they did.'

'Wouldn't ministers want APATO to follow the rules?'

'Forget it. There are joint projects that are secret. Suffice to say, Tom was making powerful enemies.'

'By asking relevant questions?' Laura remembered that phone call. Questions could be dangerous, even deadly.

'Don't be simple-minded!' A rush of breath escaped his lips. 'You don't know what he was doing.'

He leaned forward and touched her arm, but she recoiled. It was true, she didn't know what Tom was working on. It might not be what she thought.

'Laura, we're aligned with the government and we have to keep secrets. It's about commercially sensitive information.'

'Tom was researching something...I want to understand.'

'He may have been affected by drugs. They could've made him irrational, paranoid even. Have you considered that? He wasn't himself anymore; he'd lost his ability to make good decisions. You saw the autopsy report. The combination of medication and drugs were a potent cocktail. You can't follow in his obsession.'

Could this be the answer? Tom lost perspective, or maybe he'd lost hope. Laura shook her head. She couldn't believe this.

'He was on to something, wasn't he?' Laura insisted. She wanted to believe in the noble version of Tom.

Peter jumped out of his seat. 'Bloody hell, Laura! You're as impossible as he was. I begged him to talk to me that morning, but he wouldn't. You're both the most stubborn people I know.'

'What do you mean *that morning*?'

'Er...one morning...that morning...it's semantics, but I begged him, numerous times, for the sake of you, your family, and even his career, to stop whatever he was doing.'

'Did you talk to him the morning he died?'

'I didn't see him the morning he died. I've already told you that. Don't get as crazy as him, please Laura. You need to put it aside and stop letting his obsessions ruin your life.'

How could she when Peter's tic, that quick pout of the mouth, the thing he did when he was lying, flashed across his face? Peter's resistance made her more suspicious, not less.

After Peter left, she opened a bottle of wine, poured a glass, and took it back to her chair. The deep red liquor slid across her tongue and numbed her nerves. Was Peter shielding her or protecting himself? Laura picked up Tom's 2006 diary and flicked to the back pages. Cryptic comments and initials scrawled across here too, although one entry, U-Store-It, caught her eye. It was a container storage company near the airport. Could this be connected to the key? If only she could decipher the code he'd left with it. Maybe it was a memory prod for Tom, deliberately obscure to anyone else.

She rang Eva, but her phone went to messages. Laura looked up the U-Store-It address. It was only a small detour on her way to lunch with Eva.

Chapter 13

John entered through the side entrance as a chorus of raucous shouts and jeers erupted from the bar. Men, in an assortment of shorts and sports gear, gathered near the TV screen and gulped beer from large glasses. The lounge was quieter, with only a handful of customers in muffled conversation occupying three small tables. He scanned the room and saw a hand wave through another doorway. Eyes strayed to the small meeting room as John approached and he wondered if they'd recognised Casterlow.

Casterlow's round and plump body sagged into the padded seat behind a large mahogany table. Wood panels separated the formal conference room from the dining area. Inside, the dark timber furniture and walls stripped the entire space of light.

Sitting opposite him was Kleb.

'Take a seat, John. You've met Kleb Sharpe before, haven't you?' Casterlow waved at the chair next to Kleb's. Clearly, Casterlow remained unaware of their friendship.

'We've seen each other around,' Kleb lied.

They shook hands as though they didn't know each other.

'Kleb assists me from time to time. He has a good nose for people and he deals with some of the legal issues that crop up,' Casterlow explained. 'Unfortunately, I'll have to interrupt our discussion when Furness rings.'

'Anything serious?' Kleb asked.

'Just Furness and his…concerns,' Casterlow sneered.

Casterlow paused while the waitress set a glass of red wine and a bowl of peanuts in front of him and a pint of beer in front of Kleb. John guessed she was in her late forties, mature, and her large purple rimmed glasses and edgy haircut added a flamboyant style to what looked like a medium build and medium height.

She turned towards John. 'And for you, sir?'

'What'll you have?' Casterlow repeated.

'A coke, thanks.' John smiled at her.

She looked away and scribbled on her notepad.

Casterlow guffawed. 'Surely we can have something stronger than that?'

'I'm driving,' John replied.

'One can't hurt.'

'I'd prefer to keep it light for now.'

'As you wish.' Casterlow sounded disappointed. After the waitress left, he turned to Kleb and added, 'I'll explain later.'

'This isn't your usual meeting venue.' Kleb waved at the slightly worn room.

'My old wine club used to meet here, in the good ol' days, before I spent all my time in Canberra. We'd have a three-course meal, and each course was matched with the appropriate wine.' Casterlow's features softened with reminiscences. 'It's been a long time – far too long.' He sighed, then abruptly turned to John. 'Now John, you've been helping us for the last two years, haven't you?'

John nodded. 'It's almost three.'

'That's right, you came on board after the war.'

Casterlow's phone rang, and he checked the number before answering.

'I've got Masters and Sharpie here, so let's make it quick,' Casterlow barked and turned to face the corner.

John overheard a 'bloody hell,' and 'that's not going to happen!'

but not the other mumbled responses. The conversation was one-sided for a while and when Casterlow finally spoke, he'd lost his controlled mumble.

'Tough luck! It's too late for this,' Casterlow said firmly. 'Like hell it is. You know why. It's not changing because of your wimpy concerns.'

A moment of silence followed, with only an indistinct, tinny sound emanating from the phone.

'That's final. It's time you grew a pair. I don't want to hear another word.' He exhaled heavily. 'I also want to know why you didn't tell me you met the girl.'

John listened more intently. Was this about the meeting in the park? If so, what did it have to do with Casterlow?

Furness's answer was long and Casterlow twitched silently. On the other side of the glass doors, the waitress swished between tables, serving customers with a smile and sometimes lingering for a short chat.

'Not good enough! You'll give me a full explanation tomorrow, first thing.' A snort escaped Casterlow. 'Don't be naïve, the PM knows the score.'

John was intrigued. Hopefully, either Carlo or Kleb could fill him in later.

'First thing.' Casterlow hung up.

'Sorry, I had to…never mind…where were we?' His fists pumped several times.

Kleb called the waitress. Casterlow checked the time and ordered a scotch. He munched peanuts and closed his eyes until the waitress returned with their drinks.

She was all business and efficiency with their table, not making eye contact or exchanging pleasantries. John was disappointed. They didn't even get a smile.

Casterlow asked her to close the door as she left. 'I wanted to have a private word. The PM and I have our eye on you.'

What could the PM want with John?

'You're discreet. We like that. We're also on the same wavelength. You have the same *Christian* values.'

'I've supported the direction you're heading.' John confirmed. He could talk in riddles too, although he hoped this wasn't a party recruitment talk. He wasn't interested in going into politics. There was too much scrutiny and too many blowhards, spinning three-word slogans while feathering their own nest. The pay was a disgrace and the hours would put any sane person off. Business was much more lucrative and rewarding.

Casterlow nodded, obviously oblivious to John's derogatory thoughts. 'This is very sensitive, and I can't tell you everything yet, but we've developed a new product. Something that can be used to ensure recalcitrant nations fall into line with us. Our Indonesian neighbours have a political situation and we're going to use it to test our product's efficiency and effectiveness. Without their knowledge, of course. This product has potential in international arenas but it depends on the results in Indonesia.' Casterlow paused and stared at John. 'You're discreet and your advantage is your connection to Iraq; it's an opportunity too good to miss.'

'We shouldn't waste opportunities.' John remembered Casterlow mentioning Indonesia at the soiree, although he couldn't recall the details.

'That's exactly right. This is a big development, but it's also controversial.'

This explanation sounded like a commercial or election campaign slogan, implying much, but saying little. John's company transported construction equipment to Australian installations in Iraq and returned with agri-pharmaceutical products. Even the latest contracts didn't vary that much. Why was this product different?

'John, we need your help. It's tricky, but we think you're the right man for the job.' Casterlow cast a glance at Kleb and nodded.

'What do you need?' John was flattered, but also wary.

'Up to now, Furness has overseen all the everyday Iraqi trade operations. We'd hoped he would eventually handle this new, and extremely sensitive, top-secret production and distribution operation, but he's ...'

'Go on.'

'We've had some ... complications and I need someone, not directly connected to me, to step in.'

'My transport options are—'

'No, no, it's not about your transport company or the regular shipments you handle. This is totally separate and a highly confidential operation, you understand? It concerns national security and requires utmost discretion. Frankly, I need someone I can trust; who isn't constrained by misplaced ethics; and who understands we sometimes need to break the rules to achieve results.'

'I see,' John responded although, he didn't see at all. These public service types talked in riddles or vague generalities. He was gradually learning patience, although, only slowly.

'Kleb assures me that you'd be willing to help, in the national interest.'

'I'm the epitome of discretion. Why don't you tell me what this is about?'

'I need to iron out some issues first.'

'Go on,' John said. Why this cloak and dagger game? Casterlow couldn't be talking about Dimi's mundane Iraqi drug importation business. It must be something else.

Casterlow smiled. 'I'm talking about *unofficial* business. Not even all the Cabinet members know about this. Because of that, we can't use your trade routes. Fortunately, this new commodity is small, but it's also extremely dangerous. It will have to be transported with care, but that's what makes it so valuable. Other groups would do anything to get hold of our commodity if they learned of it. That's why I've been less than forthcoming.'

'How do I fit in?'

'First, we need your help to enlist the services of a third party. Your advantage is you haven't been involved before, so you'll slip under the radar. It's too risky to give you too much information now, for you and for the project. You'll work directly for me. It's paramount that Furness not know.'

'What exactly are we talking about?' John was tired of talking in riddles.

'If you do a good job, we'll offer you more and then I'll explain fully.'

'You're testing me?'

'This project is too important to approach someone we didn't already trust. However, we don't want to be guilty of going too fast and ruining everything. Have faith.'

John's catholic upbringing meant he knew all about faith, guilt, and fear.

'OK. What's in it for me?'

He was keen despite not knowing the details. The cloak and dagger antics made it intriguing.

'That's the spirit. I'm told that you're travelling to Europe next month.'

John nodded.

'We've arranged a meeting with a potential logistics partner in Italy. We want access to his special client list and his distribution channels. He can also arrange a continuous supply of new subjects to expand our research base. It's a positive partnership if we can negotiate it successfully. His business can work in tandem with yours, giving you an added benefit too.'

'Are you going to tell me what you're *distributing*?'

'I'll brief you more beforehand. It's critical that this remain secret. This is the first stage but rest assured, this is important work.'

Casterlow chewed at his cheek, waiting and watching. John grimaced; Casterlow's request to work on *unofficial* business without divulging all the details was risky.

'I don't want to look like an idiot, talking to people about things I know nothing about.'

'It's OK, John. I'll brief you before you enter into any dialogue. I'm sure you can bluff your way through the small details if need be.'

'I don't like surprises.'

'Neither do we.'

Kleb gave John a slight nod. The message was clear. Despite John's misgivings, this mysterious project had him hooked, anyway.

'OK,' he said.

'Good. We'll meet in Sydney the weekend before you leave. You'll need to extend your trip by a few days.'

He rose and extended his hand. John's entire hand disappeared into the clammy folds of the broad grip.

'Don't discuss this with anyone, especially not Furness. Kleb will be our link.'

'Is there a reason Furness isn't in the loop?'

'The fewer people involved, the better. As it is, he's retiring soon or shuffling into, shall we say, a less stressful portfolio. It's the way it goes.'

John stifled a smile. Furness was obviously on the way out.

Casterlow grabbed his coat and together they walked out to the carpark. His driver was waiting and as soon as he got in, they sped off.

It was the end to a good day. Casterlow had the PM's blessing, Furness had burned important bridges and finally, John had a role in the top-secret project.

As soon as Casterlow's car was out of sight, John offered Kleb a lift to the airport.

John accelerated the sports car through the loops and twists of the coastal road, skimming the dramatic cliff edges and dipping into the valleys between. His adrenaline was flowing.

'That went well.' Kleb relaxed into the leather seats.

'It looks like an interesting opportunity,' John responded. 'What is this mysterious product? And what is this Indonesian issue?'

'Casterlow keeps it close to his chest. He hasn't told me everything either. The current Indonesian government is distancing themselves from Australian policies and decrying the agreements that give our companies unlimited access to their minerals. It's a political tactic for the upcoming election. They don't mean it. The opposition is the real headache. They're stirring up trouble and their stance is popular with the people. Casterlow needs the current government to retain power. I'm not sure how that product will help, but I guess all will be revealed.'

'Furness looks done for.' John chuckled.

'He never wormed his way into the inner circle. Not sure how he got the portfolio in the first place, but now it sounds like he's stuffed up.'

'He's a pompous ass and getting what he deserves.'

Kleb cast John a sideways glance and smirked. 'This latest crop of politicians are fucking cowboys. Furness thinks he's so clever and can outwit everyone, but he *and* Casterlow have stuffed up our international relationships. Their arrogance made the Canadians more intractable after the Wheat Board scandal and their bumbling created one diplomatic mess after another with the EU. They've let Iraq get away from them and all Casterlow can say is, "God's on our side." I'm not sure if he actually believes that himself. We might not recover that easily.'

'Maybe Wayne Skollov will ride in and save the day.' John liked the cowboy analogy.

'Yeah, Skollov will help. He'll help himself. He's been hankering after unfettered access. He's grubbed his sidelines into Iraq, but now Casterlow is attempting to keep him in check. Skollov's too unpredictable. He's drawing too much attention with his meddling in other conflicts and Casterlow is furious.'

'I didn't know that.'

'Beware of Skollov; he's ruthless.' Kleb's insights came from helping Skollov's legal defence whenever Skollov ran into trouble. 'I wonder if Furness got cold feet.'

'On what?'

'Whatever they're involved in. Whatever happens, you and I will share our separate pieces of the puzzle. Make sure they don't suspect we're working together.'

Their conversation turned to finances. Kleb was a master at clever investment strategies. Wealthy people valued his schemes that minimised tax and maximised their profits.

'Diamonds are a great strategy. They retain value and can be squirrelled away,' Kleb said. 'I have a reliable contact in Amsterdam. He sources diamonds through contacts in Africa and can secure top quality at the right price. He's worth his cut.'

'I hadn't thought about diamonds as an investment strategy. I usually avoid them, especially in ring form. They'd be easier to store than gold bullion.' John didn't have diamonds or gold bullion, but it was fun to dream.

'He'll look after you on my recommendation.'

John dropped Kleb at the airport and drove home the long way, enjoying the smooth grace of his sports car along the scenic road. Its power thrilled him and he opened it up on the long straight stretch of road before the congested traffic slowed him down. He enjoyed the risks, but would he enjoy the risks he was about to embark on?

Chapter 14

Laura awoke with her head jammed into the corner of the recliner backrest. She moved, and a pain shot down her neck. Her right eye throbbed in unison. A shiny crust coated the red wine residue in the nearly empty wineglass on the coffee table. An empty bottle lay at her feet.

She unclenched her fist and smoothed out the slip of paper on which she'd written the U-Store-It address. She moaned, but the ache in her head made her stop immediately. Laura dragged herself out of the chair and collected the wine bottle, glass, and snack packets. She hesitated, then grabbed her car keys and strode out the door.

At Sir Donald Bradman Drive, blue and red lights flashed. Two police cars blocked the inside lane in front of an office building and a tow truck wound a badly crushed car onto its tray. The traffic crawled as two lanes merged into one and she was stuck in the inside lane. The storage company was down this road, but she couldn't park along here. Laura turned left at the next side street, but there were no available parking spaces. She'd hoped to sit and observe who went in and out before approaching, but that was impossible now. Her search took her in ever-expanding circles, further and further away.

'Shit,' she muttered.

Finally, she found a park. She used a laneway to cut through to the main road. The disused office block carpark didn't look inviting, but it provided a shortcut and she'd be able to observe the storage company entrance before deciding what to do. Stepping through the debris, she scowled at how these neglected spaces around Adelaide lay dormant for years.

Vandals had been busy. Glass from broken windows scattered across the abandoned concrete carpark while litter and discarded clothes bunched against walls and fences. She held her breath to diminish the strong smell of rotting matter. A sound made her jolt. A movement caught the corner of her eye and paper rustled near her feet. She jumped back as a rat scurried from under the strewn newspapers and fled. Laura screwed up her face, but pushed forward. There was a less littered pathway via the upper-level carpark to the front of the building and she headed in that direction. It offered a better vantage point too.

As she changed direction, she noticed an intact and stylish woman's shoe beside a rubbish pile. Curiosity got the better of her and she detoured to take a closer look. Beside the shoe was a lumpy shape, covered in a tattered and dirty blanket. She recoiled. It could be a homeless person sleeping rough. Although, a manicured, red nail-polished fingertip poked from the blanket's edge. Laura's stomach lurched. This wasn't a homeless person.

'Hello,' Laura called out, 'Are you alright?'

There was no movement.

Laura hesitated, not wanting to be delayed but unable to leave someone in possible need of help. She crept forward, her heart thumping wildly.

She inched back a section of the blanket. Two eyes stared back blankly. A bruise darkened the cheek of a woman's swollen face and dried blood caked her cut mouth. Her contorted body lay with arms by her side, but her head twisted awkwardly. Laura dropped the blanket edge and, although a scream lodged in her throat, she made no sound. She stood frozen to the spot. Could the woman still be alive? She needed to make sure. Laura forced herself forward and put her trembling fingers to the wrist. It was deathly cold. There was no pulse. Laura shrank back.

There was no help around. She couldn't stay here, but her brain wasn't functioning. She ran. She kept running until she reached the main road. One of the police officers directing traffic was still there, completing paperwork, and she raced up to him.

'There's a body. I found a dead body. It's —' She pointed in the direction of the building.

A plane took off at the airport and its loud rumble drowned her out. She repeated herself slowly and deliberately.

The policeman's puzzled expression turned into one of authority. 'Where? Show me.'

Laura led him back along the street and into the car park. Her legs grew weak as the policeman examined the scene and murmured into his radio. She felt faint and propped against the dirty broken wall, watching but unbelieving. Her phone jangled and broke her trance. It was Eva.

'Sorry, I missed your call last night,' Eva said.

'Hello Eva, I'm sorry—'

'Are you OK? You sound shaky.'

'I've found a body...a dead body.' The words were strange on her lips. It felt unreal. 'The dead body of a young woman.'

'Oh my god! Where are you?'

'A disused office block,' Laura gave directions. The policeman approached her. 'I'll ring you back.'

'No, I'll come to you. I'm not far away.'

The policeman pulled out his notebook and studied Laura.

'Are you OK?' he asked. When Laura nodded, he continued, 'Can you tell me what happened?'

Laura explained, her voice quavered, and she kept clearing her throat. As she talked, more police arrived and cordoned off the area.

She flinched when a hand touched her elbow, then realised it was Eva. Laura couldn't help much and she struggled to remember the sequence of what she'd done and seen. Her eyes filled with tears recounting how she'd looked under the blanket. After giving the policemen her contact details, he let her go, handing her into Eva's care.

Eva offered to take her home, but Laura wanted to surround herself with noise and liveliness to drown out the images stuck in her brain.

The walk to the café was like a dream. She mechanically moved one foot in front of the other and was surprised when they finally slipped into the half-empty space in a café around the corner. The lunchtime rush was finished, and they had a choice of unoccupied tables tucked into quiet alcoves. They settled into a corner table away from the windows. She kept her coat on despite the café's warmth.

'What were you doing there?' Eva asked.

'The key. I was going to check out U-Store-It. I took a shortcut—' Laura clasped her hands tightly to steady them.

'Why U-Store-It?'

'That's why I rang you last night. Tom wrote it in his diary.'

'I hadn't thought of storage hire places.' Eva grimaced. 'A lot of homeless people camp out around this area. The sheltered spots are popular. The cold nights lately may have taken their toll.'

'I thought it was a homeless person at first, but…her shoes and her nail polish…her hands… she wasn't sleeping rough.' The image of the battered face flitted across Laura's mind. Then a vision of the young woman in a red cocktail dress, and very much alive, took its place. Her animated features were full of emotion. Laura sat up abruptly. Where was that image from?

'Are you OK?'

'I have the strangest feeling I've seen her before?'

'It's shock,' Eva suggested and ordered them both a coffee.

'If I hadn't parked so far down the street, she could've lain there for days, undiscovered.' Remembering the rat made her nauseous.

Eva touched her hand. 'It's OK. She's been found. It's a shame you had to find her. You've been through enough.'

'I'm alright.' Laura shivered and unsuccessfully tried to put the scene out of her mind.

The waitress served the coffees and Eva accepted two sugar sachets. 'I've heard sugar is good for shock.'

Laura patted her tummy. 'Better not.'

She stirred the coffee without adding sugar and cupped the mug in her hands to steady them while trying to steady herself too.

'Shall we order something to eat?'

'I'm feeling lightheaded, but I don't think I could eat anything.'

Eva ordered at the counter cabinet and brought back two glasses of water.

'How long have you been working at your office now?' Laura tried to distract herself.

'Too long! Almost three years now. I enjoyed it until the new boss took over. He says all the right things but…he used to work for one of the big banks. I'm not sure what he did; his previous title doesn't give any clues. He's too aggressive and unscrupulous for me. I'll give him a chance, although I think it's time to retire.'

Laura couldn't be distracted enough. 'That woman wasn't homeless. What do you think happened to her?'

'She could have been walking through after work or going home from the bus stop.'

'It gets dark early in winter.' Laura shuddered at the vivid image of the swollen eye and bloodied mouth.

The waitress placed two focaccias on the table and whisked away their table number. Laura managed two bites before putting it back on the plate. Talking to Eva settled her quivering and outward reactions, but inside she was still fighting the images.

They sat in silence. Once Eva finished her lunch, she suggested they drive to a favourite hotel and chat over a quiet drink.

They drove onto Sir Donald Bradman Drive. A crowd assembled by the derelict building where she'd found the body. Two camera crews rushed down the side street and a policewoman talked to a cluster of people while cordoning off the area.

After a few twists and turns, Eva parked at the Crown hotel carpark.

Four men in casual gear, about retirement age, sat at the bar chatting to the barman. Laura walked past the bar into a small, rounded alcove and sank into a booth. The smell of cooking hamburgers reminded her of the derelict site, and she again felt nauseous. Eva brought a rum and coke for Laura and a scotch and dry for herself.

'We'll have to change our names from Gynne and Tonique to Rum and Scotch,' Eva laughed.

'She was so beaten up and swollen.' Laura couldn't get the young woman's bruised face out of her mind.

'I didn't realise you'd seen so much.'

'I thought she might need help.'

'Oh, Laura.' Eva touched Laura's arm.

'You'll be careful when you leave work, won't you?'

'I have a secure carpark although it makes me feel on edge. It's close but, what can I do? I can't leave work early to avoid the dark. I take all the usual precautions; we're women, we just do. But I'm not going to live my life in fear.'

They were strong words, but Laura couldn't dispel her worrying after seeing that young woman's untimely death. 'We'll find out what happened soon enough.'

Eva bought Laura a second drink, while she sipped on a glass of water. The alcohol had the desired effect; Laura's equilibrium was returning and eventually, Eva drove her home. They would collect her car tomorrow.

That evening Laura yet again opened a bottle of wine and tried unsuccessfully to avoid the news. There was nothing new, no identity, or details about the woman. The news reporters speculated that she'd been attacked and her body dumped there. For Laura, the coverage brought back a vivid myriad of recollections: the rat, the scattered debris, the smell of rotting food and excrement, and most of all, the battered defenceless body sprawled underneath a tattered dirty blanket.

That night, Laura's dreams turned to nightmares, filled with images of the dead woman and Tom. Their sallow and expressionless faces stared at her and mouthed words that Laura couldn't hear. The young woman suddenly appeared wearing a red cocktail dress, her face pleading as she reached out a hand. Laura recoiled. Tom joined the charade, pleading with her too. Laura woke with a start, bathed in sweat and the sheets entangling her limbs. Sleep eluded her, and she tossed and turned. Who was this woman? And why were she and Tom in her nightmares together? Her hand swept across the barren centre of the king-sized bed. It was cold and empty and right now, so was she.

Chapter 15

Laura rubbed her gritty eyes. Why did the dead woman's swollen and bruised face transform into a blemish-free, young, and vibrant woman wearing a red cocktail dress? And why did Tom appear in those nightmares, too?

Laura resisted the temptation to burrow back under the duvet. The images wouldn't let her rest anyway. Instead, she dragged herself out of bed, and after a breakfast of coffee, buried the images under a barrage of work and sweat cleaning up. At least the house would be ready for the real estate agent's visit tomorrow. After an hour, her muscles ached as much as her head. The constant tug of memories and the gruesome images melded into an unpleasant melting pot where her emotions were sandwiched between memories she happily followed back in time and those that made her angry or sad.

The house turned sombre. Outside, rain clouds gathered in readiness for a storm, and her mood followed. She made herself another coffee and flopped into the recliner.

A loud knock at the door sent the coffee mug crashing to the floor, smashing it into sharp shards at her feet, and sending inky black liquid splashing across her shoes and onto the rug.

On the doorstep stood a uniformed policewoman, and behind her was a short, older policeman. His shirt gaped, revealing a tuft of dark, straggly hair where it strained over his protruding belly. Laura focused on the fresh-faced policewoman.

'Hello. Ms Gynne?' the policewoman asked. 'Can we come in?'

Laura led them into the dining area and as they passed the smashed remains of her coffee, she explained, 'Your knock startled me.'

'Nerves?' the policeman muttered.

'We're here to ask you some questions about the body you discovered yesterday. We've identified her and believe you may know her,' the policewoman explained. 'She used to work with your husband.'

'She worked with Tom? My *late* husband.' She sat down and looked up as the policewoman held out a photo.

'Do you recognise her?'

Laura hesitated. The face was the one from her nightmares. 'There is something familiar about her,' she finally said.

'You didn't mention that you knew her at the time.' The policeman scribbled in his notepad.

'My late husband worked with a lot of people, most of whom I never met.'

A fragment of memory danced in Laura's mind, but it wouldn't come at her bidding. The bruised and beaten face under the shabby blanket crowded everything else out.

'Her name is Corrinne Lamberthy. Does that mean anything?'

Laura shook her head. CL. They were the initials in Tom's diary. 'No, but I think I may have seen her before.'

As she grappled with the memory, she again looked at the photo and suddenly she remembered.

November 2003

The home belonged to one of the APATO senior managers and was regularly used for special work functions. It was grand, almost too grand. Tom was on edge before and during the party. As usual, he'd coached Laura on what she mustn't talk about and she'd relaxed as much as she could while being on guard. Laura didn't like these functions; they were formal, and too much work and not enough social.

Peter, at his schmoozing best, laughed and joked with the bosses. He caught her eye, smiled and, after clapping one of the bosses on the back, wandered over.

'Haven't seen you for a while,' Peter slurred. He clapped Tom on the shoulder but winked at Laura. 'You're not avoiding them, are you?'

Tom grimaced. 'Of course not!'

'Are you enjoying the do?' Peter's comical emphasis on the word do made her laugh.

'Where's Abbie tonight?'

Abbie often worked the room as effectively as Peter. She was a natural at turning on the charm, for the right people.

'The babysitter cancelled and we couldn't find a replacement at such short notice. She wasn't happy.' Peter made a sad face, although he'd make the most of her not being there.

Tom placed his empty glass on a passing tray. 'I'll pop over to say hello to Furness and the crowd. I won't be long.'

Laura nodded and watched Tom walk, straight-backed and tall, towards the upper management group.

'Good. They like you to act like they're important.' Peter leaned in conspiratorially. 'Doesn't matter what you really think, you have to keep up appearances.'

'You wouldn't have said something like that in the old days.'

'I've grown older and wiser, I suppose.'

A white-haired man with a slight stoop approached. 'There you are, Peter. I wondered where you'd got to. Furness wants a word.' His short and wiry frame belied the strong voice.

Peter made his apologies and followed the man out to the hall. Laura scanned the room but couldn't see Tom anywhere. The management group he'd been talking to had also gone. She grabbed another drink and strolled out onto a moonlight bathed balcony.

Shrubbery partly obscured the other balcony, but a flash of red caught Laura's eye. She leaned forward. A young woman in a luscious red cocktail dress waved her hands furiously as she talked. Her dark hair was pinned back into a severe but striking style, and the light from the patio accented her expressive face. It was obvious she was upset and Laura sensed anger in her body language. A hand reached out and touched the woman on the shoulder. Laura was curious, but she couldn't lean forward enough to see. She contemplated going down into the garden but thought better of it. The young woman stepped back, and the torso attached to the hand moved with her. It was Tom. He dragged the woman to him, cradling her in his arms in a gentle embrace.

Laura tore back out of sight. Her heart pounded. She was unwilling to believe the worst, but that tender and intimate moment seeded a kernel of doubt which pierced her confidence.

On the way home, Laura questioned Tom, gently at first and then more vigorously as he became evasive. He finally explained that the young woman was his ex-research assistant, Corrinne, and she'd broken up with her boyfriend. Tom comforted her, that was all. Laura couldn't challenge the explanation; it was plausible, although for some reason it seemed unlikely. There was something about the encounter that made her uneasy.

***

It was the same Corrinne. After re-examining the photo, Laura was sure.

'I remember now. I only met her once, actually, I never *met* her. She was at a work function a few years ago.'

'If you didn't meet her, why do you remember her?' the policeman asked.

'I saw Tom console her. She was upset. I didn't even know her full name, only Corrinne.'

'Do you think your late husband and the victim were in a relationship?' the policeman continued.

'Of course not!' A kernel of doubt surfaced and lingered after her denial.

'How can you be so sure?' the policewoman asked.

'I know … knew Tom. He wouldn't.' She sounded convincing, but she wasn't convinced.

'Is there anything you can remember?' The policewoman took back the photo and stowed it in her clipboard.

Laura shook her head.

'Your husband died suddenly too, didn't he?' The policeman continued taking notes.

'In February. From a heart attack.'

'Weren't there other circumstances besides a heart attack?'

'His heart attack was brought on by a combination of drugs.' Laura struggled to say it out loud.

'It was suspicious circumstances then?' The policeman watched Laura intently.

'No one suggested his death was suspicious. It could have been accidental.' Her voice shook as a tremor travelled up her spine.

'What drugs did they find?' The policeman focused on his notes.

'Digoxin and E-bomb, I think it's called.' Her tongue caught on these words; it was like speaking a foreign language.

The police officers glanced at each other briefly.

'Where did he get the drugs?' he asked.

'I didn't even know he was taking them.'

'You didn't see changes in his behaviour, see him taking pills, or acting strangely.'

This policeman had a simple view of life and marriage. The changes Laura saw hadn't suggested drug-taking. She'd interpreted them as disenchantment with their life together, trouble at work, his regrets, and his worries. She still couldn't believe Tom took drugs or was having an affair, although the evidence was stacking up.

'Your son, Robert, has been hanging around with some unsavoury characters too. Could he have supplied your husband?'

'Robby? He wouldn't do drugs. Robby is…' Laura couldn't finish that statement. What was Robby; misguided, stubborn, naïve, or all of the above? He was her son, and that was the most important thing to her.

'We may need to talk to you again. In the meantime, if you think of anything that might help, please contact us.' The policewoman handed Laura a card with her contact details.

'What happened to her? Her face…it's given me nightmares.' Laura needed to know.

'We can't reveal the details,' the policewoman explained.

'I think she had a boyfriend.'

'We've spoken to her husband.'

Laura showed them out and as soon as the police car pulled away, she phoned Eva.

'The police have been here, asking me if I recognised her.'

'They flashed up a photo on the news and I've seen her before. Her name is Corrinne something or other. She worked at APATO,' Eva said.

'Corrinne Lamberthy. The police said she worked with Tom. I saw her at one of the work functions.'

'How odd. I thought she was one of Peter's— A friend who works near APATO told me she saw Peter with a young woman several times. From his cagey response, I assumed she was another of his *flings*.' Eva sighed. 'By then I was past caring. I was leaving him.'

'Wasn't he with Abbie when you split up?'

Eva laughed. It sounded hard and perhaps it was ironic, but there was a touch of pain too.

'You know, he was never a one-woman man,' Eva replied.

'They asked me if Tom had a relationship with her.'

'What did you say?'

'Of course not.'

'But?'

'But, the more I think about it…I'm not sure of anything. I never thought Tom would take drugs either, so having an affair isn't much more of a stretch.' Her world was falling apart. She didn't know what to believe.

'He was devoted to you and the family.'

'They called Tom's death *suspicious*.'

'I'll call my friend. Her husband works in the police department. She might know more.'

'It's bizarre that we both know her,' Laura said sadly.

'They're questioning her husband; the news mentioned a possible abusive relationship.'

'The policewoman said they'd *talked* to him.' Laura's brain whirled with small details but settled on the gruesome picture of a badly beaten face.

'It's an unlikely place to dump a body. Surely the husband would conceal it somewhere more remote, where she might never be found.' Eva was thinking out loud, a common behaviour for her, but her thoughts on this topic made Laura queasy.

'Tom's diary listed an appointment with a CL the morning he died. Now Tom's dead and Corrinne, who worked with Tom, and whose initials are CL, is also dead. Is it a coincidence or am I becoming paranoid?' Laura shivered.

'Did you mention this to the police?' Eva asked.

'How does it help? I don't know anything substantial. It's all supposition and suspicions.' Questions whirled through her mind and she didn't like any of the possible answers. 'But CL matches Corrinne Lamberthy.'

'You need to tell them,' Eva said forcefully.

Eva arranged a time to drive Laura to pick up her car, then hung up. Laura returned to her recliner. Tom said Corrinne had broken up with her boyfriend, but the police said they'd talked to her husband. Had she married since or had Tom lied? Were they having an affair or was this about something else? She hadn't suspected Tom's drug-taking and even when Tom became distant and more unreachable, she'd assumed it was work. Perhaps she hadn't known Tom at all.

Laura shivered. This mystery engulfed her no matter how much she tried to ignore it. Tom's death was considered suspicious and now Corrinne had died suspiciously too. That phone call. Could it have been Corrinne? Warning her?

Laura's head ached. There were too many questions. Maybe Peter was right. She was becoming as crazy as Tom, puzzling over mysterious things she knew nothing about.

Her stomach grumbled. She was hungry but didn't feel like making dinner. The usual indecision beset her. Should she make something simple and easy, get a takeaway, or make herself cook. She'd wait until Eva took her to the car and decide then.

When the phone rang, she stared at it, willing it to silence, but immediately felt guilty. It could be Robby returning her calls.

It took Laura a moment to recognise the voice. 'Oh hello, Jacques.' She was surprised but not unpleasantly.

'Have I caught you at a bad time?'

'It's been an awful day. Never mind. You surprised me.'

'Anything I can help with?' His voice was soothing.

'No, it's nothing.' She couldn't explain now.

'Would you like to meet for a coffee or lunch on Saturday? Perhaps whatever made today so bad, can be rectified.'

'That sounds lovely.' Laura surprised them both. The phrase, *Life is short*, echoed through her mind, and the evidence was following her around. 'I'll meet you. Where did you have in mind?'

Jacques suggested Café Milanese on Rundle Street. It was central, casual, and had a versatile menu.

'It's the one with the big tempting cake display,' Jacques said with a smile in his voice. 'Shall we make it 11 a.m. or would you prefer to meet for lunch?'

'11 a.m. is fine.'

Laura marvelled at her own audacity. She'd never accepted an invitation so easily before, but she wanted pleasant company and interesting conversation and the question 'why not?' replayed in her head. She had no convincing answer. Like all the other questions being raised in her life, although this one didn't need an answer.

Chapter 16

The slice of toast hovered midway to John's lips. The photo on the morning news program was her. The woman from the park, Corrinne, was dead. Her badly beaten body was dumped in a disused office block in Adelaide, not Sydney. Carlo said he'd fix it. Is this what he'd meant? Casterlow was angry at Furness for meeting the girl, but was he angry enough to silence her? Even Furness may have a reason to eliminate her, especially after Casterlow's angry rebuke. She'd posed a threat to very powerful people, any one of them could be responsible for her death. It was a puzzle John was keen to solve.

Skye shuffled in, snuggled deep into her fluffy dressing gown, her hair still tousled from sleep. She leaned across and kissed him. He automatically put his arm around her shoulders and squeezed, his mind still plucking at the mystery.

'Are you going to take me out tonight?' she purred.

'Mmm.'

'We don't go out together very often anymore.' Skye opened the fridge door and extracted almond milk and strawberries.

John liked the dreamy, freshly awake Skye and her languid and less self-conscious movements. She sliced the fruit, preparing her usual breakfast smoothie.

'I have things to sort out. You know how it is. Business comes first.' He studied her as she tipped the strawberries into the blender and added nuts and a handful of kale.

'Let's go out for dinner?' she suggested.

'I'm not sure when I'll be home.' He leaned in to kiss her goodbye. It was a good time to leave.

'Can I come to Amsterdam with you?' Skye asked.

Not again. Obviously, she'd been stewing about it. 'No. I can't be distracted.'

'I could shop and amuse myself.' Her eyes pleaded with him. 'Please. I'd stay out of your way. I wouldn't distract you. I've never been to Amsterdam.'

'I said no. It's all arranged already. Besides, you have work.'

'Nothing I couldn't change.'

'I'll see you tonight.' John turned to go.

Skye stomped her foot. 'That's it, is it? You ignore what I want. You take me for granted. I'm stuck here, waiting for you to get home. You never take me anywhere anymore, unless it's for business. I'm sick of this.'

John didn't tolerate temper tantrums, and he wasn't making an exception now. 'You know what you can do if you don't like it,' he said coldly. 'You have a good life, nothing too taxing, nothing much expected of you, so what more can you ask? Yet, when I need your help, you're useless. That party. You got your nose out of joint because Lucinda bloody Murphy didn't cosy up to you.'

'What do you mean? Those old biddies ignored me, treated me like dirt. Is that *my* fault? I can't help it that your business involves such old farts and their dull and boring wives,' Skye scowled.

'You need to try harder to be an asset.' John glared, signalling an end to the discussion.

She hadn't received his signal or if she had, she ignored it. 'Don't you dare put this on to me! This is about us; our relationship. I want to be loved and appreciated, not be an *asset*. That's not much to ask.' She glared back.

Skye didn't get angry often, and it would be amusing if it weren't annoying. He was going to be late.

'Do you love me?' she yelled.

'What sort of question is that? I've given you a home, a car, designer clothes, and even paid for the plastic surgery to help your career. What more do you want?'

'You can't say it, can you? Say you love me.'

'You know I do.'

'Say it!'

'Of course I do,' he began, but now he was angry too. 'If you don't know how I feel, then what's the point?'

Skye cranked the blender into top gear. No conversation could compete with that, and he stormed out, slamming the door behind him.

Why did women always need to be reassured? Why couldn't they be satisfied with having a good life and being taken care of? There were some wives, millionaires' wives especially, who were happy to live the good life, even when the couple essentially lived separately. They came together in mutually beneficial ways. That's what he wanted. He was finished with love and exclusive relationships. He didn't want restrictions or to be responsible for someone else's happiness. He was comfortable with Skye; they'd become close and fit together well. Why did she have to spoil things?

At the office, his receptionist, Fleur, brought him the day's files. Her smile improved his mood. He phoned Kleb, but he was busy and promised to ring back later. John's research into Casterlow's secret project had hit a dead-end; he'd need specialised help to crack their security. He scoured the files on the Iraqi defence transport contract. His first contracts delivered construction and technical equipment to Bassarti and returned to Australia with small consignments of supplements and pharmaceuticals for APATO. He'd replaced the dodgy Wheat Board transport arrangement. That's how he'd discovered Dimi and her Bassarti E-bomb supply. Did

Furness or Casterlow know about the synthetic drug and turn a blind eye, or were they entirely unaware? Maybe the leaks jeopardising Dimi's business endangered Casterlow's project too. But how?

In the newer contracts, the equipment he transported from Australia was delivered into a central warehouse and distributed by others to building programs in secret locations. These must be the installations producing Casterlow's secret product. In addition to the construction machinery, there were several scientific laboratory fixtures. But, Casterlow's narrative didn't fit with mundane illicit drug manufacture.

His private mobile rang. It was Kleb. John explained what he'd seen in the park and about Corrinne.

'It doesn't make sense. She worked for Trade, not Defence. My boffins have failed to hack into the system so far, but I can check what projects she worked on. That might be a clue.'

'Are there any other developments?' John asked.

'Furness is provoking Casterlow and Casterlow's livid. You don't want to get on the wrong side of him. The PM backs him all the way. I've heard that Skollov's complaining about being left out of a new trade opportunity. I think you've interrupted his plans. He's not happy, poor love.'

Skollov's cunning and shrewdness were the kind of traits Casterlow usually admired, so why was he now out of favour?

'I'll keep quizzing Casterlow, especially before the Amsterdam meeting. I'd like to know what he's not telling me too,' John said. He hoped he hadn't made an enemy of Skollov now.

'I'll keep you posted, John.'

'I've scheduled several meetings in Amsterdam. The Russian contacts will provide another distribution arm here in Australia and help my takeover plan.'

'Good. They can't recognise you.'

'I know, but what else can I do?' All his plans depended on his identity staying hidden until he was ready. John shivered. His reconstructive surgery had effectively disguised him until now. If it didn't work there, he didn't like to think about what would happen to him.

'How else can I help, John?'

'I'd like to know which families support Dimi and Babbo's succession plan. They can't all be happy. I'm sure some of my uncles would prefer the son to take over, but I can't approach them without exposing my identity. It would be useful to know whose support I can count on when the time comes.'

'I could find out what support Dimi has, but not much more.'

'Let's see what you can come up with.' John had a couple of ideas. One was Franco, nicknamed The Ferret. He'd been an instrumental source of information in John's father's world. Carlo could arrange it discreetly. Carlo was an asset in the old world.

'Talk again soon.' Kleb hung up.

John stared out of the window, summoning up the enthusiasm to tackle his supply issues. The South American cargo was arriving in steady shipments at last, but there was trouble brewing. The KT Cartel was his main supplier, but the rumours suggested there was a leadership challenge coming. These gangs acted as badly as politicians. John was more intent than ever to find an alternative. The family business was within reach and his meeting in Amsterdam would start the ball rolling. He'd be able to act soon.

Chapter 17

Laura put down the phone and shuddered. The apartment she'd fallen in love with was generating a lot of interest and she'd increased her offer. It was a big step. There were no guarantees she could sell her house for the right price. She tried to quell her nerves by flicking through her tattered recipe book, searching for her favourite Mediterranean chicken and feta filo pie recipe. Dinner for Mel tonight would be special. She wrote a list of ingredients and grabbed her keys to drive to the shops when the phone rang.

'Robby, what a nice surprise.'

'I'll drop by on the weekend to clear out my boxes,' Robby said. 'You can give me a new key then.'

'I haven't done the keys yet,' Laura said. 'I discovered a dead body and the police—'

'Dead body? How?' He sounded excited.

Laura explained. From the muffled voice in the background, Shayida was with him.

'Was this the body found near the airport?'

'Yes. It turns out she worked with Dad.'

'That's a weird coincidence. But how cool,' Robby said cheerfully.

Laura thought cool was code for good and couldn't agree. 'It was ghastly.'

'Have you found out what that key is for?' Robby asked.
'How did you know about the key?'
'You must've mentioned it when we came over.'
She couldn't have. She hadn't found it before their visit, had she? Maybe her memory was playing tricks on her.

Robby interrupted, 'Any clues?'

'Tom wrote a series of letters and numbers, but they mean nothing to me.' Perhaps Eva had mentioned it to Robby. 'Have you talked to Eva lately?'

He cleared his throat. 'Not for a while, not since—'

'And?'

'Stop interfering. I know what I'm doing,' he hissed.

Laura couldn't think of anything tactful to say and she didn't want to argue, so she let it go.

'I'll clear out my stuff this weekend. Without my key, I can't come when I'm free.'

'I'm going to lunch on Saturday.'

'Lunching with Eva?' Robby's tone was accusing, as though Laura and Eva were conspiring against him.

'No, with Jacques. Someone I met at a dinner party.'

'You're going on a date?'

'We're having lunch.'

'It's a bit *early*,' Robby accused.

Laura's cheeks flushed. 'I'm allowed to eat and have friends.'

'Sure,' he muttered. 'I'll work out a time and ring you, OK?'

Laura clenched her fist. Her younger children sometimes tried to control her life, yet he shrugged off her concerns about his association with Shayida's dodgy family. Laura sighed. Robby believed he was mature enough to make his own decisions, but he was young for his age and impressionable. Still, she needed to tread carefully, not blunder into his issues and make things worse. If only she could work out how to tackle this without pushing him further away. She hoped it wasn't too late for her to learn.

She gathered her bag and took her list of ingredients to the supermarket. By the time she'd prepared dinner, Mel arrived.

'I saw the news report about that body. I've seen her before. She was here that morning when Dad—' Mel faltered momentarily. 'She rushed out of the house and almost hit me with her satchel. Dad said she was an old work colleague.'

The diary entry said he'd met CL that morning. It confirmed that CL was Corrinne. But why was she here?

'The police said she worked with your father. I saw her at a party once.' Laura couldn't go on. Maybe he *was* having an affair, and the drugs were part of that relationship? She felt the blood drain from her face. Had she been living a lie all these years? An image forced itself into her thoughts. The unknown woman at the funeral. Was that Corrinne? The other woman? Could they have both been murdered by a jealous husband?

'Are you alright Mum?' Mel came around to Laura's side of the table and hugged her.

'I obviously didn't know…the real Tom. I believed in him,' Laura stammered.

'It might not be what it looks like.'

'Or it might be exactly what it looks like,' she argued. 'Were they having an affair? I don't know what to think.'

Laura's mind choked on questions. How long had the relationship been going on? His diaries were the clue, and she *needed* to know the truth. She was tired of thrashing around in the dark, unable to get answers, and she didn't want to live a lie.

'Dad might have taken you for granted, but he loved you. I can't believe he'd have an affair, but he's my dad and I believed in him, too. He was principled, even when it was annoying or inconvenient or hard. It's not in character. He even jeopardised his friendship with Peter over principles.'

'That's true, but lots of men separate their personal principles from public or business ones,' Laura reasoned.

'Dad wasn't like that. He did the right thing and that included being true to his wife and family.'

'He changed.' Laura hadn't been aware of how much he'd changed. His regrets and sullenness showed her a different side, but she'd ignored it, turned a blind eye, and hoped he'd sort it out. 'I wish he'd talked to me.' Deep down, she wished she'd asked more questions and persevered too.

'This could all be work-related. She worked on a system called Fast-Track. I remember Dad accused Peter of deliberately misleading him about Fast-Track.'

Fast-Track, that term struck a chord with Laura.

August 2003

The press conference announced a new approach to border control, encompassing a reorganisation at the docks to facilitate more efficient processing. So much jargon for such a simple change, Tom said. This, they vowed, would save taxpayers money, lots of money, that could be redirected into other imperatives like security. Some of the savings would be used to upgrade the machinery and technology at the wharves, further increasing efficiency and showing the world Australia was open for business.

Tom grunted.

'It's a step in the right direction, isn't it?' She turned to Tom, who huddled in his seat. A cup of tea sat untouched on the table beside him.

'That's what they want you to believe. On the surface, it looks great. Fast-Track means our shipments to and from Iraq will no longer go through a thorough check or red tape, as they like to call it. Instead, they'll be processed quickly and not held up at our border.' Tom grunted. 'It means that these shipments are trusted.' He shook his head. 'Do you know how dumb that is? How can we guarantee anything coming in from Iraq? How can we be sure of the companies we're dealing with?'

'Why do you always have to question everything?'

'It's not a good idea to wind down the oversight of shipments. It leaves it open for…exploitation.'

'Surely they wouldn't set it up without some safeguards or assurances.'

'The way it's set up, anyone can use the Fast-Track process for things it's not meant for. There've been problems with people trying to smuggle in antiquities, even drugs.'

'They have contingency plans, don't they?'

'Ha. For them, it's about "get as much trade and make as much money as we can and don't worry too much about the collateral risks or damage," not efficient trade. That's the spin. That's what they want the public to hear but—'

'You've become cynical.'

'Who wouldn't be with the way things are run these days? The joint contracts opened my eyes to what companies can do with impunity. No one cares about ethics. We're willing to do things that are irregular, and even illegal, in the name of profit.' His eyes rested on her. 'I'm sorry, I shouldn't blow off like this. I've raised my suspicions with management, but they insist I'm wrong. I don't trust them, but there's nothing I can do about it.'

'Maybe you need to let it go, Tom?' Was she being selfish to want to focus on their life together?

Tom shook his head slowly. 'Perhaps you're right; I should accept it. I'm out of step with this modern world. Maybe I should just work with the system and take the easy option.'

Laura wasn't sure if he was being sarcastic or meant it, but she was too exhausted to ask.

***

Laura swallowed down a twinge of guilt. She'd dismissed his concerns and wanted him to stop worrying, but had she pushed him towards something he'd regret. Was this why he'd taken drugs? Maybe Fast-Track was a clue.

'I don't know what to think. Maybe he saw conspiracies where there aren't any, but then…'

'But then, what, Mum?'

'The burglary, the key, and the mysterious phone call, they add up to a more sinister explanation. It could have been Corrinne warning me about Tom's files.' Laura shook her head. 'I think finding her body has spooked me.' The other explanation was too disturbing. *Maybe I should work with the system and take the easy option.* Those words stuck in her head, but she couldn't say them out loud, especially in front of Mel.

Mel refilled their glasses. 'You should tell the police.'

'They'd want to know why I didn't mention these things earlier. Will they believe that I've had too much going on and I forgot? I'm worried about Robby; I'm trying to prepare this house for sale, and then I stumble on the dead body of Tom's old colleague, and it's being suggested Tom was having an affair. His mysteries are drawing me in and, as if that isn't enough, I've increased my offer on that apartment and now the pressure is on,' Laura explained. The more pressing reason stayed unvoiced. Maybe they would find that Tom was part of the problem rather than the solution.

'Let's get Becky to talk to Robby. I'll ask her. I'll help with researching Dad's *mysteries* if you pass them on.' Mel's reassuring and efficient mode had the necessary effect.

'Enough about me. What about your trip to New York?' Laura asked. It was time to focus on good news.

'I'll be working with an informal committee called the Australia Group.' Mel's voice almost sang.

'That's a very vague name. Is it a secret?'

'Not secret, but sensitive. They work in international arms control. I'm not sure what my role will be, but I'm excited.'

Unlike Mel's excitement, Laura felt that familiar churning in her stomach. She handed Mel Jacques' business card and mentioned she was meeting him for lunch tomorrow. Thankfully, Mel's attitude was the opposite of Robby's.

After dinner, Laura filled their glasses with a newly opened Shiraz and flicked through Tom's DVD library. His favourites were the old classics and Laura's mind filled with images of him watching, and often sleeping through, his black and white collection. She didn't often watch them with him, but maybe she should have. There were classic westerns and musicals, at least they were in colour. She selected the *Billy Elliot* DVD she'd bought him for Christmas one year. He'd enjoyed it once she'd convinced him to watch it.

'Some escapism would be good,' Mel agreed.

Laura opened the cover but instead of *Billy Elliot*, the handwritten label said *Omar, 23 Jan 06*.

'This looks home-recorded. It must have been put in the wrong case.'

Mel peered over her shoulder. 'That's a weird title for a home movie,' she said, echoing Laura's thoughts.

'Let's have a look,' Laura suggested.

She loaded the DVD, flopped into Tom's well-worn recliner, and pressed play. The video started immediately with a blue-grey, blank screen. A man's deep voice whispered an introduction while the grainy picture focused on rough, dirty, stucco walls and a small figure crouched in the corner.

'What can you tell us about Bassarti, Omar?' the deep voice hissed.

'My father…we need to get him out before he dies. We need your help. My mother, my family, we need help to save him. Please.'

Laura frowned. What was this? It didn't look like a home movie.

'Tell me what's happened,' the interviewer asked.

'The soldiers took my father away. We are not permitted to visit. They say he is a terrorist, but they are wrong.'

Laura and Mel glanced at each other. The word terrorist set Laura's nerves on edge.

'Are you sure?' the interviewer questioned.

'He speaks against the government. They beat him in front of us. They say this is a warning and then last month they take him away. We are forbidden to talk to anyone about it.'

'You said there was more.'

'A friend smuggle me in to see him. His body is covered in bloody sores. I have never seen my father like this. He is very sick and in much pain. He will die. I know it. He said the medicines they give him don't help. Others have died. He will die too.'

'Can your friend smuggle us in too?'

'He has disappeared. I ask to see my father again, but they tell me, no.'

Omar swallowed a sob and closed his eyes. 'He said he was the only one still alive.'

'Did he tell you what is happening to him? How he got sick?'

'He has seen terrible things. Men have died. They fall to the floor, their eyes roll back into their heads and their tongues hang from their mouths. It is shocking. It is—'

Omar closed his eyes but immediately opened them again, wide and bright.

'His sores don't heal. He can't breathe, eat, or even lie down. I must get him out.'

Omar reached his arms towards the camera. The camera jerked back, and so did Laura. A tear glistened down Omar's cheek and the camera trembled.

'I will do everything I can.'

A noise sounded in the background and the video stopped abruptly. Laura stared at the screen wordlessly. Suddenly a different voice spoke, although the picture remained blank.

'Omar's father died 24 January 2006, one day after this interview. His death has not been officially reported, therefore we have no cause of death.'

'What is this?' Mel grabbed the DVD case but the cover lied. 'Where did Dad get this? And why?'

'Is there an epidemic somewhere? I don't understand what this DVD is about. Is it from Iraq? What's Bassarti? A place? A hospital? What? APATO supplies medicines, so are they accusing them of not helping?' Laura voiced her confusion.

She trembled. This DVD filled her with dread.

Mel examined the DVD. 'Could there be more?'

They searched Tom's collection, not trusting the covers, they opened each in turn.

'This is the only one,' Mel said, staring at the mess of DVDs on the floor.

'Omar looked Middle Eastern. Can we assume it's Iraq?' Laura asked as they began replacing the DVDs in the cabinet.

'Not necessarily. Saddam Hussein's torture prisons are all closed.'

'Mel, with your connections and access—'

'I couldn't,' Mel replied. 'If this is about security, I'd lose my job.'

'This must be connected to APATO. Tom kept it for a reason.' Laura sounded rational and calm, but inside, a torrent of nerves was ready to explode.

'There's not much to go on; a date and a name.'

'And the mention of Bassarti. What else can we do?' Laura didn't want to get Mel into trouble or risk her newly established career, but how else would they get answers? She needed the truth. 'There must be a way to look into it without raising alarm bells. If it turns out to be something important, we can hand it on. But right now, we don't know who to, or what it's about?' Laura's throat constricted. 'I understand, sweetie, if you can't do this. I'll ask Eva; she has resources and means.'

Laura could almost see Mel thinking as her frown grew deeper.

'No, I'll take it. It's better that I look into this discreetly.'

'I'm not sure now. It could be dangerous and I don't want to put you in that position.'

'I promise I'll be careful.'

Their conversation petered out. Finally, Laura made up the spare bed for Mel and they said good night. Laura pulled the duvet up over her head, but the disturbing images and thoughts slipped under the covers with her.

Chapter 18

Laura dawdled through her morning, and now she was running late. Twice she poked herself in the eye with the mascara and tears threatened to ruin her handiwork. Her makeup barely disguised the dark circles under her eyes anyway. She rifled through her wardrobe and selected her favourite, go-to black pants, but when she tried them on, they were too tight around her waist. She sighed. Wine, too many easy meals, and not enough gym were taking their toll. Finally, she settled on the blue dress, which slid smoothly over her bumps. The colour complimented her eyes too. She grimaced. Hopefully, Jacques would appreciate her efforts.

Jacques sat by the café wall facing the entrance. He was engrossed in the menu, but as though sensing her arrival, he looked up and smiled at her. She automatically smiled back and patted down her dress.

As she approached the table, the group of six sitting near the rear of the café burst into raucous guffaws. The noise combined with music from the radio and someone in the kitchen clattered crockery. She frowned. She didn't like noisy cafés.

Jacques leaned forward and kissed both her cheeks. 'I'm glad you could come.'

'Thank you for your invitation.' Laura grimaced. She hadn't meant to sound so formal.

'You look lovely.'

Her cheeks warmed. It had been some time since she'd been complimented or even noticed. Jacques offered her the menu.

'For lunch? Otherwise, there's a magnificent cake cabinet. I discovered it on my first days here.' He patted the small bulge around his middle.

Laura chuckled. 'Let's order coffees.'

'You're going to see how well this goes first.' He watched her, a wry smile replacing the more generous one.

'That's not what I meant,' she said rather too quickly, although it was exactly what she'd meant. 'I'm not sure if I'm hungry enough to eat yet,' she lied.

'Would you like a coffee or something stronger?' Jacques clearly liked options, but decisions were not currently her strong point.

While he ordered coffees, Laura glanced at the tables nearby. Couples sat silently, transfixed by their phones; together yet each one cocooned in their own world.

'I wasn't sure you'd come,' Jacques said, bringing her back to the world at her table.

Laura hadn't been sure either.

'I enjoyed your company at dinner,' he continued.

'I'm out of practice… meeting new people since Tom.'

Laura leaned back in her chair. When their coffees arrived, they simultaneously returned the sugar sachets to the waitress, then descended into silence. Laura fidgeted with her ring.

'No more mysterious phone calls I hope.' Jacques said.

'Er, no. No phone calls, but I discovered a…dead body.' Laura explained the sequence of events. 'Now the police suggest Tom and Corrinne were having an affair.'

Jacques frowned.

'I didn't recognise her at first. She was too badly…but I'd seen her before. She'd worked with Tom,' she added quietly. The gallery of images reappeared along with the putrid smell.

'Are you alright?' His hand moved forward, then dropped onto the table next to hers. 'Why do the police suspect she was involved with Tom?'

'It's a theory, I guess. They worked together. I saw them together once. He was comforting her but—she worked with Peter too, before she moved to the Fast-Track program.'

'Fast-Track?' Jacques' frown deepened.

Loud laughter and conversation again rose from the back table and drowned Jacques out. Laura shook her head. She wanted to be like that table, enjoying a trouble-free and fun-filled lunch.

'Perhaps we could order lunch. I need distracting,' she suggested.

'I'm good at distraction.' His frown disappeared and his eyes sparkled.

She studied the menu while he sipped the last of his coffee. The waitress returned with a carafe of water and two glasses and took their orders.

'You're still planning to move?' Jacques asked.

'I'll have to sell quickly if my offer on an apartment is accepted. It's scary.' Every topic contained a nerve-twitching component. 'I've lived there for thirty-five years, but the house and the garden are too much for me now. I need a change.'

'I've never lived in one place that long. You are a gardener?'

'Not anymore,' Laura replied. 'Are you?'

'Not me. It was one of the issues between my ex-wife and me.' He shrugged.

They sat in an awkward silence, surrounded by memories of those who weren't there.

'Tom spent a lot of time travelling for work,' Jacques said. 'Did you mind?'

'I worried, especially given the issues in Iraq '

'There was little justice before the war, but it hasn't improved.'

Laura's mind returned to the DVD and its sad story. 'Are political prisoners still kept in their jails?'

'Besides Abu Ghraib, which the USA is keen to maintain, not that I know of.'

Maybe the DVD wasn't Iraq.

'Are you going there? To Iraq, I mean. To see for yourself.'

'I'm touring some Middle Eastern refugee camps soon, but not looking at the political prisoner issues. That's not my area of responsibility.' Jacques sipped his water. 'Did Tom confide in you about his work and what he saw?'

'Much of it was confidential. He worried about…things, but he didn't tell me what,' Laura swatted away the question.

'Peter seems more relaxed. Does he talk to you about it?'

'Don't let his façade fool you.'

'But you and Peter are…close?'

'No, not close.' Laura bristled. Why would Jacques say that?

'Oh, I'm sorry. Peter said —'

'What did Peter say?' Her face flushed. Had Peter been overstating their friendship?

'I'm sorry, maybe I misunderstood. I didn't mean to suggest anything. He's very…protective…of you.'

'Peter and I are friends, nothing more. When he married Abbie, it made things awkward. His ex-wife, Eva, is my best friend. Tom and Peter's endless disagreements about work stretched their friendship, and it strained my relationship with Peter too.'

'You agreed with Tom?' Jacques put his glass down without taking a drink.

'I don't know what his issues were.' Laura shook off a wave of sadness. She'd spent too much time looking backwards. 'It might have been the drugs—'

'What drugs?'

'There were drugs in Tom's system when he died.' Laura swallowed and again guilt niggled at her. 'Can we talk about something else?'

'Sure.' Jacques touched her hand softly.

While the waitress placed a plate of steaming fish and chips in front of Jacques, Laura studied him. His gentle face and smiling eyes were appealing and despite wandering into difficult topics, she enjoyed his company. She'd been lonely for some time, even while Tom was alive.

The waitress served Laura's chicken curry and her stomach rumbled at the spicy aroma.

'Do you work, Laura?' Jacques asked once the waitress left.

'I'm retired. Originally, I worked in a hospital haematology lab, but when the twins came along, I guess I chose stability over ambition. I could manage my family commitments better in the public service. With Tom often away, and four children, I needed a part-time job with stable hours. Back then, most workplaces weren't flexible.'

'Caring for the family and home fell to the women in our generation, didn't it? Maybe it will be easier for the next generation.'

'Do you have children?' Laura asked.

'A daughter, but she's grown up and busy. Her mother and I split up a long time ago. I didn't put enough effort into my relationship with either of them. Work got in the way, and I regret that. I've lost so much ground; it's hard to win it back.'

'They have their own lives. Parenting absorbs you when they're young, then suddenly, everything changes.' Robby loomed in Laura's thoughts.

She told him about her children, her hopes and aspirations for them, finally returning to her biggest concern.

'Robby's girlfriend's brother is a bikie. Robby's too old to lecture, although it doesn't stop me trying.' Laura grimaced. 'He doesn't listen to me anyway. Any suggestions?'

Jacques laughed. 'I'm no help, I'm afraid. I muddle through as best I can. Who's the family?'

'Saviento.'

Jacques's eyes widened.

'Do you know them?' Laura asked.

'The big political donors? They're influential. I've met Mr Saviento.'

'That's her father. Shayida seems nice enough but... I'd ask Becky to help, but she's struggling. She adored Tom, even though with his constant travel, they hardly spent much time together in recent years.'

'Did Tom go to other countries like Syria, Iran, or South America?'

'At first, he travelled to neutral territories like New York and London, but immediately before the war, it changed. They always met in Iraq after that.'

'And always for the same products?'

Laura shifted in her seat. She needed to stop dwelling on problems, hers or Tom's, and rehashing them.

'I don't know. If you want the details about Tom's work, perhaps you should invite Peter to lunch.'

Jacques put up his hands in surrender. 'I'm sorry. Forgive me. I've lived alone for a long time and work fills up my life. I have difficulty putting it aside. I'll stop talking work now, I promise.'

He kept his promise and told her stories of Canada and the different places he'd lived. He had a storyteller's gift. The tales of his travels to New York, Washington, and Geneva were laced with humour and astute observations about the people he met and worked with. He made her laugh and finally relax.

Jacques glanced at his watch. 'I hope we haven't got off on the wrong foot.'

'You've redeemed yourself.' Laura meant it.

Outside, he kissed both her cheeks, and they walked off in opposite directions. She turned to watch him. He was intriguing and good looking, and she enjoyed his company. At the corner, he stopped and waved. A memory of a stormy afternoon about a year ago flashed into her mind.

October 2005

Tom stormed out of the house. His agitation yet again spilled over, and Laura reeled from arguing over trivial things. His temper, anger, or whatever it was, consumed and transformed him and she paced the lounge, back and forth, unable to contain the anger bubbling inside her.

She made a cup of tea, sat down, opened a book, turned on the television, but eventually, she again paced. Finally, she tipped the cold tea down the sink and grabbed her car keys.

Laura parked on a side street off King William Road. She dodged the Thursday night shopping crowd as she walked along the footpath. Dark clouds threatened rain. The October sunshine at the start of the day had been overtaken by the stubborn wintery weather she hated and she'd forgotten her umbrella.

She waited at the pedestrian crossing and glanced at the newly renovated King's Arms hotel. It offered shelter if needed. Its fresh and modern look was inviting, and she made a note to have a meal there sometime. She was about to turn away when Tom stepped out of the side door, turned and remonstrated with someone. What was he doing here? Tom gesticulated in a way that was a regular feature of his conversations, but the other person was hidden. Then Tom stomped towards the car park.

Laura's pedestrian lights changed to green, but she waited, her curiosity prevailing. Who had he been arguing with? A few moments later, a person stepped out of the same doorway, strode across the footpath and got into a waiting taxi.

***

That profile. It looked exactly like Jacques. Had Jacques followed Tom out of the hotel? Or was her mind playing tricks on her?

'Shit.' The past wouldn't let her go; regardless of how much she wanted to put that episode of her life aside.

Tom was unfinished business. Was his research drug-addled paranoia? The DVD, files, and phone call, all suggested otherwise, and the mysterious code and key probably held the answer. If only

143

she could decipher that code. She had a choice, either she investigated, or let it go. Did she want to know the truth? Was she ready to face it? She must decide. Maybe tomorrow she'd start by visiting the U-Store-It.

Chapter 19

Amsterdam's July weather was unwelcoming, with clouds shrouding the sky and blocking out the summer sun. Soil from a construction site eddied in circular sweeps across the road in front of John Master's taxi. As they pulled up outside the hotel, he grimaced. Kleb's recommendation was outmoded. John grew up with traditions, the old ways dominated Babbo's thinking, and John had happily discarded them at the first opportunity. The flashier Hilton tower, where the conference was being held, rose on the other side of the main canal and looked more inviting.

The elderly porter heaved John's bags up the steep front stairs and John smiled at the thought of the porter lugging the oversized, overstuffed, and probably overweight luggage from the airport carousel up that incline. He imagined the owners of those bags would end up oversized, overstuffed, and overweight by the end of their river cruises too. His workout gear was in the suitcase for that reason.

In the compact lobby, three consoles lined the wall, each with a young woman standing behind it. The fresh-faced receptionist at the first console looked like an apprentice. She stared at her screen, frowned, stabbed at buttons on the keyboard, then sighed, and stabbed again before finally looking up and fixing her mouth into a smile.

'You have a reservation?' she asked, ready to attack the keyboard again.

She tapped in his details and almost instantly, the manager mysteriously appeared at John's side. He welcomed John, then ushered him into a petite office, where he was offered a seat and a drink, both of which John declined. The manager launched into a spiel to explain the amenities while completing the booking process. The spa sounded inviting.

A small tour of the ground floor revealed a dining room and bar joined by a cavernous foyer with grated teller-like windows and a zig-zag patterned white and black tiled floor. The marble walls, white with dramatic vertical black slashes, conjured up an opulent past, but the woodwork needed a coat of varnish and the building needed some general maintenance.

'Was this a bank?' It seemed too big for that.

The manager laughed. 'This building was a shipping administration. It was built in 1916 and we have kept many of the features. They are historic.'

The lift carried them to the fourth floor, where a maze of hallways led to his suite. Corridors branched off at different angles.

'I hadn't expected to need a GPS *inside* the hotel. I'll need a trail of breadcrumbs,' John joked, but the manager didn't even smile.

The suite was also old, spacious, and dark. He could hold a meeting at the round table and still have room to stretch out. Everything in the room was dark wood: the wall panelling; the cupboards; the window frames; the doors; and even the four-poster bed, which took pride of place in the middle of the room. It felt sombre, maybe even sinister. The dull lighting was strategically placed but absorbed by the wood before it could illuminate the space. John swallowed down his disappointment.

He stared at the river and the modern, attractive Hilton Hotel across the water. Its clean lines were so appealing and he'd read there was a bar with a view on the fifteenth floor. The railway station plaza was on the left and, on the right, was a curious green building, perched like a brussel sprout on the river edge.

Grey clouds gathered menacingly overhead, yet people outside wore short-sleeved shirts or T-shirts. He opened the window and the rumble of cars, buses, and the occasional van assailed his ears. As he watched, an open sight-seeing boat navigated along the river to the canal entrance. Cameras pointed at his hotel and he stepped away from the window.

The adjoining lounge décor was also dark with chocolate coloured wood surrounding deep maroon upholstery on the sofa and chairs, but here the two floor lamps lit the area more effectively. The bonus was a well-stocked fridge in the corner.

John unpacked and checked his phone. There was enough time before today's appointment to conduct some research of his own. The factory was supposedly an easy walk from the hotel.

He strolled beside the canal with a swathe of tourists. He didn't usually suffer jet lag, but today his stomach ached and pain prickled above his right eye. Even in business class, his mind raced with plans and ideas, and he couldn't sleep. He refused to take sleeping pills, preferring to stay in control.

His phone trilled with a message confirming his meeting with the Russian power couple tomorrow at 6 p.m. in room 475 and a shiver ran up his spine. He needed to be at his best for that. They represented an oligarch with connections to the Russian mafia. Their fledgling Australian operations would be useful, especially the link to the Devil's Guard bikie gang.

An open, hop-on-hop-off boat sailed by, and John stepped onto the bridge and watched it disappear underneath him. He passed through a small square lined with a rabble of stalls and then ducked down a narrow lane.

A young woman sat provocatively inside the window. Her red bra and red knickers drew his eye. She looked up at him, eyebrows arched, questioning, and he abruptly turned away.

Beside him, a couple stopped in front of another window. The husband stared and smirked while the wife moved back, her mouth twisted in disapproval. In another doorway, a middle-aged woman in a minuscule skirt, black stockings, and suspenders haggled good-naturedly with a middle-aged man.

After another lane of women in windows, he stumbled onto the main square. He'd come too far. Characters dressed in costumes, from Star Wars or superheroes, were dotted through the crowd. Tourists, holding maps, cameras, guidebooks, and phones, paid before posing for photos with the characters. He spotted a mafia-style costume and smiled. The Hollywood-style image was so farfetched. A horse-drawn carriage ferried people around the square, navigating between tourists and costumed characters with clumsy grace. He steered clear and checked his map.

John followed a different lane, crossing yet another bridge and trailed the canal to the Diamond Factory. He registered for the free tour, along with six others. He and the tourists from Brazil, the UK, and the USA were herded through a display area and into the factory where a blue overall-clad woman sat impassively at a high bench, protected by a Perspex shield. Her hair was tied back severely, but several strands escaped and gave her a cheeky edge.

The guide gathered them close to observe the polishing process as the demonstrator pinched the tiny diamond fragment in a clamping device. She set a grinding wheel in motion, fixed an eyeglass to her right eye, and peered at the gem before delicately touching it to the rotating wheel. She repeated the process several times, oblivious to the watching tourists, as she alternately scrutinised and polished the gem. Her light touch and precision were impressive.

Finally, the guide showed them into a small room and explained the concepts of carat, clarity, and cut. John's limited research touched on these concepts, but this simple talk suggested intelligent questions he could ask later. He studied the samples carefully, trying to identify the difference between exceptional white and tinted colour. He twinkled the diamonds in the light, observing the effects of the different cuts. It was fascinating. He peered at the small gem to find any distinguishing facet that made it a low or high-quality diamond. There was an art to this, although he hadn't quite mastered it.

When the guide started her sales pitch, offering a significant discount for anyone who bought immediately, the British couple left. John stayed to watch. The American couple and the Brazilian mother and daughter engaged in the pitch, examining the bigger, better quality stones, re-examining the different cuts, while asking about price. The fire in their eyes matched the sparkle of the diamonds. The American husband drawled as he bartered, pretending to be willing to walk away, but John smiled. It was a sham. The wife's keenness was too obvious. He loved watching the battle, the toing and froing with the insistent but calm guide and her expertise in reeling in a sale. It was magic. She clinched it, selling him two to get the level of discount he wanted. His bride giggled and clapped her hands when the deal was done. Would she have a ring and a necklace or earrings? The ring and necklace won.

The Brazilian mother and daughter left with John as the Americans finalised their deal. John loitered in the shop, examining the different designs and prices. The Brazilian mother and daughter bartered for a ring. Their purposeful examination broadcast their intention to buy. John's phone pinged with a message from his Brisbane office but he stowed the phone back in his pocket. He'd call later.

Walking back, he stopped for a break at a small hole-in-the-wall café. The upstairs dining area overlooked a canal and a four-storey, chocolate brick home with small white-ringed porticos, white framed attic windows and an orange slate roof. John grimaced. So much dark brown, it overshadowed the touches of colour. Below, cars parked along the canal edge and cyclists merged with pedestrians as they streamed over the bridge. His image of Amsterdam had been canals and bicycles, not cars.

He fidgeted with the menu, then ordered a coffee, a duck ravioli to be followed by a Nutella and banana crepe. His mind turned to the upcoming meeting. He didn't like to admit it, but he was nervous and keen to impress.

After the short rest-break, he ambled through a square and past the Magna Plaza shopping centre. Its impressive archways formed a historic backdrop for the quasi-tram-terminus. The tram networks in Amsterdam surprised him too. He dodged people running for trams or distracted by the building façades, or maps, and turned into Raadhuisstr. He followed a winding pathway beside another canal. Tourist boats floated by, adding splashes of colour and the occasional booming commentary. The tourists' heads turned in choreographed unison to view highlights on either side of the canal. Were they missing things they might find more interesting? People saw what they paid attention to, but their observations were being directed by someone else's judgement. Occasionally, a rebel looked in the opposite direction and made their own observations. John liked to think he was a rebel, but he wasn't setting his own direction. He was still striving to succeed against Babbo's criteria. His father had been a severe and demanding critic. Harper had been the last straw. If Harper had survived, he'd have taken a different track. At least, he thought so, although he wasn't sure anymore.

He checked his watch and hurried forward, turning his focus to his meeting with Kleb's recommendation, the diamond merchant, Werner, and inventing intelligent questions. Maybe the clear blue sky and sunshine was an omen. This meeting held exciting prospects.

Werner's tiny office disappointed. Rather than reflecting success, it suggested a small-time operation. The man himself reminded John of the TV detective, Poirot. They didn't linger on small talk for long, although John learned he was a man of many talents, speaking five languages, Russian, Italian, French, Dutch, and English and he was an expert on raw diamonds. Unlike the cut and polished diamonds John studied this morning, Werner dealt in the uncut variety, which required special paperwork to satisfy UN requirements and declare the product *guaranteed clean*. John hadn't heard of the Kimberley Process before and made a note to investigate.

The discussion moved on to numbers. John would have preferred to see more enthusiasm when he explained his business plans and how he'd have more capital soon, but Werner's poker face stayed fixed. From his questions and comments, it was clear his soft outer appearance hid a shrewd and sharp mind. John liked that.

John was ready to progress. His new Swiss bank account was available, but the Poirot-like figure hesitated. He'd compile a formal proposal and present it at a follow-up meeting tomorrow. The final details of a deal would be discussed then.

The meeting finished earlier than expected and John's mind clouded with concerns and uncertainties. A hop-on-hop-off boat stopped in the canal in front of him, and on a whim, he jumped on. Skye would have enjoyed this, although she'd have cramped his style, unlike Harper. She'd been more carefree, although he'd still admired other women even then. He turned his focus onto the passing scenery to unclamp his heart. No matter how often he tried to put Harper behind him and move on, his mind returned to what he'd lost.

John ambled back towards his hotel. A trip to the gym was needed to work off his overindulgence. He turned his phone back on and checked his watch. It was 6 p.m., but he couldn't calculate the time difference and gave up trying. He rang anyway.

After several rings, a sleepy, gravelly voice answered.

'Do you know what time it is?' Kleb finally sounded awake.

'I've met—'

'It's 4 a.m. here! Unless it's urgent, ring me back later.' Kleb obviously wasn't good at mornings.

'The meeting went well but I thought you'd be interested to learn—'

'I'll ring you back later.' Kleb wasn't going to negotiate.

'I thought—'

'Later.' Kleb hung up.

John stared at his blank screen. 'Bastard.' He shoved the phone back in his pocket.

He crossed a bridge and continued walking. Before he knew it, he was outside his hotel. He baulked. Across the river, the Hilton Hotel glistened in the early evening light. He turned, strode over the bridge and finally took the lift up to the scenic 15th-floor bar.

The open space, flanked by picture windows, oozed modern décor. No dark brown anywhere; all beige, grey, and neutral tones, the way he liked it. The music synchronised with his heartbeat and he carried his Americano cocktail to a bench seat near the window, drinking in the panoramic view across Amsterdam while also surveying the clientele. He didn't recognise anyone. A group of American tourists perched at a table nearby, drowning out the music with loud southern drawls and raucous laughter.

He ordered another drink at the bar. Two attractive young women entered and glanced around the room. They bought a drink each and settled into the table behind him, giggling as they took photos of each other, their drinks, and the view. They spoke with British accents. He sat down at his table, facing them, caught their eye, and smiled. They smiled back. He offered to buy them a drink, and they glanced at each other before agreeing. He bought a bottle of white wine, then carried it and three glasses back to their table. The evening was improving.

Chapter 20

Laura walked to the bus stop, still puzzling over her vision of Jacques when her phone rang and pulled her from her preoccupation.

'Why haven't you been answering your phone, Mum?' Becky admonished. 'Robby's been trying to reach you.'

'Robby? Why, what's wrong?'

'It's OK. He slipped away before anyone saw him. But the police stopped the guy he was meeting. He was carrying drugs.'

Robby. Involved with drugs? She'd hoped to never hear these words connected to her children. It was bad enough they were part of Tom's story.

'Where is he?' Laura grabbed a pen and a scrap of paper from her bag and scribbled down the details, along with Robby's new mobile number.

'What is he getting himself into, for goodness' sakes?'

'Oh Mum, don't be melodramatic. It was probably for personal use.'

'The police wouldn't arrest him if it wasn't serious.' Had Robby spun Becky a story or was she sparing her mum the details? 'I'm getting on the bus now. As soon as I get home, I'll go straight out.'

'No rush. It'll do him good to sweat it out.' Becky chuckled, then hung up.

Laura dialled Robby's new number and left a message.

Kmart and a Coles supermarket dominated the local shopping complex, which also had two small cafés, a bakery, and a chemist. Robby was slumped on a low concrete wall beside the Kmart car service centre, his body crumpled as though searching for invisibility.

Dark bags underscored his eyes and his sour smell reminded her of the pungent unwashed reek of the drunk and belligerent homeless man bellowing at the traffic in the carpark. Robby's gaunt face collapsed in on itself, making his lips and nose more prominent. This wasn't the same Robby she'd seen last month.

At her touch, he smiled warily, and she pulled him close.

In the passenger seat, he hung his head low and his silence made her more anxious.

'Are you using drugs?' she asked.

Robby's head jolted up. 'No. It was a…friend.' He didn't have his usual bravado.

'What friend?'

'Just a guy I know. He's got a record, but it was only a small cache. I got away. I was careful.'

'What does that mean? Robby, what are you getting involved in?'

She felt Robby's eyes flare without even looking at him.

'It's business, for christ's sake,' Robby sneered. 'I'm helping them to provide a service.'

'What? By dealing drugs? Is that your business?'

'It's basic supply and demand. There's money to be made and it might as well be—'

Laura jerked the car to the side of the road and glared at him. Her whole body trembled, but she kept her voice firm.

'Don't parrot that shit to me. It's illegal and —'

'I'm helping out,' Robby snapped.

'This wasn't a *friend*, was it? Who are *they*?'

'Your generation was into drugs. Now you're all paranoid and don't want anyone else to have fun. I can look after myself.'

'You haven't done such a good job of looking after yourself so far. Is this connected to Shayida?'

'Christ! Get off my back.'

Robby shoved the car door open, jumped out, and slammed it shut. The car rocked with the impact. He'd fled down the footpath before Laura could switch off the motor and unbuckle her seat belt.

She yanked her door open and called, 'Robby, come back.'

He was swallowed up by a laneway and by the time Laura got to the entrance, he'd gone. She ran down the lane, peering into every alcove and niche, but he'd disappeared. The lane opened onto another regional shopping centre carpark and inside the mall, she scoured the aisles. He'd vanished.

She rang his number. It went straight to his upbeat message. 'Shit.' Why hadn't she waited to talk to him? They could have talked more rationally at home.

She trudged back to her car, still trying his number and leaving messages.

'Robby, I'm sorry. I'm worried about you and for you. Please come home.'

Eva arrived soon after Laura got home.

'He stormed off. I've left messages, but he's not answering. I have no idea where he is.'

'There's nothing you can do until he gets in touch.' Eva provided her usual, rational perspective.

Laura used up her nervous energy by fussing in the cupboards. 'Coffee, biscuits?' she asked.

'Yes to all the above.'

She organised a tray and took it out to the patio. Robby should have been sharing coffee and biscuits with her. They should have been talking.

The winter chill nipped at her face, and the splashes of afternoon sun contained no warmth. A line of pigeons congregated on the fence. Their cooing wasn't working its magic this time. Laura's frustration raged, but her phone stayed remarkably silent.

'How is your book progressing?' Laura forced her eyes away from the blank phone screen.

'I'm re-interviewing, but it all takes time.'

'Did you negotiate to keep that controversial story?'

'They say it restricts the book's appeal, that is, sales. I'm not convinced, but all I can do is replace it. I've found one the publishers prefer.' Eva scowled. 'The man who helped people escape persecution in Iraq. They think he's a hero, yet the man who helped people travel to Australia is labelled a people smuggler.'

'The provocative story might find its way into a second book. Then the public can decide for themselves.'

Eva laughed. 'A choice would be a fine thing. I have to sell a serious number of copies before they'd contemplate a second book. Besides, I need a new focus for a while. Their stories get to me, especially in the current political climate. I'm getting burned out. What's happening to them is anything but fair and I can't, or don't want to, stay impartial.'

'Newspaper articles are more opinion pieces than news nowadays. Facts aren't reported seriously and the government rhetoric is rarely challenged. When people say, "oh well, they're politicians, what do you expect?", it's code for "I don't care if they're cruel or dishonest, I'm ignoring everything",' Laura said fiercely.

Again, they railed about politics and how they thought people were sleepwalking through issues. They didn't find solutions this time either. With her life in such turmoil, perhaps she should pull back and protect herself too.

Laura went inside and returned with two wine glasses and a bottle of rosé.

'Here's to finding Robby safe and well, and hopefully contrite,' Eva said and they clinked glasses.

'He's not himself and I don't know how to reach him,' Laura

confessed.

'He needs time to think. He knows what's right. You and Tom made sure of that.'

'I don't see any evidence that he's thinking at all lately. He's getting in too deep'

Silence descended as Laura sipped her wine, keeping one eye focused on her blank phone screen. Had she indulged her youngest children too much? She hadn't pushed them as hard as the older two. Was that the problem? They'd become self-indulgent and aimless? Another source of guilt.

'I know it's not a good time, but I've organised for us to meet Tom and Peter's driver from Iraq, Fayyaad.'

Laura sighed. Robby needed her now, but it was too late for Tom. 'Can't it wait?'

'He says it's urgent and I think it could be helpful.'

Laura shrugged.

'By the way, my friend's husband, the policeman, said that Corrinne died from organ failure and an unidentified chemical was found in her system.'

'What sort of chemical?' Laura's spine tingled. 'Like the E-bomb found in Tom's system?'

Eva hesitated. 'Her husband insists she didn't take drugs and avoided prescription medications. They don't know what it is. It must be new.'

'She was so vibrant and alive when I saw her. She was angry, remonstrating with Tom, and he consoled her. It looked…intimate.' If the link between Tom and Corrinne was drugs, was that better than an affair?

They sat in silence for a moment, the dark clouds reflecting Laura's mood.

'They knew each other and I know it looks suspicious but…' Laura said forcefully, but the niggling doubts wouldn't disperse. 'Tom was evasive. The signs were there. Mel confirmed that they met that morning; at our house. Perhaps they were experimenting with drugs, although it seems so unlikely. It hurts because I believed in him, but maybe I didn't know him as well as I thought I did.' What more proof did she need?

'Oh, Laura, he wasn't like Peter. Peter believed he could do whatever he liked and say sorry if he got caught.'

'He was always a flirt, but—' She'd thought Peter's infidelities were aberrations. 'You and Peter were happy.' Laura said it like a statement, but she was asking too.

She remembered Eva's face, beaming with happiness but also tinged with embarrassment, when she'd announced her impending marriage and pregnancy, in that order.

'At first, then Peter got bored. He panicked when I fell pregnant again. Two children were one too many, and knowing Peter, perhaps it was two too many.' Eva sipped her wine.

'That's harsh.'

'But it's true. He rarely came home early on Friday nights. He'd sneak in late, always smelling of alcohol but also perfume. I thought it was my fault.'

'Oh Eva, no.'

'Eventually, I realised it was him, not me.' Eva topped up her glass. 'Peter even wanted to get back together a few years ago? He'd moved in with Abbie, but she wasn't pregnant yet.' Eva's face was unreadable.

'*After* he was living with Abbie?'

'He said he'd made a mistake. I couldn't take it seriously, not while he was still living with Abbie. I didn't want my old life back and although I probably still loved him, I didn't want him.' She shrugged and smiled. 'I still don't.'

'You're very strong. And wise.'

'He's probably cheating on Abbie.'

'He tried it on with me, just after Tom died.'

'He's a bastard.' Eva raised an eyebrow. 'What happened?'

'What do you think?' Laura felt strangely aggrieved by the question. 'I threw him out.'

The twinkle in Eva's eye danced in the shifting light. 'Good for you.'

'Well, he's a friend, and he's also married. Although I'm not that close to Abbie, he has responsibilities.'

Eva patted Laura's hand. 'You do know he always fancied you?'

Laura shook her head. More to remove the image of that stolen kiss than to deny it.

'It's true.' Eva sat back.

'You've been alone for a long time. How do you cope?' Laura moved on to safer topics.

'I like living on my own. Being married to Peter was all about compromise and acceptance. I compromised, and he accepted it.' Sadness tinged Eva's chuckle. 'I took care of him and so did he. Take care of himself, I mean. I didn't matter. I cooked, cleaned, and raised the boys and he came and went as he pleased. His work always came first and his ambition took him into higher stress and long hours. For amusement and relief, and probably to stroke his ego, he had affairs. He gave his best to others. The funny, charming, smooth man I fell in love with charmed others, and the boys and I got what was left, a self-absorbed, tired, bored man. At work or social functions or when it suited him, he'd turn on the charm for us, for show, but it was fleeting. It only reminded me of what I was missing.' Eva looked lost in the memories.

Laura sipped her wine. 'Tom was different. Work seemed to take more than he wanted to give. He was a good dad, but as they grew older and needed us less, he withdrew. Instead of building a new life together, I lost both lives. I thought I knew him. I thought he'd snap out of it and he'd come back to me, instead of brooding in his study. I never thought he'd be unfaithful, except with his work. I thought he would always talk to me, eventually. I miss him, but it's the Tom I married, the caring and loving husband and father, the man of principle, I miss. Not the grumpy, self-absorbed man he was when he died.'

'Even good marriages can disintegrate and I don't have the energy to start again.'

'I don't know. I want arms to hold me tight and reassure me. I want the intimacy of love and to have someone care for me, but you're right. It will be hard to start again. The things I want aren't the things I had at the end, anyway. I think we might have found our way back if we'd had time.'

'You'll never know.' Eva studied Laura's face and her eyes clouded.

'But you date,' Laura said.

'Yeah, but it's more *going out with friends* than dating. I'm up front, there's no future *us*. I'm not going to live with a man again. I've become selfish and I don't want to look after anyone anymore. I saw the writing on the wall when Peter had his heart and blood pressure issues. He saw caring for him as my responsibility. I'm not sure he'd have felt the same if I'd had the health issues. I like my life. Now I watch what I want on TV, I go out with my friends when I want to, I eat out alone or with others, I don't mind.'

'You've become tough. What happens if love sneaks up on you?'

'It hasn't yet.'

'I'm not sure about being alone.'

'You've recently become a widow. Give yourself time. I enjoy being single.'

Laura struggled with her mixed emotions. There were times when she enjoyed the aloneness, the lack of stress, and expectation. She didn't need to compromise on anything. But and it was a big but, she missed having someone to share life with, to discuss issues or problems, to hold her and reassure her when things were going wrong. She couldn't have both, not really. Her friends, especially Eva, helped and provided support, but was it enough? Right now, she needed Tom and his help with Robby. He would have helped moderate her words, offered a different perspective, and helped bring everyone together. At least the old Tom would have. Maybe the latest one would have too if he'd felt needed. How was she going to mend the rift between her and Robby by herself?

Chapter 21

Fine grey fog blanketed John's view. Droplets trickled down the outside of the window, splitting the scene into fragments. A dark ribbon identified the river and the Chinese floating restaurant was a shadowy outline on the opposite bank. The Hilton Hotel was entirely obscured. He clenched his fists. The English girls were an unrealised promise. They'd said they were looking for a good time but, despite applying all his charm and buying them wine and cocktails, he'd gone home alone.

Outside, wet pinpricks tingled his face, but it wasn't cold. At the railway plaza, commuters jostled him as they rushed to catch a tram or train. He successfully avoided collisions, sometimes only narrowly, and rode the escalator to platform 2B. The Klasse 2B café entrance was a turnstile, and he groaned when he saw the dark-brown wood décor, dark wooden chairs, tables, and benches, and walls clad in dark mahogany. Any light streaming through the full-length windows was filtered by orange curtains and huge potted palms, barely brightening the room. The Poirot-like figure of the diamond merchant sat directly under a low hanging, saucer-shaped light creating a halo effect. After formal handshakes, they sat opposite each other.

'They do a nice breakfast here.' Werner passed him a menu.

John ordered the eggs and continental breakfast while Werner selected a single croissant. They talked about the weather and John's conference. Werner explained that the café was a popular business meeting point, especially for commuters from other Dutch cities. Their conversation momentarily stalled when the waiter served their coffee and placed a croissant in front of Werner.

'Now, down to business,' Werner said once the waiter left. 'I've looked at your proposition and find myself in a difficult situation.'

He scrutinised John's face as he dipped the croissant into his coffee and took a bite without splashing a drop.

'What do you mean?'

Werner munched on the remainder of the croissant and followed it with a sip of coffee.

'I've reviewed the numbers and, you have to understand, I don't usually handle such, um, *small* investments.'

'I thought I'd made it clear; this is a start.'

'Yes, but the set up fees for a new account, acquiring the necessary documentation, the risk…' He pursed his lips. 'My services alone cost…'

Werner slid a sheet of paper across the table and the blood drained from John's face. His investment would be wiped out by the fees.

'You can't be serious!' It must be a joke.

'My services are highly valued. I cannot offer them to you for less, even though our friend recommended you.'

John bristled. Kleb had recommended Werner to John, not the other way around.

'My prospects are excellent. Once my plans are enacted. I—'

'Yes. We can talk again when it is done. It is better to wait. There is no rush.'

John was speechless. He'd been confident that he'd walk away with an investment plan and diamonds added to his portfolio. He'd counted on it.

'This is outrageous. My investment is substantial; it should be enough to start.'

'Substantial is a relative term and in my world, it is not the *correct* word. These investments are risky and I require a bigger start-up to make them worthwhile.'

John fumed as Werner gathered his briefcase and coat.

'Please stay and finish your breakfast. The bill is taken care of. Don't be discouraged, I'll be ready to help you when your growth is secured and the investment is greater.' He offered his hand and John hesitated before shaking it. Then the Poirot-like figure left through the turnstile exit.

'Discouraged! Discouraged! I'll show you discouraged!' John muttered and then, under his breath, called Werner arrogant, pompous, and worse names. He felt better for it. He didn't need Werner; he'd find a way to do this for himself.

The waiter served John's breakfast, two boiled eggs and a selection of pastries set neatly on a tray. It was some time before he turned his attention to the food. He was hungry and finally, he swallowed his pride and ate. His day hadn't started well and was all the more difficult to cope with given last night.

After he'd eaten, he gathered his belongings and left. The cool air and short walk momentarily soothed his bruised ego, but he couldn't forget that Poirot-like figure and the smirk on his face as he refused John's investment. He'd fix him. He'd tell Kleb he didn't trust Werner and that his future business might be better placed elsewhere. Werner would regret insulting John like that.

He stalked down a maze of streets until his agitation eased. He detoured into the arched entrance of the Magna Plaza shopping centre. Patterned white and pink stone arches rose three floors while curved walkways spanned the foyer. Opulent chandeliers finished the effect. John loitered, enjoying the aura of affluence. He'd come to Amsterdam to attend the conference. That was the public explanation, but the meetings outside of the conference were more important. These next steps would put the finishing touches on his takeover plan. Soon his little sister, Dimi, would be disenfranchised. She'd be finished and John would finally get what he deserved. He left the centre refreshed and enthused.

His next business meetings laid important groundwork. John hoped Skollov's contacts would offer insights into the emergence of a cartel in South America. Skollov dealt with them too, weapons not drugs, but they had the same supply chain hassles and unreliability. He hadn't told Kleb of Skollov's introductions. What Kleb didn't know wouldn't hurt him. This was a preliminary scouting expedition after all and there was no point annoying Kleb unnecessarily.

That evening, John knocked on the door of room 475. This Russian power duo's business interests reached across the world and into Australia. Boris and Svetlana's associates owned large manufacturing plants in the eastern bloc and, of particular interest to John, controlled the Devil's Guard bikie gang, rivals of Dimi's partners, the Pythons. He shivered. He didn't meet with Russian mafia representatives every day.

Boris' physique benefited from regular gym sessions and he was younger than John expected. Boris uncoiled his tall frame and leaned forward to shake hands. A flashing gold tooth drew attention to his thin lips as they curled around mispronounced words. Spittle collected in the corners of his mouth and his thick accent tested John's concentration. The flamboyant ruby and gold ring on the little finger of his left hand was more ostentatious than his dull shirt and trousers would suggest. Svetlana was much more pleasant to watch.

She was icy, with sparkling dark eyes that drew his attention away from her over-large nose. Her flowing black hair, long legs, and lean fingers appealed to John. When she smiled, she defrosted and her face lit up. Her screeching voice and grating laugh, however, were a distinct disadvantage.

He'd passed the first test. They accepted his credentials and backstory without question. It amused him to think that the accident had helped John to establish a new identity. Giovanni Mastriani was dead and in his place was John Masters, a transport company owner. They'd have been more inclined to kill Giovanni than make deals.

Svetlana led the questioning. Business jargon tripped off her tongue with natural ease.

'We are glad you choose to talk with us about your business needs.' Svetlana smiled. 'We would like to help you.'

'Your Australian gang are well placed to work with me on my expansion plans,' John explained. He didn't doubt they wanted to help, but it was more to help themselves than help him. He knew the score. He was no different. He had his own agenda.

'We hear you have access to a potent new synthetic drug, E-bomb. It is a great opportunity, even in Europe,' Svetlana continued. 'We looking to offer new and improved products like this to our clients.'

'I'm concentrating on the Australian market at the moment, but we can see how that arrangement works first,' John said. The Russian connection wasn't part of his long-term plans for Europe, but he wouldn't tell them that.

'Our Sydney peoples will talk logistics when you are ready,' Svetlana confirmed. 'We are happy that are you are more ready to work with us.'

Dimi's exclusive arrangements with the Pythons irked the Devil's Guard and threatened to explode into a bikie war, which would severely hamper his business plans. At least this partnership would negate that risk.

'This partnership will benefit us both,' John said.

They discussed the details of a business agreement. They negotiated hard for a commission, but he'd expected that. And although he couldn't identify any issues, he'd talk to Kleb before he formalised an agreement.

'Your interests in South America are strong?' Svetlana asked. 'The new breakaway group is a problem for you?'

'It's causing intolerable disruptions, but I think my supply is under control.' He didn't voice all his concerns. His plans to use Dimi's E-bomb to leverage a better deal with Mexico and Guatemala weren't fully formed. The heroin, cocaine, and now methamphetamine imports were still too lucrative to dismiss. They might help him move into the diamond investment sooner rather than later.

'We can help there too?'

'Perhaps.'

Boris had left Svetlana to ask the questions, but now he stretched forward, ready to strike. Both of them faced John.

'You have much business in Amsterdam?' Boris' gold tooth flashed in the light. 'Your transportation business needs a partner?'

'What makes you ask that?'

'The conference. You make valuable contacts.' A fleck of white spume collected in the corner of Boris's mouth and John's stomach turned.

'The transport business is a means to an end. Setting up a smooth running drug importation process is my main focus for now.'

'But there will be new products too? More valuable but different, isn't that so? Are you offering us that important business too?' Svetlana asked.

Were they referring to Casterlow's new secret project? Did they know about that, or were they fishing? 'For now, I'm offering you access to distribute my drug products, especially E-bomb, in Australia,' John responded.

Boris and Svetlana exchanged a short burst of Russian, and John thought he heard a heavily accented *Stavros* as they spoke. His stomach lurched. What did they know about Casterlow's contact Stavros? He'd deliberately arranged the meeting for after the conference to avoid scrutiny. How could they know about that?

'Forgive us. You are a resourceful man and trusted by important people. I just asking if there's anything else we can help with,' Svetlana said sweetly.

'There's nothing more,' John said firmly.

'In the future maybe, hey?' Svetlana asked.

Their conversation finally turned to more casual topics and John happily moved on. They were only fishing. Svetlana laughed and joked while Boris sat stony-faced. She fixed herself another drink, but Boris declined a second. John's acceptance earned him a warm smile. She leaned back, crossing her legs and tilting her head provocatively, and John enjoyed the display.

Boris offered to arrange a *friend*, someone to prevent John from being lonely so far from home. John declined, but after another cocktail, the idea grew on him, especially remembering last night's disappointment. Maybe he could indulge a little, especially with stuffy conference sessions awaiting him. The rest of his important meetings were scheduled for after the conference. He should have some fun now, while he could.

Back in his room, John fixed himself another drink when a knock sounded at the door.

'Boris sent me,' the impossibly-thin woman purred.

John scanned the empty corridor before inviting her in. Her slim legs and arms jutted from a tight, revealing dress, and her carefully coiffed hair and thick makeup reminded him of a model like Skye. She was more high-class than the women in the windows. When she smiled, the tilt of her head made John wince. A flash of Skye morphed into Harper. He hardened his conscience, the way he'd learned to do. He was going to have fun because he deserved it.

Chapter 22

Laura's jaw ached from grinding her teeth. Twenty-four hours without a word from Robby. His phone rang but disconnected without going to voicemail. Again, family filled her life with worry, planning, second-guessing, and puzzling, rather than happy, carefree moments.

She phoned Robby's twin, Becky, again. This time, she finally answered.

'Hi, honey. Have you heard from Robby? He ran off on me and now he's not answering his phone.'

'You didn't lecture him?'

Laura ignored the comment but registered Becky's mood. 'Are you alright?

'I'm sick of this essay, sick of the flat, and sick of myself.' Becky had a dramatic flair.

'Shall we meet for dinner?'

'I'm a bit low on cash.'

'My treat,' Laura offered. Some things were predictable.

Becky suggested an Indian restaurant near her flat and Laura offered to pick her up at six-thirty.

With time on her hands, Laura selected a book from the shelf, scanned the blurb, then put it back. It was no good. She couldn't concentrate. She ambled into the kitchen, but then changed her mind and grabbed her coat, scarf, and car keys. Before she knew it, she was outside Robby's rundown unit.

Normally, Robby's music could be heard from the street, but not today. It was eerily quiet. She knocked on his door and waited. There was no sound of movement in his unit, and Laura knocked again. Nothing. He wasn't home.

A dog in the unit next door yapped and Laura noticed the lace curtain in that front window twitch. Maybe the neighbour could help.

Her knock on the neighbour's door sent the dog into a frenzy of snarling and yapping. Laura stepped back in anticipation, but no one inside stirred. She knocked again. No response. Laura frowned. It was clear she was wasting her time.

Back in her car, she checked her watch. The U-Store-It was on her way to Becky's unit and she had enough time. Images of her grisly find again assailed Laura, but she batted them away. Maybe she could at least get one answer today.

She parked away from the deserted site, but she noticed the fluttering, bright police tape sealing off the carpark area as she drove past. Again, the panic and fear from that day surfaced, and she swallowed it down. She walked down the pleasant tree-lined street, as far from those memories as she could. If only she'd walked this way last time.

A young man sat in the U-Store-It office. His desk was almost obscured by a pile of paperwork and he sat, tilting his chair back to balance on the two rear legs, as he scrolled on his phone. Her knock on the window startled him and he jerked backwards, almost losing his balance. His hand grabbed the desk's edge just in time and he slowly pulled himself up. He grinned as he approached the window.

'You scared me.'

'Sorry. I wondered if you could help me.' Laura faltered. She hadn't prepared her questions or story. 'Can you tell me if my husband rented a storage locker here?'

The young man raised his eyebrows. 'Umm, lotsa people have lockers here.'

'My husband's name is, er, was Tom Schultz. Can you look up the records?'

'We're not s'posed to give out personal information.'

'He died. I found a key in his things and I need to sort out his affairs.' The word affairs tripped her up. 'Papers, er—'

The young man grimaced. 'I'm not s'posed to but…'

He tapped on the keyboard, and after a moment, shook his head. 'Nah, no Tom Schultz on the list, but this list only has the names of people who have a locker now, or maybe gave it up in the last couple of weeks. All the earlier records are archived.'

'Could you check? If I give you my number, could you ring me if you find it?' Laura wrote her phone number on a scrap of paper and he glanced at the back door before pocketing it.

He lowered his voice. 'I can't promise anything.'

'What about Corrinne Lamberthy? Is she on the list?' Laura was pushing her luck, but you didn't know if you didn't try.

The young man narrowed his eyes and Laura added, 'She worked with him and they may have shared a locker.'

He frowned but returned to attack the keyboard. 'She used to. She emptied it about a week ago.'

'What are you doing?' A deep voice called out from an adjoining office, and Laura flinched.

A broad-shouldered man, in a short-sleeve T-shirt with heavy dark tattoos covering his entire left arm, walked into the cubicle. He stared at the young man's screen before fixing Laura with a stern glare.

'This lady wanted to know—'

'We don't give out people's details. We have privacy rules.' He glared at the young man. 'You know that.'

'Yeah, but—'

'Yeah, but nothing, that's the rules.' He turned back to Laura.

'Unless you have authorisation, we can't help you.'

Laura's hands shook as she pulled the key out of her pocket. 'Is this one of yours?'

The young man pulled a face, while the tattooed bulk took it to look more closely. 'Where'd you get this?'

'I found it when I was cleaning out. Is it from here?'

'Nope, not one of ours. Did this belong to this Ms Lamberthy you're asking about?'

Laura felt uneasy. His stare, his manner all felt threatening. 'No, it was among our general stuff. It could be old—'

'What does this have to do with Ms Lamberthy then? What are you asking about her for?' His stare made her quiver.

'She worked with my husband. I thought they might have shared a locker.' This hadn't been such a smart idea.

The tattooed man handed the key back and frowned. 'If you find any documentation about a locker, bring it in and maybe we can help you, but without that…'

He studied her and Laura put on her best smile, thanked them both, and stumbled away.

Corrinne removed whatever she'd stored here just before she'd died. How did this information help, given Tom's key wasn't from here? Was the manager telling the truth? The young man's reaction suggested he was. Hopefully, she hadn't got him into trouble.

She drove across town to Norwood, her mind preoccupied with everything but driving. She'd been foolish to barge into this. What if she'd alerted Corrinne's killer to Laura's research? It could even put Laura in danger. Her whole body shook as she drove, and she could barely control it.

She pulled up at the kerb outside Becky's apartment and coincidentally, Becky appeared at the window and waved. A few minutes later, Becky ambled out of the front door and greeted Laura cheerfully.

The aromas inside the restaurant made Laura's stomach rumble;

she'd skipped lunch again.

'Would you like a drink?' Laura asked once they'd sat down.

Becky raised her eyebrows in question.

'I know you're a struggling student. I said it's my shout.' Laura patted Becky gently on the arm.

'Wine would be nice.'

'You'd tell me if you'd heard from Robby, wouldn't you?' Laura asked gently.

'He hasn't been in touch.'

'I'm worried.'

'OK Mum. I get the message. Maybe you shouldn't lecture him all the time,' Becky said, then added in a softer tone, 'he's mixing with strange people and he won't listen.'

'I push too hard and he retreats into his shell, but if I don't ask, he thinks I don't care. I'm in a no-win situation.'

Becky's look softened. Maybe it was the light.

When the waiter returned, they ordered wine and Becky reeled off a list of dishes from the menu.

'The people he hangs around with look like thugs,' Becky confirmed once the waitress left. 'I've seen Shayida at uni recently. She was meeting this tough-looking guy. She's up to something.'

'Her brother, Nick?'

'Not the way they're acting. It looks like she's two-timing Robby. I should tell him.'

The waiter returned and set a glass of wine in front of them both. Becky and Laura made a toast and promised to spend time together more often.

'My assignment was due last Friday. I hadn't prepared properly, you know, with Dad...' Becky explained.

'It's been hard.' Laura meant for everyone, not only Becky.

Becky wiped her eyes. 'Are you still selling the house?'

'I've put together a box of stuff you can pick through before I donate it.'

'Don't throw anything away until I've had a look. I don't have room at my flat, can I keep things at your place?'

Laura shook her head. 'I won't have much storage space. You already have several boxes in the garage.'

Becky chewed at her trembling bottom lip.

'We could hire a lockup and share it with the others too,' Laura suggested, then shivered. Not U-Store-It though.

'That's a great idea!'

The waitress set their dishes down on the table. While they ate, Becky talked about her upcoming trip to Melbourne with friends, her university tribulations, and everyday stresses. When they finished, Laura pushed her hand into her cardigan pocket and extracted the envelope and key.

'Have you seen this key before?' She handed it to Becky. 'There's a code too. Does it mean anything to you?'

'It looks like the keys at the swim centre, only they're blue and don't have any letters.' Becky turned the key around in her hand.

'Which swim centre do you go to?'

'North Adelaide.' Becky stared at the fireplace and then abruptly turned to Laura. 'I ran into Dad when I first started. It was a nice surprise.'

'Do you remember anything unusual? Did he say anything? Anything at all Becky.'

'Why? It's a key.'

It was their usual dance; the more Laura wanted something; the more resistant Becky became.

Laura took the intensity out of her voice. 'Yes, it's only a key, but Tom hid it with this cryptic note. Maybe it's important.'

Becky squinted at her mother. 'Now? It's too late now. Anyway, he might've been hiding it from you.'

'He could have. Please, I'd appreciate your help.'

There was no point in arguing. Becky believed Laura hadn't supported Tom enough. Laura would always come up short. They sat quietly, Laura almost holding her breath. Finally, Becky looked up.

'I showed him where I worked out and explained my fitness training program. The membership was my birthday present, remember? It was a long-term membership for the Marion Centre. Luckily I was able to change it when I moved.' Becky sighed then added, 'Oddly, he hugged a briefcase to him, protectively, the whole time. I went off to change, and he left.'

'Can you remember anything else?'

'No, nothing particular. He was very distracted.' Her eyes scanned the restaurant. 'But those lockers are cleared every night.'

'Can you think of anything else?'

Becky shook her head. Her eyes glistened.

Laura paid the bill, and they left.

In the car, Laura's phone rang, and she scrambled to answer. It wasn't Robby.

'Have I caught you at a bad time?' Jacques asked.

'I'm out with my daughter.' Laura turned away to muffle her conversation.

She could feel Becky's eyes on her.

'I'm sorry to interrupt. I'd like to invite you on a day trip to the Barossa next Saturday. A wine group have organised an itinerary for me and I would love your company.'

Laura hesitated. Becky was listening.

'It sounds lovely…' She searched for the right words to decline.

Becky shifted in her seat and looked at her watch.

'That's great,' Jacques said. 'I have a driver for the day, so I'll pick you up. Shall we make it about 10 a.m.?'

'No, um—'

'We could make it later if that suits you better.'

'It's OK. I'll see you then.' It was easier to agree than argue.

'You'd better give me the address,' Jacques said.

'Can I text you?' Laura needed to get off the phone.

'Great. See you Saturday. I'm looking forward to it.'

'See you then.' Although doubts dampened her anticipation, she was inclined to dismiss the flashback as a mistake. Spending more time with him might be fun.

'Who was that?' Becky interrupted her reverie.

'Just a friend. I was hoping it was Robby. Can you think of any friends I could ring or places he goes regularly?'

Becky shook her head.

At home, Laura studied Tom's cryptic note on the envelope. She remembered him buying Becky's Marion swim centre membership. He'd organised it. She'd been surprised, especially since remembering birthdays or special occasions hadn't been his strong point. He was usually the ideas man, and she made it happen. She stared at the code. It suddenly made sense. B1002SC. Of course. Becky 10th of February Swim Centre. That was it. It must be at the swim centre. She might finally get some answers. Unfortunately, Eva had arranged to meet Fayyaad tomorrow, so the swim centre would have to wait, but not too long.

She turned her attention back to Robby. She rang him, but again there was no answer. She tried again before going to bed. Nothing. She sent him a text. There was no other way to contact him. Where was he?

Chapter 23

Eva drove through unfamiliar suburbs in relative silence. Laura sat in the passenger seat, trembling. Was she ready for the truth, whatever it was? She didn't voice her fears, especially with Eva's obvious optimism on show.

'Do you believe someone is watching Fayyaad's home? Is what he knows that important?' Laura strained to keep the quiver out of her voice. She wanted answers, at least she thought she did.

'Fayyaad believes he and his family aren't safe, and I can't convince him otherwise. To be honest, I don't know how real the threat is, but if it gives him peace of mind then…'

They arrived at a group of shops nestled into a cul-de-sac. The faded façades were sunbleached, leaving only black or grey tones. The small shop fronts were cluttered with odds and ends, yet the footpath was clean. Signs in foreign languages were chipped and peeling, and too dull to read. They parked across the road and strode to the old-fashioned café.

Inside, Eva pointed to the corner and a shadowy figure untouched by the muted lighting. As they approached him, the dark red scars marking his cheeks became visible. His bushy grey-black beard added age to an already old and gaunt visage, and his thin wrists and ankles revealed a small, wiry frame swallowed up by a loose coat. Laura swallowed down her reservations.

'This is Laura, Tom's widow,' Eva said.

At the mention of Tom's name, Fayyaad bowed. He studied Laura. Dark circles underlined his watchful eyes and he oozed sadness. She hoped it wasn't contagious; she'd had enough sadness to last her a lifetime.

'My heart is heavy for your loss. Mr Tom was also my friend. He helped me and I am sad that I could not help him more,' Fayyaad said in a heavily accented voice.

Laura thanked him.

Fayyaad's eyes blinked furiously although the left eye trailed to the right, and she worried about which one to focus on.

'I am glad to meet you, at last. I needed to speak with you.' His hands trembled in his lap. 'To warn you. Mr Tom did not die by accident. I worry for you.'

'What makes you think it wasn't an accident?' Laura said a little too loudly.

Two young men sitting near them stared in their direction, caught Laura's eye, then immediately looked away.

Fayyaad continued in a hushed voice. 'Before Christmas, Mr Tom tell me he is worried. He tell important people what he knows but they do not act. Maybe Mr Tom tell the *wrong* people. This is why you must hide everything from his work, all his papers, any recordings, everything. Give them to me and I can keep them safe.'

Laura stiffened and watched his face. Why did everyone want Tom's papers and recordings?

'Tell them what? Who are these *wrong people*?' Eva asked.

'And, why are the papers so important?' Laura added.

'I don't know the answer to all your questions, but when she died too, I know it is them. You are not safe, Mrs Tom.'

'You mean Corrinne? How is she connected to this?' Laura hoped he could provide answers.

'I meet her when Mr Tom help me with my visa. They work together too. She say she'd learned important things. They don't tell me what they learn. It is dangerous for me. I should not have let them do this alone.'

'Fayyaad, you can't blame yourself,' Eva said gently.

'You're saying that Tom and Corrinne were working on something together? The police suggested they were having an affair.'

Fayyaad shook his head. 'It is not true. They learn about a serious problem. The Australian government is involved.'

Laura released her breath slowly. Was this enough to convince her that Tom and Corrinne weren't having an affair? If so, what were they doing? Were they researching a problem or working on a scheme of their own? Is that why the police were so interested?

'Fayyaad, can you start at the beginning and help us to understand what this is about?' Laura asked. Again, her body trembled. This could be the moment of reckoning, and she hoped she was ready for the answer.

'You must understand, in Iraq, criminals have much power, especially since the war. Their control reaches Australia too. They do anything for money and to keep their power. Even kill.' He looked down at his still quivering hands. 'Criminals control the security forces and make inconvenient people disappear. They were Saddam's people and now they work for the new government, or anyone who will pay. They lock up *enemies of the state*, torture them, and make them *confess*. Not all are guilty. They do what others will pay them for.'

That DVD mentioned people accused of terrorism and being imprisoned without a trial.

Fayyaad continued, 'When we have sanctions, criminals do what the government can not. They get more and more influence, wealth, and power, but it is never enough. They control everything. Everyone knows *of* them. No one wants to *know* them because they are dangerous. They control all the trade, even the black market, and will trade anything; people, weapons, drugs, goods, anything to make money.'

The mention of drugs made Laura shiver. 'I don't understand what this has to do with Tom.'

'After the war, there is chaos. Everything change. Mr Peter go to meetings alone, and he say it's secret. I must not tell Mr Tom or I will be dismissed. The other cars and their drivers belong to the criminals. The government turns a blind eye. The criminals are good for the *economy*.'

Laura sighed. These suspicious activities proved nothing, and she still didn't understand why Tom would be murdered.

'For many years, I drive Mr Tom and Mr Peter to their meetings. After the war, Mr Peter visit Bassarti. Sometimes I drive Australian Government ministers too.' He shifted in his seat.

The name, Bassarti, was familiar to Laura.

'Do you know what these meetings were about?' Eva asked.

'Mr Peter doesn't tell me. I tell Mr Tom but only after I come to Australia, not before.' He sighed. 'I want to find out what they did there too. My father. He died in Bassarti, in the prison.'

'Bassarti is a prison?' Laura remembered. She'd heard the name on that DVD. 'How did he die?'

'I do not know how he die. Bassarti holds *enemies of the state* but no one come out alive. Some of the prisoners are there because they speak against the war, against the coalition corruption, and the government. They torture—'

'Didn't it close when the war ended?' Laura asked.

'My uncle and nephew are still in there. Maybe they are dead or maybe they are alive.'

The Omar DVD told a similar story and if Fayyaad was telling the truth, the DVDs could be about recent prisoners.

'Why are your relatives in prison?' Eva asked.

Laura's stomach churned. This could be why he was being watched.

'They speak to the western press about the coalition corruption.

They see men put money in pizza boxes and give to the rebuilding company, so they can win the contracts. After that, security forces come to my uncle's home in the middle of the night and take them away. They beat and kill the younger son. My aunt. She die two days later. She was badly beaten.'

Laura searched his troubled dark-brown eyes. It was common knowledge that Saddam Hussein terrorised his people and his brutal dictatorship cost many innocent lives, although the war hadn't ended their suffering. She'd read insurgent groups were thriving in Iraq now the war had created instability, and allegations of corruption dogged the government and coalition rebuilding programs. There'd even been a news report about cash transferred in pizza boxes to buy off officials and win contracts.

'The rise of ISIS and the continuing al-Qaeda threat puts everyone at risk,' Laura said. She needed reassurance that Fayyaad and his family were not part of the problem.

'They are my enemy too. They want power. They kill anyone to get it, Muslim or not.' Fayyaad's eyes turned fierce.

Eyes again turned towards their table, and Fayyaad shrank down into his seat. Eva and Laura did the same.

'Who were the government ministers that visited?' Eva prodded.

'Two different Australian ministers visit. The one who goes to meetings at night with Mr Peter is called Patrick. I see him on TV this morning.'

'That could be Patrick Furness, the Minister for Trade and Imports. He oversees APATO,' Eva explained. 'He's doing an exposé. It'll be interesting to hear what he says.'

'Maybe he tell about the meetings.' Fayyaad's voice and face didn't reflect his hopeful words. He leaned forward. 'He is a very cold man.'

Laura recognised him from the current affair program advertisement. He'd been at the party that night when Laura saw Tom on the balcony with Corrinne. Laura shivered. He was a pompous man with a distressing habit of licking his lips like a windscreen wiper on a drizzly day. But, if his exposé was revealing what happened in Iraq, there'd be no reason to kill to keep secrets.

'You said they met with criminal elements? The Wheat Board transport corruption stopped when the war started.' Laura was intrigued. 'What else could it be?'

'Who was the other minister?' Eva questioned.

'I don't know his name. He go to Bassarti twice but mostly he visit country areas. His driver is too afraid. He would not tell me where they go.'

'I still don't understand why I'm not safe. I have nothing to do with all this.' Laura's head ached. How could these activities threaten her?

'In Iraq, people ask questions and they go missing or die,' Fayyaad explained.

A shiver ran up Laura's spine. Tom once said, "There's no room for anyone to question what's happening."

Fayyaad continued, 'Mr Tom want to know more about Bassarti and go to his own meetings.'

'Did he meet criminals too?' Laura dreaded the answer. She didn't want to believe Tom could be involved in something sinister, but belief didn't represent the truth.

Fayyaad nodded. 'He go to secret meetings and I drive him. But I know Mr Tom would not do it for evil.'

Tom too attended secret meetings. Why? Fayyaad believed in Tom, why couldn't she blindly believe too?

'Before he die, Mr Tom talk to a journalist. Not Australian.' Fayyaad looked down at his hands. 'You must hide Mr Tom's papers, and recordings, or give them to me. Don't trust anyone else.'

Laura hesitated. Could she trust him? He seemed sincere and his concern for her was real, but why did he want Tom's papers?

'Who's the journalist?' Eva asked.

'He is from Canada. He was very sick but now I can not find

him. You must not tell anyone about this. It will put you in danger. They are evil men—'

'Until I know who's behind this, I'm not safe no matter what I do,' Laura said.

'The forces of evil are not countries like the *axis of evil*, but leaders who unleash war on innocent people. The men that sacrifice my people, turn my country to ruin, then walk away.'

Laura nodded. While the Wheat Board, and eventually APATO, corruptly handed millions of dollars to Saddam Hussein, his people suffered. The oil-for-food program was supposed to protect the Iraqi people from the sanctions and starve Saddam Hussein of funds. It hadn't worked. Then, the exaggerated weapons of mass destruction evidence became an excuse for war and many innocent lives were lost for a lie. Insurgents now flooded Iraq, and the pain continued. There were no easy remedies. War had been a simplistic answer to a very complex problem and had created more problems, not less.

'Saddam Hussein was a brutal dictator. I wanted him gone, but now my country is broken and the criminals run free.' Fayyaad slumped in his seat. He looked exhausted.

When he stood to leave, Eva offered to drive him home.

'I walk and come home alone,' he said. 'I give you another way to contact me, please, don't ring me. It is dangerous for us both.'

Laura's skin erupted in goosebumps. His fear was contagious. They walked outside and watched him stumble down the uneven footpath. The pigeons took flight and generated a strange whistling sound. Laura thought that's how panic would sound. Shrill and urgent. It was how she felt right now.

'If Tom and Corinne were both murdered, how will we find out who's behind this?' Laura asked. Murder seemed farfetched but plausible, and the police called Tom's death *suspicious*.

'Obviously, Tom and Corrinne were working on something important. Maybe the Furness exposé will help us understand. He's being called a whistleblower.' Eva unlocked the car, and they both got in. 'I wonder if I could find out more about the secret meetings Peter went to.'

'With *criminals.*' Laura buckled her seat belt. 'Peter could have been negotiating for APATO alone because they didn't want Tom involved. On the other hand, Peter could have been working on a personal project.'

They couldn't ask Peter directly, and without inside connections to APATO, they had no way to find out.

'Tom could've been excluded from those meetings because of his objections to paying bribes.' Eva suggested.

'The minister's involvement suggests the meetings were sanctioned company business. Anyway, why send Tom to Iraq if he couldn't participate in the negotiations? Tom worried about Fast-Track's lower level of scrutiny too,' Laura said. 'Fast-Track was Corrinne's area.'

Laura chewed at her lower lip. Every point raised more questions. So far, she had a swathe of notated paperwork, diaries, and a mystery key but little hard, recognisable evidence. Except for that DVD.

'I found a DVD among Tom's movies. It's a recorded interview, like a documentary.' Laura described the DVD's content. 'It was in the wrong case. I watched it with Mel and she's investigating.'

'I'd like to watch it too,' Eva said and finally turned onto a road Laura recognised.

Back at Laura's house, they again reviewed what they'd learned. They reiterated information, confirmed, refined, and restated it until they were both exhausted.

'We should talk to Corrinne's husband. Maybe he knows more,' Eva suggested. 'This is important. I can feel it in my bones.' She chuckled. ' Call it my journalist's instinct. We need to get to the bottom of this. And, of course, you're not truly safe until we do. Fayyaad could be wrong, melodramatic, or even overstating this.

He's a very nervous man but...'

Eva wasn't reassuring. Could they trust Fayyaad? He seemed sincere, yet Laura's doubts weren't easily swept away. He wanted the papers too.

If Tom had uncovered a conspiracy, he hadn't been willing to confide in her. Had he felt that she didn't support him or wasn't willing to help? Would she risk her life and the lives of her children now, to unearth his concerns and uncover the truth? Surely, that was too much to ask.

When Eva left, the flashing light on the home phone caught Laura's eye. A message from Robby announced he was safe, *lying low*, whatever that meant. She cried with relief. If only he'd phoned her mobile, they could have talked. She rang him back, but his phone disconnected with no opportunity to leave a message. At least he was safe.

Chapter 24

At the Hilton Hotel, attendees gathered at the conference suite entrance, balancing cups of coffee and biscuits as they chatted. John steeled himself for the pompous grandstanding that always happened at these conferences. At least he was in a good mood. He replayed his evening with last night's accomplished young woman. Her obvious experience was exactly what he'd needed, and she'd left him satisfied. Her excellent English and smooth conversational skills provided an unusual dimension, one he'd enjoyed. She'd shown a real interest in him and talking about himself came easily. Casterlow and Furness' faces flashed across his mind. Publicly they were upstanding Christian men, but luckily the media baron, Paddington would ensure that the public never learned about their private indulgences, at least while they remained in his favour.

John's phone lit up just as he accepted a coffee. It was a message from Kleb and John cursed. Had the Poirot-like diamond merchant, Werner, already reported back?

Kleb's message read, "The shit's hit the fan. Furness has turned whistleblower. The TV interview will be aired on Saturday night. Stay tuned."

John read it twice before it registered. This couldn't be good. What could Furness reveal? And why was he calling himself a whistleblower?

John recognised two European transport company bosses standing by the doors and he joined them. Their conversation followed the pattern of a carefully choreographed advertisement. My business is thriving, I'm very successful, I'm making lots of money, and so forth. John participated without divulging his real money-making enterprises, although he was sure the others hid secrets too. Finally, they turned their attention outward, into the world of politics and control and the Wheat Board scandal.

'On the international stage, Australia is suffering a branding crisis. Being criticised by the President of Indonesia and the Canadian Prime Minister is a new low,' the bespectacled and muscular Belgian said.

'We may be small, but sometimes we have to stand up for ourselves,' John responded. He wasn't sure what the criticism was about but, in his opinion, the Wheat Board rort was getting more coverage than it deserved.

'Australia is being less than open about the details,' the tall, wiry man said.

'Who is Furness? Will he disclose any juicy secrets about the enquiry, do you think?' the Belgian asked.

His friend shook his head and brushed back the lock of hair falling in his eyes. 'Surely, he'd talk to the inquiry first, wouldn't he?'

John shrugged. Furness turning whistleblower on any topic was worrying. If only he could get more details.

'I've heard it's about Iraq,' the tall man added.

The file Corrinne gave Furness seemed to have started this. Clearly, it had shaken him. He'd argued with Casterlow about it and after that, Furness' career was on a downward slide. Had Furness suffered a crisis of conscience? John laughed. Furness didn't have a conscience. Whatever this was about, it could become a total train wreck.

The doors opened and attendees were ushered into the presentation. His companions greeted others, and John peeled away to take a seat up the back.

The sessions on new technology to improve loading efficiency, and new software to track and process payments, droned on. If he'd brought his receptionist, she'd have saved him from having to pay attention. He glanced out of the window. Perhaps this tracking software could help with the supply issues in Central America. The rival intra-gang factions blamed each other for the sabotage of his shipments and he didn't know who to believe. These factions were rumoured to be breaking away, but it was unlikely to improve his issues. No matter what, he always bore the inconvenience.

The day's succession of presentations bored him and he was relieved when it was finally time for the afternoon break. As he entered the hallway, his phone rang.

It was more bad news from his Brisbane office manager. The manager explained that rival groups had set up labs to produce methamphetamine to interrupt heroin and cocaine supplies. John's face flushed. This mess created cash flow issues and once his customers turned elsewhere, it wouldn't be easy to win them back. The Brisbane manager suggested no solutions.

The no-fuss synthetic E-bomb had a guaranteed supply from the special government labs in Iraq. Dimi didn't have to suffer these inconveniences. Of course, now there was Casterlow's mystery new product too. Was that another drug he could sell on the streets or something else? As long as Furness's whistleblowing didn't bring it crashing down.

His sour mood mellowed during the sumptuous group dinner and afterwards, he joined the attendees at the bar. Their excitement bored him, and he felt oddly subdued. The transport business was a means to an end, although the wheeling and dealing after a conference usually inspired him. Now his mundane business in Amsterdam was finished, he could focus on meeting Casterlow's contact, Stavros Carnegie. He smiled. He'd allowed himself a little personal indulgence in Milan too.

John scanned the room and noticed Wayne Skollov step into one of the side rooms. He hadn't told John that he was coming to the conference. Who was he talking to and why? John threaded through the crowd towards the door, but by the time he got there, Skollov was gone.

It was late when John left the hotel foyer. He stumbled slightly on the step, although he was sure he hadn't drunk that much. He passed the taxi rank; breathing in deeply to let the cool breeze refresh him. He looked up and saw Wayne Skollov slink out of the hotel. Skollov furtively glanced left and right, and John pulled back into the shadows. What was Skollov up to?

Skollov crept down the path along the edge of the canal. John stepped off the curb onto the road, ready to follow, but suddenly jumped back when a cyclist careered across his path. John swore loudly. He carefully scanned the area before stepping off again.

He tracked Skollov. They'd left the hotel precinct and now the area was strangely free of people, cyclists, or water traffic. He hadn't ventured this far along the canal before. The shadow ahead shuffled close to the outer edge, where the river opened into a large bay-like basin. A river cruise boat was moored at the dock with its lights dimmed. It was shrouded in an eerie silence. John approached quietly but it was unoccupied and probably awaiting passengers. Tiny security lights flickered; their reflection dancing on the water like low-quality diamonds. John hugged the darkened edges and his eyes remained fixed on Skollov's eerie round shape.

They passed more empty vessels, looming in the semi-darkness and casting a sombre veil over his mood. He felt a strange unease. He'd re-engaged with the murky illegal business world without question. When he was younger, trying to prove himself to his father, Babbo, he'd been comfortable in that world. His little sister, Dimi, thrived in it. He clenched his fist. He hated the injustice. He'd struggled to build his confidence, rarely earning his father's praise or approval. It was never given easily except to Dimi. If he'd left, as he'd planned to do with Harper, he'd have been content. He shook his head and swore. Contentment wasn't happiness. He'd take over the family business because he wanted the kudos, the status, and most of all, he wanted to see Dimi lose. Hard, cut-throat, and callous fighting were the price of revenge. And he was ready.

'For god's sake.' It was time for unconditional commitment.

With a jolt, he realised he hadn't noted his surroundings. The shadow slipped around a corner and he was too far back. He needed to hurry. He didn't recognise any landmarks, and the river was deserted. The shadows played on the water, a gentle breeze creating ripples that broke up the images into strange shapes. John shivered. Should he go on?

He rounded the corner and large storage sheds loomed at the water's edge. His eyes slowly adjusted and the sporadic placement of security spotlights high on the shed walls illuminated patches while large tracts remained dark. Nothing here resembled a human shape.

A movement next to one shed caught his eye. The squat and beer-bellied shadow was indisputably Skollov. He strode towards the warehouse entrance, then stopped. A fiery red pin-prick of a lit cigarette pinpointed him. A dark limousine approached from the opposite side and swept into the parking area. John moved back against a wall. The headlights exposed the shadow and Skollov's signature colourful jacket.

The limousine halted in front of Skollov and a tall, well-built man heaved himself out of the passenger door. The light spilled from the cabin, but John didn't recognise the dark-haired man in the dark suit until a ring on the man's left hand flashed. The red sparkle from a flamboyant gem told John what he wanted to know.

John itched to get closer, but there was nowhere to hide. What business did Skollov have with Boris out here in the dark? And without Svetlana. John envied the power and status of Skollov's weapons business, but he dealt mostly with new punks trying to make their mark. Boris wasn't like those usual contacts. He was an old punk who'd already made his mark.

Finally, Boris slapped Skollov on the back and guffawed loudly. He curled himself back into the limousine. John didn't move until Skollov also sauntered to a waiting car and they'd both gone. Now all he had to do was find his way back to his hotel.

Chapter 25

Laura dragged herself out of bed. She felt all of her fifty-nine years. All night she'd jumped at every sound as the wind howled, the thunder rumbled, and the lightning flashed. Danger lurked in every unusual sound and her fears followed her under the sheets and blankets. Trying to reason Fayyaad's warnings away hadn't worked.

The breakfast radio news report confirmed the chaos Fayyaad spoke of. The rebuilding program had stalled and the CPA, short for the Coalition Provisional Authority, had lost approximately $US8.8 billion since 2003, with much of the money unaccounted for. Iraqi infrastructure hadn't even reached pre-invasion levels yet. Corruption was rife, not only in Iraq. Australia was mentioned too.

After her morning coffee, Laura stared at the mysterious key and envelope. It was time to find out the truth. She stowed them in her handbag and grabbed her car keys. She opened the front door and almost collided with Abbie. What could she want? She never dropped in unexpectedly.

'I brought homemade cookies.' Abbie flicked the hair from her face and attempted a smile.

'How kind, thank you.' Laura dropped her bag by the hall table. 'Would you like a coffee?'

Abbie placed a container on the kitchen bench and pointed at the coffee machine. 'Is that new?'

'Mark bought it for me.' Laura laughed. 'I haven't used it much. To be honest, I prefer going out to cafés for the atmosphere, and I enjoy reading the paper amid a sea of conversations. Coffee at home feels…lonely.'

'I guess it's been hard for you.'

'Especially trying to figure out how to work this blasted contraption.'

'Here, let me. It's the same as ours.'

Abbie ground the beans, filled the portafilter, tamped the grounds, and filled two cups with steaming black coffee. They carried the biscuits and coffees out to the patio.

'You're a whizz in the kitchen, Abbie. I never learned, just made it up as I went.'

'I learned young. Mamma's recipes were passed down from Nonna and her mother.'

'Do you have any brothers or sisters?' Laura knew little about Abbie. Laura's closeness to Eva created a barrier.

'An older brother…he died…'

Abbie stared across at the garden and Laura was reluctant to intrude.

'I'm sorry,' Laura said gently. What else could she say?

Laura relaxed back into her patio chair and quietly watched a parade of pigeons, twigs in their beaks, land on the roof next door. They ducked under the solar panels and disappeared. They were building a nest again. Nature's life cycle in motion.

Abbie sighed. 'Anyway, I have an ulterior motive for popping in. I'm curious how your date with Jacques went.'

'It wasn't a date.' This relationship with Abbie was taking odd twists. They rarely shared confidences or girl-talk.

Abbie waved her hand, sweeping the air before her dismissively. 'Whatever it was. How did it go?'

'We had lunch and we're going to the Barossa on Saturday.'

'He's keen.'

'It's a day out. Don't make too much of it.' Laura's voice became unusually shaky. It mattered that others made this serious when she was trying not to. 'I don't know him that well.'

'He doesn't seem to want anyone to know him well. He's cagey, especially about his work.'

'Both Tom and Peter were secretive about their work.'

'Details, yes, but they talked about their trips and their work in general. What have you found out about Jacques? Do you know what he does, who he's working for, or why he's here?' Abbie's gaze rested on Laura while she nibbled on one of her biscuits.

'He's divorced, has a daughter, and doesn't like gardening. Will that do?'

'That's just superficial'

'He works for a humanitarian organisation connected to the UN and he's developing charity funding models for refugees. What more do I need to know?'

'He fits right in with you and Eva then; the bleeding-heart brigade.'

Laura bristled. Abbie ruined the friendly tone with that one thoughtless comment.

'Did you talk about Tom or Peter's work?' Abbie asked.

'Why would I?'

'Maybe he's snooping. A little commercial espionage? There's something amiss with him. You would tell us if he gets too inquisitive?' Abbie sipped her coffee, watching Laura over the rim of the cup. 'Anyway, I hear Eva's book is being published. How did she find her *subjects*? Have you met any of them?'

Laura stifled a laugh. Abbie's mind was not usually so scattered.

'I, er, no, I haven't.' When Abbie raised her eyebrows, Laura added, 'She's told me so much about them. I *feel* like I've met them.'

'Oh.' Abbie sounded unconvinced. 'You've read the stories, though? Any of particular interest? Did any of them work with APATO?'

'I haven't read them all.' Why would Abbie ask that? 'You'll have to buy a copy of the book to find out.' Laura chuckled.

Abbie grimaced. 'Peter said she's very protective of her sources. Surely now they're in Australia, they're safe.'

'Their experiences make them wary; they don't trust people easily. She's looking after their welfare.'

'I guess it keeps her occupied.'

'This is important work,' Laura insisted.

Again, they reached an impasse and their relationship was back on its usual footing; Abbie trying to score points against Eva and Laura defending her friend.

Abbie looked at her watch and smiled. 'I must be off. Katie finishes at kindy soon.'

Laura held out the biscuit container.

'Keep it. I'll get it back another time.' Abbie swished out the door.

Laura cleared up in the kitchen. Her plan to visit the swim centre had lost momentum. A loud knock at the door made Laura smile. Abbie must have forgotten something. Two well-groomed and immaculately dressed men stood on the threshold. They reminded her of the President's bodyguards from a movie she'd recently watched. Something about their military-style haircuts and neatly tailored suits made her step back.

'Can we come in?' the tall man closest to the door said. His jaw flexed as he flashed his badge.

Both stepped forward and stood so close that Laura again moved back. They took advantage and moved into the vacated space. Finally, she led them to the dining room.

'Mrs Schultz, I understand you knew the deceased, Corrinne Lamberthy.' The tall man's hard-edged face and square chin didn't stretch to a smile.

'I'm Ms Gynne,' Laura corrected.

He rolled his eyes. 'We understand you knew her,' he persisted as his colleague's sharp unblinking green eyes watched her.

'I didn't *know* her,' she emphasised. 'She worked with my husband. I saw her only once. It was at a work function. I've already explained this to the police officers the other day.'

'You didn't tell the constable you knew the victim when you reported finding the body.'

'I didn't recognise her. She was badly…I didn't look that closely.'

'Mmm.' It was his colleague's turn. His piercing green eyes combined with a crewcut to give him a sinister and menacing look. 'And your husband died in February under suspicious circumstances.'

'You know the details.' A combination of anxiety and anger stoked a nervous earthquake, and she clasped a chair to steady herself. Unlike the uniformed police officers, their manner was aggressive.

'You said you had no knowledge of him taking drugs, yet a pill bottle was found in the bathroom.'

'I've never seen that bottle before. I never saw him take anything, regularly, only the occasional pain killer or vitamin supplement.'

'You don't know where he got the drugs?'

Laura shook her head. A spark of anger ignited her outrage, but she stifled it.

'The phone records show Ms Lamberthy rang you soon after your husband died. What did she want? Did she arrange to meet you?'

'What?' Laura gasped. That confirmed the mystery phone call was Corrinne.

Both the detectives stared unblinkingly.

'Well?' The shorter detective ran his hand over his bristly crewcut and the onyx ring on his little finger flashed.

'She was, er, offering her condolences.' Laura twisted her wedding ring. Lying could lead to trouble but she didn't trust them.

'That's all?' He glanced at his tall partner and an unreadable look

196

passed between them.

'Was your husband having an affair with Ms Lamberthy?' the tall officer's voice startled her.

'No. They weren't having an affair.'

'Come on now. How can you be so adamant? Why else were they spending time together after he retired?'

'I'm not sure they were.'

'According to information we've received, they met regularly.' His jaw flexed and he watched her closely.

Where had this information come from? She'd only recently discovered it from his diary. Who else would have known?

'I can't state categorically that Tom and Corrinne didn't have an affair. All I can say is that I had no suspicions. If they were having an affair, I knew nothing about it.' Laura glared at him.

'Perhaps you know more than you're willing to admit. Maybe his drug abuse made you angry. Their deaths are convenient for you. You're rid of both of them now. You're living comfortably. You've inherited the house and the super? Won't lose everything to a grasping girlfriend.' His green eyes burned bright.

Instead of sparking anger, a laugh escaped Laura's throat. A glance at their faces showed they were not joking. She'd doubted Tom once, but not anymore. His relationship with Corrinne was not intimate, but she couldn't assure them.

'I loved my husband, and he loved me.'

'We know your marriage had hit a rocky patch. Things were not as rosy as you pretend. We've seen it before. The spurned wife, angry at being cast aside, finally acts in a fit of rage. Rage makes people do terrible things,' the tall one accused.

'That's absurd.' They couldn't be serious.

'You saw them together at the party, so tell us what you know.'

'I don't know what you're talking about. I don't know anything.' Laura's heart pounded in her throat, making it hard to speak.

'She was last seen at Adelaide airport. She was met, it's on

CCTV, and she went with them, willingly. She knew them.' The shorter detective glared at her.

'You have a new man already. That's pretty quick. Did you know him before your husband died?' The tall officer continued the allegations.

'What? What new man? Are you referring to Jacques? I met him for the first time in July, months after Tom died. You can ask my friends. They introduced us. Have we finished now?' It was time to halt this fishing exercise. She was afraid she'd say something she'd regret.

'Tell us about this, Jacques,' he demanded.

'There's nothing to tell.'

'Who is he? What does he do? Is he connected to your husband or Ms Lamberthy?'

'You'll have to ask him. We've only just met—'

'You should answer our questions truthfully. We're asking you to help us with our enquiries so if you'd rather do it at the station …' the tall detective threatened and pulled himself up to his full height.

'How is this helping with your enquiries? You put forward wild ideas that have no basis in fact and I'm supposed to prove you wrong. Perhaps you should find evidence to prove what happened, not waste time and energy on wild guesses. The CCTV should prove it wasn't me.'

'You haven't answered us yet. Have you been having an affair?'

Bile filled her throat with acid. 'How dare you! I've lost my husband of thirty-seven years; my house has been burgled, and I stumbled onto a dead body. I'm having nightmares and I've been traumatised and you have the nerve to come here and accuse me of plotting murder. I think you're clutching at straws and you're too lazy to do your jobs properly. You think you can bully me into saying something to hang all this on me and save you from searching for the real killer?'

'We're not bullying you, or trying to pin anything on you, but it's a legitimate line of enquiry. The CCTV isn't clear, you knew both of the deceased, their affair would be a strong motive. You have another relationship and you have a family connection to bikies. You have a lot of questions hanging over you.' The tall man listed the points off on his fingers as he spoke.

'It's all…circumstantial.'

'Your husband worked for APATO, didn't he?'

Laura nodded.

'Ms Lamberthy also worked there for a time?'

'So I understand,' Laura said cautiously.

'Did your husband ever talk to you about his work? The details of what he was working on?'

'Why?'

'We're asking the questions here, Mrs Schultz, er, Ms Gynne. Please answer our question.' The courtesy was only in the words, not in his manner or tone.

'No, he didn't.'

'Not at all?'

'I knew he worked on trade contracts with Iraq, but that's all.'

'You said you were moving. Does that mean you've cleared out his office?'

'I've thrown out or shredded everything.' It wasn't completely true, but she wanted these men out of her house. She'd had enough of their questions, their sneering and rude attitude. 'Are we done?'

They ignored her question.

'We may need to ask you further questions at a later date,' the tall officer said firmly.

Laura bristled. 'You have no evidence, nothing concrete, only rumour and innuendo.'

The detectives nodded to each other.

'One more thing. What were you doing in Brooklyn Park that morning, the morning you found the body?' His green eyes darkened.

'I was checking out storage companies.'

'Were you now? Connected to your husband's business, perhaps?'

'I'm moving, clearing out my house, and I'll need extra storage.'

'That's a long way from here. Why that one?'

'I'd seen an advertisement. I don't know any others.'

'Are you sure you're telling us everything?'

'I don't know what you want me to say.'

'We've finished our questioning today, but don't leave the country or go away without advising us,' he cautioned.

'And if you think of anything else, call us immediately.' The tall man handed her a card.

Once they left, Laura closed the door. Her entire body shook. They couldn't seriously suspect her of killing or arranging to have Tom and Corrinne killed.

She phoned Eva, who recommended a lawyer. But that could be interpreted as a guilty conscience. Wouldn't it make things worse? Surely justice would prevail. Eva's calm analysis reassured her, but Laura's hands were still shaking as she put down the phone.

Chapter 26

When the white Palazzo Hotel first came into view, John congratulated himself on his choice. The Milan hotel was everything he'd imagined. A grand exterior encased an equally grand interior. The white marble staircase behind the sumptuous hotel foyer with its art-decked walls and refined chandelier-reflected light. Not a dark-brown feature anywhere.

He unpacked and, despite the pull of the private garden bar and the spa, he strolled the short distance to the commercial district. Although still early, the heat brought a sprinkling of sweat to his brow. The northern hemisphere peak summer vacation time meant crowds slowed his errand. He avoided the tour groups and dodged the individuals scrambling in a mild panic to stay close to their guide. Tour leaders, with raised umbrellas or flags, surrounded by bored but often old faces, filled the square. Beside him, a tour guide earnestly related facts and figures that John was sure no one would remember before darting to the next sight.

At a small, incognito mobile phone shop, he purchased a local phone and the assistant patiently demonstrated how it worked. Technology was not his strong point and John struggled to maintain attention to learn the basics.

Back in his room, he plugged in the phone, hoping the battery would be sufficiently charged by the time he needed to leave. His chore complete, he changed clothes and found a comfortable chair in the hotel coffee shop to indulge in an espresso and flick through some paperwork. He sent Kleb a text with the alternative number.

Invigorated by the shot of caffeine, he collected his phone and a jacket. He stepped outside into the sticky heat but returned and ordered a taxi. A moment later, John strode through the broad white entrance to Milan Central station and rode the escalators up to his train's departure platform on the second floor. He searched for carriage number two, but the train began at carriage number six. People milled about, looking confused. Some loitered, taking turns to harangue the conductor and John found an assistant who waved his hands with exasperation.

'This is a very *extraordinary* train,' the assistant said flamboyantly. 'Just get on and find a seat.'

'But I have a first-class ticket. Where is the first-class carriage?' John protested.

'There is none. Please get on and find a seat.'

John stared in disbelief. Taking a train was bad enough, but having to sit in economy was worse. He joined the throng of embarking passengers and found a seat by the window. A couple stowed their luggage across the aisle and settled comfortably, only to be moved on by a family who'd booked those seats. The sounds of chaos and distress, and a growing smell of sweat, filled the carriage. A large round woman plonked into the seat beside John and he instinctively shifted closer to the window. Her heavy, sweet perfume made him gag. She nudged him as she fussed in her bag for a handkerchief, then delicately wiped her brow, nudging him again as she stowed her bag by her feet.

She turned to John and demanded, 'You a tourist?'

He turned to face her and immediately choked on a waft of overpowering scent. 'No, I'm here on business.' He turned his head away, signalling that he didn't want to talk.

'This is terrible. I have a first-class ticket, but there is no first-class carriage,' she complained, obviously not getting the message.

'I know,' John muttered. It was a sore point with him, too.

'I have a meeting in Zurich, but this train doesn't go through, so I have to change at the border. It's a disgrace.'

'Oh?' John wasn't interested.

The woman continued, 'Of course, we are late and I'm going to miss the connection. Swiss trains don't wait.' She sighed and nudged him to gain his attention. 'I'll have trouble getting a seat on the later trains. It always happens.'

John nodded and turned back to the window as the train finally pulled out of the station.

'Are you going to Zurich too?' She was determined to engage him.

'Como.' Thankfully, it was a short trip.

'For business? Lake Como is beautiful with wonderful hotels along the lake's edge. You should have stayed there.'

'Yes, I should have,' John said and again turned back to the window.

His shirt stuck uncomfortably to his back despite the air conditioning and he ground his teeth as he stared out of the window. Finally, the woman found a more willing conversationalist across the aisle and he was left to simmer on his own.

John was startled when his new phone rang.

'Furness suffered organ failure,' Kleb announced before John could speak.

'When? What brought that on?'

'*Before* the interview.'

'The stress got to him?' John had seen it before. Not many whistleblowers could withstand character assassination and media campaigns. Given Paddington's unrelenting support of the current government, his media outlets would've called Furness's motives into question and unleashed a vitriolic media campaign. Paddington hated government whistleblowers.

'It wasn't stress. It's suspicious. I can't talk now. I'll ring again later.'

John reluctantly agreed. The people around him had ears, and unfortunately, they also had lips. You never knew who they were or who they would talk to. Especially the large woman who'd stopped chatting and was flicking through a magazine.

Furness's death was convenient for Dimi and possibly Casterlow. There'd be no uncomfortable revelations now and nothing to explain. John smirked. Furness's death was convenient for him too. It maintained the status quo.

He was the first to disembark at Como station, and he commandeered the first taxi at the rank. They skirted the old town and in no time, the taxi pulled up at the ferry terminal. He bought a return ticket to Bellagio but struggled to find a quiet space on the crowded ferry, eventually joining the tourists on deck.

His mind was preoccupied and he couldn't dispel his sense of dissatisfaction. Was it Werner's delays or his unease at Skollov's meeting with Boris? Or was it dissatisfaction with his life in general? He'd expected to gain a sense of achievement from this trip, but in reality, he was still striving for an elusive idea of success. And now he also worried about failure. The meeting in Bellagio was important, but he suspected he wasn't sufficiently briefed. What would happen then?

He calmed as the ferry set off. A gentle breeze ruffled his hair and brought a faint whiff of heavy, sweet perfume. He searched the deck, but the woman from the train was not nearby. She said she was travelling to Zurich, she shouldn't be on the ferry.

The sweat on his face cooled as they cruised along the lake's fringe before docking not far from their departure. He swore. He'd caught the stopping all ports ferry, not the express. He couldn't be late. They slowly rounded a promontory and passed a grand pink mansion and manicured gardens spread over an entire clifftop. He glanced at his watch and clenched his jaw.

Loud squealing and shouting suddenly interrupted his thoughts. A middle-aged woman wriggled in her seat, jabbing at her companions and pointing vigorously. John's eyes followed her pointing finger. The Clooney residence was there, perched on the lake's edge, and her companions erupted into a high-pitched and feverish discussion.

The ferry meandered, pulling into small docks to embark and disembark a trickle of passengers. John's blood pressure rose with each stop.

Pink villages clustered in the dips and curves of the mountainous terrain and large, palatial mansions took pride of place closer to the lake. The mansions represented old money and a time when wealthy aristocrats splurged on grandeur. Many were no longer owned by local or traditional families. Change was inevitable and, although he agreed it wasn't always good, the old ways weren't relevant anymore. In his business, the old families were stale, devoid of energy and ideas, and they were being outmanoeuvred. Too much tradition and doing what they'd always done. John was the new direction, the one who could make the business strong again, and he'd make sure of it, no matter what it took.

The ferry pulled away from yet another stop and a surging wash swept past the boat. He should relax and enjoy this slow ride, but his mind wouldn't rest. He was as prepared as Casterlow had allowed, but it wasn't enough. The man was all promise, and John worried that he'd been set up to fail. Stavros Carnegie was powerful. His reputation made John nervous. This was a man he didn't want to cross.

The ferry threaded across the lake and around protruding headlands, passing more orange-pink villages clinging precariously to the hillsides, creating streaks of colour in the mountain backdrop before finally pulling into the dock at Bellagio.

John was caught unawares by the rush and was the last to leave. He shuffled down the pier behind groups of ambling tourists and purposeful locals, blocked from moving past. Swarms of tourists clambered up the hill or to the esplanade to walk along the water's edge. Once the crowd fanned out, he rushed forward. Following the directions, he took the other path along the lake, then turned and climbed a series of steep steps. Small clusters of tourists followed, and he searched to be sure the woman wasn't among them. He was being paranoid. She wasn't significant, but he searched again anyway when he rounded the corner.

He was out of breath when he arrived. The *trattoria* was perched above a silk shop and stairs lead up from the alleyway. He wiped his brow, took a deep breath, and climbed.

Inside the room sat an assortment of tables that accommodated different-sized groups. The homely teak furniture looked quaint and, in its favour, was not dark brown. One beefy man sat beside the wall and his clone sat by the entrance. Dark sunglasses underlined their slicked-back hair, biceps stretched their jacket sleeves to bursting point, and their shirt buttons pulled with dangerous tension. They stared impassively, despite the sheen of sweat layering their foreheads. His contact sat by himself in the corner near a picture window overlooking the lake. His bulk spread across the equivalent of two seats and his chin sagged over his shirt collar. His rugged face was pockmarked and rutted like an ungraded outback road. His tough skin echoed his demeanour; everything about this man said tough. He glanced at his watch, tilted his head, then reached awkwardly to offer his hand.

'Stavros Carnegie.' John's contact introduced himself. 'Pleased to meet you.'

John stifled a grimace as the handshake crushed the bones in his hand. 'John Masters,' he responded. 'Sorry, I caught the wrong ferry.'

Stavros dismissively waved his hand in the air and swept away the apology. 'Please, sit. I have taken the liberty of ordering a selection of dishes to share. The chef is top class and the food here is delicious. I come here whenever I am in Bellagio.'

The café seemed unremarkable and not the top-class establishment that would earn such glowing praise, but John wasn't a gourmand. His mother's face came to mind. For her, food was a substitute for love. She'd fussed over recipes to cook the *right way*, but neglected her family's other important needs.

Delight lit Stavros' face as he listed the dishes he'd ordered. John vowed to use the gym tonight.

'Where are you based?' John asked.

'Turkey. It is my home, as much as any place can be called my home.'

They engaged in small talk, but when the banquet arrived, it stifled any conversation. Stavros urged John to sample all the dishes. The pasta included his favourites, agnolotti pan-fried with sage and butter sauce with a touch of white truffle, and the coin-shaped crosetti with meat sauce. The Sicilian specialty, Ziti, baked in a marinara sauce and topped with generous lashings of ricotta and mozzarella cheese, was authentic and delicious, although it brought with it too many unwelcome memories for John. The seafood platter was a meal in itself and the side dishes of salad and potatoes remained almost untouched. Despite moderating his helpings, John felt overstuffed when he'd finished.

'I don't like to do business on an empty stomach,' Stavros explained.

John smiled. Stavros probably did nothing on an empty stomach.

'I hear you run a very successful transport business. If this works out, maybe we could work together on other projects in the future. I'm always keen to expand.'

'You have interests in Australia or Iraq?'

Stavros pursed his lips. 'Mmmm, yes. My business takes me all over the world. Lately, I've been concentrating on Syria. Now, there's a conflict that will not end soon. The Russian and American governments will see to that.'

'And which side are you on?' John asked.

'Whatever side pays me.' Stavros laughed, and his whole body shook.

John laughed too. His research of Stavros Carnegie's business revealed a man involved in a host of shady deals, including hints of people smuggling and supplying arms to rebels. John didn't understand why Casterlow had sought him out, especially after shunning Wayne Skollov's help.

Stavros reached for a cigar, and the closest minder lumbered over to light it. The waiter took that as a cue to serve two Negroni cocktails. The blood-red liquid contrasted ominously with the white tablecloth. The aroma of herbs was much more pleasant than that overpowering perfume from the train. Stavros raised his glass in *salut* and sipped. John did the same. He shuddered at the first taste, but then the Campari and gin's bitterness combined with the smooth vermouth refreshed him. John sipped again, then turned his attention back to Stavros Carnegie.

'Syria has become too crowded, too many vested interests supporting different groups. We now drop our weapons shipments and go,' Stavros explained. 'The Americans and Russians use Syria for their personal dispute. Their support blocks competing commercial interests and frankly, I can do better elsewhere. There are plenty of conflicts in the world.'

'You're moving into new areas?' John hoped he wasn't displaying his ignorance.

'Yes and no. We are interested in getting in on the start of this new product. I hear it's a potent chemical agent, better than what's currently on the market and it's not easily treated. It has big prospects.' He clapped John on the back and laughed. 'Enough small talk. Let's talk business.'

John shivered. 'We have several areas to discuss. First, we are looking to expand the research, our current operations are becoming too small. That means we'll need access to large-scale in situ testing options in other locations, including a supply of subjects for our own facilities in Iraq. Second, I'm sure you know we're interested in the confidential new markets you've proposed. Once we've tested the efficacy of our product, we're prepared to negotiate a mutually beneficial deal. Third, we hope to draw on your business to supply our new consumers, if we can come to an agreeable arrangement. You are confident that you can create a secure and reliable supply and distribution mechanism?' John repeated the key elements of his briefing.

'You are not handling the transport yourself? It looks easy to shift.'

'I'll be involved in Iraq, but not with the transfer into Europe and Africa.'

'There are rumours that inquisitive people are threatening to expose this scheme. This could be detrimental to my other operations. I must be certain they won't be compromised. I can't be caught in any fallout.'

John swallowed hard. He knew this would happen. Casterlow mentioned a *snooper* but hadn't elaborated. 'Everything is under control and our plans to expand production are well-advanced,' he improvised.

'You can swear to this?'

John hesitated, then added, 'I can,' more confidently than he felt.

They discussed the finer details over coffee. Stavros' Iraqi contact would work with John or Casterlow, while Stavros would manage the importation of the dangerous chemical into Africa via Europe. Breaking up responsibilities ensured there was no single trail, although it was riskier to have more people involved, it made sense. They were dealing with lucrative markets and there was enough to go around as long as no one got greedy. It wasn't as easy as it sounded, though. Greed fed this business.

'This is a unique opportunity,' Stavros admitted.

'If done well, it will be a win-win,' John parroted Casterlow's favourite cliché.

'Production must increase quickly. There is a huge demand. So many conflicts and protestors, and so many leaders needing help to maintain control. The large-scale testing will help refine the product to make it even more effective. I can help with this. I have an unlimited supply of undesirables we can use for this.' Stavros leaned in close. 'Although you must take care of the Russians.' John's frown was met with a laugh and Stavros added, 'They don't *know* anything, but, of course, the whispers of a new and improved chemical agent is making them nervous. They don't know where it's from and they don't like surprises. They're calling in favours to get information, so make sure everything is secure.'

John grimaced. Casterlow hadn't mentioned Russian interest.

As they parted, Stavros drew John in close and said quietly, 'Be careful, my friend. This is a dangerous game. Watch your back.'

John nodded as a shiver ran down his spine.

On the outer deck of the Como ferry, John found a sheltered spot with a calming view towards the Swiss snow-covered mountains and their startling white peaks. They seemed close enough to touch.

He rang Kleb on the new mobile phone.

'It's me. Tell me about Furness,' he ordered.

'He was planning to expose details of top-secret government operations in Iraq. This wasn't about Dimi's business. It's related to Casterlow's project. Furness only recently learned about the full extent of the Iraqi operations and apparently objected. He was willing to put his career on the line. His home study was ransacked and his office has been sealed by the government, so the information has been lost to us.' Kleb sighed. 'And the government's refusing to order an autopsy. They're saying it's a waste of taxpayer money.'

'Wasting taxpayer money isn't usually high on their list of concerns.' John pulled a face. That file must have contained new, powerful information. He wished he'd seen it.

'Furness's wife insists his specialist gave him a complete physical a month ago. He'd been given the all-clear.'

'It wouldn't be the first time a specialist got it wrong. Is she implying—'

'Casterlow was determined to stop Furness talking. He'd even talked of arresting him.'

'Would Casterlow commit murder? He's ruthless and very wily, but murder?'

Kleb sighed. 'He won't let anything stand in his way. He's willing to do anything to protect his secret project. We can't underestimate him.'

'Casterlow's contact said the Russians are interested in this chemical agent and it's better than theirs. Is it a secret weapon of some kind ?'

'It's called Formula Z.'

John shook his head. It was more than an illicit drug like E-bomb.

'I'm guessing it's a chemical weapon.' Kleb added.

'That would explain the Russian's interest.'

'They already have Sarin gas, novichok, and nerve gasses. Where do you think small nations get their supplies? Their dominance is indisputable.'

'Would Australia try to compete with the Russians?' John frowned. He'd sought Russian help for his business expansion plans through Boris and Svetlana. Could that threaten Casterlow's project? Svetlana's question about his *other* product suggested they knew, but how much?

Kleb was still explaining, 'Russia can ignore bio-security regulations and safeguards that inhibit our research. It gives them a competitive edge. We need more information.'

'Can you speed it up?' John's plans were becoming bogged down. 'I saw Skollov sneak away to meet my Russian mafia representative.'

'What's he up to now? He always stokes more problems than he solves.' Kleb sighed.

'Maybe I should talk to him.'

'Not a good idea. He's only interested in what benefits him. Stay clear for now.' Kleb sighed again. 'So, you met my diamond trader?'

John swallowed down his annoyance. He'd put that meeting out of his mind. 'He didn't impress me.'

'I've known him for years. He's impeccable.'

'Are you sure you can trust him?'

A muted voice interrupted Kleb's conversation.

'I've got to go. I'll be in touch.' Kleb hung up.

The fast ferry was true to its word and back in Como, John sauntered through the old town, admiring the muted colours of the stonework and building façades. The detail reminded him of his childhood visits to family. They were happier times. His uncles fussed over him and told him he was the heir and successor to the family business. He'd felt important then.

The sun hung low in the sky. The lake surface sparkled and shimmered with street lights and lanterns. He was tired but detoured to stand at a café counter to down a strong, bitter espresso followed by a gulp of water. The rush was exhilarating. He hadn't done that for a long time.

At the station, he checked his messages and dialled the number Carlo had given him.

'Hello, Franco. I'm confirming our meeting tomorrow.' John avoided his nickname even though Franco the Ferret had a tempting ring to it.

'Something's come up. I can't get away now,' the sharp voice replied.

'You agreed. I've come especially.' John wasn't going to be stood up.

'Look. It's tricky. I'm busy.'

'Carlo assured me, and, it will be well worth your while.'

'Fuck!' a wary Ferret muttered. His cautiousness meant he must still be in the thick of things. At least Carlo still had his old persuasive power. Ferret had been a reliable source of inside information for Babbo in the past, and John was counting on his help now.

'OK, but I can't leave Santa Margherita. You'll have to come here.' Ferret's lack of respect was unexpected.

'You agreed to come to Milan.'

'I'm needed. We can meet between jobs. It's the only way.'

John didn't like Ferret's surly tone, but reluctantly agreed.

When John's train pulled into Como, he rushed on, this time finding a first-class carriage minus the perfumed woman. He stretched out and rang Skye. No answer. John clenched his jaw. Where was she?

In Milan, he ambled back to his hotel, enjoying the soft evening breeze. He'd anticipated a sumptuous dinner in the flashy gastronomic restaurant, but he was too late and he was still full from lunch. The modern bistro lounge boasted a well-stocked bar, and three couples and two small groups filled the seats around the perimeter. He chose an armchair close to the bar, facing away from the mirrored wall, and once his Americano cocktail was served, he again phoned Skye. Still no answer.

Around him, people laughed or talked quietly. No one paid him any attention. He finished his drink and left.

The only English news service on the TV in his room was CNN or BBC, and neither featured up-to-date news from Australia. They briefly mentioned Furness's untimely death before his planned exposé and how the Australian PM branded Furness a disgruntled politician who was about to be demoted. He emphasised that Furness had been under a great deal of stress lately.

Before switching off the TV, a report of a suspicious factory fire caught his attention. There were allegations of corruption and pay-offs. Babbo's rivals supplied the concrete for the recently collapsed main bridge near Genoa and now their factory was going up in flames. John grew up with the families and their blame-shifting. No one accepted responsibility for failed projects, but blame was allocated anyway.

There was talk of the local crime families joining forces to combat legal action and Russian mafia attempts to take over their key industries. Video footage of yachts formed the background visuals and John drew closer to the screen. Was that who he thought it was, stepping into a lane behind the restaurant? That was the resort of Portofino, he was sure of it, and it was only a short drive from Santa Margherita. He could check it out tomorrow if he had time. Travelling to Santa Margherita for his meeting with Ferret might not be such a waste after all.

Chapter 27

Laura sank into the limousine's soft leather seats and eyed Jacques. The casual jeans and jumper suited him.

'A charity patron arranged today's itinerary to show off the Barossa Valley,' Jacques explained.

'Why isn't *he* showing you around?'

'He got a better offer.' Jacques laughed. 'And I couldn't rearrange my schedule.'

She frowned. Was she only a fall-back option?

'I haven't visited the Barossa for years.' The memory of wine tasting with Tom before the John Farnham *Day on the Green* concert flashed across her mind and the image danced with laughter and intimacy. She swallowed down the ache and continued. 'I had second thoughts about today—'

He studied her face. 'What is it?'

'The police. They suspect me…Tom's death…and Corinne's death. They even suggested you and I are…lovers.' Her face warmed as she stumbled over her words.

'Why would they think that?'

'They believe Tom and Corrinne were having an affair, and that's my motive. Tom and Corrinne worked together before she took over responsibility for Fast-Track. I think they shared work concerns, but that's all.'

'What concerns?'

'I don't know.' Laura shivered again. 'Those detectives scared me. Their questions. I'm still not sure what they were getting at.'

'Were they local police?'

'They weren't in uniform. I'm not sure if they were detectives. That makes it more serious, doesn't it?'

'Have you talked to a lawyer?' Jacques watched her shake her head and added, 'Why not?'

'Eva suggested that too, but I thought it'd look like I was hiding something.' Laura wrung her hands.

Jacques frowned. 'I think you should get advice.'

An uncomfortable silence engulfed them as the limousine carried them out of the city.

'I'm glad you came. I return to Melbourne next week,' Jacques said.

'What brought you back for such a short visit? Besides the Barossa tour.'

'You, of course.' He winked at her. 'That was hard to resist. Of course, I was looking forward to seeing you again, but I have meetings.'

She frowned again. Which explanation did she prefer?

'It's difficult getting commitment to a long-term charitable legacy. The Australian government's punishment of refugees influences business attitudes. Our data shows that money spent on programs within trouble-torn countries prevents the exodus, provides aid, and improves living conditions so refugees are more likely to stay.'

'People can't stay in war zones, though,' Laura protested.

'Much of the migration is caused by famine, drought, or rebel incursions. They simply don't have the resources to combat them.'

'Australians are very generous; appeals get a good response.'

'That might be true of the Australian people, but it's less true of government and business, in general. Foreign aid is the first expenditure cut in the budget. I know it's not only Australia, but the current government's rhetoric stifles discussion. It makes my job harder.'

'Why Australia? The US causes countless problems meddling in other countries' affairs. They grabbed the rebuilding contracts in Iraq. Maybe some of their obscene profits could be diverted into aid.'

'I admit US companies are getting rich and we've yet to see much improvement in Iraqi infrastructure. The rebuilding hasn't achieved the results promised.'

'I wish Australia was more generous and took responsibility for the damage we caused. We should take more refugees, instead of demonising them.'

'It's a fear of difference. Despite Australia thriving through successive waves of migration, fear resurfaces with each new wave. Of course, politicians use it to their advantage. Tampa, children overboard, and now terrorism; all feed that fear.'

A sense of helplessness again settled over her. 'I used to joke that if our politics didn't change, I'd move to New Zealand or Canada, although Canada is probably too cold for me.'

'I'm sure you'd love it.' Jacques smiled at her.

'I can't imagine fleeing my home only to be jailed in the country I escaped to. It's like Fayyaad. Despite helping the Australians during the war, he's struggled to get permission to stay. He'd be killed—' Laura bit her tongue. She wasn't supposed to tell anyone about Fayyaad.

'Fayyaad?' Jacques asked. 'Is this someone you know personally?'

'No, I—' How could she recover this indiscretion? 'Tom helped him with his visa application and ranted about the complicated red tape. I don't know what happened to him.'

'He was trying to stay in Australia?'

'Tom met him in Iraq.' Laura sidestepped the question, hoping she wasn't making it worse. 'It's sad that Australia turns a blind eye and deaf ear to people in dire need.'

Jacques studied her face for a moment, then nodded. 'Australia joined the coalition of the willing. Instead of diplomacy, they used bombs and now, they all wash their hands of the consequences. In a way, the western world uses the chaos for their own gain. Iraq is a mess and people like, Fayyaad is it, are collateral damage.' Jacques leaned back and smiled. 'I guess wars are good for our economies, though.'

Laura gasped. Was this irony, a joke, sarcasm, or was he serious? His face didn't betray his intent.

Approaching Sandy Creek, the sign to the Whispering Wall caught her attention. She told Jacques about bringing her children here when they were young. They'd take turns to run to the end and whisper messages to each other along the curved dam wall. They'd squeal with delight when they could hear the instructions clearly at the other end, many hundred metres away.

Jacques asked the driver to detour down the bumpy dirt road. Their tyres kicked up dust and stones on the short drive to the parking area. A narrow, neglected-looking pathway led to the wall. This was once a popular tourist stop, but apparently, not anymore.

Laura led Jacques to the beginning of the wall, then continued to the opposite side of the dam. She bent down into the curve and whispered, 'How are you today?'

'Wow, that's so clear,' Jacques exclaimed. 'Wait there, I'm coming over.'

A few moments later he was beside her, admiring the view of majestic gumtrees and marvelling at the colourful rosellas flying past.

'What's on the itinerary today?' Laura asked.

'Wine tasting and lunch are booked in. I can't remember all the names, but the last wine tasting is at about 3.30 p.m. at the Carol Minton winery.'

'That sounds relaxed.'

Returning to the car, they passed a man at the narrow entrance.

His car's number plate made Laura laugh.

'I've seen a number plate like that before. The letters N.U.T. attracted my attention. I was, er, running errands and took it as a sign that I was going a bit crazy that day.'

In Lyndoch, they stopped at a bakery and ordered coffee and slices of *beestings* cake. They sat outside under the vines in the dappled winter sunshine.

'Your kindness fuels my frustrations. I can't often express myself so openly, I have to be diplomatic. In the interests of enjoying our day together, perhaps we should steer clear of controversial topics,' Jacques suggested.

Laura nodded. At least this cleared up his previous comment. She longed to trust him.

They passed pruned vines punctuated by compact red rose bushes at the end of each row. Cars in front and behind them peeled off into winery driveways but were replaced by others, creating a mini traffic jam. Passing the Shirazfeld mausoleum, they slowed, joining a queue of cars along the winding palm-tree lined road. They talked easily, discussing their wine preferences and the abundance of options in South Australia.

At the Shirazfeld winery complex, they were met by a dark-haired woman who guided them on a tour through the operations. The fermentation smell was strong and not entirely pleasant. They finished at the tasting room where two small bus groups tasted wine at the end of the bar. Two couples admired the exhibits along the far wall. The guide cleared a space and offered tastings from a specially compiled list. Laura accepted the sparkling wine, followed by a not-too-sweet-but-fresh Riesling. Its fruity aroma was a pleasant replacement for the tour smells. She declined the rest of the whites and although Jacques tasted all three, he tipped the remainder into the bucket.

'You must meet many interesting people through your work,' Laura noted.

'They're not so *interesting* really. Countries I visit don't have the same legal or democratic structures we western countries enjoy. I need to talk to whoever can help achieve the outcomes. Some are perhaps, shall we say, dubious.'

His pragmatism stoked her anxieties. 'I'd love to travel. There are so many exciting places to see.'

'Travelling for work is rarely *exciting,* especially in war zones. Work keeps me too busy to sightsee, anyway.'

'Tom used to say that too.' Laura immediately regretted bringing up Tom's name.

'I'd love to have the time to go out to see some of the great historical sites in Iran and Iraq, but—'

'I didn't think you'd been?'

'Not since the war.'

'Before?'

'I—'

Their guide introduced a Shiraz and splashed a sample into Laura's glass. The deep red liquid shimmered as Laura swirled it against the light. Jacques raised the glass to his nose, breathed in deeply before taking a sip, then swirled it in his mouth and swallowed.

'The reds are best,' he said and turned to Laura. 'You were asking?'

'Tom mentioned meeting Canadian delegations, and I thought maybe you'd met.' Her face warmed. She needed more practice to lie convincingly.

Jacques sipped his wine and looked thoughtful. 'I never met Tom or Peter in Iraq.'

'What about in Australia?'

'No, not here either.'

Jacques poured the remnants of his glass into the bucket and they both declined a taste of the port. He chatted to the guide, his manner animated and warm, and Laura wondered at her tension around him. He couldn't have been at the hotel that night. She must be mistaken.

Jacques took an order form, checked which wines she preferred and purchased six bottles.

A string of traffic again accompanied the drive to their lunch venue. Melancholy settled over her. Jacques confused her. He seemed to care. His role suited that side of him, but there was an edge she couldn't interpret.

Stark rows of denuded vines pruned into small hard kernels of promise flashed past the car windows. Her and Tom's visit during harvest time was very different. The lush vineyards burst with ripened fruit and green fulsome leaves. Like her life. It had changed dramatically, and she was struggling to adjust.

At the next winery, they tasted more wine and selected a bottle of Shiraz to accompany their lunch. Again, the past intruded; this restaurant had been one of Tom's favourites.

Couples or small groups occupied almost all the tables. The waiter brought table water, poured the wine, and took their orders. The surrounding chatter and laughter helped, or maybe it was the wine or Jacques' relaxed company, but finally, she allowed the light and sunny ambience, and his storytelling, to carry her along.

Their conversation stalled as they ate. She savoured the tender and moist duck confit with the tangy plum sauce. Jacques attacked the succulent lamb shanks with gusto. They ordered coffees but decided against dessert.

'When is your daughter travelling to New York?' Jacques asked.

'Next month. She's in Sydney at the moment.'

'I'll be back in New York then. Send me her dates when they're confirmed.'

Laura smiled. Maybe Mel could identify what kind of man Jacques was.

The driveway into Carol Minton winery revealed a small boutique winery nestled in a valley. A creek divided the vineyard into stark parcels and rows of stunted vines led the eye towards a line of trees. Inside, a large wooden table with director's chairs lining one side dominated the compact tasting room. Two sets of glasses and six bottles were arranged in anticipation. The middle-aged employee introduced himself and explained the planned proceedings.

The view spanned the vineyard, and the tree-lined creek sparkled with patches of soft afternoon sunlight. Laura savoured the deep, full-bodied wines and her cheeks warmed with the alcohol. She wasn't a wine connoisseur, but she knew what she liked. She took her time to enjoy all six wines. Jacques asked her opinion and drew attention to the rich colour, spicy aroma, or a specific hint of fruit or chocolate. He joked with ease, and she laughed as they slowly worked through the selection. Their guide didn't hurry them and neither did Jacques. They stayed longer than planned and she was sorry to see the day end.

Their driver meandered through the valley towards the highway. The traffic eased, and she and Jacques slid into a gentle camaraderie. Laura suspected that the wine they'd consumed helped. His attentiveness made her dismiss the flashback entirely. She must have imagined it.

On a narrow bend, a white car roared past, then swerved sharply to cut in front. Red brake lights flared. Laura was propelled forward. The seat belt ripped into her shoulder and she cried out in surprise and pain. The limousine veered into the centre of the road, clipped the tail of the white sedan, then accelerated to pull alongside. A four-wheel-drive wagon rounded the bend; coming straight at them. The limousine surged forward, speeding on the wrong side of the road. They pulled level with the white sedan but couldn't pass him. A horn blared. The four-wheel-drive veered left and plunged into the culvert. The limousine jerked back onto the left-hand side of the road in front of the white sedan. They sped smoothly into the next bend.

'That idiot nearly ran us off the road!' their driver shouted. 'He cut in front of us, then slammed on the brakes. He nearly ran us into those trees.'

'We have to make sure the occupants of the 4WD are alright.' Jacques turned to Laura. 'Are you hurt?'

'I don't think so. Are you OK?' Laura rubbed her sore shoulder. He nodded.

By the time they'd turned around, the white sedan had disappeared. The 4WD vehicle perched in the ditch, its driver stood rubbing his head as he surveyed the damage. It had narrowly missed a thick, metal stobie pole. Jacques and the other driver exchanged details and Jacques offered to pay for damages, suggesting they didn't need to involve the police. Laura undid her seat belt and shakily got out.

'We've had a lucky escape,' the driver said to Laura. 'It wasn't just bad driving. He was deliberately trying to run us off the road. If we'd crashed into that huge gumtree by the side of the road, we'd have come off second best.'

Laura trembled. Who would want to run them off the road deliberately? Was he trying to hurt her or Jacques? Laura shivered. It was that car, the one with the N.U.T. number plate.

Back in the car, Jacques dismissed any suggestion it was deliberate.

'It was an accident? Either a bad driver or maybe he was under the influence of drugs or alcohol.'

Laura wasn't convinced, especially when she caught the driver's eyes in the rear-view mirror. He didn't believe Jacques either.

223

Chapter 28

John Master's limousine was on time and as the driver navigated the busy city streets, John phoned Skye.

'I'm helping Anton throw an impromptu party for the crew,' she explained when she finally answered. A voice mumbled in the background, and she giggled. 'How are you?'

'A bit tired. I've got a long, boring drive ahead of me right now.' John sighed.

'It's good of you to find time to call me in your busy schedule.' Was that sarcasm in her voice? 'I've been working hard too, I had—'

'I've booked an extra night in Milan to unwind. I'm staying at the Palazzo Hotel. I—'

'Where? The one featured in last month's magazine? You're staying there? By yourself?'

'Why not? I've earned it.'

'I've wanted to stay there but—'

John frowned. It was always about her. She never acknowledged his hard work.

'What have you been doing?' he redirected.

'Anton has offered me some new work.'

'Anton. You're working with him again?'

'I've been working on a new spring catalogue —'

'And of course, that's with Anton.'

Skye sighed. 'As a matter of fact, it is. He's great company, and he came to the industry event as my plus-one.'

'I've told you before, don't get mixed up with Anton or…' John clenched his fists.

'Or what? You're swanning about in Europe, living it up without me. What do you want me to do? Sit at home and knit?'

'I don't have time for this. I'll call again tonight.'

'That's right. You don't have time for this. By this, of course, you mean me. Don't bother ringing me later. It's now six-thirty at night, so I'll be asleep unless I'm out partying.' Skye hung up.

John clenched and unclenched his fist. Anton was a bad influence. John caught the driver's eye in the rear-vision mirror and shrugged. He'd sort out Skye when he got home.

Once free of the drab apartment blocks on Milan's outskirts, they sped along the *autostrada* passing rural scenery interspersed with small villages and industrial sites. John sagged back into the seat; his eyes were heavy, but simmering anger wouldn't let him relax.

They stopped at an Autogrill for a cool drink and toilet break. Holiday-makers buying chocolate bars and assorted junk food filled the shop. John took his iced coffee outside, but the petrol fumes chased him back inside to a small table by a window. A mix of sad and happy memories assailed him. As a young boy, he'd loved the Autogrills and their colourful packets of usually forbidden treats. Chocolate was still his favourite; any flavour would do. He took the last gulp of his drink and bought a chocolate bar.

The past held irritations and unexpected obstacles. A familiar ache throbbed in his chest. Babbo's unrealistic expectations weighed on him. John craved his father's approval. Dimi, on the other hand, charmed their parents with ease. Her prettiness and demure attitude gained their adoration. He shivered. His little sister became John's tormentor when out of sight of their parents. She provoked him and somehow he always got into trouble while she escaped any blame.

Revenge would be sweet. Back in the limousine, he tossed the chocolate across the seat. He didn't need the past. He had the future.

Near Genoa, the road dived in and out of tunnels, eventually skirting around the perimeter of the city. Between long stretches of darkness, he caught glimpses of hilly terrain and snatches of coastal blue. The hills were greener than those at home and not as tall. He remembered Babbo hiding in a cave for three months to avoid the prosecutor and his lieutenants. John laughed. It was an extreme tactic, the kind that Babbo so often employed, and he'd risked becoming a laughing stock, but the prosecutor was dead and Babbo was still alive.

Of course, Babbo hiding away for three months caused other, more personal, issues. Kleb's father had consoled John's mother. At least that's what everyone thought, but they became close; too close. They broke the rules and their behaviour threatened the family's security. Someone had to step in and put a stop to it.

John had started the rumour about Kleb's father's betrayal, but John would make sure that Kleb never found out. Letting Kleb believe Dimi was responsible was much more useful. His desire for revenge on Dimi was a perfect result and advanced John's ambitions.

The car sped along an older stretch of *autostrada* with ugly corrugated iron barriers and weaved through the convoys of trucks and vans. Closer to the city, clusters of apartment blocks appeared on the hillside and they gradually formed a dense wall. Behind here would be the charred remains of the factory he'd seen on the news last night.

Thinking of this upcoming meeting with Franco reignited his simmering anger. In the old days, Franco knew his place. He'd been a reliable stool pigeon; Babbo's eyes and ears into his traditional rivals, the northern families, and hopefully, he was still well connected.

The driver dropped John near the Santa Margherita marina and he strolled through the open space by the water's edge. The village was bigger than he'd expected and a trickle of tourists spilled onto the marina and foreshore. It was the gateway to Portofino, the playground for the rich and over-resourced, rather than a destination of its own.

John ambled into the town and found an inviting trattoria. A table by the front window, in the fan-cooled room, provided a view over the piazza. Shorts and T-shirt clad tourists wandered past but, in the café, he spotted the locals in their shirts and trousers. The occasional well-dressed businessman strutted past the window, the tailored designer suits showing not only their style but also their success.

He ordered an entrée sized *penne al forno* and a glass of local red wine. He ate his early lunch slowly, savouring the flavours and channelling calm, although he missed the peas and *caciocavallo* cheese his mother always added. John's hands shook slightly. Franco was an important link and it was risky meeting people from his past. John stroked his chin, fingering the slight ridge of the scar. He'd escaped recognition so far and hopefully, he'd fool Franco too.

At 1.30 p.m. he walked to the Via Della Vittoria. Tucked into the archways, opposite the Basilica, a choir sang. Onlookers filled the piazza and butted against the church doors. John squeezed through, uttering 'scuzi' without much result. He held his breath against the overpowering combination of sweat, perfume, and aftershave.

Once through the church doors, he brushed himself down and straightened his clothes, then checked his wallet and change pocket. Sunlight streamed down from the dome and the gold-leaf decorations and colourful frescos glistened brightly. Dramatic religious scenes adorned the transept dome's canopy and scolding stuccoes covered the massive columns separating the three naves. Space closed in on him. John shivered as his childhood priest's stern face flashed across his mind.

People, bent in silent prayer, were dotted along the pews. A trickle of tourists talked and camera flashes popped. Lit candles flickered in the corner and smoke laced the air. John sat beside an ornate, but small, side chapel partially obscured by a pillar. From here, he could watch the entrance unobserved.

As soon as the short but sinewy man entered, John realised Ferret had hardly changed at all in the last five years. His hair was shorter and noticeably thinner on top, his moustache was gone and he was thicker around the middle, but that was all. His furtive glances sharpened his ferret-like features, and he seemed uncomfortable in the stylish suit. He sat near the back, watching. John waited, ensuring Ferret was alone, before quietly walking over to sit beside him.

'*Merda*!' Franco the Ferret startled. 'You are John?' he asked in a whisper.

'How are you Fe—Franco?'

'There's no time for small talk.'

John bristled. 'I need information.'

'I don't do that anymore.'

'I thought you didn't want to waste time,' John said sternly.

Ferret blinked repeatedly. His features turned wary, and he nodded. '*Andiamo!* OK, but hurry up.'

'Do you know Stavros Carnegie?' Ferret nodded warily and John continued, 'I need information on him and his business.' Casterlow's contact had powerful connections, and John was keen to learn more.

Ferret twitched and without turning to look at John, shook his head. 'That kind of information is worth more than my life,' he whispered.

'It can be, whether you tell me or not.'

'What do you mean?'

'People will learn about our meeting and they'll believe you talked, anyway.'

Ferret resumed his rapid blinking.

'So why don't we cut the crap? You agreed to meet and now tell me what I want to know, *Andiamo*, and no one needs to know.' John whispered.

'You could set me up, anyway.'

'Why would I? Give me what I need and you become a valuable man to have as a friend.'

Ferret's eyes darted to John's face and John turned away.

'Have we met before?' he asked. 'Your voice—'

'Let's get on with this. I want to know everything about Stavros Carnegie and his business. I need details of his connection to Iraq and Australia and anything else he's mixed up in.'

John squirmed under Ferret's stare.

'Can you get what I need or do I have to—'

'OK, OK. But it's... *pericoloso*...dangerous. Carnegie is being watched.'

'By who and why?'

'He dabbles in conflicts and has made enemies of both the Russian and American governments. He steps on people's toes. Rumours say the Australians have enlisted his help with something new. Maybe some kind of new chemical weapon.'

'I need to know everything; his contacts and his business interests,' John said. Casterlow's project wasn't as secret as he'd thought. 'And the Russians? How much do they know?'

'One of their mafia families is working on it.'

John leaned forward. 'Boris and Svetlana?'

'How did you know? The government has offered them immunity for information—' Ferret shrugged and blinked slowly.

Boris and Svetlana were John's connection to the Devil's Guard, but he hadn't known they could endanger Casterlow's project. Suddenly he remembered the woman; his *entertainment* with the great conversational skills. She'd been impressed by his family business, but had he been indiscreet? What a mess!

'I also need to know everything about Wayne Skollov.'

'The Australian arms dealer? Is he connected to Carnegie?'

'That's what I need to find out; who he's dealing with.'

They agreed on the details and a timeframe, then haggled over the price. Although he wasn't cheap, John accepted, he'd already proved valuable.

Ferret slinked out of the church first and John waited. He scanned the ornate surroundings and, out of the corner of his eye, noticed a dark form leaning against a pillar. The shadow straightened and followed Ferret out through the huge wooden doors. John dashed to the exit, but Ferret and the dark shape were swallowed by the crowd leaving the finished concert. Had Ferret brought security or was Ferret, the eternal watcher, being watched?

John searched the faces and the dark-haired crowd. He spun around and glimpsed ferret-like features in the alley leading to the marina. He followed.

At the square, Ferret jumped into the driver's side of a white Renault and as soon as the traffic allowed, he pulled out from the kerb but didn't progress far. A traffic jam blocked the road ahead, giving John time to grab the first taxi at the rank. He directed the taxi driver to follow the Renault. Finally free of the town traffic, they skirted along the narrow, coast-hugging drive to Portofino. Despite a blue fiat pulling in between them, John kept the Renault in his sights.

In Portofino, Ferret parked the Renault in a private area reserved for yacht owners. The blue fiat veered off and John directed his taxi to pull over at the entrance to the small, colourful square.

John stepped along the dock, eying the row of impressive boats bobbing in the water. Each expensive yacht flanked an even bigger one. This was the view he'd seen on the TV report last night. He just needed to find out who owned which yacht. Crew members cleaned the decks on the first two, and a couple enjoyed a sumptuous lunch on the deck of the third. The next looked empty and forlorn until a short, rotund man, dressed in an expensive polo shirt and slacks appeared. Behind him stood Ferret, body language pleading and a pained expression on his face. John froze. He pulled back into the shadows and watched.

John vividly remembered Babbo's rival as a cold, hard punk, ego aplenty and seriously overconfident back then. Now, as head of the northern family business, he had a firm grip on the controls, dominating building projects and construction contracts, at least until the latest scandals. It was his factory that had been destroyed by fire in the report last night. His power and influence stemmed from a history of treachery. John shivered. His enemies often disappeared, permanently.

The rotund mafia punk welcomed a group of equally rotund and immaculately dressed old men in designer suits. Ferret moved to the side and John frowned. His father and his henchmen. He stared. John hadn't seen him for five years, either. Babbo had grown fatter but still had a thick head of hair.

John scanned the surroundings for anyone suspicious also watching the yacht, but saw no one. The men shook hands. Babbo and the northern punk sat down in the corner while their men stood guard near the entrance. There were stiff smiles and nods as they spoke. Perhaps the looming threat from the Russians made them put aside their usual tensions and rivalries. If so, it must be serious.

As John watched, a loud boom echoed from the end of the dock. A boat exploded, and the force sent John crashing to the ground. Debris rained across the marina. Flames shot into the air and the splintered yacht tilted dangerously. John saw, rather than heard, screams. Fragments splashed into the water while heads bobbed and hands grabbed at the wreckage.

John pushed past the people moving towards the action, instead joining the stream of people fleeing. He ran. Sirens wailed, and he stumbled up the cobblestoned path, trying to find refuge.

Who'd set that blast and why? Was it designed to kill or just a warning? Where was Babbo now? Was he dead? John shivered. Was that possible? The mafia families spawned many enemies, not just the Russians. Any one of them could have tried to eliminate these powerful men.

Police vehicles sped past into the piazza. A small, plain church near the dock entrance offered respite, and John slipped inside. The cool interior summoned the calming memories of Harper. She'd loved simple churches and often made him detour to look inside. He bent over, gasping to catch his breath and willing his heartbeat to slow. Then he saw a small group gathered in front of the altar. They stared at his interruption and John stepped towards a pew. That's when he saw a dark-brown coffin perched on a stand. The raised lid revealed pink, gnarled hands clasped across the chest of a dearly departed. John stepped back into the aisle. He tried to look away, but the hands drew his eyes. Death. It was following him.

Chapter 29

Happy laughter, squealing, and shouting accompanied by mothers' stern commands, echoed through the Marion Swim Centre undercover parking station. Laura joined a procession of women laden with bags, kickboards, and sundry swim gear, corralling their children towards the lift.

When the lift doors opened, two of the waiting families moved in and scrunched along the walls, leaving space for Laura. She smiled a thank you, but the mothers' eyes were already glued to their phones. Laura ignored the occasional knock or slap on her legs from the play-fighting children. She plunged her hands deep into her pockets, tracing her fingers along the outline of the envelope with the mysterious key. Her nerves twitched.

Inside the swim centre, she lined up at the front desk waiting as family groups confirmed class times and memberships. When it was her turn, she placed the key on the bench in front of the attendant and explained her dilemma.

'It looks similar, but ours aren't red.' The attendant examined the key. 'The lockers are cleared every week.'

'It's been months.' Laura's spirits sank; Tom would have ensured his collection was safe. Maybe the key was a red herring.

'I'm new here. I'll ask what happens to belongings that are cleared.'

He walked up to his colleague engrossed in her computer screen. A blue streak zipped across the front of her dark hair, matching her cobalt blue framed glasses. Otherwise, everything else about her was grey. She reluctantly tore her eyes away and, after a short discussion, accompanied the attendant to the counter.

'What exactly did the locker contain?' the woman asked.

'I don't know. This key was among my late husband's things.'

A pained expression sped across her face. 'I'm sorry, but this isn't ours. We don't have red keys.'

'Do you have any suggestions?'

She shrugged. 'Our other swim centre at North Adelaide uses the same system.' She shook her blue streaked hair and returned to her computer.

The attendant smiled. 'Good luck, ' he said and turned to the next person in the queue.

As Laura stepped back, she tripped over the girl standing immediately behind her. She grabbed the girl's arm to steady herself.

'I'm so sorry.'

The redhead smiled. 'It's OK. I didn't mean to listen, but I could help with that key. It looks a lot like mine.' She showed Laura a key that was identical except for the number etched into the red circle. 'It's from the long-term lockers at the gym upstairs. I can show you.'

'It looks the same.' Laura's hopes soared.

'I have a combined membership. It's handy because I can use both the gym and the pool. During school holidays, the reduced number of swimming lanes turns this into a big holiday play centre,' she grumbled as they walked down the corridor together.

Swim centre sounds: splashing, the boing of the diving board, and squealing, echoed from beyond the pool entrance. The smell of chlorine assaulted Laura's nose.

'I see what you mean,' Laura said, then added, 'Thanks for your help. I was running out of ideas.'

'The gym offers long-term lockers to regulars.'

'You have to apply for it?'

'Yes, the cost is added to your membership if you want one.'

The three-year combined membership that Tom bought for Becky as a surprise present had been a considerate gift, but maybe he'd had an ulterior motive, too.

They climbed the stairs to the first floor, where banks of beige lockers formed a U-shape against the foyer walls. The upper rows could fit a sports bag, but the lockers along the bottom were bigger. Red topped keys protruded from some doors and each locker sported a number prefixed by the letter 'L'.

'Thanks, you've been a great help.' Laura's hands trembled as she reached for her key.

The redhead nodded. Laura scanned the numbers and there, at the bottom corner, was L132.

'It's here. Thanks again,' Laura said.

'Great, glad I could help.' The redhead turned and disappeared back down the stairs.

Laura poked the key into the lock, but it jammed. She didn't want to apply too much force. What if it broke? But everything matched; it must be the right key. She cursed and tried again, this time jiggling the key up and down. Finally, it scraped in. One turn and the door sprung open. Laura scanned the foyer before pulling a bulging black satchel free.

A BioPharma advertising logo adorned the front pocket. Tom's old business card filled the plastic window beside it. It was one of Tom's conference freebies. Laura unlatched the flap and stared at the files spilling from the main compartment. The large zippered section contained two notebooks and another file. She groaned. She already had enough files and paperwork to last her a lifetime of searching. Her heart sank. She'd hoped to unravel the mystery, but how would she make sense of all this paperwork?

Voices broke through her thoughts. Two men, toting sports bags, raced up the stairs and strode towards the lockers. Laura straightened, but they passed without giving her a second glance. She was about to close the locker door, then hesitated. She swept her hand inside and her fingers brushed against a small parcel tucked into the back corner. The Canadian stamped packet was postmarked January 2006 and addressed to Tom at home. She stuffed the parcel into the satchel, relocked the locker, and raced down the stairs.

Laura stowed the satchel in the boot, then sat in the driver's seat with her head propped on the headrest. She could see Tom systematically gathering this information.

March 2003

'What made you think of a gym membership? It's a great idea.' Laura wasn't saying it was odd for him to think about Becky's enjoyment of the gym and swim centre, but it was odd nonetheless.

'It'll help her to stay fit.' Tom shuffled his feet as though he'd been caught doing something he shouldn't.

'I'm sure it'll be good for her.' She bit back the *'and so unlike you to think of it'* threatening to escape.

The TV volume ramped up with an advertisement for a program featuring Andrew Wilke. His resignation from the Intelligence Service headlined the news for days. A short excerpt showed him declaring that he had no choice. He had *'an ethical conflict between his duty and his respect for the truth.'* The program would discuss allegations that the government was distorting intelligence about the weapons of mass destruction.

'He's a brave man,' Laura said.

'Yes, either brave or foolhardy. Anyone who puts their career, indeed their life, on the line has to be one or the other. Is it worth it?'

'It's a personal decision, but where would we be without whistleblowers?'

'That's true, in theory. In practice, the government machinery shuts you down and makes you look suspect. They attack your credibility, they sling so much mud, that most people don't believe you, anyway. You lose your reputation and get branded a troublemaker. People prefer to believe the government even when they know they lie.'

'I'm sure the personal costs are astronomical, but we need people of courage to speak out, otherwise, we'll become like Russia or East Germany. The dictators control the media, keep tightly held secrets, and escape scrutiny.'

'Yes, well, the media isn't so free here either,' Tom said, then retreated into his thoughts.

***

That was three years ago. She'd waved it away as a theoretical exercise. The Wilke episode had proven Tom right. Intelligence hadn't supported the existence of weapons of mass destruction or going to war, and no weapons were ever found. Wilke's life was turned upside down. His reputation was attacked, but Australia joined the war with Iraq, anyway. Had Wilke's sacrifice for the truth been worth it?

Whistleblowers were important. How else could the public hold the government to account? Honesty and integrity couldn't be maintained if whistleblowers were silenced and afraid to speak. It was getting worse. The government was threatening to prosecute all whistleblowers and intimidate them into silence.

Tom's pangs of guilt for withdrawing his protests about the Wheat Board scandal worsened once the hearings started. It confirmed he'd been right. The papers and documents in this satchel were more recent, from another concern. What had he been working on? A shiver travelled up her spine. Tom and Corrinne were silenced and now a government minister, Furness, had died before he could reveal what he knew. It was an unlikely coincidence.

The stakes could be higher than she'd bargained for. In that case, was she strong enough, or determined enough to go on? Did she have the courage to finish Tom's work? More questions she couldn't answer.

At home, Laura propped the satchel beside the sofa. She should feel triumph now she'd found the mystery package, but her feeling was more akin to dread. Maybe they would reveal a very different picture. She believed Tom was an honourable man, but what if his disillusion had transformed him. Pushed him into doing things he wouldn't be proud of.

She strode to the wine rack but stopped midway. Instead, she sat down again and began sorting the dog-eared and creased contents. Laura created neat piles by her feet, laying folders to the right nearest the wall, and stacking the loose papers next to them.

Laura scanned the APATO letterhead emblazoned documents. Bassarti was mentioned. Fayyaad explained that it was a notorious prison. Could it also be the name of a town? A bright pink Post-it note bookmarked a Fast-Track order form and a hand-drawn black arrow pointed to a partially obscured signature. Thick black text slashed through the name and only the beginning, 'F u r' was clear. Furness?

As Laura dragged out the notebooks, the Canadian parcel toppled onto the floor. She opened the flap. Inside were three DVDs; each with a handwritten label like the one she and Mel watched. A different name and date were printed on each one.

She shivered. It was time to face up to what this was about. Laura laid the DVDs on the TV console and turned both the TV and DVD player on. She ejected the movie she'd watched last night, dropped the disc onto its case, but the news report on TV grabbed her attention.

Chapter 30

The camera panned back. That street! The unit in the background was Robby's. Her knees buckled as the camera scanned the damage. Smashed windows in nearby homes, front yards showered in shrapnel, and a shard of twisted metal plunged through the front window of the house across the road. The elderly occupants, reading in their front room, had narrowly escaped being speared.

Witnesses reported seeing a man wearing a balaclava and dressed in dark clothing pitch a flaming bottle under the parked car and speed away on a motorcycle. A neighbour explained how he'd been repelled by the intense heat. He'd watched, horrified and distressed, not knowing if there was anyone inside. The camera crossed to a blackened, torturous wreck, a barely recognisable car. The charred Toyota with a patch of red visible on the twisted back door was like Robby's new car. Laura fell into the chair. Her hand clasped to her mouth. Robby?

With a shaking hand, Laura dialled Robby's number. It rang and rang. Eventually, his answering machine barked instructions, and she stuttered a semi-coherent message.

What else could she do? She was stunned, speechless, dumbstruck, all the clichés applied. She grabbed her car keys and jacket, then dashed out of the door.

Her knuckles turned white as she gripped the steering wheel and listened to the radio news. A car had been firebombed in Robby's street. Fortunately, no one was inside the car. Air rushed from her lungs. Robby was alive. Tears trickled down her cheeks. A new worry formed. Where was he? Was he in danger or maybe hurt?

Robby's street was blocked off and she could only find a park a block away. Three police vehicles and two fire trucks blocked her view of the scene, and she couldn't even see Robby's unit. She pushed past onlookers until she stood at the main barricade. The smell of smoke and petrol brought more tears to her eyes.

One of Robby's neighbours, the older lady from next door, stood dazed and disoriented beside a policewoman. Laura shouted and waved her hands, trying to get her attention, but the noise and activity drowned her out. When another fire truck arrived, the crowd was bustled aside and Laura darted past the barricade and rushed towards the older woman. A firm grip pulled her back by the arm and yanked her to a stop. In front of her was the charred remains of a car. Robby's car. She froze. The blackened shell sat crumpled on the kerb where Robby so often parked. Fumes bit at her throat and the smell of burning petrol made her cough. She couldn't speak. Her eyes watered as the fumes combined with her rising emotions to leave her feeling overwhelmed.

'You can't come in here,' the policeman said firmly.

Laura finally found her voice. 'My son's car.' She pointed.

'The burned one?'

She nodded. 'Is he alright?'

'He wasn't in the car,' he said gently.

She slumped, and the policeman held her up. Once the tears started, she couldn't stop crying.

'When did you last hear from him?' he asked.

'About a week ago when I picked him up.' She didn't explain. He'd escaped the notice of the police then. 'Why would someone firebomb his car?'

'We don't know the details yet.' He led her to the police car and encouraged her to sit. Laura accepted the offered tissue and wiped her eyes.

'Can you tell us anything that would help?' he asked gently.

Laura shook her head. Words failed her.

'Perhaps you should go home. There's nothing you can do here. We'll talk to you once we've established what's happened. We may have some questions for you then.'

Laura nodded. He was right, but she didn't want to leave. A news cameraman pointed at her and the reporter beside him turned from the onlooker she was interviewing and stared. Laura shivered. She couldn't talk to them now.

A policewoman wrote down Laura's details and gently talked her through the next steps. The words were soothing, although Laura's attention was elsewhere. Her whole body trembled and her mind raced, trying to understand what, why, and most of all, where Robby was now. She was just getting in the way and stopping the police from doing their job, but she couldn't leave. She felt closer to her son sitting here than if she were at home.

It took some time, but the policewoman eventually convinced Laura she should go. Loud shouting sounded at the barricade. A large, round man, carrying two bags of shopping, stood by the tape. He shouted incoherently at a policeman, creating a disturbance around him. With the reporter sufficiently distracted, Laura took the opportunity to dart through the barricade beside the fire truck and scoot around the corner.

In the cocoon of her car, the tears again trailed down her face. She phoned Robby again, but there was still no answer. She phoned Eva and left a message.

At home, Laura left a message on Becky's phone and then found her address book containing the phone numbers of some of Robby's old friends. He must be somewhere. The first two calls went to message services, and the next two friends hadn't seen Robby for years. She kept trying, working through the list slowly but unsuccessfully. Her heart sank further with each call. He could be lying hurt somewhere or in trouble. She needed to find him.

When Eva appeared at the door, Laura let herself sink into an embrace and be consoled.

'No one's seen him. I don't know what to do next,' she explained.

'These young ones never answer their phones. If you have addresses or know where they work, we could visit them,' Eva suggested.

The phone rang, and Laura's hopes soared.

'How are you, Laura?' Peter's voice dashed her hopes. 'I just heard about Robby. Is he alright?'

'I can't find him.'

'Did you know this is bikie related? How long has Robby been mixed up with them?'

'His girlfriend…Shayida's brother is president of the Pythons or something like that…' Laura couldn't go on.

How could she believe her son was not involved with a bikie gang anymore? He was connected to the lawless, criminal world of drugs, guns, and whatever else. She and Tom had worked hard to instil values of common good and fairness into their children, yet Robby was on the wrong side, in trouble, and she had no idea how to help him.

There was a moment of silence before Peter asked, 'Is there anything I can do?'

'Eva and I are going to look for him. I don't know what else to do?'

'Promise you'll call me if you find him. He'll need my help. The police can't adequately protect him, those gangs are too strong. I'll do whatever I can. Make sure you let me know.'

A wave of gratitude washed over her. This was the Peter of old, her helpful and good friend. One positive from the latest events.

The doorbell rang. Laura ended the call and raced to open it.

Two uniformed police officers, a man and a woman, stood on her doorstep.

'You've found Robby?' she asked before they could speak.

'Er, no. We hoped Robby might be here,' the policewoman said. She stepped forward into the doorway and her head barely came to Laura's shoulders.

'I haven't seen him for weeks,' Laura said. Eva stepped up beside Laura, giving her strength.

'We were hoping to talk to him.'

'I've rung around, but no one has seen him. I was just going out to visit his friends. I don't know what else to do.' Laura wrung her hands. 'I can't sit around and do nothing.'

'He possibly knows who did this, which puts him in danger. We need to locate him quickly,' the muscular policeman explained.

Laura's hand flew up to her throat.

'We can protect him,' the policewoman added.

'Since dating Shayida, his life has totally changed—'

'Shayida? Is that Shayida Saviento, Nick Saviento's sister?' the policeman asked.

Laura nodded.

'Has Robby been associating with bikie members? Have you seen him wear bikie colours? Or wear a leather jacket with the Python's insignia or rank on it?'

'I've never seen him wear anything like that, but he doesn't live here. He doesn't even have a motorbike.'

'You are aware Shayida is allegedly connected to the Pythons?'

Shayida was involved in her brother's gang and, after their talk about drugs, she was suspicious about Robby's involvement. This world he was mixed up in was foreign to Laura, belonging in novels, on TV, or in a movie, not real life; at least not her real life.

'There's a gang war escalating and we need to find him urgently,' the policewoman explained. At least she didn't appear to be judging Laura.

'What do you think has happened to him?'

'He's either scarpered, which would be wise, or they've kidnapped him.'

Despite the matter-of-fact delivery, the scenario shocked her. Kidnapped?

'We'll keep you informed. If you hear from him or anything that could help, call me.' The policewoman handed her a card with her name and contact details, and Laura put it in the hall table drawer.

After the police left, Laura took a deep breath. 'Let's go. I need to find Robby. I need to know he's safe.'

Chapter 31

At The King's Arms hotel, the bartender was serving a customer when Eva and Laura walked in. Two scruffily dressed men watched a horse race on TV at one end of the bar and a middle-aged couple lounged in a booth in the corner; otherwise, the pub was empty. The ka-ching of pokies from next door combined with the soft drone of the TV commentary to create an old-fashioned pub ambience. Along with the disinfectant smell, it reminded Laura of old times.

'Hello, Laura,' the young bartender's face showed surprise. 'What can I get you?'

'Hi. I'm not here for a drink—'

'Although we could use one,' interrupted Eva with a half-laugh.

'Have you seen Robby lately?' Laura asked. This young man and Robby had been close friends before Robby dropped out of university.

He looked up from wiping the bar. 'I saw Robby about a month ago, in a club in town.' He began wiping again, avoiding Laura's gaze. 'He's mixing with a very different crowd now.' He looked up again and frowned. 'Why?'

'I think he's in trouble. He's gone missing.'

'He'll turn up.'

He hadn't heard the news and, as Laura explained, his face transformed from impassive to shocked in one easy movement.

'No way! Shit, he's got in deep!'

'You can see why I'm worried.' Laura wrote down her phone number. 'Ring me if you see him or hear anything, please.'

He nodded. 'Sure thing.'

Laura dragged herself back to the car. She consulted her list, striking out his name.

The next two friends on the list weren't home. She wasn't sure if they still lived there or if their phone numbers were still the same, but she phoned and left messages anyway, stressing how urgent it was.

They found another of Robby's friends at home. His haggard face and tousled hair looked like he'd just got out of bed. He cleared a space on the sofa, explaining how he worked the night shift at the local hospital.

'There isn't anything more I can tell you from yesterday. I haven't seen him for about six months.' He sounded irritated.

Laura frowned. 'What do you mean from yesterday?'

'When you rang, I told you I hadn't seen Robby—'

'I didn't speak to you yesterday. I couldn't get through and left a message.'

He grimaced. 'Don't you remember? You told me what happened and asked if I'd seen Robby.'

'Did she say she was Laura?' Eva frowned.

'She said she was Mrs Schultz, Robby's mum.'

Laura's heart lurched. 'I didn't talk to you yesterday and I go by Laura Gynne. I don't use Schultz.'

'She sounded a bit muffled, but I figured you were upset. The voice was different; more high-pitched.'

'Did you ever meet Shayida, his girlfriend?' Eva asked.

He nodded. 'Yeah. What a stunner! She's a bit tough for me, though. Not sure how Robby pulled that off,' he said before catching himself and muttering, 'sorry.'

Laura gave him her phone number, entreating him to ring if he

246

heard from Robby.

They learned nothing new from the rest of their visits. They confirmed that Robby had drifted away from all his school or university friends, even before he'd met Shayida, although she'd intensified the narrowing of his life. She and Tom hadn't been generous, to push him towards something constructive, but now Laura wondered if it had pushed him into the first easy option.

Back at Laura's house, Eva opened a bottle and poured two glasses of wine.

'Did Shayida ring him and pretend to be you?' Eva handed Laura a glass.

'Who else could it be? Why would she pretend to be me?'

'Maybe she thought they'd tell her the truth if they thought it was you. After all, a girlfriend can be looking for a guy for different reasons.'

'She hasn't rung me.'

'If there's a gang dispute, she might be in the middle of it.'

'I'm getting desperate. I have to find Robby, to know he's safe. Maybe she's trying to help him.'

Eva stared at Laura and laughed. 'You think?'

Laura shrugged. She could let the police handle this, but maybe Peter was right. She didn't want to expose him to more danger? If Shayida was looking for him, it meant the gang hadn't kidnapped him. Maybe Shayida could answer Laura's questions.

Laura picked up her glass and took a deep drink. 'I'm not sure if I'll learn much, but I'm ringing Shayida.'

'If it's gang warfare, the firebomb could be a rival gang, not the Pythons,' Eva suggested.

'If so, why aren't they protecting him?' She didn't want them to protect him and draw him deeper into the club, but she wanted him safe.

'Maybe they are, and Shayida is pretending, to throw people off the scent.'

'Why ring Robby's friends?'

Eva sipped her wine. 'We don't know that she did.'

Laura's head ached. She didn't understand the criminal world Robby was mixed up in. There seemed to be bad guys, good bad guys, bad bad guys, and who knew what. It was a mess.

Laura searched her phone contacts, the pile of business cards in the hall table drawer, and the notes beside her lounge chair before finally finding Shayida's number in her diary. Before she could change her mind, she dialled.

A man answered. 'Ink Inc.'

'Can I speak to Shayida please?' Laura asked, successfully keeping the nervous quiver out of her voice.

'Who's calling?'

'It's Laura.'

Voices mumbled in the background and a door slammed.

'Hello. Laura?' Shayida asked.

'Yes, Robby's mum.'

'Oh,' Shayida said. 'Have you got any news?'

'No. I was hoping you did.'

'I haven't a clue where he could be.'

'Have you rung any of his friends?'

'I've rung mine, but no one knows where he is. I don't know any of his other friends.'

'I must find him,' Laura pleaded.

'You and me both,' Shayida emphasised.

'Have the police talked to you?'

'Not yet. My brother…he's going to kill him. I have to warn him—'

Laura gasped.

A door slammed in the background and a deep voice shouted, 'Who's that Shayida?'

'Just a customer, err, make an appointment when you're ready and we can work out the details.'

'Why is Nick angry with Robby?' Laura's throat constricted and her hand shook.

'I can't talk now. He has to stay low.'

'Let me know if you hear from him,' Laura said.

'Will do. You let me know too,' Shayida said before hanging up.

'So? What do you think?' Eva leaned forward in anticipation.

'Shayida didn't phone Robby's friend.' Laura believed her. 'How would she have his phone number?'

Eva drained the last of her wine. 'If *she* didn't, then who?'

Laura shrugged. 'Nick's angry with Robby. I don't know where Robby's hiding, but he must stay away from these thugs.'

Eva nodded. They sat quietly, Laura's mind whirring with confusion and fear. What should she do now?

'Sorry to mention this, but Fayyaad left me a message. He says it's urgent. He wants you to bring him Tom's files.'

'Oh, Eva. I can't think about that right now. Robby is my priority.'

'I understand.'

After Eva left, Laura's mind swirled with mysteries. Why would Nick *kill* Robby? What was all this about? And why did Fayyaad want Tom's DVDs and files? She couldn't let Tom's mystery distract her now. Robby needed her.

Chapter 32

'Hi, Mum. I can't talk for long; my mobile credit is running out,' Robby whispered down the phone.

'My god, Robby! Where are you?' Laura's eyes brimmed with tears of relief. Two days of worry, stress, and sleeplessness were taking their toll and made her feel much older than fifty-nine.

'Not over the phone, Mum.'

'The police are looking for you.'

'They're not the only ones.' Robby sighed. 'Don't tell the fuzz anything. I'll become a bigger target.'

'Oh, sweetheart, what are you mixed up in?'

'Can you bring me some clothes and money without going near the unit? You've got some things at your house, they'll do. I can't come to the house, it's too obvious.'

'What's going on, Robby?'

'I can't explain, but she's been using me. I was just a decoy.'

'Shayida?' Frustration lapped at Laura. His car was firebombed, and he was hiding. It couldn't be about him and Shayida arguing.

'I found out. Shayida and Bulldog are…lovers. I can't believe it. It's been going on since before we met. She's been using me to hide their relationship from Nick.'

'What's this got to do with your car being firebombed?'

'Bulldog's the enemy; the sergeant at arms for the Devil's Guard

Adelaide chapter. I told Nick about him and Shayida. I didn't mean to. Nick was furious, but Shayida denied it and now he believes her. I'm caught in the middle.'

'I still don't understand. This is about Shayida?' It wasn't about drugs or firearms, but jealousy and a lover's tryst?

'Shayida encouraged Bulldog's jealousy. He almost killed me. Nick thinks I'm making it up and Shayida's mad at me for telling her brother.'

'How did you get mixed up with these people?' Exasperation seeped into her voice. Robby was an easy scapegoat and this tangled web of lies and deceit proved it.

'Mum, I don't need lectures. I can't explain now. Where can we meet? It can be busy but not too public. Not anywhere you always go, just in case, or anywhere I'll be recognised.'

'I don't know where to suggest.' Laura didn't categorise her cafés as *safe* or *uninhabited by bikies*.

'Do you know Coffee Temple? It should be safe.'

Laura wrote down the address and Robby's directions.

'I need money, too. I can't use my cards and I need to get away, preferably out of the state.'

'I can sort out clothes and money. Do you have transport?'

'I have a car for now. I'm staying at a mate's flat while he's overseas. Can we meet today?'

'I could be there in about an hour.'

He wouldn't give Laura his new phone number *just in case* and his caution, 'Make sure you're not followed,' unnerved her more.

Laura swallowed down the lump in her throat. Elaborate conspiracies and deadly intrigue were hard to take seriously, but she must, for Robby's sake. She remembered Peter's offer of help and rang him. She was about to hang up when Abbie answered.

'You've heard from Robby?' she asked.

'I'm meeting him in an hour. I'll tell him about Peter's offer then.'

'Where are you meeting him? Maybe Peter could come too,'

Laura hesitated. It made sense, but she wanted time with Robby to talk to him, and to make sure he understood how much she cared. 'No, I'll sort it out with him first.'

'Don't be silly, Laura. He can take care of it straight away.'

It was tempting. If Peter came, Robby could be safe almost immediately.

Laura had an idea. 'I'll ring from there and Robby can talk to Peter to sort it out.'

'It would be easier to just tell me, Laura,' Abbie insisted. 'I'll make sure Peter gets the message right away.'

Her pushiness made Laura pull back. 'Maybe, but I need time with him first. I'll call from the café.' She hung up.

She folded some of Robby's old clothes into an overnight bag, throwing in some of Tom's T-shirts and a jacket, too. She stowed the bag in the car boot, then drove to the ATM to withdraw cash. She wasn't sure how much he'd need, but she was generous. She stuffed the envelope of money into her handbag while scrutinising the people around her. No one paid her any attention, but she walked back to her car via the shopping mall, backtracking several times to be sure.

Laura drove to the café, taking every twist and turn on the residential roads to cover her tracks. She constantly checked her rear-vision mirror. She wasn't certain, but a dark-brown Holden sedan appeared to follow her along the road, turning towards the café. At the roundabout, the Holden turned in the opposite direction and she exhaled noisily. She turned into the hotel carpark Robby had mentioned, then glanced in her rear-vision mirror just as the dark-brown sedan drove past. Laura waited. She wiped her palms on her jeans, her eyes fixed on the rear-vision mirror, but the Holden sedan didn't reappear.

Once she was assured the area was clear, she walked down the street, away from the café. Her heart raced. Footsteps behind her echoed her rhythm, and she turned to see a man in black trousers and a navy jumper, stop by a gate, two houses back. Her skin prickled. A dog barked and snarled as the man grabbed the gate lock. Laura walked on slowly and when she reached the corner, glanced back. The man had vanished. Had he gone into the house or the lane beside it? She doubled back and slipped into a lane on the other side of the street. A few minutes later, the man passed the end of the street. It was obvious he was searching for something or someone, but was he looking for her?

She couldn't take any risks. She waited, planning her next move. The bag felt heavy even though it contained mainly clothes. She hadn't expected to be carrying it on long walks around the suburbs. She walked out and doubled back. She turned into laneways to throw anyone off the trail. She almost got lost.

Finally, when she was satisfied she was no longer being followed, she ambled to the café strip and stared in the window of a mobile phone shop, watching the reflections. No one resembling the man in the dark clothes was nearby, and she darted into the café.

She rarely visited the suburbs where Robby lived, and this café was new to her. He'd said it was safe, but studying the clientele, she baulked. She found a table to the side, away from other patrons and stowed the bag beside her. The waitress eyed Laura with suspicion. Her petite face was framed by stringy black hair and piercings on her eyebrow and nose made her look fierce. A skull tattoo on her neck slipped in and out of view every time she flicked her hair, and it contrasted strangely with the rose tattoo on her forearm. She offered Laura a menu.

Laura ordered table water.

Her mind played with her options to keep Robby safe. If Peter's ideas weren't suitable, what options could she offer? Mark was a short-term solution, but was it safe, not only for Robby? Did the gang know Robby's brother lived in Brisbane? Even if they didn't, it wouldn't be hard to find out.

The only other option was Laura's sister, Claire. They weren't exactly estranged, but they may as well be; regular birthday and Christmas cards were their only contact since Laura's twins were born. Their relationship was complicated. Life had thrown too many obstacles in their way and it would be hard to ask her. Maybe it was better to let Peter help.

Laura looked up from her thoughts in time to see a short but solid man walk into the café. This human wall had long and straggly mousey hair and indistinguishable ink *art* covered his arms. He looked familiar. Nick's photo on Google showed a man with close-cropped hair, clean-shaven, and wearing a suit as he entered the courthouse, but there was a resemblance. He was flanked by two men; a wiry man with a scruffy white beard and hair to match. His skull emblazoned black T-shirt hung loosely on his thin frame. The redhead, who was also wider than he was tall, had an impressive scar running the length of his face. Faded patches decorated the sleeves of their well-worn leather jackets. As they walked towards Laura's table, she raised the menu to partially hide her face. Her heart thumped and the menu fluttered in the air, drawing the skinny man's attention.

They sat in a circle around a table beside Laura and boxed her in. She couldn't leave without squeezing past them. How was she going to warn Robby? She sent a text to his old mobile number but wasn't confident he'd get it.

'What are we gonna' do, Nick?' Black T-shirt's reedy voice muffled through his scraggly beard.

Laura shivered. It was Nick.

'Bulldog should've finished him off. The pigs are watchin' and it's a fuckin' mess,' Nick replied.

'What about Shayida? What are you gunna do to her?' the redhead asked. His sneer disappeared when Nick glared at him.

'Leave her out of it. We got more important things to sort out.'

Laura fidgeted with her menu. She needed to warn Robby, but

how? Perspiration broke out on her forehead. She felt ill.

'What're we doing for Friday?' asked black T-shirt.

'Nothing much,' Nick replied. 'There's gunna be a delivery. Not our usual small-time crap, but important people'll be protectin' us now.'

Four young women, wearing impossibly high heels, staggered into the café. They collapsed into chairs at the table on the other side of Laura. Their laughter and shouting drowned out the bikie conversation and drew the men's attention. The bikies smiled at the women, who smirked back. Laura shrunk into her seat and hid behind the menu. She was stuck. She couldn't leave without drawing attention to herself.

The waitress brought beers and focaccias to the bikie's table and Nick leaned back, letting his eyes meet Laura's. She looked away. That look. Did he know who she was?

She scanned the other customers. There was an assortment of different people, but she was the only older woman in the café, sitting on her own. She'd drawn others' attention too. Was that it? Although, it seemed too much of a coincidence that they were here now.

'The idiot's running scared, but we need to find him.' Nick said.

'We don't want him squealin,' black T-shirt confirmed.

Nick's phone chimed with the theme song from an old western movie. It seemed an odd choice.

'Nah, we haven't seen him yet,' Nick explained.

Laura trembled. This wasn't a coincidence.

The three men finished their lunch in a few bites and slugged down their beers.

'We better go. Scarface, stay here and keep a lookout. Viper and me are gunna get things ready,' Nick ordered and caught Laura's eye before striding out of the café with black T-shirt, also known as Viper.

Laura slumped in her seat. If it wasn't so serious, she'd laugh.

They were scary, but not because of those ridiculous names. Outside, Nick and Viper stood beside a black ute and argued. Laura waited.

Her phone shocked her out of her inaction.

'I saw them in time,' Robby said breathlessly. 'Why didn't you warn me?'

'I don't have your new number, remember?' The women beside her erupted in raucous laughter just as Robby spoke. 'What? I couldn't hear you.'

'We can't meet there now. It was a bad suggestion. Where else can we go? You better choose.'

Laura cupped her hand over the mouthpiece before speaking again. 'We could meet by the beach or a park.'

'I'm starving, Mum. Can't we try somewhere you usually go?'

'What about the Mediterranean Café? It has a private section and is far away from here. I can meet you there in an hour, OK?' It was a favourite of Laura's, although it wasn't close.

Laura almost forgot the bag in her rush to escape. She squeezed past the young women and fled the café. Thankfully, Scarface wasn't much of a lookout. He stared at his phone and didn't look up.

Laura approached the hotel carpark from the opposite direction, stealthily moving between parked cars. She scanned every parked car and every passing vehicle before unlocking hers. She was still trembling as she started the motor.

Chapter 33

John's receptionist, Fleur, sneezed as he walked through the office door. She pressed a tissue to her mouth, nodded hello, and stifled another sneeze. Handing him a sheaf of papers and a file, she turned her head and sneezed again. John recoiled.

'I don't want to catch your cold. Take the day off.' He screwed up his face.

'Thank you,' she snuffled. 'I've printed everything and cancelled the appointments, as you requested.'

'OK. See you tomorrow.'

She smiled weakly, collected her coat and handbag, and left. John grimaced as another sneeze echoed from the hall.

He removed the report and dropped the rest of the paperwork on his desk. He felt tired and listless. The Italian press reported Babbo's death as a triumph over evil, but John had heard from Carlo that Babbo was not dead. The explosion was a smokescreen for the benefit of their enemies. Despite his age, Babbo was a wily bastard. John wasn't pleased or disappointed at the news. He didn't really want his father dead, not yet anyway. He wanted Babbo to witness his triumph when John finally took over the business from Dimi.

Redirecting his thoughts to his supply problems, he flicked through the report, but couldn't concentrate. Luckily, nothing required urgent attention for once.

He checked his diary, then dialled Kleb's private number.

'What do you know about Portofino?' Kleb asked

'Neither the northern boss' nor Babbo's body has been found. More's the pity. Talk is the Southern Alliance group took out a contract on them both. A dispute about money and territories. But I think it's a smokescreen. Suspiciously, the crew of the exploded boat were given the day off. They're still being questioned.'

'Are we sure it's not related to your meeting with Ferr…Franco?'

'We can't be certain of anything. If people were following him…' John grimaced. 'It's becoming messy. The Russians are involved in everything. They're manoeuvring to take over the family businesses and watching Casterlow's contact,' John said.

'I'd assumed Casterlow meant journalists were snooping. It's safer to leave Casterlow's project until we're sure it won't endanger our main business. It's getting mired in too much controversy and might draw attention from the wrong sources.'

'Talking of controversy, what happened with Furness?' John asked.

'I haven't tracked down that report. He's hidden it. I'm sure he had a backup plan though. He wasn't naïve. I've offered to help his widow sort out his affairs, so if he set up a backup plan, I'll find it.'

'It was organ failure, wasn't it? How could Casterlow be responsible?'

'Furness was poisoned, I'm sure of it. I'll lay money on Casterlow's National Security branch rogue unit being involved. They're effectively his private militia. They follow orders without question. They've raided journalists working on the exposé and are intimidating witnesses. Skollov brought in special recruits from overseas, on the quiet, for this special group.'

'If Skollov set it up for Casterlow, why isn't he involved with this chemical agent? His line of business involves weapons of all kinds.'

'Skollov's become too powerful and they're wresting back some control. With his international connections, he even scares me.' Kleb laughed. 'Anyway, what else did you accomplish?'

'The Devil's Guard will provide security for my future meetings. As I'd expected, they're more than happy to muscle in on Python's territory.'

'It'll cause complications.'

Although Kleb argued strongly against the plan, John wasn't going to change it. He needed them to counter Dimi and her gang. It was time to be ruthless.

'Competition will do the Pythons good.'

'Don't start a war,' Kleb warned.

'Wars can be useful.' John was already embroiled in wars with Dimi and even Skye, but he planned to win them all.

'Sounds like it's safe to move on the takeover.'

'We should move forward on the Casterlow deal too.'

'They're separate issues. Don't complicate things. The plan is, take over the family business, and with her supplies from Iraq and your contacts in Guatemala; we'll have the drug trade in Australia sown up. The gangs will keep small-time operators off our backs. The Casterlow project is a distraction and until we know what happened to Furness, we should stay cautious. Play along and do what Casterlow asks. We can string him along, but don't jeopardise the takeover. We still haven't confirmed what opportunities Casterlow's chemical agent offers.' Kleb had strong ideas, but John bristled at his use of *we*. The business was John's.

'I won't jeopardise the takeover. I know it's now or never,' John confirmed.

'Good. I've waited a long time for this. I vowed I would avenge my father and I'll keep my promise. Dimi will finally pay.'

It was personal for Kleb. He believed Dimi was responsible for the rumours that led to his father's murder, and John wasn't going to argue. It was a useful belief.

Before he could respond Kleb added, 'Why didn't you like Werner?'

John hesitated. 'I don't trust him. He seems shifty.'

'I've used him for years; he's trustworthy, and an expert in blood diamonds. I've made serious money from his efforts. He spoke highly of you and said he was looking forward to working with you in the future. Don't dismiss him too easily.'

John smiled. The trader was discreet; perhaps he wasn't such a bad option after all.

That evening, John sorted through his wardrobe in search of something subdued. He skipped past the expensive black Italian leather jacket in favour of the casual fleece-lined one. He grimaced. He was struggling to summon up the necessary enthusiasm for this meeting.

'Are you going out *again*?' Skye asked.

'I told you.' John checked his image in the mirror. It would do.

'I thought we were spending the night together.'

John sighed. 'It's business.'

'It's always business. You never think about me, do you? I can't accompany you overseas, although plenty of businessmen take their wives, and—'

'You're not a wife though, are you?' John wasn't in the mood. He was having enough difficulty concentrating.

'No.' Skye glared at him. 'No, I'm not.'

'We'll have a night in soon, but this is important.' He fidgeted with the tie, putting it on, taking it off, then repeating once more before deciding he didn't need it.

Skye stormed out of the room.

'What?' he shouted. Her timing was always off.

She poked her head around the door. 'Maybe it's too late. I've heard it all before.'

He glanced at his watch. He'd deal with her later. Carlo was already late.

When the front doorbell rang, John yelled goodbye, but Skye

didn't respond. He slammed the door and strode to the car.

'Why are you meeting them? I don't understand,' Carlo grumbled. His protective vest added bulk.

'I don't like bikie gangs any more than you do. I know they're unpredictable, but they're a necessary evil; they'll keep the others in check.'

'They're rivals, they won't cooperate. Why not let me get a group together, independent ones?'

'It's better this way. It'll be alright, I told you.' John hoped this was true. Carlo's offer was tempting, but he couldn't have his success dependent on one man. John winced as he remembered Babbo's advice: "Spread the power." It seemed the sensible thing to do.

'We should have brought more backup,' Carlo groaned.

'I'm keeping it low key. I don't want to attract attention. I've got some security stationed outside the venue.' Kleb's idea was good.

As they crossed the bridge, Carlo asked, 'How many will be there?'

John shrugged. 'Carlo, stop complaining. You're losing your touch. You're not indispensable, you know.'

Carlo was a comfortable link to the old days. His support had eased John into the family business at the start. But things changed. He didn't remember Carlo being so nervous. His confidence and strength had inspired John back then. As reluctant as John was, maybe it was time to find a new right-hand man.

'The boss doesn't think I'm losing my touch,' Carlo shot back.

'Dimi won't be the boss much longer. It's what I think that matters, remember that.'

Carlo concentrated on the winding coastal road, and John ignored his muttering. The meeting was in an unfamiliar part of town and John wondered if Carlo had been right. They should have insisted on neutral territory. It was too late now.

They parked around the corner and Carlo checked and rechecked that the car was locked. John scanned the area but couldn't identify any extra security. They were very discreet. Dilapidated shop fronts stretched along the road. Strips of blistered paintwork peeled from the walls creating a scattered snow-like effect and cracks gaped above the windows. The Golden Lotus restaurant sign might have been golden at one time, but now it was faded with only the G and the L still glittering. Advertisements for past events covered the windows. Peering through the frosted glass doors only revealed shadows of black in a grey sea. John straightened and followed Carlo through the door.

The man at the bar was taller than Carlo but not as wide, and his straggly grey-flecked beard drooped down to his chest. Piercings across his eyebrows and nose supplemented a long, colourful tattoo spreading up his neck. His T-shirt stretched across his biceps. John expected something more subtle. Before he could ask, a voice called out from the corner.

'Knuckles, check him out,' ordered a man wearing a leather jacket covered in colourful patches.

John looked at the hand and then across at the table. The man beside the leather-jacketed figure looked like an accountant, clean-cut, suit, and tie.

Knuckles stuck out his hand. 'Phone,' he grunted.

Carlo stepped in front of John, crossing his arms and firmly planting his feet.

'Phone,' repeated Knuckles.

'Give him your phone,' yelled the voice.

'What the fuck —'

'Phones are not allowed at our meetings,' said the voice. 'Knuckles will give it back when we're finished.'

John tapped Carlo on the shoulder. 'They're playing safe.' He didn't like being ordered about, but he'd go along with this for now.

He smacked his phone into Knuckles' hand and Carlo slid his device onto the counter, out of Knuckles' reach. John strode to the table. Carlo remained stationed by the bar.

The leather-jacketed figure stood, reached out his hand and for a fleeting moment John thought he wanted something else, then realised he wanted to shake hands. Up close, he was trim and muscular, with a thick and sinewy neck. Club badges and patches covered his leather jacket, and a muted tattoo on his right cheek showed a circle surrounding 1%. It was brazen, telling the world you belonged to the lawless one percent of the population by stamping it on your face.

'Mungo,' he said. 'This is my Vice President, Butcher. Knuckles over there is our sergeant at arms. He's a lookout.'

Butcher looked like he'd come straight from the office. John shook his hand and sat down facing the two men. He crossed his legs, feigning nonchalance.

'Well, Mungo.' John almost laughed as he said the name, but he reined it in. 'As you understand, I couldn't go into detail over the phone.'

Mungo nodded.

'I've spoken to your bosses in Amsterdam,' John said.

'Bosses? You mean associates? So, exactly what did you discuss?' Mungo asked.

Boris and Svetlana assured John they'd confirmed the arrangements before this meeting. He shook his head. Playing games wasted everyone's time.

'I'm sure you know,' John said testily. 'I need a small security team.'

'We can put one together immediately. We do security for nightclubs and other businesses.'

'They can't look like…' John didn't know how to finish the sentence tactfully. He glanced at Knuckles and Mungo. That's not what he wanted.

Mungo laughed. 'They'll be, shall we say, acceptable.'

They discussed John's requirements and agreed that once the meeting date was confirmed, they'd finalise the plan. Their people in

Adelaide would take care of it.

'You were going to offer us an…opportunity,' Butcher interrupted.

'I discussed establishing an ongoing partnership with Boris and Svetlana. It includes the new imports, but only once I have Adelaide secured.' John kept it vague. They had his phone, but they might still have their own.

'We could be interested,' Mungo said. 'It depends on the deal.'

They were haggling? 'Remember. I'd prefer to have a distribution base in Sydney, but I don't need you.' he warned.

'You're doing us a favour?' Butcher smirked at Mungo.

John hadn't expected this reaction. Were they too stupid to see how good this deal was?

Their eyes didn't waver from his, challenging and provoking him. He stared back. 'Your established network is attractive and I'm offering you first refusal. There's a shipment on its way. An arrangement would be mutually beneficial but, if you're not interested—'

'We want more. A better deal. The Pythons need to be put back in their place. We need to set up a more extensive groundwork for this too.'

John clenched his jaw. 'I'm not subsidising your operations. This is a business deal, not charity.' They locked eyes and John added, 'I have other options if the Devil's Guard can't do it.'

It wasn't true, but despite his conversation with Boris and Svetlana inspiring confidence, this gang was hostile. John clamped his lips and waited. He wasn't speaking first or backing down. He needed a partner with muscle and a large network for all his drug imports. And to keep the Pythons in check. But Carlo was right; these punks weren't such a savvy business group.

'We might be able to come to an arrangement,' Mungo finally admitted.

John gently released his breath. 'We can set up an arrangement after the Adelaide meeting, but don't mess me about.' John warned.

'Svetlana mentioned there was a new product, something big that you would be handling soon. Are we getting access to that too?' Mungo's eyes were steely cold.

'I don't know what you're talking about. I'm offering you my regular heroin and cocaine supplies and, eventually, E-bomb. That's all.' John frowned. He hadn't planned to be explicit.

'It's not enough. The new product would give us serious clout.' Butcher nodded at Mungo.

'There is no new product. Someone has made a mistake.' John's nerves were tingling. They knew more than they were supposed to. How?

'Come now, don't be shy. We know there's a new product. Without that on the table, we'll have to think about your offer.' Mungo smirked.

'I'm not a patient man. You either accept my offer as is, or I take it elsewhere. Be assured, I have other options.' John would make them regret threatening him.

'We're not letting you take advantage,' Mungo said.

'Seriously? I've offered you a fair deal. What I want is on the table. Now you need to decide.'

Another unreadable look passed between Mungo and Butcher. John stood up. It was time to go.

'We'll be in touch.' Mungo stood and offered his hand.

John hesitated. 'Don't take too long.'

He shook hands. At the bar, he demanded his phone. Knuckles waited for Mungo's nod before extracting them from his pocket. He slammed both phones into Carlo's hand. Carlo didn't flinch. He checked them, handed John his, and pocketed his own. They turned and strode out of the door.

Back in the car, contingency plans swirled in John's head. He'd expected the negotiations to be a formality. He'd done the hard talk with the Russian power couple, Boris and Svetlana. That should have been enough.

'That went well,' Carlo taunted as he slipped into the passenger seat.

'Don't say a word,' John warned and slammed his hand on the steering wheel.

He squealed the wheels in a U-turn and sped away; putting as much distance as possible between him and the humiliation. Unfortunately, the humiliation was in the car with him.

'I can't come to Sydney so much for a while. The boss needs me for the big meeting,' Carlo said.

'Who'll be there?' John didn't want any more surprises.

'This is different. It's a new supplier and requiring higher security. Even I don't know everything.'

'Those other problems are finally settled, aren't they? There are no more threats?'

'They're under control. The girl wasn't a threat to us, but she's been neutralised now, so it doesn't matter.'

'You didn't take care of her?'

'No. It doesn't matter who, it's sorted.'

John didn't agree. It mattered. This put Casterlow back in the frame. She must have had information on more than just Dimi's E-bomb importation.

'Keep me informed.' John sped off at the traffic lights.

At home, John opened the front door. There were no lights, no TV voices, and no music; the house was shrouded in an eerie quiet. Where was Skye? His heartbeat quickened.

'Get a grip,' he scolded himself.

Skye wasn't in the bedroom, or the lounge, or the kitchen. She wasn't anywhere. Had Devil's Guard pulled a stunt and raided his home? They'd do anything to gain an advantage. Could they have kidnapped Skye for ransom or to bargain with?

Chapter 34

Laura followed a circuitous route via the beach, adding as many twists and turns that she could without getting lost. She detoured to the Semaphore foreshore and parked, pretending to watch the ocean while scanning the cars around her. She needed to be sure she wasn't being followed. The ocean waves crashed onto the sandy beach and it made her nerves twitch even more. Had Nick known she was meeting Robby at the café? If so, how? She hadn't told anyone. The look in his cold eyes burned into her memory, and she shivered.

Satisfied that none of the cars near her were following, she continued along Seaview Road and, after Henley Beach, she again parked along the esplanade looking over the sea. The grey sky and swirling water darkened her mood more. The beach wasn't working its magic today. Again she scanned the traffic and any passers-by. Everyone looked normal. Walkers, joggers, and a family playing with their dog were scattered before her. Cars pulled in and out of car parks nearby, but nothing looked unusual.

She continued. Back in Glenelg, she parked streets away from the café, around the corner from a group of small shops. She bought some bread rolls from the local bakery and stuffed them into the bag, the whole time scrutinising every passer-by.

Her phone rang, and she jumped. The other customer in the shop stared at her and frowned. Laura managed a tight smile and then checked the caller ID. It was Peter. She cut off the call. He'd have to wait.

When she was certain that no one was acting suspiciously or paying her any attention, or at least as certain as she was ever going to be, she rang for a taxi. She waited by a bench seat, trying to fade into the shadows while staying alert. She dabbed a tissue at the sprinkle of perspiration on her brow and upper lip. Her head ached, and this hypervigilance frayed her nerves.

The taxi finally arrived, and she got in as quickly as she could.

'You could've walked this,' the driver grumbled when she asked him to stop at the café.

The tables in the secluded section of the café were all occupied.

'Shit,' she muttered under her breath.

She was exhausted and edgy. This must work. She crossed her fingers and stared at the couples chatting over full cups of coffee. The individuals scanned newspapers, with two of them busily doing puzzles. Laura took up a position as close to the back as she could, keeping far away from the windows but still feeling exposed. Her eyes continuously swept the small section, searching for signs of people leaving.

She looked up in time to see Robby slink into the café. A hoodie barely covered his messy hair and his crumpled clothes hung on him. He was paler than she'd ever seen him. It was an effective disguise. She barely recognised him herself. She stood up and wrapped her arms around him, feeling his body stiffen in his customary reaction before he leaned into her and finally hugged her in return. She squeezed him, reluctant to let him go.

As they were about to sit down, the man at the corner table packed up his newspaper. Laura grabbed the bags and steered Robby towards the now vacant table. Once settled, the waitress took their order for drinks, then returned with menus and table water.

'I've been so scared. How could something like this happen to us?'

'It didn't happen to *us*, it happened to *me*,' Robby snapped.

'I didn't know if you were hurt or…even alive. The police suggested you could've been kidnapped.' Laura wiped a threatening tear from her eye.

Robby stared at the wall, his gaze distant and unreachable.

'I brought clothes.' Laura slid the bag closer to him. 'I got some cash. Hope it's enough.'

She watched him. This was her son, and he was in trouble. Even if he'd caused the pain himself, she had to help him.

'Thanks,' Robby finally said. 'I didn't lose my wallet and cards but my phone went up with the car.' Robby sighed. 'It's all fucked up.'

Laura nodded. It was an accurate description. The waitress served Laura a black coffee and Robby's beer. She took their lunch order and left.

Robby continued, 'No one believes me.'

'About what?'

'It was just a small stash. I was going to take it to the distributor, but…later. I was busy, you know. It was in the boot when the car…Nick thinks I've stolen the stash and that I'm using Bulldog and the firebomb as an excuse.' Robby lowered his head into his hands and moaned.

'Oh, Robby. How did you —' Laura sighed. She wanted to put her arms around him, but it would create a scene.

'They gave me an opportunity. I earned good money and had a role. They…liked me.' Robby straightened.

'You were expendable. You see that now, don't you? What about your other friends? They *liked* you, didn't they?'

'I was the weak link. They're studying, working, and settling down and I'm still not sure what I want.'

'Robby, your family, we could have helped you—'

'You're always on my back, always on about how I'm not studying, or not working, or not building a career, or life, or something. I didn't fit in. Not anywhere. Not with my mates, not with my family, but I did with this gang.'

'How could you fit in with these criminals? They're vicious and callous. They beat people up, extort money, deal drugs and guns, and kill people. They have no morals, no decency. They don't care about people.'

'They listened to me. They said I had good ideas. They respected me.'

Laura was speechless. He'd interpreted his parent's attempts to help as browbeating and turned to criminals for approval.

'Anyway, it's all fucked up now,' Robby said.

The waitress placed their meals on the table, and Robby and Laura both declined the ground pepper. As soon as the waitress left, Robby attacked his steak with mushroom sauce like a starving man. A sob clutched at the back of Laura's throat.

'We wanted you to make a good life for yourself,' Laura explained. How had they fallen so short of their aim?

Robby shook his head. 'I did. They may be an illegal organisation, but people treat their business pragmatically. They target young professionals. Sometimes they're not even that young. They're hip, and drugs are part of their image. The business isn't enticing kids who don't know what they're getting into. They supply adults, people who are old enough to make their own decisions.'

'Like you?' Laura couldn't stifle her sarcasm.

'Respectable people, not only criminals, get involved,' Robby said defiantly.

'Some people might be *respectable*, but that doesn't mean they're honest or ethical.' She pushed her chicken salad back. 'What these gangs do is illegal and immoral. It's not simply business,' Laura said quietly and shook her head. This wasn't the time for a lecture. 'We need to sort out what you're going to do next. Peter has offered to help.'

'You didn't tell him we were meeting?' Robby's face turned paler.

'I did, although I didn't tell him where. Why? His offer may be our best chance to keep you safe.'

'That's how they knew.'

'What do you mean?'

'Peter and Nick are business partners. They're in it together,' he explained.

Laura's mouth gaped. 'Surely not. What could Peter have to do with—'

Robby glared. 'I've seen them together.'

Laura's heart lurched. Is that why he'd offered his help?

'This business makes serious money. Nick and Peter meet, secretly, of course. It's funny.' Robby chuckled. 'Peter acts like he's in charge, but Nick has it all over him. The gang has fingers in lots of pies. That's why the Devil's Guard is trying to muscle in on our turf.'

'It's not your turf anymore.' Laura didn't want to talk about the bikies' *business* model and their turf wars anymore. She didn't want to think about Peter and what he was doing, either. Now they needed a plan to keep Robby safe, without Peter's help. 'We need to work out where you can go. You could stay with Mark in Brisbane.'

Robby shovelled in another mouthful of steak and shook his head vigorously. 'Brisbane is no good. The Devil's Guard has a chapter there and the Pythons are growing their influence there too.'

Laura sighed. 'Your Aunt Claire lives in country NSW. Would that work?'

Robby pulled a face. 'I don't know her. She didn't even come to Dad's funeral.'

'She had medical issues,' Laura explained. 'I can't promise anything, but if she's willing, she might be our best option.'

Robby placed his knife and fork on the empty plate and downed the last of his beer. 'Maybe. But only until I can get something else sorted.'

Robby read out his new phone number and temporary address,

then together they checked outside for lurkers. Robby left first, promising to ring her soon and stressing his new number was only for emergencies, suggesting her phone could be tapped. However unlikely, it didn't help her twitching nerves.

Laura ordered another coffee when her phone rang.

'Hello. You haven't been answering my calls. What happened?' Peter's voice startled Laura despite its cheeriness.

'He…didn't show up. I don't know what's happened. I haven't heard from him,' Laura improvised.

'You must be frantic. I don't understand why he hasn't phoned to reassure you.' Peter sounded concerned and caring but Laura wasn't fooled anymore.

'He's frightened. Those bikies terrify me.'

'But you said he wasn't mixed up with bikies.'

'Going out with Shayida seems to be all it takes.'

'I'm sure he'll be OK. Do you want to come over? Abbie's out tonight, so I'm home babysitting.'

'I'm fine. I have to go.'

'Let me know as soon as he gets in touch again. I'll arrange help once we have the details.'

'Sure.' Laura wanted to get off the phone before she said something she'd regret. Sending Nick to the café, having people follow her, that wasn't the kind of help she'd had in mind.

'Are you OK? You sound a little strange.'

'For goodness sake, of course, I'm not alright. I'm worried and afraid. Now, I need to go.'

She hung up and pushed her half-finished salad away. Peter and bikies could only have one thing in common? Drugs. Laura shivered. It was consistent with his behaviour in Iraq too. The bikies must be linked somehow.

She finished her coffee, paid the bill, and drove home, taking twists and turns through back streets, although it probably didn't matter now.

Chapter 35

Laura poured a glass of wine and sunk into her comfortable recliner while cradling the phone. Wine was her medication of choice lately, and hopefully, it would give her courage. Her finger poised over the green phone symbol under Claire's number, but she hesitated.

Their history got in the way. It's not that Laura didn't care, but Claire had burned bridges. Laura stared out of the window. She wasn't blameless either, was she? Claire stoically carried her grievance. She'd sacrificed her dreams to support their parents after Dad's accident. The company cheated him out of his entitlements, and Mum's stroke added to the strain. Laura's contribution wasn't enough for Claire. Claire gave up her studies, her life, and she didn't let Laura forget she hadn't given up anything of consequence. When their parents died, only three months apart, Claire moved as far away as she could.

Guilt tugged at Laura. She should have kept in contact. They'd avoided talking about issues during those early visits before the twins were born. Avoiding confrontation was a family trait. Laura squirmed. It was a familiar pattern. Avoiding difficult relationships and avoiding conflict. She'd dodged the difficult conversations with both Tom and Claire, and even with the children. At fifty-nine, maybe she should stop running away. She needed to sort this out and maybe she could make turning sixty a real milestone.

She thought about what she could say then, on impulse, pressed call. Laura was both disappointed and relieved when it rang and rang. She almost hung up, but a frail voice finally answered.

'Hello, Claire, it's Laura,' she said.

'Laura?'

'It's been a long time since we've talked. I'm sorry,' Laura said sincerely.

'Yes, well…'

Laura faltered. She hadn't expected a welcome, but she'd hoped for cautiously friendly.

'I'm sorry I couldn't be there, at the funeral. Tom was a good man.' Claire offered a small olive branch.

'It was…a shock.'

Laura continued with stilted and uncomfortable small talk, the weather, the children, anything to postpone asking her the favour.

'Well, you're not ringing to catch up, are you?' Claire finally challenged.

'No. I couldn't think…' Laura stopped and took a breath. 'Let me start again. I need to ask a favour. It's to help Robby.'

'Go on.'

'Robby is in trouble. He needs somewhere to hide, where they can't find him.'

Claire's shallow breaths travelled down the phone. 'Who are *they*?' she finally asked.

'It's complicated. Suffice to say he needs, no, *we* need your help.'

'Who is he hiding from?' Claire persisted.

'His girlfriend…she's connected to a bikie gang. He's in trouble.'

'And you were thinking he could hide here, with me?'

'I don't know what else to do?'

'I'm the last resort, am I?'

'You're my only resort.' Laura sighed. This was as hard as she'd imagined, and the strain of the last few days wasn't helping. 'I'm sorry I haven't kept in touch.' She didn't mention that Claire hadn't maintained contact either. 'I know things haven't been good between us…but…Robby's life is at risk if he stays here and…he's your nephew.'

'Don't play the family card with me. We've never been the model happy family.'

Laura bit her lower lip. Whatever their differences, she'd thought Claire might put them aside at a time like this. She'd been wrong.

'Alright,' Laura said. She couldn't chat and pretend she wasn't disappointed. She needed to find another option.

'So that's it. You haven't got anything else to say to me.'

'I'm sorry Claire. I know we haven't been close. I understand the history. But right now, my son needs my help and I need to arrange something quickly. Maybe when this is done, we can talk again.' Laura meant it. It seemed silly to carry grievances when life could end tomorrow. It was too late to mend her relationship with Tom. It shouldn't happen with her sister too.

'I didn't say no. After all this time, everything that's happened, the family card doesn't work.'

Laura shook her head; did this mean she would or wouldn't help? 'So, will you?'

'Yes, but there are rules. I run a small, self-sufficient farm; he'll have to pull his weight. I've lived alone a long time so sharing my space is a big deal. I don't want any funny business like…drugs or stuff. He has to remember it's my house, so it's my rules.'

Tears rolled down Laura's cheek. 'Thank you, Claire, thank you so much.'

'OK, OK, don't gush,' Claire admonished.

The rest of the conversation was easier. Claire explained that Sutton Valley had cherry orchards, strawberry farms, and olive groves.

'It provides a good living if you aren't greedy.'

She sounded content. She'd recently branched out and regularly tramped about the district taking photos that inspired her. Claire's voice almost sang as she talked about how she'd set up a studio in one of the sheds to display and sell her photographs.

Robby might find Claire challenging, but it wouldn't hurt him, and the more Laura thought about it, the more she thought it might do him good.

After she'd hung up, Laura punched the air. It was a good result, not only for Robby. The biggest hurdle was getting Robby to Young, where Claire could collect him. Driving wasn't an option and public transport might be too obvious.

She began to refill her glass but stopped, resealed the bottle and foraged through the kitchen pantry for a snack.

The doorbell rang and Laura's heart lodged in her throat seeing Peter on her doorstep.

'I thought I'd check on you.' He stepped into the hall and leaned forward to kiss her cheek.

Laura pulled away, and he grimaced. She remembered the satchel and papers in the lounge and led Peter to the dining room. He sat down.

'I thought you were looking after Katie,' Laura said.

'We got the babysitter again. Abbie's always so busy lately. The babysitter is almost on permanent payroll.'

'There isn't anything more that I can tell you since your call. Robby messaged me. He's safe.' Laura kept close to the truth.

'He still has his mobile?'

'The number was private.'

'He needs to ring me. Abbie and I can protect him. We know people.' Peter smiled.

Laura nodded. Yes, she was learning all about the people he knew and they weren't what she'd expected.

'I'll tell Robby if he rings, but you know him. He rarely listens to me.' She twisted her wedding band, drawing his attention to her trembling fingers.

'I could stay and keep you company.'

'It's OK. Mel will be here soon,' Laura lied.

'She's going OK, in her new job, I mean.'

'She's fine. Look, I need to clean up a little before she gets here. There's nothing you can do right now. I'll call you.'

'I wouldn't mind saying hello to Mel too. I haven't seen her in ages.'

Laura's mind raced. She pointed to the wine rack. 'Could you select a special wine?'

He smiled and nodded.

Laura dashed into the lounge and pushed the satchel back against the chair just as Peter walked through. He noticed her empty wineglass and re-corked bottle on the coffee table and raised his eyebrows. Laura ignored it. She stationed herself between him and the piles of papers and folders. The APATO letterhead in bold green and yellow lettering screamed up at her, but what could she do?

Slowly, she turned around, leaned down, lifted the bundle, and turned them over. The double-sided print meant the letterhead screamed from the back too. Her hands shook. She dropped the papers onto the floor beside her chair, grabbed the files, turned them over, and placed them on top. Finally, she turned to face Peter.

He narrowed his eyes. 'What's all that?'

'Bills and financial records. Tom took care of all this stuff before but now—'

Peter moved towards Laura. 'I could help.'

'I'm going to have to learn sooner or later. I'd prefer sooner.'

He grabbed a wineglass from the cabinet and she directed him to Tom's old chair. He couldn't see the pile from there. When he sat, she moved to the TV console, picked up the legitimate DVD case, and placed it on top of the others.

'What have you got there?' Peter asked.

'Just putting my DVD away.' Laura held up the disc she'd extracted earlier.

'You seem a bit obsessed with tidying up,' Peter observed.

'I'm nervous. I'm worried about Robby. I need to keep busy.'

Peter's eyes fixed on the coffee table and the diaries. Two bright orange Post-it notes protruded from the 2006 diary pages.

'Are they Tom's?' he asked. 'Have you found more of his stuff?'

'They're mine,' Laura said, picking them up and laying them on her lap.

Peter shook his head; he knew she was lying.

'You know, it's time for you to drop Tom's issues and start living your life.' Peter stood up, filled their glasses, and placed them on the low table between them.

'You think?'

'Yes, I think!' Peter chewed at the inside of his lip.

'The alternative is that you tell me what's going on and save me from searching.'

A range of different reactions washed across his face.

'It's business and the secrets are not mine to tell. They don't concern you.' He waved his hand dismissively and gulped from his glass.

'Surely not everything is secret. Some things are about what you saw as Tom's, what did you call them, his bugbears?'

Peter raked his fingers through his hair and they locked eyes. He twirled his glass until the red wine swirled dangerously close to the edge.

'You know what happened to him. You need to move on.' He put his glass down and glared at her.

'What are you up to, Peter? What did Tom find out about you? What are you doing that you shouldn't?' She had to risk it.

'You know what, Laura, I've tried to tell you. I've tried to explain. Tom was paranoid. This latest issue, it was nonsense. He worried about secret defence installations that had nothing to do with us. There's nothing more to tell.'

'Maybe you need to go home now.'

Peter grimaced. He stretched forward and his foot disturbed the satchel by Laura's chair. She sprang up and pushed it back, conscious of his eyes following her.

'Is that one of Tom's old satchels?'

Laura shrugged.

'I found it in the wardrobe. Mel might like it.'

'It looks a bit ragged for her.'

'She's sentimental about her father.'

'Look Laura, I don't want to argue with you.'

'Then don't. It's still time for you to go.'

'You're not going to tell me about Mel and how she's going?'

'No, I'm not. I'm tired and wrung out. I need time on my own.'

Peter reluctantly took his glass and put it on the sink, something he rarely did. He scanned the notes on her calendar and the fridge.

'I'm trying to be a good friend,' he explained.

'Good friends give you space,' she responded.

He turned and walked towards the door, hesitating only slightly when he drew level with her. Her step back, out of arm's reach, didn't go unnoticed.

After he'd gone, Laura collected the paperwork and notebooks and neatly stowed them back in the satchel. She couldn't face sorting through them right now. Under her bed was safe and out of sight. She was about to sip the wine when she stopped. It was time to face the truth. No more drinking alone and self-medicating. Maybe it was also time to tackle those files. It all seemed to be connected. Peter, the bikies, and at least two deaths. There was nothing more she could do for Robby, but maybe she could unravel this mystery and achieve something positive.

The sound of the doorbell made her scowl, but she smiled when she saw Mel and Eva on the doorstep.

'We both had the same idea,' Eva laughed. 'But I brought gifts,' she added, waving a bottle of wine. There went her resolve, but at least she wouldn't be drinking alone.

'I must have known you'd be here, and I didn't need to bring wine.' Mel shrugged and produced a packet of assorted chocolates. 'Was that Peter we saw driving away just now?'

'He's offering to help Robby, but—' Laura looked at Eva. How was she going to explain?

'It's such a relief to know Robby is safe.' Eva fell onto the sofa.

'He's not exactly safe yet. I've arranged for him to stay at my sister's.'

'Aunt Claire?' Mel raised her eyebrows at Eva.

'Yes, I rang her.'

'*You* rang *her*?' Eva sounded as surprised as Mel.

'I know. But Claire was my only option.'

'It must have gone well if Robby's going to stay with her,' Mel said.

'I think we're talking again.'

'That's great, Mum.'

'Well done, Laura.'

'I don't want to be a party pooper, but I was about to sort through the papers and files from Tom's locker. There are DVDs too.'

'You found what the key was for?'

Eva was about to uncap her wine when she saw the opened bottle on the table beside Laura's filled glass. She raised her eyebrows at Laura.

'Peter was trying to convince me he could help. And of course, that I needed to stop bothering about Tom's bugbears.'

Eva laughed and poured herself and Mel a glass from the open bottle. 'So where are they?'

'I'm helping too,' Mel declared as she poured chocolates into a bowl.

Laura carried the satchel into the study and they gathered around the desk. She picked up the diaries. 'He used initials instead of names for his appointments. Cross-matching dates on the DVDs with the diary might be helpful.' Laura handed Mel the 2006 diary and laid the 2005 diary in front of her. Both started flicking through the pages.

'On 24th January 2006, there's a note. It says "Omar has died." Isn't that from the DVD we watched, Mum?' Mel said.

Scanning the pages before and after, Mel noted, 'He made a note of meetings with PF around then.'

'PF must be Peter,' Laura said, glancing across at Eva.

'Patrick Furness is also PF,' Eva pointed out. 'He's the minister in charge of APATO.'

Peter seemed more likely. The references to Furness and Casterlow mentioned them by name rather than initials.

'Casterlow is in charge of defence. How's that related to trade and pharmaceuticals?' Mel showed them the entry on 7 February 2006. Question marks trailed after both names and next to Casterlow's name, "*number 2*" was circled several times.

'Peter said Tom worried about secret defence installations that had nothing to do with APATO. They'd be in Casterlow's portfolio,' Laura suggested.

Laura turned a few pages in the 2005 diary. In December, heavy dark pen lines caught her attention. She riffled back. *Conrad's been exposed* was scribbled in bold black texta and circled several times, tearing a small hole in the page.

'Who's Conrad?' Mel asked.

Laura shrugged.

She kept turning pages. Tom's cryptic notes resembled contract numbers. Meetings with CL occurred during the following months. They were sure this was Corrinne Lamberthy. In October, a hastily scrawled note in green ink caught Laura's eye. It covered the whole page and said,

"7.30 meeting with Nick? King's Arms hotel."

Was this Nick the bikie? If it was, why was Tom meeting him? Laura's stomach lurched. Had Tom also been involved with the bikie gang?

281

She marked the entry with a Post-it note to follow up later. She couldn't blurt this out now, not with Mel here.

She squinted at an underlined note scrawled across the adjacent page. She could only decipher *"J.a.c... interested?"* and what looked like a phone number. Laura picked up the phone and, before her nerves intervened, dialled the number.

'What are you doing?' Mel quizzed.

'Oh, Jacques.' Laura had planned to hang up, but hearing his voice shocked her. 'I'm sorry, I must have rung you by mistake.' She shrugged at Eva and Mel.

'It's a lucky coincidence. I was going to ring you to make sure you were OK after the accident. You also left your jacket in the car. I'm flying out to Canberra this evening, but I could drop it off.'

He couldn't come to the house. 'I'm about to go out.'

'Perhaps I could meet you somewhere. I have to be at the airport at 9 p.m., so we could meet for coffee, around 6.30 p.m.?'

She agreed to meet him at Café Braci in Hutt St. Mel and Eva protested. She couldn't meet Jacques, not on her own.

'We'll be out in public and I'll be careful.' This was an opportunity to learn more, and Laura needed to know why his number was in Tom's diary?

'Mum, it's dangerous.' Mel objected. 'I'm coming too.'

'I'll be OK. I'll have the car. You start on the paperwork. I'll be back before you know it.'

'One of us should wait in the car,' Eva suggested. 'Just to be sure.'

'It's no different from waiting at home. I'll be fine.' Convincing them helped her to convince herself too.

Laura's nerves weren't under control, but she was resolute. All her life she'd rampaged about injustice and mistreatment of others yet believed, naively, that justice would prevail. She'd been wrong. For justice to prevail, it took vigilance and hard work, and it was time she did both. It was time she stopped being a bystander.

282

Chapter 36

John feared the worst. Skye was gone and the Devil's Guard bikie gang was unscrupulous enough to use kidnap and ransom to gain an advantage. As he repeatedly clenched his hands, he noticed an envelope propped against an empty vase on the kitchen bench. His name was printed across the front in purple ink. It was Skye's handwriting, but it looked careless and rushed. He ripped it open. He read it twice before he understood, and then anger replaced his other emotions. It wasn't a ransom demand. Skye had left him. She accused him of not loving her and cheating on her. She said John didn't care, and she'd gone.

He screwed up the note and threw it at the wall. Women! Skye didn't understand the pressure he was under. Building a business required hard work and perseverance. Eventually, she'd be a wealthy woman, but nothing was ever good enough or fast enough for Skye.

He opened the bottle of duty-free grappa; a rare and fine blend, and poured a generous glass. It burned his gullet, spreading a welcome warmth through his chest. He turned on the stereo and poured himself another glass.

'No one leaves me. If anyone is going to leave, it's me!' John muttered. He gulped at his drink, then held up the glass to raise a toast to Skye's publicity photo sitting on the mantel. 'You're not worth it. Anton can have you, you ungrateful whore.'

In the office the next morning, Fleur brought a cup of steaming black coffee to his desk. His head throbbed. She leaned forward to place the mug on the desk. Through gritty eyes, he admired the way her light, summery top skimmed across her bra outline.

'Thanks.' John stood and moved around to the front of his desk.

'You're welcome.' She stepped back.

John brushed a curl of hair feathering across her jaw. A tingle travelled up his spine. He'd let her wait, but he was ready now. He needed consoling.

She moved back again. He hated these games, although he admitted she was a good actress. She'd flirted and smiled sweetly at him since starting as his receptionist. Now she was playing coy. He stepped closer, placed his hands on her shoulders, and leaned in. Pulling her to him, his lips sought hers, but at the last minute she turned her head, and his lips pressed against her cheek. He pushed her, pinning her against the wall. She was no match for his strength, and this time, he kissed her lips. Her soft mouth hardened in resistance.

'Enough of the games. You want this too,' he growled, tightening his grip on her fleshy upper arms. He pulled her close.

He lifted his head, satisfied that she was finally giving in to desire, but she lunged forward. Her forehead connected with the bridge of his nose. Pain seared through his head and his grip released. His hand flew to his nose. Fleur pushed him aside and fled. The door slammed shut behind her and moments later, the outer door slammed too, leaving an eerie calm.

His eyes watered, and it took him a moment to focus. In the bathroom, John surveyed the damage. Blood trickled onto his upper lip and he wiped it with a wet paper towel. Had she broken his nose?

'That bitch teased and flirted with me for months, but as soon as I act on it, she does this,' he fumed. He dabbed a red spot on the front of his shirt, but it smeared and turned brown.

She'd blown it. He could have helped her career, but that wouldn't happen now. Not after assaulting him. He sat down at his desk and slammed his fist on the surface. He grimaced, his hand now hurt almost as much as his nose, and his pride.

The phone rang, and he grumbled, 'Hello.'

'Whoa. Who's in a bad mood?' Kleb responded.

'Bloody women.'

'What now?'

'Skye's left me and my receptionist, she just…never mind.' He dabbed at a drop of blood trickling onto his lip.

'Keep your mind on the job. I didn't invest in your resurrection for you to waste it chasing skirt.' Kleb scolded.

'It was just a little fun. Now I'll have to find a new secretary.' John didn't like Kleb's tone. He'd expected sympathy. Skye had become a fixture in his life, and Fleur was organised, efficient, and catered to his preferences. Both took care of him in their way. Now he was alone again.

'Shades of Harper,' Kleb muttered.

'What did you say?'

'Nothing. You could never read the situation with women.' Kleb sighed, then added, 'What arrangements have you made for the meeting?'

'It's not my fault women behave in such irrational ways,' John protested. 'I'm going to the meeting. When I get all the details, I'll let you know.'

'I need to know where and when. It's important.' Kleb's tone hadn't softened.

'Why?'

'You might need backup. How are you going to deal with Dimi? She won't hand over the business without a fight. You may have turned her goons, but she isn't going to slip away quietly. You'll have to *deal* with her.'

John grinned. 'I'll sort it. Carlo or even Nick can take care of her.'

'That won't do. You can't risk it. If she talks them around, you'll lose. She has to be dealt with, permanently.'

John stared out of his office window. He knew he'd have to neutralise her. Kleb was right, of course. He had to make sure it was done. There was no other way. He'd planned the takeover for years but had avoided thinking about what would happen to her.

'Maybe I could persuade her to go quietly, or admit defeat first but—'

'She'll never relinquish control willingly, not to you. You know that.'

John nodded. Of course, it was true. 'So be it.'

It was payback time. She wouldn't step aside. It wasn't in her nature. He'd deal with her and show he was determined. It was the only way he'd finally prove to his father that he was up to it. He'd be as ruthless as required. And he'd enjoy it.

'I've learned more about the Furness issue. Members of Casterlow's national security division special squad were seen outside Furness' house the night he died.'

'It seems farfetched for Casterlow to order Furness' murder to protect his project. Is he that zealous?' And dangerous?

'They're fiercely loyal to Casterlow, but they wouldn't dare take matters into their own hands. That squad follows orders. They don't act on their own initiative. I'll keep investigating, but you concentrate on the takeover and get that right. Once that's done, we'll work out what to do about Casterlow's project.'

'I think we can do both,' John argued. Kleb's caution could squander a significant opportunity.

'Why can't you focus? You'll jeopardise everything. We need reassurance before we act. With Skollov's meddling, we don't know what we're up against. Casterlow could be playing games and making it look like Skollov is on the outer when he isn't. We just don't know. You don't want to get caught in the middle.'

John smiled. 'Skollov is a side issue. We can handle that.'

'Skollov hasn't only been talking to the Russians, he's set up links with influential money-men and he has family connections. He's a major threat. He's dangerous. Don't underestimate him.'

John grimaced. He conceded that Skollov needed handling with care, but that didn't mean they should step back from the chemical agent project.

'Now, we're agreed. The Casterlow project will wait until the time is right.'

'You need to get the information sooner rather than later.' John wasn't agreeing to anything.

'Done. Now, don't get distracted by the women. What did you do to piss Skye off? Never mind. You'll get your pick, eventually. Women love power, bad boys attract them, so sort out the business and the adoration will come.'

John liked the sound of that.

He hung up. He was about to phone Fleur to make his travel plans when he remembered. It was probably better this way. He dialled Casterlow's office.

Chapter 37

Jacques was on the phone when Laura arrived at the café. His free hand pointed and waved to emphasise points and as she approached, his expressive face suddenly flared with a fierceness she hadn't seen before. He was an attractive man, and she wanted to believe he was genuine and being honest with her, but she wasn't sure. He looked up, saw her and the fierceness dissolved into a smile.

'We'll finish this later,' he said firmly, nodded and added 'Oui, yes, we'll talk later about that too.'

He placed his phone on the table, stood, and kissed Laura's cheeks. Elaborate scrawls and doodles adorned the page of his open diary, reminding her of Tom's phone scribblings. Jacques followed her gaze, closed the diary, and moved it aside.

'Before I forget.' He pulled her neatly folded navy-blue jacket from a bag. 'Coffee?' he asked.

Laura nodded. He ordered at the counter and brought back table water and glasses.

'How long will you be away this time?' she asked.

'I have to return Friday but—' His phone trilled and vibrated. Even his ring tone reminded her of Tom.

'Please excuse me, I must take this.'

He took his phone outside and waved and pointed through another conversation, this time with his back to her. Laura fingered the edge of the well-used diary, its battered corners and scuffed cover rough to her touch. She slid it closer. At the sound of approaching footsteps, she yanked her hand away. She knocked her glass, and it toppled, spilling water across the table. The waitress slid two coffees onto the table and quickly mopped the spill with her cloth.

Jacques was still on the phone and when the waitress left, Laura again stroked the diary. Arranging the cups and glasses to create a visual barrier, she opened the diary at a fluorescent Post-it marker. His scrawl was worse than Tom's and some of his notes were written in French. *"Masters?"* was written in the margins alongside *"check contract 06-B4392"*. The café door slammed and Laura looked up to see Jacques striding towards the table.

'Shit.' She released the pages and as they fluttered closed, a name caught her eye. She couldn't check, but was that *"Fayyaad?"* she'd seen written there? She shoved the diary, and it came to rest right on the edge of the table. Her stomach churned.

'Sorry about that.' Jacques' eyes fixed on her hand quivering near the diary.

Laura gently pushed it closer to Jacques. She slid her coffee into its place, then rested her shaking hands in her lap, out of sight. She'd mentioned Fayyaad during the Barossa trip, but why would Jacques write his name in his diary?

'You've been in Australia longer than I'd expected. It's taking a long time to establish this charity effort,' she said as he sat down.

'You want me to leave?' he replied light-heartedly. He stowed the diary in his satchel.

'Tom's business trips rarely lasted more than a few days.'

'You are keen for me to leave?'

'Doesn't technology make it easier to do things remotely?'

'I'm establishing new processes without a team. Some things need to be done face to face.'

'I'm confused about you.'

'Yes, I'm confusing, but so are you.'

'Me? How am I confusing?'

'You ask about my work, yet you insist you don't like talking work. You are close friends with Peter, but don't admit to knowing what Tom and Peter did. You seem to enjoy my company but appear keen for me to leave.'

Laura sipped her coffee. If only she was better at these games.

'I ask about your work because…it sounds interesting. You're mysterious—' She hadn't meant to add that.

Jacques laughed. 'Mysterious? I'm not mysterious. I've told you, I do very mundane and ordinary work.'

It's what he hadn't told her that made him mysterious. Seeing Fayyaad's name in his diary revived the flashback and her uncertainty. She gathered her courage.

'I found your phone number in Tom's diary.'

Jacques grimaced.

'Why would he have your name and number?'

Jacques shrugged. 'I can't explain it. Someone must have given him my number.'

'I thought I saw you last October, leaving a hotel with Tom,' Laura continued, emboldened by his silence.

Jacques looked deep in thought. 'It can't have been me. I've never met Tom.'

She wasn't certain it was him that night. His explanation about his number in Tom's diary was plausible, but she wasn't satisfied.

'Laura. I assure you I never met Tom, honestly. What's this about?'

'Did you come to Australia last year?' Laura persisted.

'I worked in Sydney, but I can't give you details. What are you looking for in Tom's diary?'

'I was flicking through—'

'Did you find anything else?'

His gaze was assured, clear, even warm. He seemed sincere, and yet she was reluctant to trust him.

'No. Nothing.' She wanted to ask about Fayyaad and Bassarti but it might give too much away.

'If you tell me what's bothering you, maybe I could help,' Jacques offered.

She wanted to believe him. 'I was…surprised to see your name and number in Tom's diary, that's all.'

They sat quietly for a while.

'I'm flying back to New York soon,' he said.

Laura nodded. She hadn't finished questioning him yet, but was unsure of how to continue.

The café had emptied, and the silence felt oppressive. She wanted noise, chatter, and conversations to fill the spaces. To give her time to think.

'I hope to catch up with my daughter, but she's always so busy. We struggle to connect.' He grimaced. 'I wish it was otherwise, but—'

'Children are their own people.' Laura's thoughts turned to Robby and her fears for him forced themselves in front of Tom's puzzles.

'Have you sorted the issues with…Robby is it?'

His uncanny ability to pinpoint her concerns unsettled her.

She shook her head. 'It's worse now. He's involved in…he doesn't think it's serious.'

'But you do?'

'I can't get through to him. Nothing I try works,' she admitted.

Jacques hesitated 'I'm not much help. I struggle trying to convince my daughter that I care.'

They both shrugged at the same time. Laura studied him. The image he presented didn't reconcile with the pieces of information, firing her suspicions. Maybe she didn't want to believe the evidence.

Jacques looked at his watch and sighed. 'I must go.' He stood 'If you need anything, or find anything, please talk to me.'

'Like what?'

'Anything,' he repeated.

'Is there something you need to tell me?' she asked.

He frowned. 'You can trust me. Can I drop you anywhere?'

Laura shook her head. 'I drove.'

Jacques grabbed his bags. 'Can we keep in touch?'

'I have your phone number.'

His frown deepened. 'Stay safe, Laura.' He kissed her on both cheeks.

He climbed into a waiting taxi and as it sped away, Laura cursed. She'd learned nothing important.

Chapter 38

John turned into the almost full car park and parked on a slight incline near the exit. The cars around him were empty and there was no one around. The sound of music and laughter filtered down from the Pavilion Restaurant perched on the rise above the carpark. If he stretched forward, he could see the balcony jutting out towards the sea, and if he listened carefully, he could hear the muffled sounds of waves lapping on the beach. The night sky was a luminous grey with shadowy forms, either birds or bats, winging past.

He examined his throbbing nose in the rear-vision mirror. He cursed Fleur. It was too dark to see much, but it was tender and the swelling was obvious. He swore. To make matters worse, he'd probably develop a black eye. He got out and, following the directions he'd been given, walked up the hill along the back of the restaurant to the end of the treed garden. He tracked the shadows before ducking into a wisteria-covered gazebo with a bench seat inside. He sat and waited.

Footsteps crunched on the gravel pathway. John pulled back. The outline of a familiar short, round figure appeared at the entrance and John released his breath.

'No one saw you? This is not convenient,' Casterlow puffed.

'I'm happy to meet you out in the open,' John retorted. 'I've done everything you've asked. Now it's time you told me what's going on.'

'I don't like being pushed.'

'If I'm good enough to do your dirty work, then you can fill me in,' John insisted.

'I've explained before, I must protect my project. It's too important.'

'I've kept my end of the bargain. It's time you honour yours, or else.'

When Casterlow stepped back, a shaft of light caught the fire in his eyes. 'Or else? Are you threatening me?'

'You won't get rid of me as easily as you did Furness. I'm not as naïve or stupid.'

'I didn't do anything to—'

'Save it for the press. I told you I'm not stupid.' John wanted answers now.

Casterlow's head shook slowly from side to side. He chuckled; a sound devoid of joy but akin to amusement. 'You've got balls threatening me.'

He turned and ambled up a path straddled by trees and manicured gardens. The breeze rustled the leaves. It carried faint music and laughter into the garden too.

'I think we can work together. I've proved my usefulness.' John softened his tone.

'I can't be away from the reception too long. I'll be missed. But you're right. You've been useful, and I'd planned for you to become more involved, eventually. It's dangerous. I can tell you, my project has developed a new, powerful chemical weapon. It has massive potential. We still working on developing more products, with varied uses, but this chemical weapon is fantastic. God is definitely on our side. Once the testing phase is completed, we can plan to use it to stop the rot. It's more than a political tool. It will discreetly rid us of obstacles, those people who want to stand in our way. We'll be able to promote our values and take the crusade further. It has limitless applications. We could even eliminate those advocating for abortion rights and gay rights, and bring back common decency. This product will deliver real power.'

John swallowed down a thread of anxiety. He hadn't expected this. The fire in Casterlow's eyes resembled Babbo when he plotted and planned. Religion was drummed into him as he was growing up but it hadn't taken John long to recognise that religion was a form of insurance. His family paid their dues and then ignored the rules. Casterlow was fanatical, but his belief system was convenient. It delivered power, control over others, and the moral high ground to interpret the rules for his own benefit. John needed to step carefully. Religious zealots of all kinds were unpredictable. That made them dangerous.

'How can I help you? How can I be a stronger partner?' John offered warily. A shiver travelled up his spine.

'Early indications are that our weapon is more formidable than what's currently on the market. It's easy to use, just a small coating on an object will do the trick. Victims won't recover. We want to use it strategically to eliminate the fools who stand in the way of our plans. But we must keep the product under the radar. We're not sure how detectable it is once it's done its job. The Russians are our biggest threat. That's why it's paramount we maintain utmost secrecy.' Casterlow hesitated. 'With this chemical we'll force our enemies to cooperate or else.' Casterlow sighed.

Casterlow was talking about using this chemical to kill people, but he couldn't say that. Was he squeamish? Or had his enemies become less than human?

'Rumours suggest the Russians know a product has been developed, but they don't know anything concrete,' John suggested.

'The UN are investigating too but they're not only interested in the what. They'd shut down our research and trials if they knew about them. That can't be allowed to happen. Just because we don't comply with their damned rules. It's a war for christ's sake. We have to use whatever means we have at our disposal to win. If some people suffer, it's unfortunate, but a necessary sacrifice. These people don't matter. This is for the greater good.'

John frowned. Casterlow seemed lost in his tirade, but then, suddenly, he pulled himself out of the trance, and added in a calm and cold voice, 'We've deflected them so far.'

John stifled his unease. 'It's time to trust me, otherwise, I can't trust you,' he said. The truth was he didn't trust Casterlow, not yet, but this project was important.

It was business.

Casterlow stood in front of a rocky pile on the edge of the pathway that curved back towards the carpark and the beach. The dull light momentarily glistened on his bald pate, but when he faced John, the low-level light cast his face into shadowy relief. It was clear he was calculating his risks. John waited to see what side the mathematics came out on. He watched moon flecks sparkle on the distant waves and create dancing patterns.

'I'm in a bind,' Casterlow finally said. 'Maybe you can help me after all.'

'Go on.'

'Furness fucked up. He was overseeing a side business, a useless byproduct that generates revenue to prop up our research. All he needed to do was turn a blind eye, and he did until that girl interfered. How she got that information, I don't know. Her half-finished report revealed details about my project that shouldn't have been available.'

John smirked. So he'd been right. The girl, Corrinne, had threatened Casterlow's project.

Casterlow continued, 'Furness got cold feet. He objected, saying he wouldn't sit by, blah blah blah, like he was some kind of do-gooder. He was going to threaten everything.' Casterlow seemed to be talking to himself and John didn't want to interrupt the flow. But, as though John's thoughts had stemmed the flow anyway, Casterlow shook his head and chuckled. 'The PM's moving a rookie into the portfolio, so I have to clear up the mess. I wasn't supposed to be directly involved. Furness handled the small-time issues but now.' Casterlow paced. 'I'm attending a meeting on Friday.'

John stared into the dark shadow across Casterlow's face. Not Friday. He was going to Dimi's meeting. That couldn't be postponed.

'Where's the meeting?' John asked.

'It could be useful to have you there. You can be installed as a go-between. The rookie can be kept out of it altogether. I'm not confident she'd play the game and the last thing I want is to break in a new recruit.' Casterlow's voice tapered off.

'Where is the meeting?' John asked again.

'Adelaide. We'll fly there separately. I'll send you all the details, but the meeting is at night, at a warehouse. What do you think?'

John frowned. Was Casterlow going to Dimi's meeting? The side business must be her supply of E-bomb. This was turning out better than he planned.

'Who is the meeting with?'

'A local outfit. They've benefited from the byproduct. Now I want them to help me distribute this new product too. What do you say?'

It was Dimi's meeting. John was sure of it. 'Sounds fine. I'll be there.'

'Thank you, John.' Casterlow thought John was doing him a favour and John wasn't going to disabuse him. It was a stroke of luck that the meetings were going to deliver John both the control of Dimi's business and access to Casterlow's chemical weapon.

Casterlow grabbed John's shoulder and squeezed hard. Voices from the other side of the pavilion came closer. John stood rigid, listening. His heart thumped. A woman giggled. It was high-pitched, almost shrill. A man's smooth voice responded and John relaxed. It was a couple sneaking an illicit moment.

Casterlow tapped John on the arm and pointed. John couldn't decipher the sign language in the dark but guessed Casterlow knew a back way into the function. He pushed John's chest, steering him towards the bushes, and whispered, 'I'll be in touch.'

Two loud cracks in quick succession split the silence. John turned to see Casterlow arch violently and crumple. John reached out to break Casterlow's fall but couldn't hold him and they thudded to the ground together. The heavy bulk pinned John under him. Casterlow's arms flopped over John's head, locking him in. The sound of bushes rustling preceded footsteps crunching towards the carpark. John struggled to pull himself free, finally pushing the body to the side. John's hand was wet and sticky. Gunshots? He felt no pain. Casterlow must have been hit.

In the distance, a car door slammed, followed by the sound of a motor starting. John hesitated. Should he run after them? Headlights blinked through the foliage as the car turned onto the main road and sped away. John checked Casterlow's vital signs. He was breathing, but John couldn't find a pulse. Then, Casterlow moaned. He was still alive.

Silence, then one of the couple shushed the other. The man's mumbled response was too indistinct for John to hear, but he guessed they'd heard the commotion and were debating about what to do. John scrambled to hide behind a thick bush as a tall, willowy man strode towards Casterlow's form sprawled across the path. The woman mounted the side stairs and took up a position on the balcony. Her green gown glittered in the bright lights as she brushed it gently.

John hesitated. He couldn't be discovered here with Casterlow. There were too many questions he couldn't or didn't want to answer. When he thought it was clear, he scurried across the lawn as quietly as possible and darted behind a large oak tree. He waited.

A man's voice called for help. John used the commotion to creep back to his car. He gently closed the car door and, without turning on the lights, rolled the vehicle down to the main road. He itched to speed away, but used all his restraint to wait until he'd rolled onto the main road before starting his car. Nausea threatened at his throat when he noticed the red sticky residue on his hands. It stained the leather steering wheel.

Chapter 39

Once home, Laura was met by a barrage of questions and she confessed that she'd learned little new. She was even starting to doubt that she'd seen Fayyaad's name in Jacques' diary. She wasn't ready to sift through Tom's paperwork and files. As a distraction, she turned her thoughts to Robby's dilemma.

'I don't know how Robby will travel to Young without access to a car.' Laura pursed her lips. If only she could resolve at least one important issue.

'I've been thinking Broken Hill may be an option.' Eva suggested.

Mel tapped on the keyboard. 'Bus routes link Broken Hill to Sydney via Parkes. From there, he can connect to Young.'

'That could work.' Eva grabbed her phone and left the room.

She returned with a broad grin on her face.

'Sorted,' Eva announced. 'My copy editor can give Robby a lift next Wednesday. She and her brother are driving to Broken Hill for their parent's thirtieth wedding anniversary.'

'Did you tell her it's dangerous?' Laura wanted Robby safe, but not at the risk of others.

'They know the circumstances. It'll be alright, as long as he's careful.'

Laura grimaced. Robby must do the right thing now. Others'

lives depended on it.

'Now Robby's escape is organised, we can tell you what we learned while you were out,' Mel said.

Laura nodded and Mel continued, 'We've worked out that there are two products. One called Formula Z, and another called E-bomb. They are both connected to Bassarti and Fast-Track.'

'We don't know much about what they are, but of course, we know E-bomb is an illicit hallucinogenic and being sold illegally in Australia. Formula Z is more of a mystery.'

'Perhaps the DVDs will shed light on this,' Laura suggested.

'That first one suggested some form of testing, so it's worth a try,' Mel said.

They returned to the lounge and sat where they could easily see the TV screen. Laura inserted the earliest DVD, labelled *Bokmal 28 March 2004*, into the player and instantly, a shadowy form appeared on the TV screen. It was silhouetted against a dark, indistinct backdrop.

'Are you comfortable?' asked a deep but muffled voice off-camera.

The shadowy male figure nodded.

'Now Bokmal, you have agreed to talk to us about your experience in Bassarti Prison.'

Again, the shadowy figure nodded.

'Shall we start?' The interviewer paused. 'You were imprisoned in Bassarti, is that right?'

'For a long time,' Bokmal's frail voice replied.

'How did you escape?'

'I was smuggled out.' He paused. 'My family paid. I was hidden under…dead bodies. I cannot tell more. It would make trouble.'

Laura gagged at the thought of hiding under dead bodies.

'What happened inside Bassarti?'

'I don't belong. My family made a good business. We help our neighbours and are part of the community but one neighbour, he is jealous. He want his son to marry my sister. My father forbids it. I think, maybe they want revenge. I am sure it is them.'

'Can you tell us about what is happening *inside* the prison?'

'We have very little food. What they give us is sometimes mouldy. Disgusting. A man cannot live like that. Every day we have to take special medicines.'

'You were sick?'

He nodded. 'We cannot eat and we live in dirty conditions, so we get sick. But only after we take the medicines.' The shadow shrugged. 'First, I refuse to take them, but they beat me.' He leaned aside and pulled at his shirt.

'The light in here is not good enough, Bokmal.'

Bokmal leaned back again. 'They force me to swallow the pills. Sores grow all over my body. They don't heal. They bleed all the time. I feel confused and some of the others have strange dreams, or they fight, or they think they can fly. We are watched. All the time. Every day, they ask questions and write things down.'

Laura's skin erupted in goosebumps. Omar's father, in the first DVD, suffered sores too. He'd died soon after the first DVD was recorded.

'What pills are they giving you?'

Bokmal shook his head. 'I am lucky. I am still alive. Five are taken away and we never see them again. A rumour say they died, but no one know for sure.'

A loud knock sounded in the background, and the camera tilted before the screen went blank.

'Quick run,' the interviewer hissed. His voice was no longer disguised.

Laura gasped. 'Oh my god! Was that Tom's voice?' Laura stared at the vacant screen.

'It was Dad. What was he...' Mel swallowed hard.

Silence engulfed them.

'He was still working for APATO in March 2004. Fayyaad said

Tom attended secrets meetings on his own, without Peter. He could have been recording these interviews.' Laura wrung her hands. He'd been gathering evidence, but of what?

'Then these issues are related to Iraq,' Eva suggested.

'If Bassarti is an Iraqi prison, the dates are all wrong. Most of Saddam Hussein's scientists and researchers were imprisoned after the war in 2003. This was recorded a year after the war. It sounds like someone is conducting drug trials, but the Iraqi scientists couldn't be involved.' Mel shook her head.

'Despite the interview occurring in March 2004, they could be collecting evidence about something that happened previously,' Eva mused.

'If it's historical, why did they stop filming so suddenly? Who were they hiding from?' Laura said.

'But western governments control Iraqi rebuilding. They're subject to strict bio-security and bio-safety regulations covering the ethics of drug trials, regardless of which country they're conducted in. Australian scientists take these protocols very seriously,' Mel insisted.

Laura shook her head. She'd hoped to understand what was happening by now, but this DVD hadn't provided the required clarity. It seemed to raise even more questions.

'Are you alright?' Eva asked and looked at both Laura and Mel. Laura nodded. 'It was a shock hearing his voice like that.'

She'd been afraid of what Tom might have done. He'd become disillusioned and cynical. He'd given up, and she'd been afraid that he'd used the situation for his own benefit. Gone rogue maybe. Hearing his voice on the DVD and knowing he was collecting evidence gave her a sense of relief. It also saddened her. She would have helped if he'd asked. She'd have been willing to work alongside him, if only he'd let her in.

'Can you bear to watch the next DVD?' Eva interrupted Laura's thoughts. She picked up the DVD labelled *Hadiya, 7 June 2004.*

'We can't stop now. We need to unravel what Dad was investigating,' Mel said fiercely.

'His death can't be for nothing,' Laura said. She could now pursue the truth without reservations.

Again Tom conducted the interview, but it was a different shadowy figure. Laura's heart clenched tight. Hearing Tom's voice made her miss him more and stirred feelings of remorse and guilt.

'You work in the laboratory at the Bassarti Prison complex, is that correct?' Tom's muffled voice asked.

'There is no laboratory in the prison and only quality control at the factory. I am a research technical assistant at the complex next door,' a female voice responded authoritatively. She shifted in her seat.

Laura finally understood. Bassarti was a multi-function complex, including a prison, a laboratory, and a manufacturing plant.

'What are you researching?'

'A new, very potent hallucinogenic used for psychological treatment. It was a byproduct of a bigger process conducted by another research group. I'm synthesising treatment quantities now.'

'Are you still conducting tests for this drug?'

'No. We are researching other forms, but we are producing commercial quantities. Batches are sent overseas. Our laboratory manager negotiates the destination directly with the Australians. I don't get involved in the administration.'

'Who are the Australians?'

The woman shifted in her seat but didn't answer.

'We need names?' Tom insisted.

'Peter helps to train us in the dispatch paperwork. He's my contact.'

Laura's eyes met Eva's. Peter must be the PF in Tom's diary.

'Any others you can identify?'

'Some Australian...politicians.' She hesitated. 'I'm not introduced to them. They come after the staff go home. One is

'Bernard' and the other man, I don't know a name. He licks his lips all the time.' Her chuckle was a deep and throaty cackle.

Eva frowned. 'The only Bernard I can think of is the Defence and Security Minister, Bernard Casterlow.'

It seemed likely. Defence was connected to this story. 'Patrick Furness has a habit of constantly licking his lips.' Laura grimaced. She remembered the habit had been on display at the work party.

On the TV, Tom spread photos on a low table. Tears sprung to Laura's eyes as his wedding ring flashed across the screen.

Tom shone his phone torch and lit up the photos. 'Can you identify them?'

Hadiya pulled back. 'I…I don't know. It's not safe to name names. I thought you just wanted me to talk about my project.'

The more Tom pressed, the more agitated she became, and eventually, she put her hand up to call the interview to a halt. The camera switched off.

Laura wiped away her tears. Tom was collecting evidence. According to Fayyaad, Tom then told *the wrong people* about his findings and now he was dead. Who did he tell?

'She said they're not testing the hallucinogenic drug at Bassarti. So she must be working on E-bomb. It's not consistent with the other DVDs. They're definitely about drug tests,' Mel puzzled.

'That must be Formula Z,' Eva said

'Peter is connected to E-bomb, but we don't know what else,' Laura said quietly.

'What was Furness blowing the whistle on?' Mel scratched her head. 'Could it be connected too?'

Some of the pieces of the puzzle fell into place. Tom didn't take the E-bomb voluntarily. Someone probably administered that lethal dose. Laura shivered. He'd kept silent to protect her. It's not that he'd no longer cared, but that he'd cared too much to endanger her. Yet, his silence hadn't kept him safe.

'How can we prove these DVDs are genuine?' Eva, the ex-journalist, followed the process buried deep in her psyche; check sources, verify details, and confirm a story.

'Tom recorded them and stowed them away,' Laura said.

'I don't work on domestic issues.' Mel's face was pale. 'I can't verify them.'

'It's happening in Iraq. It's foreign, not domestic,' Laura said quietly.

'Yes and no. I can't access information about Australian government projects run overseas, only those run by foreign powers.' Mel swallowed hard. 'We should hand these over to national security.'

'Currently, some very Draconian legislation and policies are explained away as *national security*. It's code for "we don't want to explain". I don't trust them. Government ministers are involved, although we don't know how, and until we know their role, we can't trust anyone.'

'Mum, this is serious.'

'I know, sweetheart, but Tom and Corrinne died because they trusted the wrong people.'

'We can't hand these over until we know more. Mel, we'll be in a better position to make the right decision once we have all the facts,' Eva added.

Mel nodded. 'But investigating this is dangerous.'

They couldn't dispute it.

'But not investigating is just as dangerous.' Laura shivered, remembering the car incident in the Barossa. Was she being paranoid, or was it too related?

'How did they find their sources, the interviewees,' Eva added. 'We need to protect them too.'

'Do you think Corrinne could have hidden evidence away too? She'd stored her papers in a container at that U-Store-It facility, but she collected them before she died. Did she take it all with her to Sydney?'

'I wonder if her husband would know,' Eva said.

'She may have kept him in the dark too, like I was,' Laura said. 'It might be worth talking to him, just to be sure.'

Laura poured some red wine to numb their feelings. There were too many questions and too few answers. Silence shrouded them. They tried to talk about other things, but the conversation didn't stick. The images from the DVDs couldn't be ignored.

Eva glanced at her watch. 'I need to go. I have an interview in the morning that I can't postpone. Shall I come back after lunch tomorrow?' Eva asked quietly. 'We can watch the last DVD together then.'

Laura nodded. Right now, she needed respite to restore her emotional balance.

'I haven't heard from Fayyaad either. His friend hasn't seen him for days,' Eva said. 'I'm worried.'

'Could he be lying low?' Laura suggested.

'Who's this?' Mel asked.

Eva explained.

'Mum, you promised you wouldn't do anything dangerous.'

'I'm at risk no matter what I do.' Laura wrung her hands and added, 'Tonight, I thought I saw Fayyaad's name written in Jacques' diary,' Laura confessed. 'I accidentally mentioned him when we were in the Barossa.'

'No! I really hope nothing has happened to him,' Eva said.

'I do too. I'm so sorry.' Laura couldn't look at Eva. If something happened to Fayyaad, it would be her fault. 'Let me know when you hear from him,' Laura urged. She shivered. Was Jacques involved with this somehow?

'I have a report to finish for tomorrow, but I don't want to leave. Will you be alright?' Mel asked. 'I'll be back as soon as I can.'

'I'm a big girl. I've appreciated you being here.'

After they'd gone, Laura found the number and phoned

Corrinne's husband. His lifeless voice broke her heart. Despite his protestations that he knew nothing about Corrinne's research, Laura insisted they meet tomorrow morning. He finally agreed.

Then she sat in the lounge with all the lights on and waited. It grew late, and she was worried. Robby was supposed to call her. Outside, it was dark and gloomy. Big raindrops pelted down on the pergola roof, creating a thunderous roar. Her thoughts turned dark and more sinister. What would she do if something happened to Robby? By midnight, she was frantic.

Chapter 40

It was after midnight when Robby finally phoned.

'I've been so worried,' she scolded.

His irritation flared. 'I said I'd call.'

'I'd expected you to call earlier.'

'I had things to do.'

'Like what? You're not doing anything reckless?'

'I'm checking out a few things. I need something to bargain with; to get my life back.'

'You need to forget about them. I've arranged a way to get you to safety. Don't jeopardise it.'

'I want to know who's behind Nick and the gang. I'm intrigued. I've had time to think about it and I want to know who's pulling the strings. Nick's been preoccupied planning an important meeting, so he's not as watchful as usual. I'm being careful, but I don't understand why a government minister is meeting them. Why would ministers deal with gangs? The world is fucked up. It's not black and white, or good and bad. You and Dad banged on about principles and ideals, but many people talk the talk but don't walk the walk.'

'I know. I trusted politicians and businesses to consider the common good, but everywhere I look, they're acting on self-interest to benefit themselves and their wealthy mates. I'm disillusioned too. I should have been paying attention.'

'No one pays attention to what's going on. I'd love to be a fly on the wall at the warehouse on Friday.'

'What warehouse?'

'The deserted APATO warehouse in Port Adelaide. It's one of their regular meeting places and they're using it on Friday. I've only been there a couple of times during shipment deliveries. It's used for their serious meetings and I don't get invited to them. It's a good venue. They can slip in and out without being seen. The rats give me the creeps, though.'

Laura took the phone outside and sat under the pergola. The pigeons were quiet, probably asleep like she should be. The rain had stopped and, as the moon appeared from behind the clouds, moonlight created inky shapes across the yard. It reminded her of the eerie images on the DVDs. She shivered. For her, at least, a cloudy mist filtered the twinkling stars' brilliance into a soft reassuring glow.

'You'll be gone before Friday.' Laura explained the arrangements.

'Aunt Claire sounds like a tyrant. Are you sure there isn't anywhere else? I don't even know her,' Robby protested yet again.

'We have no choice.'

'Who is this editor? I don't know her either. Are you sure we can trust her?'

'There's no alternative.'

'I guess.'

And on it went; Robby raising objections which became more and more half-hearted, and Laura wearing him down by becoming firmer and firmer. She couldn't offer any other solutions and neither could he. He just didn't like the solution they had.

Finally, he acquiesced and Laura breathed more easily.

She swallowed down the annoyance that built up during this conversation. 'I love you,' she said. She yearned to wrap her arms around him and say goodbye properly.

'I love you too, Mum. Thanks for your help.'

Tears sprung to her eyes. 'I will always help you in any way I can.'

She made him promise to ring when he arrived. Eva's editor would ring once they'd arrived in Broken Hill too. At least this was one problem solved.

Laura went back inside. She checked the window and door locks, then turned out the lights. In her world now, danger lurked everywhere. She hadn't bargained for this. She yearned to walk away or curl up under the covers until the issues disappeared, but no one, including her, was safe until Tom's mystery was solved. Deep down, she believed in and wanted justice. She wanted the world to be better, to be fair and just, and if she didn't dare to bring wrong-doers to justice, how could she expect anyone else to do it.

In the morning, her gritty eyes were dry from lack of sleep. She sat outside, nibbling her toast and watching a pigeon squeeze under her neighbour's solar panels to add more twigs to the nest. Her neighbour complained about the damage they caused, so his reluctance to enmesh his panels puzzled her. Inaction would cost him more than prevention in the long term.

Her current dilemma was like that too. She couldn't ignore or turn a blind eye to the conspiracy being uncovered. She'd be complicit in others' suffering.

She glanced at her watch and grabbed her car keys. She was ready to uncover the truth.

Parking spaces were scarce along Plane Tree Drive and she'd passed the Zoo entrance before she found one. She traipsed across the unmown grass, stumbling over the twigs and pine cones scattered between the sprawling Moreton Bay fig trees. The botanic garden entrance gate squeaked as she opened it and she let it bang shut behind her. Along the tree-lined path, wind rustled the leaves and flickering sunshine danced on the pavement in front of her feet.

She peered in the windows of the upmarket restaurant, then walked around the corner to the kiosk.

Laura sat at a table overlooking the lake. It was cold, but at least last night's rain had gone. A little boy squealed with delight as the ducks dived and splashed to fetch the morsels of food he'd thrown near the reeds. She smiled. His joy reminded her of her own children at that age.

'Laura?' a man's voice startled her.

Corrinne's husband was older than Laura had expected. He was tall and reedy, and all angles and corners except for his round glasses. His dishevelled hair and clothes reflected an inner turmoil. He flopped heavily into the chair beside her and self-consciously placed a bag on the ground between them.

'After we spoke, I remembered…Corrinne…had taken up a safety deposit box with our bank. We don't have anything valuable, even her jewellery is…was nothing grand but—' He clenched his lips. 'I found this in there. I haven't looked inside. I can't. The idea that this could be responsible for Corrinne's—' His eyes welled with tears. He took off his glasses and cleaned them with the band of his jumper.

Laura patted his shoulder. 'I'll look.'

He pushed the bag towards Laura. 'I want to know…but…I don't.'

'Can I ask you about the last few days before…' He flinched as Laura spoke and she couldn't finish the question.

'She went to Sydney. She was supposed to be gone for the day but, that evening, she left me a message to say she was staying another night. She hadn't yet booked a return flight, but I expected her to call me when she arrived at the airport. She never did.'

'Why did she go to Sydney?' Laura asked.

'She was hand-delivering a controversial report about Fast-Track. Something to do with defence. She'd been anxious about it. She didn't tell me who she was meeting, but she'd mentioned both

Casterlow and Furness should see it. They denied meeting her and her manager swears he doesn't know about any report. They're suggesting she'd gone …rogue and was working… with criminals. It's unbelievable. She would never do that.'

Branding Tom and Corrinne as a problem was a way to deflect blame. Laura understood this now.

'What have the police said?'

'Nothing really. Our house was ransacked the day she left, but the police think it's a coincidence. I can't even confirm that anything was stolen. They think it was probably kids. They made an awful mess.'

'I was burgled too, the night Tom…I think Corrinne and Tom were researching serious issues related to Iraq. They weren't involved in anything criminal, they were trying to expose criminal activity.' She leaned down and opened the bag. She extracted a photocopied report. 'I'm hoping this paperwork and report will provide the necessary detail.'

He nodded.

Corrinne and Tom were listed as co-authors. A yellow Post-it note on the front page read "*Original copy to Furness, 1 copy sent to Casterlow.*" Laura leafed through it."E-bomb"; "Bassarti"; "more potent than novichok"; "formula Z"; and "mafia"; caught her attention. She rummaged through the next compartment of the bag and found an envelope tucked into the front pocket. His name was printed across it.

'Would you like me to leave you alone while you read this?' she asked.

He shook his head. He lifted himself slowly off the chair and took the envelope to a bench by the pond. The toddler was still feeding the ducks and his mother eyed Corrinne's husband warily. He didn't notice. He stared at the ducks, repeatedly turning the envelope in his hands, before finally tearing it open and extracting a single page.

Horror, disbelief, and grief played out on his face as he read. He removed his glasses and wiped his eyes. Laura's eyes welled in sympathy at his obvious grief and confusion.

His shoulders slumped as he walked back to their table. 'She knew. She knew she was in danger, but she thought she could sort it out.' He lowered his head into his hands. 'She apologised. How could exposing a plot make losing her worthwhile? If she'd asked me, I'd have told her the risk was too great.'

Laura found no words of comfort. She'd felt that way early on too. But in the end, the decision had been Corrinne and Tom's.

'This paperwork is vital evidence.' Laura explained what she knew.

'I'm not getting involved. This has cost too much already,' he said, his voice gaining strength.

Laura now felt differently. Justice must be done. She couldn't rest until it was. She remembered the little boy feeding the ducks. She needed to do everything possible to make the world safer.

She left Corrinne's husband in the Botanic Gardens immersed in his thoughts and grief.

Mel arrived at lunchtime and Eva was close on her heels. Laura told them about her meeting with Corrinne's husband.

Mel scanned Corrinne's report. 'This is an updated version. It should have more detail than Dad's copy.'

They ate their lunch of sandwiches quietly, each deep in their own thoughts. Once finished, they moved into the lounge.

Laura's hands shook as she loaded the third DVD labelled *Gunter, 5 Dec 2005*. Dread pulled at her. Again, a shadowy figure filled the centre of the TV screen. The shape bulged beyond the confines of the chair, creeping under the armrest to form a cushion on each side. Gunter was a big man.

'Thank you for talking to us.' It wasn't Tom's voice this time.

'I didn't sign on for this! I've managed hardened criminals for many years, but this? I'd expected fanatics, terrorists, and hardened law-breakers. Instead, they're old, frail men and young, naïve lads. They're not hardened anything.' Gunter's hands waved in emphasis and his body swayed with emotion, creating rustling noises.

'Of course, I'm not trusted with details. None of the guards are. We control them in the cells until it's their turn. Depending on which *care cell* is looking after them, we collect and deliver them. We might see them later,' Gunter explained.

'What are they delivered for?'

'I don't think they're being interrogated. They go in groups and they don't come back physically injured. They're just weird. I've seen them have nervous breakdowns. Early on, some died, I think from total organ failure, although not so much now. Some experience severe pain, but there's nothing specific. It's mostly behavioural and their mental state. They're under a lot of stress, there's no end in sight for their detention. They show signs of paranoia, or angry outbursts or, strangely, become unusually docile. I've never seen anything like it before. They're monitored daily, but no one knows what's happening in the long run. None have been to court or trial.'

Laura frowned. Hadn't Corrinne died from organ failure?

'Are prisoners moved to other facilities?'

'My groups come back after each session, but I've heard some don't.' Gunter leaned forward and added, 'I don't know what happens to them Conrad…err sorry…I don't know what happens to them or where they go. There isn't any other accommodation attached to the complex. Any transfers are always at night. They leave from the other end of the compound and have a special guard detail.'

'Can you get us more details?'

'My friend who works there won't speak to you, I'm sure of that. He might talk to me.' Gunter's head bowed. 'Last time I asked questions, they moved me to perimeter duty.' Gunter laughed. 'I liked it better. I could pretend it was a normal prison. Unfortunately, when they got short-staffed, I was back looking after the cells.' He sighed. 'It's time to look for another job.'

'Not before we talk again, I hope,' Conrad said softly. 'We need more detail.'

'I'll try.'

The DVD ended.

'The interviewer is Conrad,' Laura said as a memory surfaced.

January 2005

Tom organised papers and stowed them in his briefcase.

'You seem happy?' Laura commented.

'I can see a light at the end of the tunnel.' He laughed. 'My life is one big cliché.'

He looked up and smiled at her. She loved that smile; it brightened up his whole face. She'd missed it.

'We can start to plan our retirement together then?' This was what she'd hoped for.

'Not yet. It's still...tricky, but I've found someone who might help.'

'Who?'

'He's not in APATO, but he's working on similar issues.'

'You're not really handing things over, are you?' She felt cheated.

He flashed a half-smile. 'I need help to sort things out first. It's complicated. The misinformation campaign needs to be stopped. That needs facts and data. He can help and I promise, I'll eventually step back.'

Laura wasn't listening. Alarm bells sounded in her head. Why couldn't he step away or let others deal with the issues now? What was so important?

'Who is this person? Why can't he take this off your hands?' she asked sternly.

Tom looked at her as though trying to decide how much to tell her.

'His name is Marx. He's nothing like either of his namesakes, Karl or Groucho.' He laughed at the joke, but he was trying too hard. 'Conrad's researching anomalies, but he can't do it all.'

'I'm waiting for you to step away from this. I won't wait forever.'

Tom looked up and his face turned sad.

'I know. It's been rough, but it's...complicated. Whatever you do — and this is important — don't say anything to Peter.'

***

Laura cringed. She'd wanted him to choose between his research or her. If he'd chosen her, he might still be alive. Maybe; maybe not. If those protecting the secrets believed you threatened them, they acted. It didn't matter if they were right or not. They didn't need facts.

Tom's regrets had pushed him forward. He was a man of principle. He couldn't have turned a blind eye to the inhumane treatment of prisoners described on the DVDs. She needed to be strong. Someone must make a stand. Why not her?

'Conrad Marx was helping Tom,' Laura said quietly.

'Who is he?' Mel asked.

Eva Googled the name on her phone. 'There are several: a baseball player, a writer, and one attached to the UN.'

'What does the UN employee do?' Mel asked.

'He's attached to a regional security group called UNMOVIC. He was seconded from Canada.'

Mel nodded. 'That's the UN Monitoring, Verification, and Inspection Commission. The US denied them access to Iraq, so I'm working with them.'

'Can we get his contact details?' Laura asked, hopeful that they could hand over their materials.

Mel offered to follow it up.

'Wasn't there a note in one of the diaries about Conrad?' Laura leafed through the 2006 diary first and finally found the entry she was looking for. On 9 December 2005, Tom wrote *"Conrad's missing"* in red ink.

'He went missing after Gunter's interview,' Mel said.

Eva's phone pinged. 'Fayyaad's friend is frantic. He still hasn't heard from Fayyaad.'

Laura stared down at her hands. She didn't dare look at Eva.

'What do we know about Jacques?' Eva asked.

Laura swallowed down her guilt. Her carelessness had endangered Fayyaad's life.

'Not much. He's asked me questions about Tom and Peter's business but denies ever meeting them before. I suspect I saw him follow Tom out of a hotel one night last October, but I'm not certain it was him.' Laura wrung her hands.

'I've got his business card. I can check both him and Conrad Marx out. Maybe I can get some answers.' Mel sounded assured and confident. It was contagious.

'Fayyaad mentioned Tom talking to a journalist.' Laura said.

'That's right. He said he was sick and now he couldn't find him.' Eva shook her head. 'We need to sift through the paperwork again now we have Corrinne's files too.'

In the office, she pulled a clean page from her notebook and drew columns. 'What do we need to know?'

'Corrinne's report confirms our theory. There are two separate issues. Importation of the illicit drug E-bomb, which arrives from Iraq via the Fast-Track scheme, and Formula Z, which is part of a project overseen by Defence. Tom and Corrinne suspected that the secret defence program was conducting trials in contravention of the international bio-security safeguards. They referred to the new International Health Regulations established in 2005, adopted by the World Health Organisation, which were added to the 1993 Chemical Weapons Convention.' Mel looked up. 'It's about chemical weapons testing and manufacture. That's Casterlow's area of responsibility. It's top-secret.'

'Is Peter involved with both?' Eva questioned.

Mel grimaced. 'It's not clear how Peter or Furness fit into the picture. Dad and Corrinne thought Casterlow controlled the testing regime and Furness wasn't involved.'

'Robby said there's an important meeting on Friday night. I've noticed that Casterlow's in Adelaide to open the new submarine building facilities that night too. Could it be a coincidence, or could he be going to the meeting Robby was talking about?' Laura said.

'It's farfetched. Why would he?' Mel said.

'That meeting on Friday night could answer all our questions. If only we could video or record it.' Eva doodled on her page.

'There's no way,' Mel objected.

'There might be a way,' Eva said mysteriously.

'How? It's much too dangerous,' Mel insisted.

'Not if we could set up the equipment beforehand.'

'Robby said it's at the warehouse in Port Adelaide, but we don't have a time.' Laura quivered. This was more than she'd bargained for.

Eva carried her phone into the hall. When she returned, she was smiling broadly.

'Peter is so easy to read. The meeting must be after 8 p.m. on Friday,' she said triumphantly.

'We should inform the police,' Mel said.

'Corrinne and Tom informed official channels and look what happened to them. We don't have anything concrete to tell the police,' Eva suggested. 'If we record their meeting, we could publicly expose them and it would also protect us. We wouldn't have to get too close. We'll visit the warehouse to identify convenient hiding places before the meeting. What do you think?' Eva's experience with amateur recording equipment made her sound confident.

Laura hesitated. 'It sounds dangerous.'

'By the time they start their meeting, we'd be gone.' Eva's eyes sparkled. 'I'll use my contacts to get some suitable equipment.'

Laura hesitated. Her hands shook and there was a knot in her stomach, but she ignored them. 'Let's do it.'

'I'm coming too,' Mel insisted.

'Mel, you can't come. It's not safe.' Laura wouldn't let her daughter take these risks.

'That's exactly why I'm coming. I'm not letting you do this alone.'

'It would jeopardise your job. Eva and I can do this.' Laura used her firmest voice.

'No way, I'm making sure you don't do anything too risky,' Mel insisted.

Formulating a plan kept Laura's focus away from the emotional earthquake flaring inside her. Could they really set up the equipment and stay safe? They'd know once they checked out the warehouse.

Chapter 41

Thunderstorms rolled across the sky and cast John's office into dreary darkness.

'The main meeting is scheduled for 9 p.m. on Friday, at the warehouse,' Carlo boomed over the phone.

'I know.' John smirked.

'How? Even I didn't know the details until yesterday.'

'I have my sources. What else can you tell me?'

'We're having a meeting immediately beforehand. To work out the fine details of the deal.'

'Who's going to do that? You, Nick, and Dimi? Is that all?'

'Yeah. The fewer involved, the better.' Carlo paused. 'I've been thinking. Do you think the timing is right?'

'Are you meeting at the warehouse too?' John ignored the comment. Carlo wasn't a strategic brain.

'I'm serious. Maybe you should wait until the deal is settled. Let the meetings proceed, then take over.'

John didn't remember Carlo having so many opinions before. 'I'll decide when the time is right. Now, where's your preliminary meeting?'

'The North Cemetery Chapel. Do you know it? I'm driving the boss. We're starting at 8 p.m.'

'You've talked to Nick? Are you confident that he's with us?'

'He doesn't care who's in charge, as long as he gets a stake. He's a pushy bastard, so he'll probably try to renegotiate the terms.'

'I can handle him. You haven't let anything slip, have you?'

'Do I look stupid?' Carlo's grumpy tone was back. 'I'm just the muscle. Anyway, she's worried about Peter getting cold feet. He might have guessed and if so, he won't take it well.'

'That could be to our advantage. If he's pulling back, maybe she'll be more likely to go quietly. He might not mind me taking over.'

'She won't let go that easily. What are you going to do with her?'

John shook his head at the slight whine in Carlo's voice.

'What does it matter to you? I'll work it out. What happens depends on how she reacts. You have to be ready.'

'She won't go quietly, you know that?'

'Just keep your mouth shut.'

'Sure. Are you bringing your own muscle?'

'I've got local help until I'm sure it's under control.'

'Who?'

'None of your business. You just play your part.'

'You better have them under control too,' Carlo said and hung up.

Carlo didn't sound keen or enthused. Was he getting cold feet? John would deal with him once the takeover was complete.

When the phone rang again, he grumbled, 'Hello.'

'Bad morning?' Kleb asked. 'Did you know Casterlow's out of hospital? It was serious, I hear. His injuries can't have been an accident.'

'I was with him when he was shot. We were talking when two shots rang out and the next thing I know, Casterlow fell on top of me. There was blood everywhere.'

'Why didn't you tell me? We agreed you'd leave Casterlow until the takeover was done.'

'It was lucky I didn't listen to you. Casterlow's going to Dimi's meeting. He asked me to step in for Furness. If he hadn't pulled through, it would've left me in the lurch.' John didn't need a lecture. If Kleb and Carlo were so clever, why weren't they running the business?

'So who shot him?'

'I didn't see. It was too dark,' John said.

'Skollov's a likely candidate.'

Skollov was the easy answer, but was it the right one?

'Were they trying to kill him or just warn him off?' John said, then another thought struck him. 'Were they after him or me?'

'Who knew you were there? I didn't. Did you tell anyone else?' Kleb sighed.

'Good point.' John avoided saying more.

'It was common knowledge that Casterlow was going to the wedding reception, but how did they expect to get a clean shot? It must have been a scare tactic.'

'Skollov doesn't have a reason to kill, but scaring Casterlow might be useful.' John scratched his head.

'Skollov could easily arrange to steal the information he doesn't need to kill or scare anyone with a gun,' Kleb said.

'I've been thinking. Given Skollov's connection to the Russians, using the Devil's Guard as my security could be a problem now.' John didn't like to admit this complication.

'I told you they were risky.'

With hindsight perhaps, but Kleb hadn't known anything. John stared out of the window. The storm clouds had passed and there was a hint of sunlight fighting its way through.

'I can help,' Kleb offered.

Kleb avoided getting too close previously. He'd ensured his lawyerly reputation stayed unblemished and fiercely safeguarded his anonymity. Why risk it now?

'It's too late to change. It'll be OK.' John preferred to keep Kleb behind the scenes as his surprise secret weapon.

'I'd love to see Dimi's face.' A hard edge infected Kleb's voice.

John was also looking forward to seeing the look on Dimi's face. She'd deprived him of his inheritance for long enough, and he was finally going to reclaim it. He was entitled.

Although he hoped she'd see sense and accept the takeover, maybe even work alongside him, he was prepared. He smiled. Family was important, but not indispensable. Whatever happened, he was going to remove her irritating presence once and for all.

'I'll take care of it,' John confirmed.

'What are you planning?' Kleb asked.

'It's better you don't know.' John understood the 'don't ask and don't tell' philosophy the politicians used.

Chapter 42

Casterlow appeared on the breakfast TV news program. He explained that he'd been injured while attending a wedding reception but gave no details. Laura studied his face. It looked hard and cold. As was so often the case these days, he was adept at answering the question he wished they'd asked rather than the actual question. The reporter was no match for Casterlow, although maybe he wasn't really trying. They joked and laughed their way through banal questions; the reporter feeding him lines that helped Casterlow's message. Casterlow insisted Australia deserved to have more power and influence on the world stage. He stressed that small nations must be made to toe the line, especially when they were receiving financial assistance and aid. Laura almost switched off before he confirmed his visit to Adelaide on Friday to open the new section of the submarine building site.

Just because he was coming on Friday didn't mean he was going to the warehouse meeting, but it seemed an interesting coincidence. Laura shivered. A scrap of memory from the day before Tom died flashed through her mind.

February 2006

Tom stormed into the kitchen. His face was almost white. Was it the phone call or had it happened gradually from burrowing away in his study? She should be taking better care of him, but the reverse was also true. He should be taking better care of her too.

Tom slammed down a knife, sighed, grabbed a block of cheese from the fridge, and swore as he struggled to open the cracker tin.

'Do you want a coffee?' he asked and turned to put the kettle on.

'Yes, thanks.' His moods exhausted her. She didn't ask what was wrong.

He rummaged in the cupboards, grabbed two coffee bags, and took the milk out of the fridge. His face showed the same exhaustion that she felt, and she relented.

'Tom. Are you OK?'

He grimaced. 'I don't know.'

'What does that mean?'

He shrugged. 'I can't explain. I wish I could turn a blind eye, ignore things, but…I can't.'

The angry voice in her head screamed to let him deal with it and leave.

'It's too…hard…complicated and I'm not sure I can win,' he added.

'Why are you fighting if you can't win? Tom, why not stop and leave whatever these issues are to someone else?'

'Because everyone does that. Because if we all turn a blind eye, no one is held responsible. The RSL motto says it all "The price of liberty is eternal vigilance" but no one is being vigilant.'

Her energy drained. The emotional toll that was destroying Tom was destroying her too. His face changed through a range of expressions so fast she couldn't accurately catalogue them. Sadness followed anger and settled into fake cheerful.

'I'll work it out,' he said unconvincingly.

Laura sighed. She couldn't keep playing this game. He handed her a cup of coffee, she thanked him and left him to make his snack alone.

***

That was the day before he died. She'd sensed something more than his usual preoccupations and knowing what she knew now, she understood at last. Not only had she ignored politics and social issues; she'd stopped paying attention to Tom. This scandal was too big to handle, too big to understand alone, and too risky to put into words. If only he'd confided in her. She couldn't promise she'd have understood, but they could have shared the burden. Taking the safe route on his Wheat Board concerns weighed heavily on him. He'd chosen to not expose his family and his reputation by becoming a whistleblower but, it was clear, he wasn't going to turn a blind eye a second time. His determination now fused with her own.

Laura was ready, or as ready as she was ever going to be, to tackle this on his behalf.

Laura drove Mel to Port Adelaide and parked in the nearly empty carpark by the lighthouse. The three hotels within walking distance were popular in the evenings, but this morning, they were quiet.

Eva pulled up beside them. She removed a bulging backpack from the boot and slung it over her shoulder. Together they walked into the desolate laneway connecting the road network servicing the warehouses. The fresh late-morning air nipped Laura's face. She couldn't stop shivering. She carefully scanned the area for stalkers as they walked. She saw danger everywhere; Tom and Robby saw to that.

The abandoned warehouses reflected varying degrees of decay and neglect. They were empty now that Adelaide stores brought their stock from Sydney, or Melbourne, or overseas. Flats and housing would eventually replace them, but until then, the sites fell into disrepair. A swirling wind whistled through broken windows and rattled rotting doors. Debris piled against fences and walls. The smell of feral cats and vermin laced the air. Laura drew her jacket close.

Hammering from the demolition works close to the river echoed around them. Portside living promised to reignite a glimmer of life so sorely needed, but these warehouses were untouched for now.

Hugging the shadows, they turned onto an access road flanked by high walls. A concrete fence edged along the left, forming a deep alcove at a driveway. It could accommodate a truck as it waited for gates to open. Along the other side, the wall was set back. A rubbish skip on the corner offered a temporary hiding space if needed. A laneway and a narrow road turned off at right angles along here, offering well-concealed areas for parking.

At the end of the street, the broken windows and rusted fences of the APATO warehouse showed years of decline. Barbed wire, like lethal icing, topped the metal fence. It looked remarkably intact, and they searched for a hole or weakness to exploit. A padlocked chain-link main gate leaned perilously inward and swayed gently with each gust of wind, dragging at the tattered strands of fencing beside it. Jagged holes in the fence were large enough to squeeze through, the flimsy strands of shredding tape and witch's hats were no obstacle. The road curved away sharply in front of the warehouse and there was a loading dock entrance on the other side of the building.

It was unfortunate that the technology Eva sourced needed to be attached close to the action. As they approached, a loud rattling sound made Laura jump. Across the road, in the shadows, a movement caught her eye. She tugged Mel's arm, stopped, and held her breath. A grey form stumbled out of the shadows and moved towards the rusty skip. A patch of sunlight revealed a ragged homeless man. His tousled hair jutted out at sharp angles, creating a Medusa-like shadow on the wall. A scruffy beard hid his features and a dirty brown coat barely covered frayed trousers. He lunged forward, digging down into the bin, and lifted two large sheets of cardboard. With surprising tenderness, he smoothed the sheets before placing them in a shopping trolley beside him. He continued to scavenge, but his curses showed there were lean pickings today. Finally, he turned, grabbed his shopping trolley, and, noticing them for the first time, stopped. He stared. The three women stood, frozen to the spot, unsure of what to do, but he suddenly turned and clanked down the road, disappearing around a corner.

They watched the space where the homeless man had been and once they were assured they were again alone, they squeezed through the hole in the fence.

They stepped past the smaller skip by the entrance and the heavy unbolted main door creaked loudly as they inched it open. Inside, a narrow reception area led to a one-person office. Dust layered everything. The dank smell of disuse was laced with stale urine and other smells she couldn't identify. Laura sneezed, and the sound echoed through the building.

A corridor led at a right-angle from reception. A broken window admitted light but also rubbish, which formed uneven piles against the walls. Footprints on the dusty floor formed a path to another door and eventually, into the main warehouse. Pigeons roosted in the corner, puffed their feathers, and cooed softly. Pigeon poo streaked the walls like a white waterfall, adding to the smell of neglect.

Shelving covered two-thirds of the space and in the corner, by a huge exit door, sat a fold-up table surrounded by a hotch-potch of metal chairs. Laura trembled. The area had recently been disturbed. They searched through adjoining doors, but the table and chairs offered the most likely option for tonight's meeting.

Eva attached a small transmitter to the underside of the table and placed two more under the chairs against the wall. She affixed a bug to the base of the wall nearest the door. Laura and Mel stacked debris to disguise her handiwork. Eva spread the devices to monitor as much of the space as possible. Mel and Eva then left to find a suitable hiding place outside while Laura remained.

Laura paced the cavernous space and stopped near the side entrance at a crate bolted to the wall. A series of unmarked small cartons lay inside. They were strapped together into bundles. A discarded pill bottle on the floor caught Laura's attention and she picked it up. Her heart raced as she read the label. Digoxin;

dispensed by the Green area pharmacy in Mosul. The prescribing doctor's name was obscured. The same as the bottle found in Tom's medicine cabinet. She stuffed it in her pocket for later.

Imagining the people who met here set her nerves quivering. The pursuit of wealth was justified in their eyes, no matter the cost. Their greed fuelled so much pain. Tom had just been collateral damage to them. The justice system only worked to a point. The law didn't decide morality, it just decided legality. Current scandals, those embroiling the Wheat Board, the banks, and property developers, had been exposed, and the victims paid a terrible price. But, strangely, those exposing wrongdoing suffered more than those doing the wrong. Whistleblowers were being punished and jailed while power protected the powerful. Tom had wanted justice. He knew that turning a blind eye or ignoring corruption didn't work. *What you don't know won't hurt you* wasn't true. Ignorance could make people suffer much more than the truth. Laura had never been courageous. Even now, she had a strong urge to run, tell the police, and let them deal with this. Doing nothing was attractive. Laura shivered. At the end of the day, she needed to stand up for what was right. How else would those committing crimes be held responsible? She must at least try to make a difference.

The phone startled Laura out of her reverie.

'Ready to test?' Eva asked. 'Move around the room and speak normally.'

Laura tightly clasped her hands. She self-consciously recited nursery rhymes. They seemed incongruous in this setting but were a stark reminder of why she cared. Her voice sent the pigeons fluttering, creating that high-pitched whistle as they fled to another corner. Eva stepped through the door, and Laura jumped.

'Don't do that,' Laura admonished.

Eva apologised, tutted as she adjusted two of the devices, then left. A short while later, a text message advised Laura they'd finished.

Outside, light raindrops splashed her face, and she gulped at the fresh air. Mel found a tiny hiding place for Eva to set up the recording equipment and they'd disguised it with empty cans and cartons.

They'd finished for now.

'I have to come back. I need to swap one of the components. It's not working properly,' Eva explained. 'I can do it by myself later.'

'No way,' Laura and Mel said in unison.

'Mel, you stay away. We'll let you know what's happening or if we need help,' Laura suggested.

'We're safer in numbers,' Mel insisted.

Everything was ready. Was Laura? Laura couldn't get away fast enough.

Chapter 43

Bulldog steered the hire car one-handed, casually cutting the corner and John tilted across the back seat. John's nose ached and a spot of blood dripped onto his trouser leg. He cursed Fleur. He'd enjoyed firing her. Wasn't it bad enough that the swelling and discolouration around his nose were ugly? Now a drop of blood stained his trousers too. Bulldog was clean-shaven and neatly dressed, but his musky aftershave barely covered a hint of sweat wafting through the car. John turned his face towards the partially open window and breathed in deeply through his mouth.

Bulldog accelerated up the winding approach road and pulled into the holding bay beside the chapel. Trees shielded them from the driveway without blocking their view. A message from Carlo said he and Dimi were on their way.

John didn't have to wait long for a black Mercedes to pull up beside the kerb. He leaned back, although their car was screened by the shrubbery and the darkened windows concealed him. This was it. A shiver travelled up his spine. Five years of planning culminated at this moment. He was going to enjoy it.

Carlo exited the car first. His eyes scanned the area, resting momentarily on John's vehicle before he looked away. He opened the rear passenger door. Dimi's short but shapely legs swung out, and she pulled herself up tall on her high heels. Her strut towards the chapel's sheltered foyer looked confident, haughty even. It had always come so naturally to her.

Again, John leaned back as a beat-up Holden sedan pulled in behind the Mercedes. Its lights dimmed. Bulldog's hand twitched as the muscle-bound hulk exited. This must be Nick.

'You're only here as my bodyguard. Your inter-gang rivalries will have to wait for another day,' John directed. Bulldog didn't respond and John added, 'Is that clear?'

Bulldog grunted.

Once Dimi, Carlo, and Nick huddled in the foyer, John gently opened his car door. He stepped gingerly onto the gravel surface, then stealthily moved to the front of the chapel. Bulldog followed one step behind. Once John was on the edge of the portico, he cleared his throat.

'Hello, Dimi,' John said loudly.

She spun around and glared. 'What did you call me?'

John chuckled. 'Don't you recognise me?'

'Who's Dimi?' Nick's face screwed in confusion.

'Dimi is Abbie's nickname. It's my *endearment* for my little sister, isn't it?'

Fire blazed in Dimi's eyes, but not the surprise he'd expected. She'd always had the gift. Her poker face never gave anything away.

'But Giovanni is dead, isn't he?' she said quietly.

'Surprise.' John grinned. He flung his arms out wide. 'I'm alive and well. I've been waiting a long time for this.' John's eyes fixed on Abbie. 'Babbo should never have given you everything.'

'How dare you call him that? You never showed any respect.'

'It's both an endearment and insult.' John snarled. 'Babbo gave me no choice. He left me with nothing.'

'You made your choice. You and Harper were going to walk away from the family business and live your irresponsible hippy lifestyle. What did you expect?' Abbie spat at John.

John's hand flew into the air, ready to strike. Instead, he glared at her, extracted a handkerchief from his pocket, and wiped his face. 'You'll pay for that. You were always his favourite, but it doesn't matter now. I'll prove him wrong.'

'You've always been full of excuses. You're the only one to blame for your failures. The truth is, you weren't up to it. Papa trusted me and I proved him right. I built this business into a success.'

'Not up to it? You've made one blunder after another. You've brought this whole enterprise to the brink of ruin. I'm taking over and if you don't back off then I—'

'You'll what?' Abbie glared at him. 'You can't waltz in and take over like this.'

'I'm the rightful boss.'

'You don't get to decide,' Abbie shouted. 'I don't give up that easily. This is my inheritance.'

Carlo stood beside Abbie and stared at his feet.

'Maybe you should stop fighting, Dimi. Go. Be a mother and let me take care of the business. That's how it should be.'

'Papa honoured tradition, but he gave me the business for a reason.' Abbie's eyes flared in defiance. 'I won't let him down.'

'I'll help him to see that I'm the rightful heir..' It was a shame she wasn't going to accept his peace offering. Now he didn't have a choice. He must get rid of her for good.

'Carlo…Nick…' Abbie stared at the pair.

'They're with me now.' John smirked. This was the moment, and it felt good.

Carlo moved to stand beside John.

Nick stepped forward, stopped, and pointed at Bulldog. 'What's he doing here?'

'He's my security.'

'Bulldog, you need to leave,' Nick growled and turned to John. 'He can't be part of this.'

'It's not up to you.' John locked eyes with Nick. 'I'm the boss now. I'll call the shots. Get used to it.'

Nick glared at Bulldog. 'I don't care who's the boss. Don't screw with me. I won't work with that son-of-a-bitch.'

Bulldog sniggered.

Nick lunged. His fist connected and Bulldog staggered back momentarily before launching a fist in return. The crack of bone on bone exploded in the air and Nick's head jagged back. Bulldog followed it with a punch to the stomach.

At the same time, Carlo grabbed John's arms. 'I'm sorry,' he muttered as he snapped handcuffs onto John's wrists.

John struggled. The cuffs tore into his flesh, but they held firm.

'What's going on, Carlo?' John demanded. He hadn't anticipated this.

Bulldog landed another punch on Nick, sending him reeling backwards and almost smashing into John. Without warning, Carlo kicked John's feet out from under him and John crashed to the ground. Pain seared through his back. The air gushed from his lungs and he gasped for breath. Carlo flew at Bulldog, grabbing his arm to prevent him from striking Nick again. With Bulldog's hands firmly held, Nick landed a punch to his midriff and one to his chin. Bulldog crumpled. He groaned and fell forward, pulling Carlo off balance. They both tumbled to the concrete floor. Bulldog cracked his head on the stone edging and a pool of blood formed under his right ear. He lay sprawled at John's feet, but didn't move. Carlo checked Bulldog's pulse and nodded.

'Carlo. What are you doing? You can't do this,' John yelled. 'You vowed to support me.'

Carlo stood up. John rocked, trying to stand up, but he couldn't get any leverage. He thrashed his legs but missed.

'Help me,' he yelled at Carlo.

Carlo looked away.

'You've double-crossed me!' He should never have trusted Carlo. It was clear their history didn't count, and he'd chosen the other side.

'In this business, we have rules. She's the boss, she's *my* boss.' Carlo hesitated.

'You fucking turncoat. Do you know what you've done?' He kicked out, but Carlo stomped down on his leg. The pain seared up to John's back and immobilised him.

'You're an arrogant bastard. You think you're smart, but I've seen you stuff up one thing after another. You treat me like an idiot; like you can push me around. I've earned my place. I know enough to be useful. I deserve some respect,' Carlo said quietly.

'That's enough. Don't waste your breath on him. Secure them. We need to get ready for the meeting,' Abbie ordered.

Bulldog moaned. Nick kicked his unconscious form and rolled him over. Carlo stripped off John's tie and searched his pockets, removing John's phone and wallet. He handed Nick the tie, and they bound Bulldog's hands. They used John's handkerchief as a gag and, when they'd finished, they dragged him to the beat-up sedan. Carlo and Nick held him down as Abbie extracted a bag from the boot and lifted out a small syringe. She uncapped it and stabbed the needle into a vial.

'We can't have you talking or ruining our plans.' She smirked at John as she plunged the needle into Bulldog's arm. John watched in horror. His heart thumped.

'No. You can't do this,' John screamed.

'Apparently, I can.' Abbie studied him. 'I couldn't believe it when Carlo told me. Ferret thought there was something weird about you. They're not as stupid as you thought. I have to hand it to you though. Your resurrection was a tight secret. I didn't know until Carlo told me. He knows he's better off with me. We'll have a future. He knows you'd ruin the business and then we'd all lose.' Abbie pulled another vial from the bag. 'Luckily, I came prepared.'

She plunged the needle into the new vial and drew up the liquid. Theatrically, she raised the needle, pressed the plunger, and squirted liquid up in the air.

'E-bomb works so much better as a liquid, it's more potent. You'll enjoy it more too. Not like poor Tom. Perhaps the other drug in his system made it work faster than I'd expected. We'll see now, won't we? You might suffer more than him.'

'What are going to do?' John's heart thumped in his throat and his mouth was dry.

'What I have to.' Abbie smirked again.

'Carlo, you can't let her do this.' John struggled, but the cuffs held firm, and so did Carlo's resolve. 'Dimi, let me go. We could do a deal. We'd be stronger if we banded together. We'd make a great team, you and I. My business could be a valuable addition. We'd be formidable.'

Abbie laughed. 'You're too much of a snake in the grass. I can't trust you. Never could.'

Carlo and Nick held him firmly. As the needle pierced John's arm, easily passing through his jacket and shirt sleeves, he jerked his shoulders. The needle snapped.

'Shit. Now, look what you've done.' Abbie threw the broken syringe back in the bag. She drew on rubber gloves. 'You're a bloody nuisance. We don't want to make it too easy for the coroner.' She poked at his arm, searching for the needle fragment. John flinched and cried out as her fingers flicked the needle end. Abbie laughed as she dramatically yanked it free.

John's body grew weak. What had she done? Would the drug kill him? She'd killed before. He was sure she could do it again. Although, was she capable of killing her older brother? He thought so. She'd grown tough and unyielding. She was her father's daughter, through and through.

'That should take care of you,' Abbie said, then turned to her helpers. 'Clear this up. We need to get moving.'

Nick and Carlo untied and ungagged Bulldog and dumped his limp body into the bushes beside the car. They pulled John onto his feet, but he felt lightheaded and they needed to hold him up. A gag tore into the corners of his mouth and a hood turned his world dark. He was going to be sick.

'You know what to do,' Abbie ordered.

John's body lifted, and he was thrown into a narrow space. His elbow smacked against something hard and his funny bone sent sharp pains down his arm. He was in the car boot. He heard the boot slam shut, and it became deathly silent. A motor rumbled into action and he was tossed from side to side. The handcuffs tore into his wrists and sharp edges jabbed him as the car swung through corners. Carbon monoxide fumes laced the air and nausea scratched at his stomach. It took all his will to overcome the urge to vomit. His head swam and vivid images flared behind his closed eyes. Knights on horseback, groves of thick vines, and bizarre snake-like creatures swirled in his vision and his heart rate spiralled.

John resisted the images. They were frightening. He knew they were hallucinations, yet they felt real. He lurched to escape the creatures, and wetness formed around his handcuffs. What a fool he'd been. His plans had come to nothing. Who could save him now?

When the car stopped, his body trembled. No one opened the boot. The creatures were attacking him and pain seared through his body. His scream was muffled and the sound of it made him more afraid. Outside, a motorbike roared into action. It crunched across gravel and sped away. In the cramped, dark space, his anger flared. They'd abandoned him to die here alone in the dark. He was going to die an undignified death, trussed up like some Christmas turkey in the boot of a car. The images asserted control over his mind. His heart raced as the snake-like creatures hissed and slithered towards him. They were coming for him.

Chapter 44

Laura stuffed the DVDs into one envelope and placed the report in another. She addressed them both to Mark with a note explaining recent events and what she was doing. If anything went wrong, her eldest son would have to work out what to do. Her hands trembled as she stowed them at the back of the DVD collection. Hopefully, it wouldn't come to this.

She drove to Port Adelaide as twilight veiled the cloudy sky. Night came early in winter. Skirting the carpark, she turned right towards the warehouses and followed the narrow side lane branching off to the left. She manoeuvred a three-point turn and parked in an alcove along the side road where the scarcity of street lights concealed the car from view. It was safe here and obscured from the main entrance. Her heart raced while she waited.

Darkness descended abruptly. The hazy twilight became a mediocre sunset. Grey clouds underscored by thin brushstrokes of gold and pink darkened into blotches of dull navy and slate grey. Street lights cast a dim glow at irregular intervals along the access road. One weakly illuminated the entrance to the lane but barely cast light further than the intersection. The lane swam with brooding shapes and dark crevices. Laura's nerves twitched even more. At least the dark recesses along the well-lit warehouse approach road could be used for cover.

A moment later, Eva's car passed the end of the lane and turned down the unlit road on the opposite side. Laura stealthily approached the corner, scanning the surroundings before waving to Eva. Her skin prickled. It took Eva longer than expected to find a replacement part. This needed to be done quickly so they could get out of here.

Eva and Laura sat in the car, reviewing tonight's plan. They had time.

'I hope we're doing the right thing.' Eva voiced Laura's thoughts.

'It's too late, I'm committed. They must be stopped.' Laura's words sounded more confident than she felt.

'I agree, we need to get hard proof,' Eva said. 'I've got the part, so hopefully, I can replace it easily.'

Mel's call interrupted Laura's anxieties.

'I'm near Peter's house. Abbie's just left. She was picked up by a flashy black car with a driver. Peter's still at home,' Mel reported.

'Are you sure you're out of sight? He wouldn't recognise your car, would he?' Laura worried.

'I'm fine, Mum. Peter hasn't seen this car before. Make sure you don't take any stupid risks either. Get in, fix things, and get out of there,' Mel cautioned. 'Peter's just come out of the house. I've got to go.'

'It's too early.'

'I'll follow him.'

'No—' Laura protested, but Mel hung up.

She should never have dragged Mel into this. What had she been thinking?

Was Peter on his way already? Had they got the time for the meeting wrong. They needed to hurry.

Laura grasped the door handle and unlatched the door. A motorbike roared down the road in front of them. She pulled back and switched the cabin light off. Eva leaned her door shut. They hadn't expected them this early. How would they get the recording equipment ready now?

Once the motorbike passed, Laura and Eva crept along the now-empty approach road to the warehouse. They hugged the wall and darted into an alcove on the left. Behind them, huge gates on rusty hinges creaked and swayed in the wind. It set Laura's teeth on edge.

In front of the main entrance, tucked alongside the gate, was a black motorcycle. The rider was nowhere to be seen.

Another motorcycle roared down the road. Laura threw herself flat against the ground and Eva scrambled into the niche. Laura cracked her elbow on the tarmac and tears sprung to her eyes. Warm liquid trickled down her sleeve, but she didn't dare move. The motorbike slowed past the alcove, then reversed beside the office entrance too. Laura and Eva froze. A phone ringtone jangled and Laura's heart leaped into her throat.

'Yeah?' a gruff, raspy voice from near the warehouse answered.

Laura released her held breath. He mumbled into the phone and footsteps crunched away. The front door squealed and after what felt like an eternity, Laura finally poked her head around the wall. Both motorcycles were parked by the fence, but their riders were gone. Laura checked her phone. A message from Mel told her Peter met someone, and she was following them still.

'What do we do now?' Laura whispered. 'How will we get inside the grounds?'

'These guys must be the advance security,' Eva hissed. 'I need to get the recording equipment working and turned on.'

Laura traced the path with her eyes. If the bikies reappeared, Eva would be trapped in the open.

'We could wait until everyone has arrived; they might be so busy we can run across,' Eva suggested.

'What if the security guys stand guard outside?' Laura asked.

'I should move now. We're not safe here and if they park down here, we'll be seen.'

Without the recording equipment turned on, they'd have no

evidence. They must act now.

'I'm going,' Eva said. 'There's some cover after the fence if I zig-zag that way.'

'I'll follow once you clear the fence. I can slip behind the rubbish skip and follow when you're safely installed in the booth.' Laura's throat constricted, and it hurt to speak. She couldn't remember when she'd last run anywhere. Hopefully, her legs would still remember how.

Eva raised crossed fingers, then slunk to the front of the alcove. She hugged the wall, paused, then launched out into the road, and ran to the fence. She was still agile for her age. Scrunching down to step through the hole, she stopped in mid-air, rebounding like an elastic band. She twisted and turned, her hands groping at the fence. Her coat had snagged on a jagged piece of wire. As Laura readied to race out to help, Eva tumbled to the ground. The gate rattled and bounced noisily. Eva sprang up, and without brushing herself down, followed the shadows. The front door squeaked open, and she hurled herself behind a canister. A sliver of light flashed across the area where Eva had stood. Laura cringed as a bulky form filled the doorway and a deep voice from inside the warehouse shouted something indecipherable. The brooding shape released the door, and it squealed closed. In the accompanying dark, Eva scurried across the dirt and dived into the cubicle.

Laura was about to move, but again, the door squeaked open. This time, the large hulk stepped out and walked towards the gate. He plucked something from the wire fence and held it up in the dim light. He turned, showing it to a second, shorter and slimmer bikie who now blocked the doorway. The colourful patches on his leather jacket shone and his scruffy white beard and hair created a frightening shadow.

The slimmer form shrugged and called out, 'Ya know, Harry hangs around here, always muckin' about, picking through the fuckin' rubbish.' He turned and let the door creak shut.

The bulky bikie strutted to the corner. Laura held her breath as his head turned towards the cubicle. He scratched his head and moved forward to check around the skip. The light caught the scar running down his face, and Laura stifled a gasp. She'd seen him before.

Slim reappeared in the doorway and scowled, 'Hurry up, ya fuckin' pussy. They'll be here soon, so come and help.'

The big guy hesitated, took one last look around, and went back inside.

Laura let herself breathe again. These men were scary. Even when she'd seen them in the daylight, they made her skin crawl. It was worse in the dark and here. She shook her head. She forced herself to stop thinking about what they'd do if they discovered her or Eva. It paralysed her. She needed to get into position before the others arrived, but her legs refused. They wouldn't obey her brain's instructions. She was frozen.

She couldn't let Eva do this by herself. Using all the resolve she could muster, she placed both palms flat on the wall and pushed. Her arms achieved what her legs wouldn't, and she propelled forward out of her hiding place. Crouching down, she manoeuvred through the hole in the fence, willing her clothes not to snag. As she straightened, she stumbled and accidentally kicked an empty drink can. It clanked loudly against the warehouse wall, bounced, and rattled to a stop in front of the door. Laura threw herself behind the large rubbish receptacle, scraping her forehead as she twisted to fit. Her breath was loud and ragged, but she couldn't slow it down.

Again, the door screeched open and the big bikie stomped out into the front area.

'What's the matter now, Scarface? Your nerves are tight tonight. It's fine, it's always fine here. It's probably the wind. Get your shit together and help me set up,' a deep voice yelled from inside.

The big guy hesitated. A loud scraping sound echoed from down the road. Laura stifled a gasp. Mel? The bikie's footsteps stomped to the fence, and he peered through the mesh. Laura followed his gaze, and a movement caught her eye. She almost called out. Surely Mel wouldn't move. With an agility that belied his size, the bikie slipped through the hole in the fence and tramped towards the sound, covering the distance in a few strides.

'Come out. I know you're there,' he yelled.

There was no response.

'I said come out. If I catch ya, it'll be worse for ya,' he threatened.

A flicker of movement caught Laura's eye. Her hands shook so hard she fumbled trying to extract her phone from her pocket. Before she could do anything, a solid figure emerged from the shadows and into the bikie's phone's dull light. Laura's knees buckled. It was the homeless man.

'What's all this noise? How's a man supposed to get any sleep,' he grumbled.

The bikie laughed. 'Harry, what're ya doing here? Go find somewhere else to sleep tonight.'

The slim man appeared in the doorway. 'What are you doing, Scarface?'

'I'm moving Harry on,' Scarface replied.

'Told ya it was Harry,' the other said and went back inside.

Harry collected his belongings, supervised by Scarface, and grumbled as he shuffled down the dark street. His indistinct grumbling faded as he pushed his shopping trolley of possessions away. Laura caught a glimpse of another shadow moving in another alcove. She couldn't be sure, but it looked like someone else was lurking along the approach road. Scarface must have seen it too because he ran to the darkened space. He reached in and chuckled loudly.

'Well, well. What have we here?' he said loudly. 'Ya better come with me.'

Laura stifled a cry. Was it Mel?

Scarface pulled a body into the faint street light and Laura gasped. It was Robby. What was he doing here? He was supposed to be on his way to Broken Hill.

Laura pulled back sharply as Scarface dragged a struggling Robby past the front of the skip. He hesitated. A slight breeze wafted across her face and brought with it the smell of rotting matter. Her stomach turned. The greasy stench suggested remnants of unfinished pizza and rancid burgers. Laura held her breath. Had he seen something? Was he listening or still looking around? She didn't dare peek.

'Let go of me, you goon. I just want to clear up the misunderstandings,' Robby pleaded.

'Yeah, right,' Scarface said as he creaked the door open. The light disappeared again in a flash.

She must help Robby. But how? She turned her head to avoid the odour-laden breeze and was about to move when two cars approached the gates. She was trapped.

Someone wrestled with the padlock and finally, the gate creaked and bounced over the uneven ground.

'Fuckin' useless bastards. Could've opened the gate,' a voice grumbled.

Tyres scraped across the gravel and one of the cars parked in front of the dumpster. The other stopped on the road. Car doors slammed and footsteps crunched on the dirt. Laura recognised Peter's strut. What would he think if he knew she was hiding behind this skip? He was accompanied by a squat, rotund man whose arm was in a sling.

Besides the smell, the skip wasn't in a prime position. She couldn't hear or see. What was happening inside, especially to Robby? She couldn't run to the cubicle now. She was too stiff, and it was too exposed. A small broken window along the side wall which belonged to the office offered an alternative.

Laura trembled as she pulled out her phone and composed her text, "They've got Robby," then she sent it to both Eva and Mel.

She scrambled between the skip and the building, hugging the shadows along the outer wall. Light from the warehouse next door sparkled gently in dirty puddles and illuminated the smattering of empty drink cans. She crouched beneath the window. An indistinct murmur hummed from deep in the bowels of the warehouse, but nothing more.

Laura shivered. Fear and anger fighting for control. She swallowed her doubts and crept forward. Tracing the office wall with her hands, she stopped under the next window. It was too high. Avoiding the clumps of empty cans and detritus settled against the building, she continued. The door hung limply on one hinge. It creaked in the wind but was jammed open, providing a narrow gap for her to squeeze through. Careful to not touch it, she flattened herself against the doorjamb and prayed it wouldn't creak. Inside, she could distinguish a filing cabinet. A desk topped with a row of cubicles for stacking letters and files butted against the other wall. Light framed an internal door and although the voices were louder, they were still unclear.

She didn't remember this door during their reconnaissance. Did it lead into another hallway or directly into the warehouse? If she hadn't noticed it, perhaps it was hidden by the shelving. The blocked keyhole didn't help.

She hesitated. If she opened the door a crack, she could glimpse the layout and work out what to do. She counted to three, then counted again. She gently clasped the door handle and pulled it. It creaked. She stopped, held her breath, and waited. Peering through the gap, a mesh of shelving created patterns on the floor. The voices were clearer, but not enough. She steadied and pried the door open a sliver more to improve her view.

The door jerked and rammed into her, hitting her head. She jolted backwards against the desk. Her elbow smashed onto the hard surface and her spine twisted. Firm hands clutched her shoulders, roughly pulled her to her feet, and propelled her into the warehouse.

'Look what I found?' Scarface called out. His fierce face and the jagged scar tearing down his face burned crimson to match his fiery red hair.

Chapter 45

Blood trickled down Laura's face and into her eyes. The brute yanked her arms back and a sharp pain seared through her shoulder. He heaved her forward into the warehouse and she stumbled into the dull light.

'What the fuck?' a voice shouted. Chair legs scraped on the gritty floor and one crashed.

'Laura …Shit.' Peter stared, mouth agape, and disbelief in his eyes.

'What's going on?' The balding, stocky man beside Peter scowled. Laura recognised Casterlow.

She didn't see Robby anywhere. Scarface dragged Laura forward, ignoring her cry of pain, and shoved her, propelling her into another pair of hands. Dust lodged in her throat and she coughed.

'What are you doing here, Laura?' Peter demanded.

'I—' Laura winced. 'What have you done with Robby?'

'Robby?' Peter stared at the door she'd come through. 'Is Eva with you?'

'No, she isn't here. Tell me, what have you done with Robby?'

Peter pointed to a doorway. 'He's not here and you can't be here either.'

'Don't lie to me. I saw Robby being dragged in here. If you've hurt him—'

'Who is she?' Casterlow asked.

'She's Tom's widow.' Peter glared at Laura. 'Calm down. Robby's safe. We're just keeping him out of the way, so settle down.'

'Who's Eva?' Casterlow queried. He adjusted the sling on his left arm and grimaced.

'My ex-wife and her best friend. They're like twins, almost inseparable.' Peter turned his attention to the wiry bikie. 'Viper, check outside and do it properly this time.'

'How did she know about the meeting? I thought you'd neutralised Tom's information,' Casterlow said.

'I guess Robby must have told her. It doesn't matter, no one will believe her.'

'What are you mixed up in, Peter?' Laura cried, hoping those microphones would salvage a positive result from this mess.

'Laura stop. This is none of your business. I told you to leave it alone, but you wouldn't listen. Stubborn, like Tom. Now I don't know if I can protect you.'

'You didn't protect Tom anyway. You're not protecting Robby now either.'

Peter banged his fist on the table. 'Tom would have destroyed everything. He had to be stopped. What choice did we have?'

'So you killed him? That's your choice? To kill your friend.'

'I didn't…He knew the risks. Why didn't he leave it alone?'

'I can't believe you'd do this. You're not the Peter I knew. That Peter was principled and cared about what was right.'

'Well, of course I'm not the same man. The Peter from university, that bleeding heart, had to grow up sometime. The world's full of winners and losers, and I wasn't going to be a loser forever. It's time to look after number one and let others look out for themselves.'

'You think you're a winner, Peter? I think I'm looking at one of the big losers, don't you?' Laura said.

'Sort out your little domestic spat another time. We have

business to conduct,' Casterlow grumbled.

'Strange business you're involved in. It doesn't look like legitimate government business to me,' Laura taunted.

'These meetings happen all the time, lady. There are heavy penalties for interfering in top-secret affairs.' Casterlow's eye twitched.

Laura laughed. 'I don't think legitimate government meetings are held in abandoned warehouses and involve criminals and bikies. Your secrets would be exposed in any court case.' Her voice was stronger than she'd expected. Her anger provided a powerful force.

'Top secret issues are kept away from the public gaze. You're naïve if you think we'd let you sprout your rubbish openly. We use secret court proceedings for people like you. You're endangering national security.'

Laura shivered. It was a potent reminder of just how powerful Casterlow was. She hoped Eva had fixed the recording equipment and captured this. Laura was going to need all the help she could get.

'What about Corrinne? Did you kill her too, Peter?' Laura asked. She didn't know where her courage sprung from, but was grateful it had.

'That was nothing to do with me.' Peter shook his head.

'Enough. Be warned. That might happen to you too if you don't shut up.' Casterlow snarled. He glared at Peter. 'Sort this out. We need to get this meeting started. Now!'

Viper sidled through the door and shrugged his shoulders at Peter. 'All's clear,' he said.

Laura sighed. Eva was safe. On Peter's order, Scarface roughly dragged Laura back towards the shelving and threw her into a chair.

'Let me go!' she cried.

'It's too late, Laura. You should have stayed out of it.' Peter shook his head.

'What a fuck-up?' Casterlow moaned. 'So, where's your mysterious boss? I emphasised I wasn't doing business with anyone but the boss. If they're not here soon, I'm going to abort this meeting.'

'Carlo says they're on their way.'

Casterlow sat down heavily. 'I'm not waiting much longer.'

'Did you…take care of Corrinne?' Peter asked Casterlow quietly. 'I thought she'd given up her research after Tom—'

'She unearthed critical details. She couldn't be allowed to threaten this project.'

The door opened and three shadowy figures entered. One set of heels clacked on the gritty concrete floor and as they approached, Laura saw the source. She gasped. What was Abbie doing here? The two men walking beside her were built like nightclub bouncers, and one of them was Nick.

Abbie scanned the room and her eyes rested on Laura. 'You're kidding, aren't you? I guess your luck has finally run out.' She laughed. 'The car accident would have been better.'

Casterlow stood up abruptly and growled. His gaze settled on Peter. 'Did you send out invitations? What the fuck kind of meeting are you running here? I'm not waiting for your boss. There are too many bloody leaks for me to trust your fucking useless mob with anything.'

The other burly guard blocked Casterlow's path. 'She *is* the boss,' he explained.

Laura gasped. What did that mean? Laura wasn't particularly fond of Abbie, but surely Abbie wasn't cold-blooded enough to be in charge of a lawless bikie outfit.

Peter's face froze into an open-mouthed stare. 'What do you mean, *the boss*? That's impossible. You've helped out but…you…*the boss*?'

'Why?' Abbie challenged. 'I've run this outfit even before I met you. Now, shall we stop the nonsense and get on with business? Carlo, you're with me.' Abbie pointed at Laura and sneered. 'Nick, keep an eye on her. You can take care of her and her lame son later.'

Nick stood beside Laura. She trembled. She'd really messed up. Now she and Robby were both in danger.

Casterlow looked at his watch. 'I was expecting my off-sider. We'll have to start without him.'

Laura shook her head. Who was the off-sider? Could it be Jacques?

Carlo directed Scarface and Viper to stand guard outside, then the group sat. Casterlow reached for his satchel.

'What are you doing? How is life so cheap to you? How many more have to die?' Laura shouted.

'Shut up, Laura, or I'll get Nick to gag you.' Abbie's eyes glinted like icicles in the dull light. 'It won't go well for Robby, either. Now be a good girl, Laura. You don't want Robby to get hurt, do you?'

Laura shivered. She didn't trust that they wouldn't hurt Robby even if she kept quiet, but could she take that risk? Perhaps their meeting would divulge enough without her prompts.

'Let's get on with this. I need to get out of here. Tell me the arrangements for the special shipment,' Casterlow said.

'Our distribution network is ready,' Abbie said. 'We have mules to take the product into Asia from Adelaide airport. Our annoying little friend in the other room might come in handy too.' She pointed at the door. 'Kill two birds with one stone, so to speak. In the long term, Adelaide will be the main hub. It's better than importing into the Eastern states and we have established routes. We'll be able to ship future supplies into Asia from all ports; Adelaide, the eastern states, or Western Australia, where-ever you need. We've devised a thorough plan, including running decoys.'

'I can't stress enough how important this is. The first shipment must arrive in Indonesia before their election, is that clear? I don't want any stuff-ups.' Casterlow's eyes flashed with fire.

'We were told this product is small and easy to disguise,' Carlo said.

Casterlow nodded. 'It may seem an easy job, but be prepared.

We have powerful enemies who'll do anything to get hold of it. These vials must be delivered into the right hands. There can be no mistakes. If we stuff up, the whole operation could be blown, and I'll accept no excuses.'

Abbie shifted in her chair. 'We need more detail to plan thoroughly.'

'What I can tell you is that Indonesia is a testing ground. It's an opportunity to iron out glitches. The Indonesian government won't win reelection as things stand, and regime change isn't in our…Australia's…best interests. This delivery will be used to rebalance the odds in our favour. We plan to eliminate the opposition leader. It'll test your distribution networks but also confirm the effectiveness of our product in that setting before we expand to other targets.'

'Are these other targets also in Indonesia?'

'You'll be told when you need to know. One step at a time. Are we ready to bring the vials around to the delivery roller door now?'

Casterlow pulled out his phone and awkwardly composed a text one-handed. On Abbie's instruction, Nick alerted Viper with a message too. Casterlow's phone chimed and on his signal, Carlo pressed a button by the roller door. It creaked open. Outside, a black sedan reverse parked at the warehouse delivery entrance and Viper stood beside the boot. He lifted out three small boxes, no bigger than book deliveries, and passed them into the warehouse. The roller door again closed.

'Is that it?' Nick frowned.

'All three vials must be delivered. All of them. Is that clear? If even one vial breaks and anyone comes into contact with the liquid, even just a drop, they'll die.' Casterlow laughed as he scanned their faces. 'That's why you're being paid handsomely. If it was easy, we'd arrange it ourselves. I can't help you with security either. You need to use your networks as we've discussed before.'

'We can do this, no worries,' Carlo's voice was confident, but his face said he was worried.

'There can be no slip-ups, you hear me? Once this operation has been successfully completed, we'll discuss the next target. If this shipment doesn't arrive in Indonesia before the election, it will cost you dearly, not just in dollars either. Don't fail me.'

Chapter 46

'It looks like you've failed yourself, Casterlow. Thank you, ladies and gentlemen, this ends here,' a voice from the doorway boomed.

Laura couldn't see where the voice was coming from. She tried to stand but couldn't get her balance. There was a strange smell of musty rags in the air. The sound of stomping feet sounded near the door and Laura coughed as dust swirled. Armed police, in combat gear, lined up beside the shelving and pointed their weapons at the group around the table. The black-uniformed officers with dark helmets and their visors pulled down were almost as scary as the thugs. Other police officers blocked the exits while three police officers surrounded the boxes.

'What the,' Casterlow cursed. He leaped up, crashing his chair noisily on the floor. 'This is official business. Get out. You *do* know who I am. You've made a big mistake.'

'The only mistake is the one you've made,' the voice responded.

A tall man dressed in dirty and ragged clothes stepped in front of the police line. Laura gaped. The clothes belonged to Harry, the tramp, but the voice belonged to someone else. She'd thought Jacques might be here tonight, but in a very different role.

A broad-shouldered policeman moved up next to Jacques. 'We need you to accompany us to the station. Let's do this quietly and in an orderly fashion.'

'This is official business. You have no jurisdiction here.' Casterlow stared at the policeman and pointed with his good hand. 'This will cost you your job. Get out.'

'Politicians aren't above the law,' Jacques said firmly.

Abbie showed her empty hands to Jacques. 'Why don't we all calm down. This is a mistake. I don't know these men. I'm ashamed to say I followed my husband here. I've no idea what this is about. I suspected he was meeting…well…another woman, so I followed him. I don't know what this is about. It's nothing to do with me,' she calmly explained.

Jacques laughed. "Really? That's how you want to play it?'

'Nice try.' The broad-shouldered police officer chuckled. 'We know exactly how involved you are.'

Casterlow glared, his ruddy features glistening with sweat. 'I demand you remove your men at once. Whatever you think you know, you've got it wrong. This is a secret mission and you have no business interfering. Your superiors will hear about this.'

The police officer motioned to the armed police behind him and they moved towards the group.

'Well, Nick. We'll make it stick this time.' A short police officer near the door said.

As Casterlow stepped back from the table to stand behind Peter, Nick lunged. He hoisted Laura up from the chair. The tape binding Laura's wrists caught on a ragged edge, resisted, and cut into her skin before finally yielding. Nick dragged her in front of him.

'I'm not going anywhere,' he yelled.

Using her as a shield, he rested a pistol on her shoulder. Laura froze. It was aimed at Jacques.

'Don't be stupid, the place is surrounded. You can't get away,' Jacques called. 'Give yourself up and it will be better for you.'

'I'd rather take my chances,' Nick snarled. 'I'll take you with me.'

He slung his arm around Laura's throat and forcefully pulled her head back. His arm tightened, and she struggled to breathe.

'Let her go,' Jacques ordered.

'Let her go,' yelled Peter at the same time.

Nick laughed. His gun dug into Laura's cheek and she stifled a scream. She willed her body not to move, but she couldn't stop trembling. Nick wrenched her head back harder. He was strangling her. She gasped, desperate to draw air into her lungs.

'We've heard it all. We know exactly what happened,' the leading police officer explained. He faced Nick. 'Now put that gun down before you do something stupid.'

'I'm not going anywhere.' The gun clicked as Nick readied to shoot. Laura closed her eyes.

The rustle of movement made her open her eyes as Peter flew forward. A shot rang out then another shot. Her cheek burned and something splashed across her face. A scream stuck in her throat. Beside her on the floor, Nick and Peter sprawled unnaturally, a red syrup pooling beside them.

Carlo stepped towards Nick and Laura kicked out with all the force she could muster. It caught Carlo's legs, knocking them out from under him. Carlo stumbled backwards. He crashed into Abbie and they both hurtled into the shelving. The unit toppled. Boxes rained down on them and green pill bottles skittled across the floor. Two police pounced. They bound Carlo's wrists before he could regain his balance. Another police officer restrained Abbie.

Peter groaned. He raised his head and groaned again. Slowly, he pulled himself up. Blood soaked his right sleeve just above the elbow. He looked dazed, but otherwise unharmed. Laura imagined she saw regret etched in his face, but it could have been the light.

Casterlow's eyes burned with defiance. Police in riot gear surrounded him, grabbing at him, but he batted them away with his one good arm.

'You're making a big mistake. You're interfering in important work. I'll make sure you lose your jobs for this. This is about Australian national security. I demand you let me go immediately!'

Casterlow struggled.

'From what we know, you're the biggest threat to Australian security,' Jacques said quietly.

'I'll bet you're one of those naïve lefties, always bleating on about human rights. Soft on security. Soft on terrorists. Too soft altogether. But you've gone too far this time. You've endangered state secrets. My project is vital. You have no right to interfere. It's government business, it's—' Casterlow eyes blazed. Spittle sprayed across the table in front of him, leaving spots in the dust.

'That's enough. You'll have plenty of time to prove this is legitimate,' a firm voice behind Jacques said.

It took three police officers to restrain Casterlow despite him nursing one arm in a sling. He continued to struggle as they lead him out of the warehouse.

A police officer checked Nick's pulse while another tied a tourniquet around Peter's arm to stem the blood flow. He moaned. Peter was wounded, but still alive. It was too late for Nick. After a moment, Peter sat up. He rested his head in his hands. Distant sirens announced ambulance units were on their way.

'What have you done, Peter? I don't understand,' Laura asked as someone untied her hands.

'It got out of hand,' Peter groaned.

Laura wasn't sure if his pain was physical or emotional.

'People died,' she accused.

'It wasn't my fault.'

'You made a choice, Peter. People died!' Laura repeated.

He glanced at Laura and frowned.

'You and Tom just had to meddle. If you'd just kept your noses out of what wasn't any of your business…' Peter shook his head. 'You wouldn't understand.'

'You're right. I wouldn't. You're pathetic,' Laura hissed and turned away.

Jacques moved closer to Laura. Dirt smudged his face and his tousled hair projected at odd angles. His clothes gave off a musty scent and Laura screwed up her nose. He wiped her face with a handkerchief. She winced. The bullet had grazed her cheek, coming very close to her right eye, but hadn't caused major injury.

'You could have been killed,' Jacques said, his eyes only straying from Laura's face momentarily.

'Robby is here somewhere,' Laura said. 'I need to find him.'

A group of police burst through a side door. Robby stumbled through with them, then broke into a run. He wrapped his arms around Laura. Despite all her aches and pains, she hugged him back.

'I can't believe you risked coming in here after me. They could've…' Robby said.

'I can hardly believe it myself. I wasn't thinking. Are you alright?'

Robby nodded. His eyes glistened as he hugged her again.

'I don't know what I thought I was going to do, but I couldn't leave you in here without help. We hadn't planned to be here during the meeting but the equipment…'

'You took a terrible risk,' Jacques said sternly.

'The DVDs…the report…tell a sinister story. Someone killed Tom and Corrinne because of them. We couldn't let them get away with it.'

'You should have taken the DVDs and reported it to the police.'

'They accused me of murdering Tom. I didn't know who I could trust.'

'You're extremely lucky. Eva raised the alarm outside. She told us you were in here.' Jacques shook his head. 'I'm glad I was here to help.'

'So am I,' Laura said. Relief at being safe added to the relief of knowing Jacques was one of the good guys.

The warehouse buzzed with activity. Dust flecks glistened in the half-light. Uniformed and non-uniformed officers scoured the warehouse, bagging and securing evidence. One by one, the prisoners were led outside to the waiting vans. Paramedics escorted

Peter to an ambulance, and a medic tended to Laura.

As the medic examined Laura's cheek, Eva raced in through the warehouse door.

'I'm so glad you're alright? I was so frightened.' As soon as the paramedic finished, Eva hugged Laura fiercely. 'When the police surrounded the warehouse, I told them about you and Robby. What else could I do? I'm so glad you're safe.'

'It's OK, Eva. This is Jacques.'

Eva scanned his tattered disguise and raised her eyebrows at Laura.

'Casterlow and the others won't get away with this, will they?' Laura asked Jacques.

'The UN, my government, and the Five Stars Alliance have been trying to crack this for a while,' Jacques explained.

'Five Star Alliance?' Eva asked. Her journalistic impulses were strong even at a time like this.

'It's a cooperative intelligence-sharing group involving agencies from Europe, USA, Canada, New Zealand, and Australia. They identified an illicit drug importation ring, and eventually, we realised it was much more than that.' Jacques looked at where Nick's body lay. 'It remains unclear how much Peter and the Pythons were involved, but they're knee-deep in the drug importation racquet.'

Jacques squeezed Laura's hand, and the medics led her and Robby outside to a waiting ambulance.

As she was helped to the vehicle, a voice called her name. A policewoman stepped back and Mel rushed through the line towards Laura.

'Oh, thank God you're safe. I can't believe how close you came to—' Tears brimmed in Mel's eyes. 'And as for you, Robby, what did you think you were doing? You were supposed to be on your way to Broken Hill. If you'd done what you were supposed to, Mum wouldn't have been put in danger.'

Robby nodded. 'I know. It was stupid.'

'You can say that again. It's time you grew up, Robby.' Mel embraced him roughly. 'Are you alright, Mum?'

'I think I've broken my elbow,' Laura said. Her whole body ached.

'I hope that's the worst of it. I was frantic. I didn't know what had happened to you. I—'

'It's OK. We're safe now.' Laura still struggled to believe she'd been so rash.

Chapter 47

Even with his eyes open, the dark enclosed John. His heart throbbed erratically. He was alive, or at least he thought he was. Sweat beaded across his forehead and his shirt stuck to his damp armpits. How long had he been here? Why hadn't anyone come to get him? What were they waiting for?

His body trembled with rage, but clenching his fist made the handcuffs bite deeper. They were sticky with crusted blood, reminding him of his helplessness. Carlo's betrayal stung. He'd trusted Carlo, but he should have known that he wouldn't have the resolve to double-cross Dimi. John's body shook with fury. No one double-crossed Giovanni Mastriani and got away with it. Carlo would get what was coming to him. But first, he needed to find a way out of here. Alive.

Dimi wasn't merciful. His survival was either an accident or she planned to make him suffer. She was Babbo's daughter. She had his mean streak, and John shivered, thinking about what was likely to happen next. He'd planned to demand Babbo take him seriously and show him the respect he was owed. But he'd failed. Babbo would be laughing at him now. Yet again, he'd say, "See, I knew you couldn't do it."

He shuddered. The hallucinations brought blinding fear, terror, even. The smell of stale urine filled his nostrils. It mixed with the smell of sweat and engine oil and he gagged. He'd never experienced anything like it before and hoped to never experience anything like it again, ever. It had almost driven him mad.

John summoned up images of Harper, trying to use them to steady his nerves. Here in the dark, his memories lit his guilt. His second thoughts about leaving the family business had sparked the argument that day. Harper wouldn't compromise. It was the family business or her, he couldn't have both. A tear welled in his eyes. Now he didn't have either.

John's head throbbed. His mouth was parched and his nerves raw. How was he going to get out of here? He needed a plan, but his brain was foggy. John curled forward, the pain in his wrists only slightly less than the pain in his heart. He closed his eyes. His mind wandered, going back through the decisions leading him here. He'd made many wrong moves, and he hadn't achieved anything. He hadn't won anyone's respect, and he'd signed away his life. John pressed his eyes closed to stem the rising tears.

There was no one left to care about what happened to John either. Skye had left him, Fleur, his receptionist, was gone, and Harper was dead. Kleb wouldn't know where to find him, and John wasn't sure Kleb would risk his reputation getting too close now anyway.

The whiff of engine oil made him choke, and he breathed in and out in rapid succession, but the gag stopped air filling his lungs. Panic lapped at his chest. Where was he? Where were they?

He needed to stop thinking about what was going to happen, but the more he tried to shift his focus, the more his brain stubbornly brought him back to his dilemma.

He prayed, making a pact with God. He hadn't called on Him in a long time, but now he promised that if He saved him and let John live, he'd start again, in a new direction. He'd forget about revenge and hatred. He'd start anew.

'Please, please, let me out of here.'

Outside, footsteps crunched on gravel. Muffled voices barked instructions, and John held his breath. Listening. He shivered, and a lump formed deep in his chest. Something scratched against the lock and he screwed his eyes shut just as a loud crash sent the boot lid flying open. John opened his eyes, but the intense daylight blinded him.

'What have we here?' a deep gruff voice said.

It wasn't Dimi or her goons. His eyes adjusted and he saw the dark police uniform. John breathed in the fresh air and steadied his nerves. He squinted at the faces above him. Hands gently pulled him out of the space and began to ungag and untie him.

His mind whirred into action. He'd need a story to explain being locked in the boot, but of course, he was a victim. Dimi had planned his demise, but this time, she'd failed.

'Thank God you're here. I thought I was a goner,' he gasped. That much was true.

Now it was time to create a new truth. He'd exact revenge on both Dimi and Carlo. They'd pay dearly for this humiliation. His chest filled with fire and rage. He'd finally achieve what he'd been planning, and he'd spare no one.

Chapter 48

Laura rubbed at the ache in her shoulder. Her broken elbow and bruises had taken time to mend. At age fifty-nine, her body didn't recover quickly and her many bruises transformed from ominous black to dramatic blue to ugly yellow, before fading. Her emotions had also transformed and now grief, anger, and sadness remained.

She prepared the coffee machine while Eva pulled out three mugs and lined them up. Jacques sat at the dining table, deep in thought.

'I'm getting too old for this,' Laura said as she tamped the coffee grinds.

'You'll get the hang of it soon enough.'

'I wasn't talking about making coffee.' Laura laughed and handed Eva a freshly filled mug.

'Neither was I,' Eva said. 'It's been both exhausting and exhilarating.'

Laura brought two coffees to the table and sat beside Eva, opposite Jacques. She warmed her hands on her mug while her mind plucked at the different strands of the past month's events.

'Are you ready for your move?' Jacques asked.

Laura scanned the neatly stacked boxes in the corner. 'I think I am. It's time to move on and put a line under this year. As Eva says, it's time for closure.'

Outside, the garden burst into new growth and colour. It, too, was making a new start. Tradesmen clambered over the neighbour's roof, clanking and drilling as they cleared the pigeon nest and encircled the panels with mesh. The neighbour had finally acted, acknowledging that it was more costly to ignore the pests.

'These last few months have taken an enormous toll on you,' Jacques said. His lopsided smile aimed at Laura.

'Tom and Corrinne paid the ultimate price,' Laura replied.

A wave of sadness engulfed Laura. The casualties were innocent people standing up for what was right.

'At least we've prevented more deaths,' Eva added.

Laura nodded. 'I never suspected Peter. I thought of him as my friend and I didn't believe he could do anything illegal. I trusted him even though I knew he'd changed, especially since marrying Abbie, but I didn't think he was capable of this.'

'Abbie was a bad influence, but I think Peter made his own decisions. He got greedy. I'm shocked that he didn't consider the consequences for the boys.' Eva said. 'Neither he nor Abbie cared about what would happen to their little girl.'

Abbie and Peter's daughter, Katie, was being cared for by one of her step-brothers, Eva's son. It was a strange situation. Peter's guilt weighed heavily on Eva and their family.

'How can they think about consequences when they don't expect to get caught,' Jacques said. 'Criminals often believe they're too clever. Luckily, they're usually wrong.'

'Was Peter involved in the chemical weapon testing too?' Laura asked. She hoped he hadn't fallen that low.

'Peter imported E-bomb but didn't know about Formula Z until Tom told him. He's confessed. You're right Eva, he got greedy. He knew something sinister was happening at Bassarti, but decided he didn't need to know.'

'I never thought Peter could peddle illicit drugs. Working at APATO, he knows the harm they do, yet he didn't care.' Eva shook her head and stared out of the window.

'My naivety almost cost Robby his life.' Laura's skin erupted in goosebumps. 'I'll never understand how Robby succumbed to the lure of a bikie gang; no matter how much he explains. I thought we'd instilled a sense of right and wrong in him, but he ignored it so easily. At least now, he's starting anew with his aunt Claire and I hope it will set him straight. I never want to experience a scare like that again.' Laura shivered, thinking of how close she'd come to losing her son too. The car firebomb was a narrow escape.

Eva patted Laura's arm.

'Children aren't only influenced by their upbringing, other forces have an impact too. Abbie and her brother are an example. They grew up in the midst of ruthless criminals and followed a lawless path from childhood, convinced their wants, greed, and success were worth killing for. Their sense of entitlement is stunning. Their upbringing was harsh and unyielding, and they suffered but, does that justify their behaviour and actions? Not everyone who suffers turns bad. Some even turn their lives around. Abbie is a hardened criminal. She isn't remorseful and still trying to lie her way out of this,' Jacques explained.

'I can't believe Abbie's involvement,' Laura said quietly. She'd suspected Tom, who'd been true to his principles, yet hadn't once suspected Abbie, who'd masterminded an organised crime gang and their illicit drug importation business.

'Criminals don't *look* different. Their eyes aren't closer together, nor do they only wear black hats like in the old westerns. We can only see criminality in people's actions.' Eva laughed.

'And criminals can come from any level of society. Look at the politicians,' Jacques added.

Laura nodded. Politicians were seen as a different breed. Even though most people thought politicians lied and were dishonest, they accepted it without holding them to account.

'I'm glad we finished Tom and Corrinne's work, but no court

judgement will ever make up for their loss.' Laura wiped a tear from her eye. Casterlow had left a lethal legacy for many families.

'Justice provides some consolation, but it can't bring Tom and Corrinne back,' Eva agreed. She comforted Laura with an embrace.

Underneath Laura's sadness, she was also angry.

'And the Paddington press still supports Casterlow. I know they're hard-liners, but I'd expected them to be shocked at the truth.'

Laura expected public condemnation of Casterlow and his project, but the Paddington press loudly dismissed any criticism as left-wing extremism. Some of the public appeared to be swayed by the arguments.

'The truth gets buried in opinion columns,' Jacques said. 'Those who align with Casterlow's world view will defend his actions, even if it's not rational. Belief trounces reason and facts everywhere in the world. This time, I think we have the law on our side.'

'Spin and propaganda work. I thought our society was better, that we've evolved somehow. We point a finger at China and Russia, outraged at how the government-controlled media manipulates public opinion, yet we're no different. This government is prepared to lie and avoid any responsibility and the big media barons help them. Truth is a casualty.' Eva said.

'Casterlow developed Formula Z, but was he also involved in E-bomb?' Laura asked. There was so much about this conspiracy that she didn't fully understand.

'Technically, he wasn't. Casterlow's project used the chaos after the Iraqi war to set up research facilities. He wanted chemicals for interrogation and chemical warfare. E-bomb was an unexpected byproduct,' Jacques explained. 'The nerve agent, Formula Z, was exactly what he was looking for and it can kill swiftly. The next step was to perfect its untracability. Dissent isn't allowed in Casterlow's world. He's an authoritarian at heart. His enemies aren't human beings, they're collateral damage. Of course, it wasn't only ideology, his plans also fattened his bank accounts.'

'His callous and single-minded zeal is incomprehensible. He talks of Christian values, but lacks all of them.' Laura shivered, remembering the fire in Casterlow's eyes. 'Casterlow scared me.'

'Such zealotry is scary. The research methodology wasn't only illegal and inhumane, it was immoral. Casterlow suspected people might object, so he kept it secret. It wasn't that he was admitting wrongdoing, he just didn't want to waste time justifying his position. He's the breed of politician who thinks rules only apply to others. He believes he knows what's best. Thanks to you, we got the vital evidence we needed to stop him. Without the recording, they might have got away with it.'

Laura smiled at Jacques. She was a poor judge of character. Doubting Tom and Jacques while not suspecting Peter or Abbie.

'I must confess, when this all started, I thought that Tom had perhaps lost his way,' Laura said. She stared into her coffee cup. Could she forgive herself for mistrusting him?

'What do you mean?' Jacques asked.

'I wasn't sure what the documents and reports would reveal. I feared he'd lost his sense of right and wrong too. He'd become disillusioned, and I thought he'd given up the fight. Before he died, he sounded beaten. I wasn't sure what to believe. I didn't have enough faith.' Her initial reluctance to investigate had been because she'd feared the worst.

'You didn't say anything.' Eva raised her eyebrows at Laura.

'I was ashamed.' Laura looked down at her hands.

'It's never wise to have blind faith,' Jacques said matter-of-factly. 'People change. Just look at Peter. We need healthy scepticism. Challenging and being vigilant is hard and can carry a high price, but how far is too far? This is our society's moral dilemma. People need to be prepared to speak out and not turn a blind eye to injustice. If they don't, the perpetrators win.'

'I feel like society accepts a lot more unethical behaviour before we're outraged.' Laura said quietly. She didn't like the trend, but hadn't she been guilty of looking away too? 'Even Tom turned away from the Wheat Board controversy. APATO was corrupt, but he let it go. He felt the cost was too high. He regretted it so much that this time, he couldn't ignore the corruption.'

'Being a whistleblower is harder than it should be. There's more risk of losing everything for the whistleblower than for the criminals. It's getting worse, with the proposed legislation threatening to prosecute all whistleblowers,' Jacques said.

'So what were they doing in that warehouse?' Eva asked. She'd listened to the recording but wanted confirmation.

'Casterlow was setting up an alliance with the Mastriani family. That's Abbie's family. They were to eventually deliver Formula Z to clients in Australia and, in this instance, to distribute it to Indonesia for the first live test. Casterlow wanted the current Indonesian government to retain power and to secure his agreements with them. The opposition leader was gaining in popularity and it looked like he might win government. Casterlow had to avoid that at all costs. The opposition leader had already threatened to cancel all agreements with Australia and renegotiate access to his country. For Casterlow, this was a catastrophe and his way of solving it was to kill the opposition leader before the election. It would also pressure the current government leaders to stick to their agreements or else. He probably wouldn't have stopped there. Once this test was conducted, he had plans to sell the product to others and to expand his own use. Casterlow planned to manipulate the political leadership in other countries for his own benefit. We're not sure where, but we're glad we've stopped him.'

Laura shivered. Images of the warehouse flooded her mind. The dangerous men, the decaying smell, the fear she'd felt, but most of all the zealous fire in Casterlow's eyes. She still couldn't believe she'd been so audacious and risked her life that night.

'Were there others involved too?' Eva asked.

'We found Abbie's brother locked in a car boot at the Python's clubrooms and he insists he's an innocent victim,' Jacques said, then laughed. 'His company imports illicit drugs from South America and everything we've learned about him indicates he's sleazy and self-seeking. We're keeping an eye on him. He'll slip up sooner or later.'

'Nice family,' Eva said.

'I thought Abbie's brother died in a car accident.' Laura remembered her conversation with Abbie a few months ago.

'He was reportedly killed in a horrific car accident in Crete, along with his fiancé Harper. We're not sure if it was a mistake, or a carefully executed plan, but the dead driver was identified as Giovani. After extensive reconstructive surgery, he changed his name from Giovani Mastriani to John Masters and moved to Sydney, where he built up a successful transport business. It's a shame that the energy he put into building his illegal importing business wasn't diverted into legitimate activities.'

Laura stood up and walked over to the window. She wasn't as worldly wise as she'd thought. The callous disregard for life by some in positions of power shocked her. Luckily, their plans had been thwarted.

'We don't really know people as well as we think. I don't understand what motivates Abbie and her family. They run racquets, control bikie gangs, and import and sell illegal drugs. Yet, she seemed a very ordinary person, albeit a bit cold.'

'Even Peter didn't know the extent of her involvement. Either he wasn't paying attention or she was a terrific actress,' Jacques said.

'What role did Furness play? What happened to him?' Laura asked. She'd almost forgotten about his whistleblowing threat and sudden death.

'Casterlow dealt with him too. Furness knew about E-bomb, he was pragmatic about it, but Corrinne's report provoked a crisis of conscience. He was like so many politicians, coerced by power and a sense of superiority until he learned the full details of the testing regime, the use of prisoners, and the plan to expand and use refugees, and then, he refused to accept it.. When he threatened to blow the whistle, he was killed.'

'He was murdered too?' Eva gasped.

'We're still gathering the evidence. Both he and Corrinne suffered organ failure, and we think Casterlow's special squad is involved. Casterlow will discover he's not above the law after all.'

'This government still doesn't accept responsibility and voter loyalty is strong. Some people won't vote against their favoured party no matter what they do, not even when they act illegally.' Eva's voice rang with despair.

'Casterlow went rogue. Why did he need to do this? What was he trying to achieve?' Laura asked.

'The chemical weapons offered the power and control he craved. He could threaten and bully leaders to kowtow to his policy whims and for the benefit of his own business interests as well as his big-business supporters. The prisoners and refugees used for testing were collateral damage to him. They were expendable. They were easily demonised and labelled subhuman.'

'There's no compassion or humanity. Casterlow was prepared to do anything in his quest for power, even kill.' Laura sighed.

She hadn't been paying attention to politics. Vigilance was exhausting, and she'd foolishly trusted politicians to make the right decisions without scrutiny. It was a dangerous strategy.

'Power corrupts and absolute power corrupts absolutely.' Laura said bitterly. 'It's better to stay vigilant.'

'We suspect Casterlow was even negotiating with an international arms dealer, Stavros Carnegie, to secure more prisoners and refugees from other world conflicts to expand his testing regime. He planned to research for more and better chemical weapons to use in interrogation and mind-control. Carnegie also had access to black markets for the chemicals. Casterlow didn't care who he sold his product to. All that mattered to him was how much they'd pay,' Jacques explained.

Laura placed their empty mugs on the kitchen sink. Despite the risks, she was glad she'd helped to expose the conspiracy.

'I wanted to let you both know that Fayyaad is safe too,' Jacques explained.

Both Laura and Eva exhaled loudly. Seeing Fayyaad's name in Jacques' diary had terrified Laura. She'd thought she'd endangered him, but it was clear that her slip had saved Fayyaad's life. Jacques confirmed he'd found Fayyaad before Abbie could.

There was one question that still niggled at Laura.

'I asked you about meeting Tom in a hotel in Parkside in October last year. Have you told me everything about that?' Laura tentatively asked Jacques. She wanted them to be friends, but it was time to face up to the truth.

'I never meet Tom. I didn't lie to you about that. However, that night, I followed Peter to the hotel, to gather information. Peter met the bikie president and while they were talking, Tom interrupted them. They argued, and I wasn't sure if Tom was involved with their scheme or not.'

'And why did Tom have your number in his diary?'

'I honestly don't know. A journalist friend may have given it to him. I can't think how else Tom would have my number.'

It seemed that Laura had finally reached a point where she could move on with her life. The mystery resolved. Her life was now heading in a fresh direction and she felt stronger. It was both exciting and daunting.

Epilogue

Laura sat on her apartment balcony looking out at the sea view. She hadn't unpacked everything yet, but she'd said goodbye to her old life. It was time to focus on the future and hold on to her good memories and release her anger. Her life followed a new routine. She regularly swam in the swimming pool and used the gym at the apartment complex, walked along the beachfront, and stopped for coffee at local cafés.

She couldn't ignore all the consequences of Tom's mystery. The Paddington news empire continued to support Casterlow, trying to convince its readers that Casterlow was working to keep them safe. Happily support was slipping. Their articles used the rise of terrorism and the influx of refugees to justify the development of chemical weapons and swept away concerns for the inhumane testing process as *bleeding-heart concern for terrorists and enemies of the state*. They even argued that whistleblowers should be prosecuted. Laura was pleased that public opinion seemed to be turning against them.

Despite Casterlow's special force closing ranks, cracks were appearing. Whistleblowers confirmed Casterlow had ordered Furness' murder. The allegation of murder couldn't be so easily explained away. To make matters worse, it appeared that Casterlow had been shot by one of his special squad members, attempting to stop him. People, public servants, and office staff were coming forward, encouraged by those already speaking out. Jacques was confident that justice would prevail.

Laura scanned the picturesque view from her balcony. Clouds cast dappled sunlight patterns across the grassy reserve. Beyond, waves rolled onto the beach and receded, leaving a silvery shimmer on the sand. Laura sighed. At least on a personal level, life was easier.

Robby was settled. His breakup with Shayida may have hurt, but it was for the best and he'd adjusted to life with his Aunt Claire with remarkable ease despite his heartache. The country environment suited him. Finally used to the hard physical work, he appeared to enjoy it. He was learning photography and helping Claire to set up marketing and promotional processes online. There was even a hint he would take up formal studies to learn more. Laura crossed her fingers. Since Shayida's brother, Nick, was shot and killed, and her secret lover, Bulldog, found dead, Shayida had turned to Abbie, visiting her in jail. It was a shame that Shayida hadn't set off on a different path.

Jacques and Laura shielded Mel from both formal and news reports. Laura's heart swelled with pride at Mel's courage and determination. Mel's disappointment at the government's lack of support for human rights, and their refusal to condemn the corrupt processes used by Casterlow, made her rethink her career. She was seriously considering an offer to work with the UN. It would bring its own frustrations, but at least she'd be working for the kind of change she believed in.

Becky, Robby's twin, on the other hand, again changed course. She'd given up her studies in marketing and PR and was embarking on a law course. It was a move Laura supported. Hopefully, this was the last change, since neither she nor Becky could afford any more. Becky's raw emotions had transformed into quiet grief. Tom's old recliner filled her small lounge and was a fitting memento.

The best news was that Laura's eldest, Mark, and his wife, Dee, were finally expecting their first child. They'd struggled with IVF and were about to give up, but luckily, they'd tried once more. Laura was making plans to visit them in Brisbane soon.

Jacques flew home to Canada but would return next month and Laura was making plans to visit Canada next year. Their relationship was starting afresh, and she didn't know where it would lead. It was early days, and Tom's loss was still very raw.

Laura wandered back into the apartment and scanned the remaining unpacked boxes. She bent down and lifted out the beer steins. They held happy memories, and the key hidden in there was a vital clue to Tom's mystery. She placed them gently on the display cabinet shelf and stepped back. Tom's loss still hurt and would for some time, but at least she was proud of his fight.

She couldn't escape regrets or wondering what life could have been like. The future was a mystery, but she and Eva made plans. Life held great prospects. She was committed to restoring her activism and continuing the fight, especially supporting the threatened whistleblowers. That's how she planned to start her new decade. She was turning sixty in a month and she was ready.

Leave a review

If you enjoyed this book and have a moment to spare, I'd greatly appreciate a short review on Amazon and Goodreads. It helps to spread the word, especially for independently published authors.

Don't underestimate the power of a review. It makes a huge difference. Reviews don't need to be long, sometimes the best reviews are one-liners.

Acknowledgments

When I first embarked on my writing journey, I wasn't sure that I could even complete a novel, but here I am publishing my second. I've learned so much along the way, especially how supportive and helpful the writing community is. I've met so many wonderful people, on-line or in person.

I'd like to thank the Novelist Circle writers' group who offer me their valuable feedback, critique, and advice, one chapter at a time and then, once a completed draft is ready, they critique the entire manuscript. I really appreciate their comments and commitment. Thanks to Dean Powell, Jennifer Mackenzie Dunbar, Paul Slater, Sonya Bates, Steve Davey, and Susan Neuhaus.

Thank you also to former Inkitt authors, Greg McLaughlin, Barry Litherland, Trudy Knowles, and Dominic Breiter who read and reviewed **Lethal Legacy**, offered comments, advice, and support, and encourage me still. They provide me with valuable reader insights and their encouragement boosts my confidence.

The plot for this fiction novel first came to me when I read the non-fiction book **'Kick Back: Inside the Australian Wheat Board Scandal'** by Caroline Overington. It provoked the inevitable 'what if?' questions and set my thoughts racing. Other books I drew on for this book are: '**The Weapons Detective: The inside story of Australia's top weapons inspector**' by Rod Barton; '**Glitter and Greed: The secret world of the diamond cartel**' by Janine Roberts; and '**My Italians: True stories of crime and courage**' by Roberto Saviano. These references are all worth reading.

Huge thanks to my editor, Amanda from Let's Get Booked, who also designed the stunning cover and formatted the file ready for publication. Her skill turned my manuscript into a professional-looking novel.

And, last but certainly not least, thank you to my family, especially John, Leeann, Andrew, and Michaela who have supported and encouraged me along the way. I love you and appreciate your interest, unwavering support, and encouragement.

So many authors, bloggers, and readers, have helped, supported, and offered generous advice, it's impossible to name them all individually. Your help has been greatly appreciated. Thank you.

It has taken years and commitment, effort, and rewriting to get to this point and I sincerely hope readers enjoy this story.

This novel has been edited and proofread, however, occasional mistakes and typos can slip through, so please, if you find anything that needs fixing, send the details to contact@hrkempauthor.com so I can amend it.

About the Author

I live in a beachside suburb of Adelaide, South Australia, where I enjoy regular walks in all seasons. I grew up in the outer suburbs of Melbourne, in a country setting where I also enjoyed long walks, although in very different surroundings.

Lethal Legacy is my second, stand-alone, conspiracy mystery thriller novel. My short stories have appeared in the UK anthology **When Stars Will Shine**; the Australian anthology **Fledglings**; the UK **Writers' and Readers' Magazine**; and the Canadian **Scarlet Leaf Review**.

Before embarking on a writing career, I worked in the public service in roles as diverse as Management Trainer, Team Facilitator, Statistician, and Laboratory assistant. After taking early retirement, I completed a Graduate Certificate in Creative Writing at Adelaide University. It was the springboard to finishing my debut novel, **Deadly Secrets**. (I enjoy being a student, my first degree, completed many years before, is a Bachelor of Science - majoring in Chemistry- and I have a Graduate Diploma in education.)

I'm a passionate traveller and my travel journal and copious photos (I even surprise myself with how many I take) form background images for scenes. There's a gallery on my website showing photos that inspired scenes for my novels. Even though most of the action occurs in Australia, mainly Adelaide and Sydney, **Lethal Legacy** has scenes set in Amsterdam, Milan, and Santa Margherita, while **Deadly Secrets** begins in Paris and has scenes set in Normandy, Nice, and Barcelona.

I enjoy live theatre, art, and of course, reading. Most years you'll find me hanging around the Adelaide Writers' Week in March, listening to authors and adding to my overflowing to-be-read pile of books. If you are interested in staying connected and hearing about the next novel why not join my mailing list here

https://www.subscribepage.com/signuptostayuptodate

Excerpt from Deadly Secrets

Prologue

Sydney

It was hard to concentrate with the fog blanketing his brain. An indistinct barrage of accusations flew at him, throwing him off-balance. He clasped the arms of his office chair and squinted at the red, contorted face bellowing at him from across the desk as a spray of spittle pricked at his face. A laugh tickled at his throat.

Dragging himself up, he carefully moved to the front of the desk. A wave of nausea lodged in his throat along with the taste of scotch. He stumbled and stifled a curse and immediately the tic in his forehead spasmed. He yearned for peace and quiet.

'You don't deny it?' the visitor boomed.

'I don't admit or deny anything. This is progress. Sometimes there are losers, but they are…' He scrambled in the recesses of his mind for some clever, elusive words. 'Collateral damage.' He smirked with satisfaction. 'I'd have preferred not to have so many losers but…it's out of my hands.'

The visitor's response, a sarcastic laugh, surprised him.

'Collateral damage? That's what you call it?' The visitor leaned down, drawing close, and stale hot breath flooded his nostrils. 'You're a megalomaniac. You think you're untouchable. Well, you're not. I'm going to stop you.'

The pulse in his temple throbbed more insistently now and he glared at the hard-set mouth opposite, his thoughts too slippery to form a witty retort. He was bored with the bleeding hearts. They just complained endlessly. No matter what he did, there was always someone ready to criticise or disagree. It was just self-interest.

'I'm not quitting! So piss off and leave me alone.' He pulled himself up straight to glare up at the red face. 'I don't answer to you…or anyone else for that matter. People will applaud my time in office. They'll see I was revolutionary…visionary…taking this country to bigger and better things…taking it forward.' He threw his head back for emphasis and immediately regretted it.

'You're out of control. You have to be fucking stopped!'

Spittle landed on his face again and he slowly wiped it off with the back of his shaking hand. The rest of that bottle of scotch beckoned, but as he stepped forward, he stumbled and again had to grab the desk.

'Fuck off!' he slurred.

'You *will* be stopped…' the visitor murmured before lunging at him. 'I'll make you pay, you bastard.' The word 'bastard' echoed like a chant.

His chest clenched as steely hands dug into his shoulders and shook him.

He jerked back but the visitor's hands held fast. He almost laughed at the absurdity of the scuffle. Instead, he growled, 'You'll pay for this…you, you…'

He thrust forward but his assailant didn't budge. Nausea again rose in his throat but he was bound by a rough and clamp-like embrace and he choked on the bile. They tussled falling against the desk. He twisted, using what strength he could muster but couldn't break free. His smothered jabs at his opponent's belly had no impact.

'I'm not quitting,' he croaked through the acid taste.

As his visitor's grip waned, a glint of something caught the corner of his eye. Then, without warning, a sharp stab seared through his neck. He grasped at the pain, his hand touching cold metal. Sticky wetness pulsed from its base down onto his collar. His legs buckled and he slumped to the floor.

A moan and an oath, 'Oh my God,' floated through the darkness, followed by retreating footsteps and the thud of a closing door. Silence. At last, he was alone. The pounding in his ears softened, his strength oozed onto the carpet in a steady rhythm. He tried to shout but only a hoarse gurgle passed his lips. He'd get that bastard; later.

Printed in Great Britain
by Amazon